EMP BACKDRAFT
Dark New World: Book 4

JJ HOLDEN
&
HENRY GENE FOSTER

Copyright © 2017 by JJ Holden / Henry Gene Foster
All rights reserved.
www.jjholdenbooks.com

This is a work of fiction. All of the characters, organizations, and events portrayed in this novel are either products of the author's imagination or are used fictitiously.

ISBN: 154305966X
ISBN-13: 978-1543059663

EMP BACKDRAFT

- 1 -

1400 HOURS - ZERO DAY +142

BRIANNA SHORES SAT beside her friend Kaitlyn at one of the small fire pits. The fires were for the few Clanners who didn't yet have a shelter and had to camp out in what remained of Tent City. Her mother, Cassy, insisted on having small fires scattered throughout, instead of one big fire, saying that it was warmer than a bonfire and spread the heat better. She'd had been right.

Kaitlyn said, "I feel bad there's still some people in Tent City. I can't wait until the last house gets finished so they can move in."

Brianna glanced toward the compound that had sprung up in only weeks, where there'd been only Mom's house and an unfinished house when they had finally driven out the invaders-turned-looters from White Stag Farm. They'd been under the control of a psychotic named Peter, who saw himself as a new Moses and promised to save his White Stag followers from starvation. It had turned very ugly. Eventually Cassy killed him and his main henchman, Jim.

Now Clanholme had five new houses, all made of earthbags, with earthbag walls stretching between them.

Arranged in a semicircle with the wall facing the exposed "Jungle" to the north and the opening facing the compound, it made for better defenses. Two spots remained without houses, but they'd be done soon—there just wasn't much else to do around the farm in the onset of winter, and the construction work kept people warm.

Brianna poked the fire with a stick and gazed into the short flames. "Yeah, I can't wait either, but it's better than being *out there*," she said, nodding her head to the west border of Clanholme. "But you know what I feel really bad about? No Christmas gifts."

Kaitlyn nodded super-fast. "Why did your mom say no gifts this year? It's stupid."

Brianna proceeded to quote her mother in a mocking tone, " 'Just being alive and here with good people and food to eat is enough,' blah blah blah. I still want Christmas."

Kaitlyn huffed. "It's still stupid. We should at least give a gift to Grandma Mandy. She's sick all the time, but she's up every day helping all the smaller kids, making sure we have snacks, playing games. All the other adults are busy running things, but not Grandma Mandy."

Brianna laughed. Mandy was *her* real grandma, after all, but it was pretty cool that all the kids and even most of the grownups also called her Grandma Mandy. "Yeah, she totally deserves a present. Something to cheer her up and let her know we appreciate all the things she does for us. But there's no stores, we'd have to make it."

Kaitlyn's eyes got wide. "Really? We could do that? Would we get in trouble by your mom? She said no presents. I heard her."

Kaitlyn clearly didn't want to get in trouble. Brianna almost laughed at the conflicted look painted on Kaitlyn's face. "I think Grandma would give her a lecture on giving, if my mom got mad. Any ideas on what to make? Christmas is tomorrow. That's not much time."

"Mom used to make circles out of branches to put on doors. She'd decorate them with stuff and give them out for Christmas to the neighbors. They're real pretty."

"They're called wreaths." Brianna looked into the fire again. That could be a great idea, actually. Easy to make. And over the last month the Scouts had collected a dragon's hoard of Christmas decorations. They'd used most of it at the complex, but a lot of it was still in boxes. There'd be no problem finding stuff to decorate the wreath. "It's a great idea, Kaitlyn," Brianna said with a grin. "But there's no pine trees in the food forests. We'd have to go north to that big clump of trees. It'd only take us a couple hours, I bet. We'd be back by dinner and no one would know."

Brianna saw that Kaitlyn was bouncing up and down with eagerness, and she smiled again. Kaitlyn was younger, but had become her best friend among all the Clan kids since her father had died on the trek to find Clanholme. "Okay, let's go while we have time," Brianna said. "No one will even know we're gone. I bet I can get Aidan to distract the tower guard, and he'll keep quiet for me."

Aidan, always one for mischief, readily agreed. Brianna and Kaitlyn then waited for the right moment, and once Aidan had the guard distracted, the two girls scrambled to their feet and ran toward the food forest, laughing and racing. Once they got to the food forest—the areas on the south and north edges of the farm was full of trees that grew a huge variety of fruits and nuts, with an understory of shrubs and other useful plants—they slowed to a walk, the better to avoid the traps the Clan had scattered everywhere. Everyone in the Clan knew where they were, but they could be hard to see if you weren't looking for them. Soon they came out on the other side and paused to gaze at the beautiful grassy flatlands out there, covered by a thin dusting of snow.

An hour later, they arrived at the copse of pine trees. Everyone in the Clan knew about it, of course. It was where Choony, a courageous young Korean-American pacifist they had all come to respect, had hidden when he first escaped the White Stag invasion. Brianna shuddered at the memory of that horrible time and shoved away her rising thoughts of all the people who died under Peter's rule. This Christmas there truly was something to be thankful for—being alive, and being free. That, and the few flakes of snow falling lazily, promising a white Christmas overnight.

A glimpse of movement out across the snow caused her to whip her head around, peering intently. Kaitlyn saw it and looked as well, trying to find what had caught her friend's attention.

"Are those deer?" Kaitlyn asked. Brianna thought her voice sounded as tense as she herself felt.

"Too small. What are... Kaitlyn. Those are *dogs*." For a moment she was excited at the thought, but then remembered what the scouts had reported. Packs of feral dogs now ran around, they said, and could be dangerous if they were hungry, or if there were enough of them.

In moments, the dogs were close enough to see their bared teeth and a ripple beneath their skin—their ribs, Brianna realized. They crept closer, and there was no mistaking their low posture, bared teeth, and spreading into a semi-circle. These were not the good doggies.

Images flashed through Brianna's mind, pictures of what Cassy would do in this situation. She'd take charge and do *something* rather than *nothing*, all while keeping people from panicking. "Kaitlyn, get behind me and stay there. I'm bigger than you. We're going to back up to the trees so they can't surround us, *but do not run*. If you run, they'll be on us fast. Let's try to get to that big branch over there..."

* * *

Nestor Lostracco plodded over the light snow dusting, half aware of his surroundings. He was too busy thinking over the past few months of his life to focus on anything else. He wasn't even really sure what direction he was going—only that he was moving away from the town of Waymart as fast as he could. They'd done fine after the power grid went down, after residents strung up the local government figures for getting all dictatorial, until the bicycle hordes from Scranton made an organized push to confiscate the supplies of everyone within 50 miles. There were a couple skirmishes with Scranton's "citizen deputies," and that's when Nestor realized it was time to bug out.

A good thing he'd left, too, because he later heard that Scranton had simply rolled in with hundreds of people and took what they wanted, killing everyone who resisted—which had been just about everyone in Waymart. Nestor was thankful that he was free and alive, even if the rest of Waymart wasn't. Good enough for him, but sad.

And since leaving two weeks and over one hundred long miles ago, he'd been wandering southwest and dodging militias and invaders alike, surviving off what he could scrounge up. He'd left Waymart with a rifle, but ditched it when he ran out of bullets. It was heavy and useless, at that point. He had since scrounged a pump-action pellet rifle along the way. The box had said "1,400 FPS," which he assumed was a lot, but it used .22 ammunition. Not bullets, like he'd expected, but good-sized pellets that still weighed nearly nothing and yet made short work of even some bigger things like raccoons. Maybe it would even work on people, if needed, but he hadn't yet had to try that out.

Nestor had more pressing matters, he realized. Flurries of snow had again begun to fall, but this time the wind had changed direction and the air had that smell, that winter smell of a bad northern storm coming. It wasn't safe to forage and hunt during a storm even if the animals wouldn't all be hiding, and then the fresh snow would leave a dead giveaway of his passing. No, he'd have to find shelter, and soon, or spend the next week either starving or risk going out and drawing attention to himself.

A blur of movement caught his eye and he whipped his head toward it, trying to identify the source. It took only a moment to realize it was a pack of dogs. Feral dogs, and they had surrounded some prey or another. At least he wasn't their prey... Damn, yet another danger to look for. He wondered what a pack of dogs was doing so far from any city, but of course, it had been months since the power went out. Long enough for fleet-footed canines to get anywhere they damn well wanted to go. Nestor felt sorry for whatever critter they were about to eat, shaking his head in mute acceptance of the inevitability of what would happen over there, and turned to continue his journey to nowhere in particular.

A small girl's shrill scream pierced the air, bouncing off the trees. That was no mere animal being hunted. Nestor froze, unsure what to do. His mind raced, trying to convince him he should leave well enough alone—it wasn't his problem. Then for a second he thought it could have been his own daughter out there, so much did it sound like her at the end, just before her final moments. But of course it couldn't be his princess. He shook away the grim memory.

There was simply no way he could just walk away and let some child get eaten alive. No one deserved that. Death should come by accident, or peacefully in one's sleep, or even quickly at the intimate hands of one's own killer—not slowly at the fangs of Man's Best Friend.

He unslung his air rifle and pumped it three times in as many heartbeats, then scanned through the scope to find the girl in danger. Damn, there were *two* girls. The older one stood between five feral dogs and a younger girl curled up against a tree in fright. The brave one held a branch and used it as a spear against the dogs as they crept toward her. Nestor began to run toward them, keeping the air rifle up and aimed as he rapidly closed ground on the girls.

Each of the girl's thrusts caused one dog to leap away, but then the other four would inch in closer. Rinse and repeat. They were gaining ground, albeit slowly. She could never keep that up long enough to save them, but thankfully those weren't wolves. If they'd been proper wolves, the feasting would already have begun.

Nestor slowed to walking and squeezed the trigger. A puff of noise, and then the dog closest to the girl yelped and limped a few paces out of the girl's reach. As he kept walking, another puff of noise and the second dog squealed; it tried to use its front paws to drag itself away, rear legs collapsed and useless. Spinal shot!

As he pumped the rifle again he saw the younger girl now looked around in confusion, and the older girl screamed and swung her branch like a baseball bat. It connected with the third dog's ribs and sent it skittering across the ground, and when it tried to get up it only limped once and then collapsed, whimpering.

The two remaining dogs barked at Nestor then fled, leaving their injured packmates behind. He wasted little time putting the wounded ones out of their misery, while black clouds rolled angrily toward them. After having to kill those dogs, the churning clouds fit his mood perfectly.

He nodded to the girls. They huddled together, pale and shaking, with the older one shielding the younger with her body. He could hear the little one sobbing in fear.

"Are you all right?" Nestor asked.

The girls remained in a fearful stance.

Nestor surveyed the downed dogs, his expression as overcast as his mood. The girls obviously did not find it reassuring, so then he looked at them directly and his frown disappeared. He smiled and raised an eyebrow quizzically. "Do you live close to here? I want to make sure you get home before the storm hits."

* * *

Cassy, founder and leader of the Clan, knocked on the third door. In the distance she heard Amber shouting the girls' names to the north. Tiffany, Michael's wife, was winding her way all through the Jungle, or what was left of it as winter began. Beyond, in the southern food forest Ethan would be doing the same as Kaitlyn's mom, Amber, though Cassy couldn't hear him shouting from so far away.

The door opened. A brief, frantic conversation, which was as fruitless as all the others—no one there had seen her daughter or Kaitlyn since lunch. On to the next door. But as she drew back her fist to pound on the door, she heard a wild shout from the guard tower. Cassy sprinted toward it, praying the guard saw her daughter and not yet another refugee.

The guard pointed south toward the food forest. In the summer, it wasn't possible to see it through the Jungle's foliage, but at this time of year she could make it out well enough. She put her hand up to her brow to block the setting sun from her eyes and searched in a near panic. There! Three figures emerging from the food forest. The girls, and Ethan— no, wait. That wasn't Ethan. She felt a perfectly rational fear jolt through her. If the girls had been alone, they could be being held hostage for food or supplies... Cassy drew her pistol from behind her waist, racked it to load a round into the chamber, and sprinted south. If anything happened to the girls...

It took her only two minutes to run the whole distance, pistol in hand. Breathing deeply she came to a halt some twenty feet away, just at the distance a person could get to her with a knife in the time it would take her to bring up her pistol and fire. Relief flooded her as she saw that his rifle was slung over his back and that Ethan was creeping up toward the stranger from behind.

Brianna shouted, "Wait, Mom, he saved us!" She took a step toward the man, which would complicate Cassy's shot if this went down that way.

"Get out of the way, Bri, until I figure this out."

"There's nothing to figure out. God, Mom, we were in *trouble* and he *helped us*. Why are you always so paranoid? He's just one guy anyway."

Damn teenager. Brianna seemed to always feel like she knew everything there was to know about any topic, apparently including strangers with guns. "Yeah? And why did he help you?" Cassy's gaze never left the man. "What do you want, mister? Step away from the girls."

The man opened his mouth to speak, but jumped when the *clack* of Ethan racking his pistol rang out from behind him. His eyes went wide for a moment. "Holy crap. Please don't kill me! I'm just a refugee, and these kids needed help. Was I supposed to just leave two kids? I had a daughter the little one's age. All I did was help."

The man stepped away from Brianna and Kaitlyn like they were pit vipers. He looked properly afraid. That was good.

Behind her, Cassy heard the clamor of Clanners approaching as well, reacting to the guard's alarm too. These days the whole Clan could turn out armed in the middle of the night from a dead sleep in two or three minutes, thanks to their fear of being surprised by another Peter. She suppressed a shudder at the memory of that sociopath dictator's brief time as slavemaster over the Clan.

The tower guard was among the approaching Clanners. Cassy didn't take her eyes off the stranger, but shouted, "Whoever the hell was on tower duty is going to have hell to pay for letting these girls go. They could have been killed, dammit. We can't take these kinds of chances anymore!"

Brianna stepped forward, posture defiant but lower lip quivering, and said, "Mom, it's not his fault. I had Aidan distract him. He can't really ignore the Clan leader's son, can he? This is my fault, not his."

Cassy fumed, but knew that most of it was just adrenaline. She wanted to be angry at the guard, but she couldn't fault him. Brianna was right about that. And she knew quite well how devious her son, now eight, could be when he wanted to. "I'll talk to the kids later about this, and about some damn common sense. Now about this newcomer —your timing sure was convenient, mister."

Brianna averted her eyes from her mother's anger, and muttered, "We just got lucky, Mom. He was in the right place at the right time."

"Or he could be a spy," Cassy stated flatly. "Ethan, take the girls inside, now that the rest of the Clan is here." She then stood by and waited for them to get out of the danger zone, though Ethan had to half-drag the girls to get them to move. Without aiming her pistol directly at the stranger, Cassy ordered him to drop his rifle.

"Sure, happy to. It's just a pellet gun anyway. Wouldn't do me any good against a pistol." The rifle clattered to the ground, and the stranger took two steps back away from it. "There you go. See? No reason to kill me. I swear I was just helping some kids get out of danger. Was I supposed to leave them there?"

Cassy had heard a tremor in his voice, though, and felt

reassured. The snow began to fall faster, but Cassy still didn't take her eyes off the man. Average height and build, and brown eyes peered out from under his shaggy dark brown hair. She saw no scars on him. "Alright, we're not going to shoot you in cold blood. Calm down. Now tell me why they needed help, what you did, and how you came to be in these parts. You a looter?"

"No, ma'am. Just a refugee passing through. Your girls were in a little stand of trees about an hour from here, but got themselves attacked by a pack of dogs. They'd gone feral. The dogs, not the girls. They looked starving, those dogs."

Over the next few minutes, the man revealed that he'd killed a couple of dogs that were getting ready to rush the kids and had put another out of its misery after Brianna clubbed it half to death. "Getting as far away from Scranton as these legs will take me," he concluded.

Cassy blinked. Scranton? That was over a hundred miles away. Then another thought hit her. "Someone go get Choony. This might interest him, his family's there." She turned back to the stranger. "What's your name, mister?"

"My name's Nestor Lostracco, ma'am. Pleased to meet you. I know you could have just killed me, and I've seen quite a few people lately who would have. But I just wanted to make sure those kids got home safely. It's rough all over out there, I'm sure you know. I swear I'll leave without a problem."

Michael's voice burst out from behind her, carrying clearly to everyone there despite the fact that he wasn't yelling. That military training of his. "My advice is to bury this guy in the woods, Cassy. If he's a scout then we can't release him. He might as well nourish next autumn's fruit harvest."

Cassy frowned. Michael was a good man, a Marine, but ever since they'd fought their way free from Peter's ruthless grasp the man saw everyone new as a threat that should be eliminated, *just in case*. "Thank you for the advice, Michael. But instead, we're going to give him a roof over his head, for the night at least, and talk tomorrow about what to do with him. He saved Bri and Kaity."

"Still could be a scout, boss. I'll go make arrangements for him for tonight." Michael's tone was crisply professional —which meant he hated the idea. Well, as her security director it was his job to be paranoid. Michael didn't like the role, but he was the best man for the job and he knew it as well as she did.

"Okay, mister. You've earned a place for the night—it's not charity. If you want, you can eat a meal with us and stay the night, warm and safe. Or we'll give you some provisions and let you get moving to wherever you're going. And thank you for saving those girls, Nestor."

For a moment, Nestor's jaw clenched but then he smiled warmly and extended his hand toward her. "I'd love a place to stay, ma'am. It's kind of you to offer. I didn't do anything special, though. Anyone would have done the same for those kids."

Cassy smiled back and hoped Nestor didn't see how plastic hers was. If he'd wanted to leave, she'd have had Michael make sure he didn't come back later. Maybe he knew it, too, because she couldn't shake the feeling that Nestor's smile hadn't reached his eyes. And she hadn't missed that little jaw clench of his, either. He was hiding something, she was sure of it. Best to keep him alive and close by.

She could be wrong about him, after all. And if she were right, then this gave the Clan a chance to find out what was coming before it surprised them like Peter and his White Stag army had. Intel was a priority, she now knew. She'd learned that lesson the very hard way.

"Alright then, Nestor," Cassy said. "Thanks again about the girls. There's a big storm coming—I feel it in my bones. Let's get you some hot food and a warm bed before it hits."

- 2 -

1900 HOURS - ZERO DAY +142

SEVERAL HOURS LATER, Cassy shook hands goodbye with Joe Ellings, who had brought her his concerns about blanket stores disappearing as cold weather set in. Although Joe had come with the White Stag people during the invasion, he had helped the Clan during their period of slavery and, with his core group of White Stag co-conspirators, had been instrumental in helping the Clan eventually overthrow Peter Ixin's malign dictatorship. As a leader of the few White Stag people who hadn't been executed or exiled after the Clan regained its freedom, Joe had even been invited into the Clan Council, a group of key advisors and administrators who helped Cassy keep the Clan ship afloat.

Joe grinned, pushed her hand aside, and gave her a brief hug. "I reckon we're beyond handshakes, ain't we?" he remarked in his laconic, almost cowboy-esque speaking style. Cassy had heard some of the older boys copying Joe's style among themselves. He was much admired by Clanholme's younger set because of his revolt against Peter, despite his White Stag roots. "Thanks for jawin' with me. I know you're busy, and I appreciate you."

"No problem," Cassy replied. "Thanks for letting me know. I thought we had more blankets than that. Someone must be hoarding them. Go ahead and put blankets on the Scrounge List—I know we have some listed on our recon maps. And talk to Michael about doing a sweep for the missing ones. We're in this together so if someone is hoarding, we need to know about it."

After another round of goodbyes, Cassy went into the kitchen, finished her cup of cider—fantastic stuff made right there in Clanholme under her own tutelage—and put on her shoes and coat. Time to make the rounds, kiss hands and shake babies, all that. Cassy smiled at the old joke, then headed out toward the new earthbag housing cluster, braving the increasingly heavy snow.

As she approached, she saw that many families still lingered outside in the little courtyard formed by the protective wall that surrounded the homes, though soon they'd have to go inside when the storm struck in earnest. Her people squatted by small fires, mingled, told stories, traded ideas. The community was coming together nicely now, despite some early difficulties integrating the White Stag people they'd invited to join the Clan. Most had earned their invitations by joining Ellings in his plot to protect Clan members and take Peter down, while others had eagerly jumped in on Joe's side in the crunch.

There were still occasional ruffled feathers among the Clanners, but nothing like in the days after the uprising, when the Clan as a whole went mad with vengeful witch hunts to "out" White Staggers who had actively joined in the violence and looting and enslavement of the Clan. Cassy felt they'd executed or exiled more people than they'd needed to, but her entire council—including her mother, "Grandma Mandy," the voice of mercy and Cassy's personal moral compass—had been adamant that the Clan needed it. Like lancing a festering boil or cleaning a fresh wound by letting it bleed for a while, the process was messy but it healed.

Cassy spotted her mother sitting on a log by one of the small fires, chatting with Choony. Her devout Christian mother and the devout Buddhist Choony got along surprisingly well, Cassy mused. But then, they were both good, brave people with kind hearts, and selfless. Everything Cassy no longer felt that she herself was, not anymore. In this dark new world, those weren't the qualities her people needed from their leader. Having those two on her council ensured that she would at least hear a moral counter-argument to her own instincts, which now ran toward decisions that were decisive and proactive, to put it mildly.

Cassy sat on the log next to Choony, where there was a bit of space, and greeted the two warmly. She smiled at Choony a bit longer than she'd intended and shifted her gaze to the fire self-consciously. Choony was a Buddhist and a complete pacifist, but he was one of the bravest men she'd met. In the Clan's battles he always ran fearlessly through the gunfire, delivering ammo or retrieving and treating wounded. He also had a way of seeing past the self-justifying lies Cassy told herself and getting her to see things more clearly. They'd become very good friends.

Choony replied, "Hello back at you, fearless leader. Grandma Mandy was just filling me in on what our visitor has been up to since his arrival."

Mandy tossed a small branch on the fire, though it didn't really need it yet. "Nestor is interesting. He helped with the dinner cleanup without being asked, and Amber's daughter has been following him around like a puppy."

"I'm not surprised," said Cassy. "He saved her and Brianna from a bad situation. Has he done something to raise concern?"

Mandy peered at her daughter, no doubt trying to read Cassy's expression. "Is there something you want to get off your chest, honey? Something you know that we don't?"

Cassy turned to look into the fire, gathering her thoughts. She shook her head slowly. "No... Nothing specific. But we're not just going to open our arms and welcome him in. We've all learned that's a bad idea. And I have this bad feeling about him. I don't trust him, even if I can't put my finger on just why that is."

"He's done nothing but good for us so far, Cassy. Kaitlyn and my granddaughter both like him, especially Kaitlyn. Maybe you're reading too much into this, sweetie. He could just be a wandering survivor who risked himself to help kids in danger, like he said."

Cassy furrowed her brow, irritated but also weighing Mandy's words. "That may be. But you know what, Mom? Since the EMPs destroyed whatever veneer of civilization we had, people keep proving they aren't all that nice when their back is against the wall. There's no police now, no consequences except the risk of death, and people lost that veneer pretty damn quickly. It seems like every time I ignore my gut, bad things happen to me and the people I care about. I won't risk our safety just because I can't see a reason for my gut instincts."

Choony spoke up. "That's your role now, Cassy, being our leader and protector. You have more to worry about than just being nice to strangers, whatever your Christ might have said. He was wise, but impractical."

Mandy huffed. "God's wisdom is beyond the understanding of the natural man," she paraphrased. "But there's a reason for His instructions to us, which is that He loves us and knows that His way is best for us, even when we don't realize it ourselves. Don't mock the Lord, Choony," she said with a grin to soften her words.

This was ongoing banter bordering on a friendly argument between the two, and Cassy paid it no mind. "Be that as it may, Mom, God helps those who help themselves. The Clan are our neighbors and our family. Do we love our neighbors as ourselves if we endanger them?"

"Villains love those who love them, Cassy. Even IRS auditors love their families."

Cassy chuckled. "You mean, 'do not even tax collectors do the same'? Yeah, I know. But worrying about God is your job, Mom. Mine is to worry about keeping us all alive so that the Christians among us have the chance to keep praying to Him with you. And I do, too."

Choony smiled, and glanced to Mandy. "Christ was a wise man, indeed. He lived up to so many Buddhist precepts. I imagine he got reincarnated as something cool, like an eagle."

Cassy looked to her mom, concerned, but Mandy only grinned and replied, "The Son of God could be an eagle if He wanted. You'll probably come back as a hornet, just so you can keep pestering me."

Cassy listened to the two go back and forth for a while, but her thoughts soon wandered back to the stranger among them, and she gazed without seeing into the fire. What was it she didn't like about him? The timing was a tad too convenient, but she wouldn't say that aloud. Her mom would rightly say that their survival up to this point had been a series of coincidences that were "a tad too convenient." Maybe she was right. Maybe God really was watching over them. But Cassy couldn't sit back and rely on that to keep the Clan safe and sound.

"...Cassy? What do you think?" It was her mother, intruding on her thoughts.

"What?"

Mandy pursed her lips. "I said, I think we shouldn't have

Nestor leave first thing in the morning. I know you were probably planning on that, but it'll be Christmas Day. At least let him stay for the celebration. After all, we wouldn't have much to celebrate if Kaitlyn and Brianna had been eaten alive. What do you think?"

"I think that I'll be having him move along, like you said. We'll have given him a warm night's sleep and two hot meals, and that's as much risk as I'm willing to take on a stranger."

Mandy leaned closer to Cassy with pursed lips. Almost under her breath, she said, "Don't you dare kick him out on Christmas. You may be concerned about safety, but there are dozens of us here. Enough that he can't hurt us, and enough to keep people with him constantly. Safety isn't an issue, and you know it."

"He could be a spy, Mom. Working for some other gang of looters."

"So? He already saw Clanholme. He saved your daughter. Unless you plan to murder him in cold blood, then seeing Clanholme is a ship that already sailed. But nothing says the man is a spy, Cassy."

"We don't know him, and I—"

"You listen to me, Cassandra Elenore Shores. We didn't know anyone here six months ago, except our own family. He's proven his worth already, and you should have more gratitude for what he did. I raised you better than that, and I'm not asking. I'm *telling* you that he can stay until the day after Christmas."

Cassy felt her face grow hot and her anger surged. She was about to start yelling at her mom when she felt a gentle hand on her shoulder. Angry, she whipped her head toward the interloper only to find Choony standing beside her. She hadn't seen him get up, much less come to her. In her anger, adrenaline had given her tunnel vision—and she knew she'd been foolish to let anyone make her so angry. Mistakes like that cost lives in this new world.

"Be calm, dear friend," Choony said. "We all know you wish only to make sure we're all safe. But I assure you, we can keep him under guard. Your Karma and your inner harmony will be harmed if you kick that man out in the morning. Give him a day of safety and food. Your daughter's life is worth that much, and so is your Karma."

Cassy took a deep breath, closed her eyes, and counted to ten. Choony was right, of course, and he'd defused the situation and got her to see reason in just a few well-spoken words. He always did have that effect on her, she mused. Once, in a moment of hot blood, she had almost kicked him out, and it would have been a terrible loss for the Clan. That recollection let the rest of the air out of her sail. She shook her head at herself, her role as leader, the fears that still haunted her after Peter's brutality, and her own jumpy nerves. And relented.

"Very well. For tonight and tomorrow, he will be our guest. Choony, please notify Michael that Nestor will require discreet guarding until he leaves."

* * *

1600 HOURS - ZERO DAY +143

Frank sat at the edges of the happy crowd gathering for Christmas Day dinner. There were fewer people at the edges and so less opportunity for someone drunk on hard apple cider to bump against the stump of his leg. He silently cursed Peter for maiming him, but of course their former dictator was dead now. It did no good to curse him, but it sure made Frank feel better. He scratched the nearly-healed stump with the tip of one crutch.

Next to him, Mary tisked at him. "Knock that off or it'll

never heal."

"It's already healing," Frank replied, and grinned.

Mary just rolled her eyes, but cut off any snappy reply when Michael approached with two plates of food. Good food, too, all either raised here on the farm or hunted. None of that store-bought crap. That was one good thing about the end of the world—if you had food, it was healthier now than in the last hundred years, or something like that. Not corporate crap, anyway. Since the '70s, up to 90% of the supermarket produce had become GMO and, while it grew faster and stronger, it also had less nutritional value than crops raised the natural way. Or maybe it was because they didn't use dinosaur-based fertilizers. There was something unnatural about pumping petroleum-based "fertilizer" into the ground year after year.

"Greetings, bro," Michael said and handed Frank his plate. "After dinner we should run off all those extra calories so you don't get any fatter."

"Har har har. Don't make me kick your ass, jarhead."

"I'm not sure kicking is your best bet, Frank."

"Fine. I'll beat you with a crutch for Christmas. How's that?"

"That works. So what do you think Cassy's going to give a speech about? I'm guessing it's about getting the last of the new houses squared away."

"We'll find out soon enough, man. Here she comes."

Frank watched as Cassy took her place at the head of the dining area—mostly still logs for people to sit on, but a few chairs salvaged from nearby abandoned homes—and coughed to get people's attention. The spot was quickly becoming ceremonial, Frank decided, and wasn't sure whether that was good or bad.

The Clan quieted down, and Cassy swept her gaze over the assembled people. The Clan now numbered some seventy adults, and half as many children, but it was a testament to the respect the people gave Cassy that they quieted down so quickly. Rather impressive...

"Merry Christmas," Cassy said, and smiled.

Frank looked around and saw a sea of faces smiling back at her. Thank God he'd stepped down to let Cassy be the Clan leader. No way he could have managed that job, or not as well as Cassy did. Of course, she had her Councilors to help. Frank, Michael, Ethan, Choony, and Grandma Mandy, plus Joe Ellings who joined them from the White Stag people. With all of them on board, Cassy had a much easier time getting things done. Frank and the others were all well liked and respected.

Cassy continued, "So now that I've got you all here and we're having our Christmas dinner, with the amazing cider—thanks to Dean Jepson, who has a knack for it—it's time to remember where we came from and give thanks for where we are today. So many out there, outside our farm, are hungry and cold tonight, but we aren't. The Clan is warm and fed, and I see a few of us got into the hard cider a bit too early."

Polite chuckles and a lot of pats on the back for Dean, the cranky old farmer who could "redneck engineer" just about anything, from anything. Due to some old bad blood, he and his politician wife didn't much care for Cassy when she brought them into the Clan, but that fell away quickly in this new world. Dean was as prickly as ever, but most Clanners now took it as just part of his crabby charm.

"It's been three months since we all overthrew Peter the Dictator," she continued. "We lost a lot of good people taking our freedom back, and gained some good new friends. Not all the White Stag people were evil, and the ones we didn't hang or exile are those who helped us while we had the yoke of Peter around our necks." People looked down, or toward friends for support, because even now the memory of that dark time haunted so many of the Clan.

"But the good news is that our way of farming, the way I've been teaching all of you, is spreading. There's other survivors out there making new lives just as we have, and we've been able to swap our knowledge for some pretty great trade deals with them. We have cows now, and we have replaced our other livestock. Goats, chickens, even a couple sheep. And these trade deals have led to some pretty good feelings between us and them. That's a good thing, because we learn most of what we know about the outside world from these friendly survivors. And we got all these apples from them! Let's get some food and celebrate!"

The crowd yelled in agreement and milled over to the serving tables, where Frank and Michael already had gotten their plates. Frank turned to Michael, who was nodding at what Cassy had said. "Michael, what's the latest on the alliances we're trying to forge?"

Michael glanced to Frank and then looked back to Cassy, and said, "Ephrata's on board. They have the same problems with those bastards in Adamstown that we do. Glorified raiders, and I hope we get to kill a lot of them come April." The scurvy survivors of Adamstown kept trying to hunt out everything in the woods that lay between them and the Clan, and they liked to raid at a distance by riding bikes down the Pennsylvania Turnpike.

The Clan had set a full-time watch out there with an irreplaceable hand radio, to give the Clan early warning of any raids. There hadn't been one in a while, on account of the Clan being ready for them every time they dropped by since setting up the scout outpost after their first attempt, which failed badly when the Clan's policy of never straying far from defensive arms proved effective. The Clan had gained a few usable bicycles from that encounter.

"What about Manheim and Lititz?" Frank asked. Those were a few miles south of Clanholme, and there was some tension between them going all the way back to the first refugee flood from Lancaster after the invaders gassed it.

"Working on it. They're leaning toward half-assed mutual defense agreements, I think. Manheim especially is getting pressure from Elizabethtown's survivors and wants us to broker a deal before they'll think about a real alliance."

"We have as much sway in Liz Town as we do Ephrata, right? So it shouldn't be too hard."

"We're working on it. Shush, Cassy's done kissing babies and whatnot."

Frank looked back to Cassy and saw that she was about to speak again. He let his conversation with Michael drop for the moment.

Cassy said, "As a special Christmas gift, I'm happy to say that we've almost got our own Constitution worked out. If America ever gets back on its feet, ours is clear that we will put it aside in favor of rejoining, but for now it spells out how we're going to do things around here. We'll let you know when we finish the draft and then everyone can have some input."

Someone in the crowd shouted, "What about capital punishment?" That had been a hot-button topic since Cassy had the worst of the White Stag goons strung up.

"War is war, friend. But we won't be killing our own. Clanners who get too far out of line will get exiled, not executed. Let's talk about happier things. It's Christmas!"

Cassy droned on for a while, covering all the bases. She talked about local issues, the growth of regional interfarm politics, the Clan's new alliances, and the need to stay vigilant. But mostly, she talked about the great things that had happened in the last hundred days. The Clan had come together and was quickly developing its own culture and traditions, many of which started accidentally with things Cassy did. It was the "Founder's Principle," a term Frank recalled from his conversations with Ethan, the Clan's skilled hacker. It was the tendency of an organization to adopt and reflect its founders' ideas and ideals.

When Cassy wound down, the Clan finished eating and happily broke up to enjoy pies and more cider—always more cider, they had barrels of the stuff—and talked about spring planting, sick chickens, and all the other things farmers talk about. Frank loved listening to the hum of happy people talking and socializing. Before the EMPs, most people didn't even know their neighbors' names, but without TV or smart phones, face-to-face socializing was again becoming the norm. If you didn't know your neighbor's name, you couldn't very well expect him or her to help you when you needed it.

* * *

Cassy sat with Grandma Mandy by the tables where the children were eating dessert. Brianna and Aidan sat on the log next to her on the other side. Dessert was a fruit-laden fruitcake slice, and half the kids were now bouncing off the walls and each other from the sugar. These days, no one ate sugary foods. There usually weren't any to be found, but one of the scouts had come back with a five pound bag of sugar and a huge grin, and the Clan had settled on making Christmas cheesecake and fruitcake. It wasn't like the stuff she used to buy in the store, but she hardly remembered anymore how all the chemically processed foods had tasted before the EMPs. She no longer missed them much, except for chocolate. She sometimes woke up in the middle of the night craving a certain candy bar that really satisfied. It was depressing to think she'd probably never get to eat chocolate again, at least not for years to come.

Aidan, her nine-year-old son, interrupted her thoughts. "Mom, why do I have to feed the hogs? Why can't Mr. Jepson's kid do it? The pigs smell bad, and after all, I'm your son. The Clan leader's son shouldn't have to slop pigs. Maybe I could feed the chickens."

Grandma Mandy smiled and answered for Cassy. "Feeding chickens is for the little kids, sweetie. You know that. You aren't special, kiddo. Everyone works, and there's more work than hands to do it. That's why you get to slop the hogs. If they smell bad, why don't you take a day off from playing in the woods and clean their pen?"

Cassy fought a smirk. "Grandma's right, son. I think that's going to be your chore for tomorrow." Aidan frowned but didn't say anything more. Whatever he said now would only bring more "unfair" chores. Cassy nodded thanks at Grandma Mandy, satisfied. It would be a few days at least before her awesome and rotten little genius tried to figure out another way to get out of his chores.

Brianna snorted with laughter, and Aidan stomped away. Then Brianna said, "Speaking of getting out of chores, I traded with Michael's kid."

Cassy fought the urge to smile. "Well, I give you an A for effort. Nick's only six, so no, he isn't going to muck out horse stalls while you feed chickens. Sorry, Brianna."

Brianna didn't even frown, so Cassy decided she'd only been kidding—not that her daughter would have complained if her mom had allowed it. Cassy watched as Brianna walked away toward the other teens.

As Cassy looked around the area she took mental notes of who sat together, which couples weren't as close together as usual, all the things a leader must notice about her people to head off potential problems.

Then she saw Nestor, the new arrival, and just watched him a moment. Nestor looked tense. As he chatted with those around him, his smile was genuine enough but he shifted in his seat almost continually. Leaning back, leaning forward, crossing and uncrossing his legs. She supposed that was only to be expected from a guy who hadn't seen another friendly person in months and was still new to the group. Cassy mulled those thoughts over as she contemplated whether to let him stay after today or to kick him out in the morning like she'd said originally.

Then Nestor seemed to lock his gaze onto something. His jaw clenched, and his knuckles grew white clutching at the log on which he sat. Cassy followed his gaze. He was looking at one of the older women, originally from White Stag. Older in this case meant about forty, as few people older than that had survived, at least not that Cassy had seen. Not out here in the rural areas.

Mandy snapped in a hushed tone, "Cassy! You stop that right now."

Cassy turned to look at her mother in confusion. "What?

"I see you squinting your eyes at him, with that look you have when you get upset. You leave that nice man alone. He saved your daughter's life, for Pete's sake."

Cassy felt trapped, like a tiger in a cage, restless and prowling. She had to move, to walk, to get out of there. What had come over her? Whatever the reason, Nestor had set off her alarms. These days they were fine-tuned and she listened to them. They'd been right far more often than not. Cassy stood, forced her face into an easy smile, made her excuses, and got the hell out of Dodge. Time for a walk. Time to loosen up her taut nerves.

A few minutes later, as she walked with head down and hands in her pockets, she heard the distinct creaking noise that Frank's crutches made, close behind her. She turned her head to see him. Frank wore his worry on his sleeve, plain as day to Cassy. Just great.

"This isn't the time, Frank. I need some alone time out here."

Frank shrugged. "Don't snap at me, Cassy. I came out because I'm worried about you, so don't grump at me. What's going on with you? I saw how you were looking at the new guy. So spill it."

"I know that look. You aren't leaving until we hash this out, are you? Fine. It's just that the guy sets off my red flags. Jimbo set them off and I ignored them, and then he tried to rape me. That was day one of darkness. Happened again with Peter when I first spoke to him, trying to negotiate Jaz's release after he'd caught her. I should have listened to my gut and just killed him, even if it had cost Jaz her life. I love that girl like a little sister now, but how many people died because of that choice I made?"

"Look, you're the Clan leader and all, but maybe take some advice... I feel like you're being overly cautious. You have to admit that your instincts are a bit on the razor's edge since the White Stag thing. You're learning to listen to your gut, and that's fantastic in a leader, but maybe you—we all, really—have a touch of P.T.S.D. from all of this. What's he done, besides save Brianna and Kaitlyn's lives when he didn't have to?"

"Frank, I get what you're saying, but how he's looking at some of us creeps me out. His vibe sets me on edge, dammit. He's too white-knuckled, like he's just about to snap. And my gut hasn't been wrong yet, if only I'd listened before."

Frank chuckled, but stopped when he saw the angry look on Cassy's face. "Sorry. I was just remembering a similar conversation about Choony when he first arrived. You'd have sworn up and down he was a villain and a varmint. Now look at him—he's one of us, and even on the Council. Yeah, you were wrong about him. Maybe you're wrong about this Nestor guy, too."

"True, I was wrong about Choony. He's a good friend, and part of the Clan's core. God, I'm confused now, Frank."

"I hate to bring it up, but you know, we aren't finding as many people out there as we used to. Not too many people survived on their own. People in a group survived maybe, but not the people out there alone. So are you going to have a funny feeling about the next guy? Or how about the woman after that? At this rate we'll never let anyone new in. And being exclusive isn't what the Clan is about, is it? Nor can you say we can't feed more people. Between the way we farm and the now-vacant land all around us, we have more room than people."

Cassy furrowed her eyebrows, and pinched the bridge of her nose with thumb and forefinger. She let out a long breath. Frank was right, of course. Keeping everyone out was never the Clan's way. No, the Clan found people and then found a way to make them useful, to fit in. And Nestor hadn't done anything specific to earn mistrust.

"Okay, Frank. We'll let him stay. But you keep a close eye on him. Tell Michael, too. I want this guy watched without souring everyone against him, or souring him against us. Keep it discreet. Time will tell, but if he turns out to be a wolf in sheep's clothing, I want to be able to deal with it before our little flock is hurt again."

Frank nodded in approval, and shifted his weight on his crutches. "Sounds good, Cassy. I'll let Michael know. Hey Cassy? This crap is why I never wanted to be the Clan leader."

"I know. Thanks for sticking me with the damn job. I hate you forever."

"Love you too, boss. Let's go get some more of that ham they cooked up."

* * *

0400 HOURS - ZERO DAY +144

Ethan screamed and sat bolt upright. The sweat that drenched him was suddenly cold, and he shivered, looking around in confusion, until he remembered where he was. Slowly, the walls of his newest underground bunker receded to their usual position as his vision cleared. Only a nightmare.

Beside him, Amber stirred. She reached up and put her hand on his arm. "Another nightmare, babe? More zombies?"

"Yeah," Ethan croaked, throat tight. He reached to the end table and took a sip from the glass of water there. "Same old stuff. I don't think I'm going back to sleep soon. I'm going to get up for a while, so you can go back to sleep."

Amber murmured her thanks and was quickly making her "baby grizzly" snore. Adorable. He smiled and spared a moment to watch her sleep, thinking back on all the challenges they'd faced to be together. First the inconvenience of her marriage to Jed, who was all wrong for her but a great guy. He'd died before they ever got to this farm with Cassy. The Clan had made it clear they weren't ready to see him with Amber just yet, so they'd had to sneak around for a while. It was only after the revolt against Peter and his White Stag army—while he and Amber had been stuck down in the bunker together—that the Clan had a change of heart.

She'd been worth waiting for.

Still smiling, Ethan got up and walked to the command center, with its computers, radios, maps... He stopped in front of the big laminated U.S. map and looked it over, as though anything had changed since yesterday. San Diego and the Marines at Camp Pendleton still had power—the only civilized place in the entire world, for all he knew, since

Operation Backdraft had unleashed EMPs around the globe. That had put a kink in the invader's abilities, but hadn't stopped them. It had, however, consigned billions to die around the world. And he had been instrumental in making that happen. Ethan suppressed a shudder, and shoved that thought into the dark, black hole inside of his soul, where all the terrible things he'd seen and done were locked away.

The Mountain—NORAD outside of Colorado Springs—had power, but they were self-sufficient. The people in the area now controlled by General Houle, leader of the U.S., went without power. Houle was also the head of the 20s, that secretive group that had done its best to prepare for the original EMP attacks against the U.S., but Ethan knew they also had a terrible agenda. And the map proved it. Much of the central U.S. was outlined in green, Ethan's color for Houle-controlled territory. It stretched far, and there were enclaves of his forces throughout Texas and Louisiana. Those were really modern-day castles, fortresses from which Houle projected power over a region he lacked the strength to conquer. Lacked it so far, at least.

Most of Florida was outlined in gray, now, and Ethan smiled. The 20s hadn't planned on *that*, the bastards. Florida was almost entirely free, except for the Invader enclave in Orlando. Someday they'd all have to go head-to-head with General Houle for control of the future. But not yet.

Virginia through New Jersey was a hodgepodge of Invader enclaves, 20s loyalists, and militia groups. Bloody ground, with constant guerrilla warfare between all three factions. General Ree, the North Korean advisor to the Islamic coalition that invaded the Eastern Seaboard, had risen from mere advisor to outright dictator. His own little North Korea, paying lip service to the Great Leader back home. Ree controlled most of New York City and its surrounding cities, where independent militias and outlaw gangs raided and he really had his hands full.

Ethan grinned widely at that thought. He'd become rather chummy with the man who kept Ree's hands full of the most trouble. Major Taggart. His efforts had kept Ree from shifting the balance in favor of the Invaders throughout the entire region, and he had no loyalty to the 20s. Naturally, the 20s distrusted him despite the great work he did, but they didn't dare challenge him. Not yet anyway. And Taggart had his own loyalists. He'd earned their loyalty the hard way, Ethan knew from various independent reports, by giving his own loyalty back to those in his command and their allies. He'd like to meet the man in person.

West of all that, it was a different story. The map was outlined in the Empire's light blue around Illinois, Indiana, southern Michigan, Ohio, and western Pennsylvania. In some places they were only 100 miles away from Clanholme. They'd been stopped at Altoona by winter and survivalist groups, and could go no farther through the mountains that lay between the so-called "Empire" and Clanholme. That vast light blue Empire, loosely loyal to General Houle, resembled some perverse imitation of an old Roman Empire client state.

Chicago was only a necropolis now. Nothing good lived there anymore. Detroit was hanging on as a city, but most of its people had migrated south into the Toledo meat grinder. Toledo was as dead as Chicago now, but before it died it had taken most of Detroit's people with it. Come spring, Detroit would probably get a pretty light blue outline of its own…

Enough. Ethan was just spinning his wheels, doing nothing productive. He went to the terminal and checked for incoming messages. He didn't expect any, but there was one from Watcher One—the contact who, it turned out, had recruited him to the 20s in the first place, though Ethan (known as Dark Ryder, online) hadn't known it at the time.

Ethan sent off the coded acknowledgement and decrypted the file. As usual, it was a series of simple text files that used a very old and very effective encryption technique. Once decrypted, the main message could be read:

> *Attn: Dark Ryder. Op Code 1216B.3 for confirmation. Hey buddy, how's life at the farm? Got some urgent mission orders for you to send out. I don't know how you get those to route, but keep it up! Someday you'll have to tell me which servers you bounce through to get them routed. -W1*

Fat chance. Dark Ryder was only needed because he was the only one who could make the communication channels work, from the Mountain out to the militia, survivalist, and rebel groups scattered all over the eastern U.S. Watcher One's mention of the farm was the 20s' way of reminding Ethan that they knew where he lived. He needed no reminding. He'd be a good little trained monkey. Or pretend to be, anyway, for the moment.

Before sending out the mission orders, he found the file that would go to Major Taggart, which he recognized by now from the header code. In a sandbox on his computer, in case the file was malicious or tracked, he deciphered it and opened the message. As he read, Ethan let out a low whistle. They were clear orders to go on the offensive against Ree's New York City positions, and promised heavy drone backup. Other units would go on the offensive hours beforehand, hopefully draining away some of Ree's increasingly limited forces.

Ethan pursed his lips and scanned the other files' header codes. This made no sense. All of the other orders were going to units in other regions. They'd have no impact on an engagement in NYC. And if he hadn't figured out how to decode Taggart's orders, he'd have never known. He still had to send the orders out, as the 20s would know if he didn't, but they didn't know that he still had backdoors to a couple of old satellites. He'd send his own little note to Taggart, separately from the orders.

* * *

Taggart sat behind his desk and tried to ignore the stark concrete walls of the tunnel. He didn't envy the guys who had to carry this desk down here. A small pile of cotton balls lay on the desk, grimy with the face paint he'd just finished removing as best he could.

Private Eagan sat in the chair opposite, but had been able to get his Army Makeup off sooner, somehow. "You look beautiful, sir."

"Cram it, Eagan. When are you going to put on your damn Staff Sergeant stripes? You're out of uniform. I ordered you to put them on before we went on this raid."

"You were serious about that, sir?" Eagan wore an infuriating smirk.

"Shitbird, you know damn well... Never mind. How are the wounded?"

"All accounted for. Two died during evac, four crit, three ready for duty in a couple days."

Taggart nodded. Eagan may have been insubordinate and infuriating, but he was like a kid brother to Taggart—his Brother From Another Mother—and he was damn good at being a soldier. As Taggart's role in the war grew, Eagan had shown himself to be surprisingly effective in the role of staff sergeant as well, though getting him to put on the frikkin' insignia was a battle.

"Not bad. But see if we can push their recovery a bit. This isn't the Holiday Inn, and we aren't in the rear with the gear."

"Yes, sir. Taggart's Titans are all combat, no play. Hooah!"

"I hate that name."

"True, but we don't have a unit designation, so what do you care? The men like it. Sir."

"The troops. Not men. We're equal opportunity, here."

"They look like men."

"For fuck's sake, Eagan."

"Sorry, sir. But the women appreciate the camaraderie, even if it is sexist. We still call coffee November Juliet—racist—so why does it matter if the women fit in how they can?"

"Yeah, that's pretty racist. But the troops joke like that."

"And so do the women troops. Sir."

"Anyway," Taggart said as he opened his desk drawer, "you want some of the good stuff?" Taggart pulled out an almost-full bottle of Wild Turkey, his favorite brand, along with two shot glasses.

"Don't mind if I do. So the whispernet says we got new orders in while we were out fighting for mom and apple pie. Care to share?"

Taggart poured two shots and drank them one after the other while keeping his eyes on Eagan. It was fun messing with the boy sometimes. The man, rather. Then Taggart poured two more and slid one glass across the desk. Eagan kicked it back like he was in college, and set it on the table.

"Damn good rotgut."

"I really hate you, Eagan. You know damn well Turkey is the best mass-produced whiskey in the world."

"I believe you, sir. Totally." Eagan's face was completely straight, no hint of sarcasm.

"I haven't had a chance to read it. Let's see what it says." Taggart pulled the two slips of paper out, and frowned. "Two orders? That's unusual. I'll read 'em by timestamp. The first one has some local intel and some orders. It says there's rumors that Spyder is still running around causing gangbanging mayhem."

"Just a rumor, sir. After what we started between him and his master, Ree, if it wasn't Spyder we hanged then the real one still has got to be dead. I know his henchman is."

"Maybe. The orders are more interesting. It says to launch an all-out at 0400 hours in two days."

"That would be suicide, sir, and suicide is a sin. Pass."

"We don't get to pass on orders from the General, Eagan. Normally you'd be right, but this says we're getting all kinds of backup. Dozens of those cool drones with the little gatling guns, a dozen delivering ammo, water, whatever, and militia all over the region should even now be causing lots of mayhem. It will draw Ree's troops thin. Wouldn't it be nice to push that smug little man back into the sea?"

Eagan didn't answer right away and had a faraway look as he thought through the ramifications. Not that Eagan knew the word "ramifications."

"Alright… Sir, I think it could work if we're lucky, based on our own intel on the OpFor. We have a pretty good idea how many of them are there."

"And it's a lot more than we have, Eagan. We're down to half-strength from our all-time high right after Operation Backdraft."

"We still have about three companies' worth of troops. Even if the Org Chart says we're a regiment. Although they're scattered all over the city. Organizing something that big in two days seems rough, sir. Let me think on it after getting some grub and a half hour of sack time."

"Very well. Let's see what the supp—" Taggart paused as his eyes caught the different timestamp and different source IP. That was his backchannel to the civvy spy, Dark Ryder, whom he trusted very little, but infinitely more than the 20s and the General.

"Sir?"

"This is secret squirrel, give me a moment..." Taggart skimmed the orders, which weren't orders at all, and clucked his tongue. "It's from 'our special friend.' He's telling us the orders we received aren't square. No drones, and definitely no rebels bleeding off Ree's troops. That explains the radio silence, come to think of it."

"Damn, sir. Should I tell the men anything?"

"No, not yet. I need to mull this over before we issue orders."

"Yes, sir. Clock's ticking, though. They'll expect to see us in action, and I imagine they got those satellites watching."

Taggart dismissed Eagan with a wave and stared at the two transmissions. With a sigh, he put the whiskey back in the drawer. He needed a clear head. He hoped this Dark Ryder was wrong, whoever he really was. For every raid Taggart launched, they hit back, and there were a lot more of them. Taggart's people were on the ropes out there, and unless he could push them back into the sea he wasn't sure he could hold out until spring. "But thanks for the heads-up," he said to himself.

- 3 -

0900 HOURS - ZERO DAY +144

CASSY, LIKE MOST of the Clanners, was mostly trying to stay warm. There wasn't much actual work to do around the farm this time of year, other than feeding the livestock and occasionally fixing fences and maintaining buildings, so most people took up a craft to avoid going stir crazy, and to take advantage of the unaccustomed brief periods of free time. Grandma Mandy and some of the other women quilted. Frank whittled bowls, platters, and other useful little items. Michael split wood or busied his day checking the traps and riding fences.

Cassy stayed in the outdoor kitchen most of her free time, canning everything she could get her hands on. She kept several rocket stoves going, which vented into pipes under the kitchen to warm it before going up a chimney pipe. Virtually no smoke escaped, everything having been burned up efficiently by the rocket stoves before reaching the air flow exhaust vent, but the underground pipes radiated a pleasing warmth once the stoves had been going for a while. They'd tarped up the sides to keep out the wind and keep the heat in better, but the tarps also made it a dark place to work.

That day she was packing vegetables into mason jars, then putting them into the pressure cooker—a homemade affair that Dean Jepson had rigged up out of a 55-gallon barrel plus several pressure valves salvaged from dented pressure cookers they'd found throughout the region during scouting trips. The contraption would pressure cook a couple dozen quart-size jars at once, saving both time and wood fuel, and the canned food would then keep for years as long as the lids didn't malfunction or get opened along the way. Cassy added melted beeswax to the rims of the jars to improve the seals, a trick she'd learned from her mother but had no way of knowing if it worked better.

She heard a horn blast—the guard in the tower had seen something. She waited, tense, hand on her ever-present rifle, for a second blast signaling an attack or raid. No second blast came, and Cassy relaxed. A visitor, then. She wiped her hands clean on her apron and put on her coat and gloves before heading out into the cold morning air to see who had arrived. Several other people were coming out of the homes in the Complex looking curious, as well. Visitors made rare, welcome breaks from the monotony of winter life at the farm.

Scanning the area, she saw the visitor approaching. In a pickup truck! A working vehicle, a black, late-model Ford F250 and not some pre-fuel injection muscle car. It belched black smoke from an odd contraption in the truck bed and pulled a trailer made from the severed bed of another truck.

Michael came up from behind and stood beside her. Cassy didn't hear anyone talking—everyone was frozen, staring in awe, probably trying to figure out how that truck could move.

The truck came to a stop a safe distance away, the doors opened, and out stepped two men. A burly white guy emerged from the passenger side, moving with the same fluidity that Michael always had. He carried a shotgun, the barrel of which he rested on his shoulder. So he'd be the bodyguard, she surmised. From the driver's side stepped a wiry, short black man with a pistol holstered at his side and a smile stretching across his face. He kept his hands well away from the pistol and walked toward the knot of Clanners. The bodyguard remained by the truck, alert and wary.

As the wiry man approached, Cassy heard muttered conversations from the people assembling behind her, which only made the man smile more. "Hello, Clanholme," he said. He walked up to Cassy and held out his hand. "You must be the Clan's leader that everyone talks so much about. Cassy, right?"

Cassy shook his hand, but her mind raced. "How do you know us, mister? Or my name?"

The man shrugged. "Everyone in these parts is talking about the Clan and its leader. They say you killed off the Red Locusts and stopped an army of ranchers who were plundering everyone around these parts. To hear the story, I'd think you did all that by yourself, with nothing more than a knife."

Of course. Tales would get around, and grow in the telling. Damn. That would mean anyone and everyone out there could know about the Clan and where its home was. "I'm sure they exaggerate—"

Michael interrupted her. "Cassy's being modest. All that is true, except the part about doing it alone. The Clan sticks together. But she did kill both the leader of the rancher army and his monster of a sidekick by herself, with a knife. Where'd you hear all that?"

Cassy resisted the urge to correct him. Peter had killed more Red Locusts than the Clan, and she'd had help killing Peter during the uprising, even if she'd supplied the final cut, and she'd used Jim's own pistol to kill him. Whatever Michael's reason for stretching the truth, it must be good.

"Yeah, well. I still have a few reminders of that battle," Cassy said and pointed to the scars on her face.

The man chuckled. "Still impressive, Cassy. I'm Terry, by the way, and the big musclehead there is Lump. I figured I might have something you want in my trailer, and maybe you have something I can use or that I can trade off later. Thought I'd see if we could talk about it and run a swap. Do some business."

Cassy raised an eyebrow. This was startling news. The guy was a wandering trader? That meant the wilds between settlements weren't as dangerous as they used to be. Of course, winter might have a lot to do with that. Still…

"Depends on what you have, Terry," Cassy said. "You didn't answer my friend's question, though. Where did you hear about us? I didn't know there were many who knew us."

Terry nodded, eyes smiling. "Heard about you everywhere I've been, really. Everything from the towns—you know, Manheim, Lititz, even the Adamstown Confederation—down to even a couple of the small settlements like you guys. Dozens of those around here, lately. Even as far north as the folks at the Falconry, which used to be called Cornwall. The survivors there renamed it and you're a legend to them."

That got Cassy's attention. More small settlements? *Dozens?* She'd have Frank and Jaz pump the two visitors for more information about those while this guy was here. "So how is it that you got an almost-new pickup to run, Terry? You some kind of genius?"

Terry grinned again. "Yeah, it's pretty awesome, right? I traded two hundred pounds of salt for it at the Falconry. They got a guy who makes that gizmo in the truck bed. It's called a 'gasifier,' if you can believe it. Runs on wood, not gas, and I get about five hundred miles off the wood I can fit in the truck bed. Something about piping 'woodgas' into the engine's air intake. If you're interested, I could probably bring you one next time I come through, in the spring. I had to modify the engine and other things a bit to bypass the old, fried electronics but power was the hard part. The gasifier solves that."

Cassy saw that Terry kept hawk-like eyes on her as he said that, no doubt gauging her reaction. He was a merchant, after all. "That'd be something we could use, for sure. But you said you knew where to get salt?" His mention of salt had piqued her interest. Amazingly, people needed salt to live. With the sodium-infused garbage that passed for food before the EMPs, people got more than they needed. Not anymore.

Terry nodded and said, "Depends. It's a long run to get it, and everyone around here wants it. But you seem like nice folks, and it couldn't hurt to have a living legend owe me a favor. Am I right, or am I right?"

Cassy knew this game. She'd been in marketing before the lights went out. She shrugged and said, "I don't know about owing anyone. The Clan pays its way. I'm sure we have something you can trade out for a profit. We already have salt from all the salvaging we've done, of course, but I'd love a bigger stockpile. Peace of mind, you know? We got some nice bolt-action rifles to spare."

"What kind?" Terry asked.

"Remington Seven Hundreds. How many do you think it would take to make it worth your while to stop here first, on your way back next spring?"

Terry looked like he was lost in thought for a moment, right hand stroking his scruffy beard. "Well… I see your guard up there has an M4. Is it semi-auto or the real deal?"

She fought the urge to grin. Those, they had plenty of. It would be better to lose the hunting rifles, but they'd get a better deal if he wanted M4s instead. "Auto. Well, burst fire. Oh, but those are so hard to come by. I could spare one for say, three hundred pounds of salt. I'd rather trade for four of the Remingtons, though." It wouldn't take long for the word to spread that the Clan had firepower to spare, which could only make them safer.

For a moment, Terry's eyes widened but he covered it with a nonchalant shrug. "Eh. I could probably do two hundred pounds, for two of the M4s. But that's almost break-even for me."

Cassy put on her sad face and shook her head slowly. "Wow, that's a lot to ask for salt. I couldn't possibly make that trade. My own people would string me up if I did that. Maybe I could spare two, but it'd take three hundred pounds of salt to keep the Clan happy."

Terry raised an eyebrow and nodded slowly. "Yeah... I guess I could do that. It will mean an extra stop for me to trade those out so I can recoup my costs, but maybe you'd remember who did such a great deal for you. Maybe give me a good trade down the road, come harvest next year."

Cassy smiled, nodded, stuck out her hand. "You drive a hard bargain, Terry, but I think we got a deal. You come back with the salt and we'll do the trade. And tell us what else you want to trade for. We manage and harvest game in huge parts of the forest around her, plus we run stock, raise a lot of fruits and vegetables... handy inventions of our in-house Redneck Engineer... there's bound to be things you can trade out at a profit. Now tell me about this 'gasifier' on your truck."

* * *

"So," Cassy said to Frank, who sat next to her later as they ate lunch, "did Dean get a good enough look to figure out how to make a gasifier of our own?"

"He's pretty sure he can do it, with only a few extra things that are easy enough to scrounge up. He's a bit of a genius, the cranky bastard. If he says he can do it, I expect he can, and he'll be a pain in the ass until he gets it right to his satisfaction. He says it could take months to get it to work right, without either a parts list or an example to study."

Cassy grinned. "If we can rig up one or more of those, we can send real vehicles out. Think of the scouting possibilities. Or contacting some of those other survivor groups the trader mentioned. We could even set up a trading center here."

Frank poked at his bowl of constant stew, the random ingredients Grandma Mandy kept slow-cooking in a big stewpot over the coals all day and all night. "Not to mention scaring the bejesus out of anyone thinking about trying Peter's idea again. Working vehicles are mighty impressive these days, and Michael says he never considered just how much advantage you get with the ability to maneuver fast until he had to be on foot or horseback."

"Yep. There's definitely that. But I had another thing in mind, too. With a five hundred mile range between loads of wood, we could get serious about communicating with other survivor groups. Maybe talk them into some sort of alliance, or pact, before the Empire finds us."

"The Fort Wayne people. Do you really think they'll get this far east?"

"If not them from the west, then the invaders from the east. There's got to be a lot of invaders out there still. It isn't like they could just go home now that the whole world's got the same problem they gave the U.S."

"And if not them, then Adamstown is always a pain in the ass."

Cassy shrugged. "Well, our weapons and knowledge are the reason Lititz and other towns usually follow Clanholme's suggestions, for the most part. They're real friendly because we put the hurt on Adamstown's troops every time they try something, and we trade our knowledge of permaculture and prepper skills for their goods and services. With working trucks? We could even force Adamstown to see the error of their ways."

"A nice dream if we didn't just provoke them. I'd rather put scouts out to the west, though. Ethan says the Empire has pushed within a hundred miles of us, and that makes me nervous. I don't know how our little hacker finds all this out, but I'm plenty glad he does."

"Lord knows, information never hurts. And to get the most current information possible, we need a gasifier sooner than next spring." Cassy shifted her weight slightly. "Alright, Frank. Let Choony know we need him to head out to this Falconry survivor group the trader told us about. He can take two horses and head out after New Year's."

"He'll want to bring Jaz. Not because she's his age and gorgeous, of course. But she's street tough and he needs her cunning. Plus, she's his age and gorgeous." He grinned.

Cassy laughed. "Of course not. He's Buddhist, and they're above the temptations of women as pretty and *cunning* as she is." Then she grew more somber. "Since we came out on top against Peter, she's really grown into her potential. It's a shame she had to shed some of that naivety, though. Now she's tough, pretty, and cunning. Trifecta."

Frank chuckled and looked over at Cassy. "He respects her newfound grit as much as he does yours."

"Yeah, I know. I figure the two of them will at least try to play house for a bit, later, when she's ready of course. She still misses Jed."

"He was my best friend, so I get that. Alright, enjoy your mason jars, Cassy. I'll go let Michael know the plan, and you can tell Choony after lunch. Think about what he can bring for trade."

Cassy watched Frank crutch away toward the Complex. Despite losing his foot—to save her life, in fact—Frank was no less appealing to her than he was before. He was happily married, though. All the good ones were and anyway, she had more important things to worry about. She shoved the thought of Frank aside, as always. Some trusts should simply never be broken.

* * *

At supper that day, Cassy sat with most of the Council. A voice from behind them almost made her jump, until she realized it was Michael. "Sorry, Cassy. I didn't mean to startle you. Got a minute?"

Cassy motioned for him to sit on the log next to her. "Sure, what's up?"

After sitting, Michael said, "I know you and Frank have this plan to send out ambassadors to the groups we just found out about, but I have some concerns. I can see the benefits, but it's my job to let you know the risks as I see them."

Frank shifted in his seat. "Your job is the security of the Clan, Michael. You're good at it, too, but keep in mind that friendly neighbors also make us safer. It's not just about right here, right now. If we had the friends then that we have now, Peter would never have made it to Clanholme alive."

"Maybe, maybe not. But not everyone we meet is going to be friendly, Frank. I think we should lay low, stay off the radar of those we haven't already met. Maybe send a spy come spring to scout them out before approaching them with envoys."

"Cassy's already a local legend. That 'lay low' ship has sailed." Frank leaned down to scratch his leg stub. "I mean, if our allies know these other groups then I imagine they've all heard of us. The trader damn near announced that Cassy's recognized across the whole region now. And if they're Adamstown's allies, well, Adamstown knows about us all too well already. We can't lay low now, even if we wanted to."

"I don't recommend sending out envoys right now anyway," Michael replied. "It's winter. Game is scarce, people are hungry. There may not be any more Red Locusts out there, gangs of cannibal bandits, but people *are still eating people* if they get hungry enough. The die off isn't done yet. I say again, waiting to send out scouts until spring is the safest path for us."

"And then what, Michael?" asked Frank. "Another couple of months for them to get back and to send out envoys? Who knows how long it'll take to negotiate an alliance. It could be well into summer by the time we get even preliminary results, and the Empire is only a hundred miles away. Think they'll sit on their asses when spring comes? Better to negotiate *before* the Empire barks at our border. And for the mobility that will let us reach out like that, we need the gasifier. Gasoline is awful scarce now."

Cassy stood abruptly. Her jaw was tight, but she smiled at them both. "Michael, we couldn't ask for a better protector. The whole Clan relies on you and your team to keep us safe. And Frank, your foot may be gone but your wisdom isn't. Bring the Council together, will you? We'll meet in half an hour. The whole Council needs to kick this one around."

* * *

1900 HOURS - ZERO DAY +144

Jaz wasn't on the Council, but she'd been with Ethan and Amber when Cassy's call for the Council came in. Ethan left, Jaz made polite excuses to Amber to leave as well, and she caught up with Ethan just outside of Cassy's house, where the Clan always met.

"Howdy, Jaz. Did you forget something?"

Jaz smiled, bright as a new morning in spring. She wasn't his type, she knew, but smiling never hurt when you wanted something. "Just wondering if I can come in and eavesdrop. I can be your plus-one. I've heard rumors about a mission that includes Choony, and I want to hear it from the Council before I freak out from not knowing."

Ethan shrugged. "Suit yourself, but Cassy might ask you to leave." He turned and entered the house. Jaz stayed on his heels.

When Ethan sat next to Choony on the couch, she sat behind the two on a folding chair and tried to seem invisible. The others were all seated already on the couch or scattered about on chairs when Cassy came in.

Cassy sat down at the head of the dining room table, the "Round Table," which was square but Cassy liked the idea that she was just first among equals, even if everyone knew it didn't work that way in reality. She wanted a Round Table—that's what the square table was.

She spread a regional roadmap on the table, but Jaz couldn't see it from the other side of the room. "Big news. I know Ethan has kept us all up to date on the threat from the Empire, west of us. They're within one hundred miles and we know almost nothing else about the situation, except that they've had to fight tooth and nail for every bloody inch of ground. It turns out the people who have survived so far don't much like the idea of bowing and scraping to some half-pint Caesar located who knows where." She looked around. "We need more information. And come spring, we need to organize the other local groups. Sooner, if we can. For that we need a vehicle. Horses are just too slow, especially once you run out of whatever feed you can carry with you."

Ethan coughed. "Don't forget the 'vaders. They're still out there, all around us."

"That situation is more stable than the Empire's, from what you tell us, Ethan. Hell, the whole reason Adamstown raids so much is to supply their fight against their own friendly neighborhood invader camp. I wish they'd just asked us all for help instead of raiding, but on the bright side that mistake put us in a bit of a leadership position with other survivors hereabouts."

Michael said, "You know my advice, but if we had a car that worked, my advice would change. Drastically. Marines hate being on defense anyway. A car would give us fast response capability when a situation does come up."

Cassy smiled crookedly. "Someone's been listening to scuttlebutt." She looked around. "It's a valid point, though. So the question becomes, 'Where do we get a working car?' And the answer to that turns out to be pretty simple. We already have a car that works—the Camaro."

Grandma Mandy frowned. "I detest that thing. And your idea has a flaw, sweetie. There's no gasoline. Where there is gas, there's no power to run the pumps. And where you can get to it without a pump, Ethan told me the gasoline goes bad after a few months. A lot of it is probably useless by now."

Jaz, sitting quietly in the back, raised an eyebrow. That was new information. She'd wondered why the Clan kept that gorgeous muscle car under cover and never used it. So, gas goes bad? If Ethan said it then it must be true, but it surprised her.

Cassy grinned and looked around the room. Jaz caught her eye and it seemed Cassy had only just noticed her, but other than letting her gaze linger for a moment longer than she had with the others, she gave no sign of surprise or disapproval.

The Clan leader then stabbed a finger at the map before her, though Jaz still couldn't see it. "That's all true, from what I understand, but we had a useful visitor today, and he let slip some even more useful news."

Frank spoke up. "You're talking about the trader that came through today, I presume."

Michael frowned. "Traitor?"

"No," Cassy said with a grin. "Trader. An honest-to-god traveling merchant and tinkerer, like in medieval times, bartering and bringing news from village to village. And he let slip a detail that will help us with our problem. There's a device called a gasifier that uses wood somehow to fuel a regular car. We must have one of these, and quickly. I am sending someone to Cornwall, the town up north through the forest—they call themselves the Falconry now, and they make these devices. I gathered you to discuss this because we need an envoy to travel there and get one. Or to get the parts for Dean to improve on."

Well now, that was interesting! Jaz ran through a few ideas on what the Clan could accomplish with this gasifier gadget. Not only letting them run the Camaro indefinitely, but they could use one to power generators, which were a lot more useful than the solar and wind Cassy had set up by the time the EMPs hit. The Clan had a few generators, but without gas they were useless for now. Not to mention sitting in Clanholme all winter was, like, totally boring. Life was too short to veg out all winter if she didn't have to.

Jaz leapt to her feet. "Cassy, I'll go. I'm totally the best person for the job. I'll get, like, the best deal. Smile and eyelashes. So yeah, I volunteer." She grinned from ear to ear. Cassy would have to let her go. She just had to!

Before Cassy could respond, Michael stood with arms akimbo. He sure looked outraged. "Cassy, the idea is solid, but you can't possibly think it's a good idea to send Jaz. No disrespect, Jaz—your heart's in the right place—but you tend to attract the wrong kind of attention and you'll be alone in an unknown settlement. What if they're Adamstown's allies, or just a bad place with bad people? A lot of that goes around these days, you know."

Jaz glared at Michael. Dammit, he should have learned by now that she could take care of herself. End of the frikkin world and she still had to deal with sexist crap! "Michael," she growled, not bothering to hide her irritation, "I think I can handle myself. Or have you forgotten I'm the one who found the Marines who help you keep our borders safe? Without them, we wouldn't have won against Peter. Do we really need more sexist bullshit in the new world? I had enough of that in the old world. More than enough."

Cassy laughed, surprising Jaz—she'd expected Cassy to get mad, not laugh...

"Jaz, Michael, please sit down. You both have valid points. And Jaz? Michael wasn't talking down about you, or thinking you're weaker because you're a woman. Last I checked, I'm a woman... and so are a few of his Marines. He's right, though—you do attract a lot of attention. The blessings of youth, I guess. And that attention is both good and bad. Depends how you use it. You're right, it'll help secure a deal, and with good terms. So I was already going to ask you to go. But I also need my people taken care of, and you're my people, too. Two are better for traveling than one. The trader who came to visit had an armed bodyguard he called Lump. It's just smart."

Frank, who had been sitting like a lump himself and

stroking his chin, started to chime in. He was a great guy, so Jaz wasn't too worried about what he'd say.

"I think Cassy has a point," Frank said thoughtfully. "But might I suggest sending some other people with her as well? Both for security and to display our strength to these Falconry people. First impressions matter more than ever these days."

Cassy paused, considering what he'd said. She was totally pretty when she got that look on her face, even with the scars. Hells, dudes probably thought scars were all sexy. Jaz tried to imagine what she herself would look like with scars, but didn't like the idea. Maybe when she got older.

"You're right, of course," Frank was saying. "Choony, I like Cassy's idea of having you and Jaz both go. You have a remarkable ability to keep people 'grounded' in reality. You calm people down. We'd send maybe four of Michael's Marines as escort, on horseback, with one of the wagons that Dean jury-rigged. You can carry supplies with you, and Jaz can trade for a gasifier on the way back. All but you would carry M4s, and you'd have half a dozen of our Remington 700s for trade as well. We all use M4s for defense now anyways. What do you think, Michael? Choony?"

Jaz grinned. Frank was really good at organizing for travel and this was the best news ever. She was totally going on an adventure, and this time there was no rapey Jimbo chasing her. And Choony was coming. It couldn't get better than that. He was the best guy she'd ever known, even if he wasn't as hot as Jed had been. Plus he was fun to play with. The more she flirted with him, the more flustered he got. If she didn't know better, she'd think he was crushing on her. That idea made her more excited than it should, though, so she squashed the thought right away. Choony was all about Cassy, as far as she could tell, and philosophy, and helping everyone in sight, so best not to get her own hopes up. That never worked out well, in Jaz's experience.

Choony shrugged and nodded. Yay! He would go with her.

The rest of the meeting was basically a planning session, with the whole Council chiming in with ideas. Jaz kept quiet but realized after a while that she was grinning like an idiot. Well, why not? It was a good day...

* * *

After the meeting, Ethan approached Cassy while the rest of the Council filed out of her house. She smiled and waved as he dodged Council people going the other direction. The poor guy spent most of his time locked away in the Bunker, even when Amber was on duty. The two kept the bunker radios manned at all times, as well as monitoring for incoming messages on Ethan's laptop. Since Ethan and Amber needed sleep like everyone else, he'd also been assigned one of the older teens to act as his assistant. It all meant that the antisocial hacker had all the company he usually needed or could tolerate, so the rest of the Clan didn't see much of him anymore.

"Hey, Ethan. Got something on your mind?"

"Sure do, boss lady. You know how we have those extra HAM radios we scrounged? I was wondering if you could authorize sending one of them over to the Falconry. They're our northern border, from what I understand, so an early warning system might be a good idea. Plus we could coordinate better that way, if the Falconry and the Clan decide we like one another. Hell, it could even be worth one of those gasifiers, if they recognize the value of a working HAM radio. Keep your other trade goods in reserve."

"How many HAMs do we have? Can we spare one?"

"We still have maybe half a dozen. That's after sending

radios to our two biggest allies, but they're both to the south of us. I didn't even know there was a working settlement to the north, at least not for many miles. But with a HAM radio they could help us tie this region together, too."

"You have a point. But I sort of think we need them protecting our northern border more than they need us to protect their southern one. But as a regional bulwark? Interesting. I think the HAM might end up being a good bargaining chip. Go ahead and make it happen, Ethan."

Ethan thanked her and left. Cassy turned back to the map on the table, and returned to considering the Clan's evolving strategic situation. Yeah, a working car would be a Very Big Deal for them, in a lot of ways. Cassy sent up a quick prayer in thanks for the trader's visit. Just in case there really was someone upstairs listening, she also prayed for her people's safe return. And for the friendly trader to stay well, while she was at it. Winter journeys were nothing to take lightly.

- 4 -

0730 HOURS - ZERO DAY +145

JAZ STOOD BY the horses and double-checked her backpack while Choony shook hands with Cassy, the two of them saying their goodbyes. Their four Marine escorts were already mounted and waiting. Jaz and Choony would ride on the wagon, drawn by two horses, with Jaz riding shotgun since Choony wouldn't.

Although they'd all become decent equestrians, neither Jaz nor Choony had much experience with wagons other than the crash course Cassy had given them the evening before, but Choony did seem to have a way with horses. Probably because he was always so calm, one of his best features as far as Jaz was concerned. She never felt her fight-or-flight instincts kick in from anything he said or did, and it was... nice.

Once the farewells were done—one could never be certain of making it home alive these days—the two stepped up into the wagon, sat on the bench, and set out slowly toward the northern border with the Marines riding out front. Most of the Clan kids ran beside the wagon as far as the now-leafless Jungle, excited at the change in daily routine, and the adults who attended kept busy keeping the smaller kids from getting run over.

Once the party had left the Jungle behind, along with the frolicking kids, Jaz lost herself in watching the trees that seemed to slowly roll by. Normally she'd be chatty with Choony, but she was too busy trying not to snap at him. She didn't want him here with her, since this should have been her own chance to shine, and to get away from everyone for a while, but it wasn't his fault. When Cassy gave orders, they were to be followed, so Jaz had acted all, like, super thrilled about it, but she wasn't really. And Cassy always did everything for the good of the Clan, so Jaz couldn't even get properly angry about it. Which only irritated her more. Rather than take it out on her friend, she chose silence. Not that Choony's company was bad. If she was truthful with herself, she kind of looked forward to spending more time with him, but she didn't have time or patience to sift through *those* sorts of feelings. Maybe later.

After a half hour, they'd passed well beyond the northern Clanholme border, beyond the food forest, and were about halfway to the copse of trees where Choony had hidden out after escaping Peter's vicious invasion. It was now well known as a safety point and hidden supply cache. The two wouldn't stop there, but it was the most well-known landmark north of the farm.

Choony coughed, a deliberate noise, and yanked Jaz from her thoughts. "So are we going to spend the next few days in silence, or are you going to tell me why you are angry with me?"

Jaz knew that, whether she spoke or not, Choony would take it in stride. His philosophy of life provided him a lot more inner peace than Jaz ever felt, but she couldn't bring herself to want to join him in that. Fire still burned in her blood, and she rather preferred her way despite its drawbacks.

Finally, she said curtly, "I'm not mad at you, y'know? I'm just bent that Cassy sent you. I wanted to go alone. No point risking both of us."

Choony only nodded. Of course he understood. Of course he didn't take it personally. Of course that irritated the hell out of Jaz. Man, she was just not good company today and she knew it, but there was no point taking it out on her friend.

* * *

1000 HOURS - ZERO DAY +145

The morning hours rolled by in silence, like the scenery around them, and Jaz kept up a sort of detached alertness that had become second nature in recent months. It allowed her mind to wander even as she kept a diligent watch on their surroundings. She was riding shotgun, after all. Their four Marine guardians weren't visible at the moment as they passed through rolling hills. Two had ridden ahead and the other two rode their flank to scout whichever side seemed more likely to conceal a threat. That didn't mean a threat couldn't slip through and jeopardize the wagon, along with her and Choony. She stayed alert.

Choony was the first to break the silence. "Thank you for allowing me to come without a fight, Jaz. The mission is important, and Cassy's reasoning was sound. More than that, I want to do what I can to make sure you're all right out here. You've come to mean quite a lot to me."

Jaz felt a little thrill in her belly when he said that, though she didn't fully understand why. Sometimes it totally sucked not being really in touch with what was going on inside her...

"Still being silent, eh? Well, I'm not going anywhere," Choony said, and Jaz realized she'd gotten lost in thought and forgot to answer him. "So, let me know if you feel like talking. It's going to be a long trip for so much silence."

"Sorry. I just zoned out is all. I'm sorry for being so crunchy. It's not you, I promise. I like the company, too. But sometimes I just wonder—"

A flash of something metallic in the sunlight, at the crest of a hill. Maybe half a mile away. "Did you see that, Choony?"

Choony turned his head to look where she'd been looking. The gleam again. Choony whipped the reins and shouted, "Hiya!"

The wagon lurched as the horses took off, accelerating into a run. Even over the mostly even, soft ground, as they sped up the wagon bounced roughly to and fro, and Jaz had to grab onto Choony's jacket at one point to avoid falling out. She brought her shotgun close to her body, a football grip, to keep from losing it. Once stable she pulled a handheld radio out of her pocket. "Mike, Mike, this is Whiskey Two. We got a union tango under one click west-northwest, over."

A brief pause before the radio squawked back, "Roger, confirm unknown tango west-northwest of your position. Head east, Whiskey Two. We'll catch up."

Jaz could barely hear through the adrenaline-fueled pounding of her heart in her ears. "Maybe it's just an abandoned car or something," she shouted at Choony over the clamor of the wagon and horses and wind.

"Maybe, but if not I'm not giving them a nice, slow target." Choony snapped the reins again and turned the wagon to the east, away from the reflection on the hill.

Jaz scanned for cover. With the rolling terrain, visibility was limited, especially as Choony kept the wagon *between* the hills to avoid silhouetting themselves on a hill crest. It was a trick they'd learned from Michael. In the distance, a small forest lay between Clanholme and Brickerville. She shouted, "There's a gap in those woods ahead at Penryn Road. If we can make it there, we'll have a forest between us and them, and Brickerville's only a mile away."

Brickerville was friendly to the Clan, and—

"No good, there's a creek between us and them, Jaz!"

Damn, she'd forgotten about that. Still, they'd have a brief moment of safety to figure out which way to go, once they were through that gap in the tree line. It was overland, but farmland like they'd been traveling on, smooth and hilly like the rest right up to the edge of the creek. It was too fast and wide to ford safely with a wagon, however.

Damn Hammer Creek. Always in her way. She'd been in a firefight with invaders along that creek before and knew its terrain. "Crap! We'll have to get through the gap and then head north, but we'll have to go through the spur of forest there, or around. That would take us west again, toward whatever's back there."

Then Jaz caught sight of the now-silent high-tensile power line ahead, running east-northeast. "No, there will be a clearing for the power lines, no trees and less snow. We can try to cross there, or follow Hammer Creek north. Remember the clearing in the middle of the woods there? We can pass northward through that."

Choony didn't reply, and didn't have to. It was the only plan they had, and God willing, it'd work. At least it gave them cover and a good shot at eluding any pursuers.

The tree line at Penryn Road came visible ahead, and Choony turned the horses just a little to the north, heading toward the gap in the trees. Behind, faint echoes of gunfire reached them.

"Shit, I hope they're okay," Jaz shouted over the wind.

Choony remained silent, focused on guiding the wagon through the sometimes rough land of abandoned farms through which they passed at speeds that sometimes felt unsafe to Jaz. They followed along with the power lines, so it wasn't too rough to pass, though the occasional sudden bounce did shake an "Oof!" out of her.

The gunfire behind them continued until they plunged across the north-south road and into the gap between the trees. The woods to either side muffled the sounds of the battle behind them into an indistinct echo. Then there was only the sound of the horses' hooves, the creak of the wagon wheels, and her own thoughts.

In minutes they arrived at the west bank of Hammer Creek. On the far side lay an abandoned farm. Despite her hopes, the creek wasn't passable with a wagon here, not without stopping and moving very slowly, at least. Choony began to pull the horses to the left, north, to parallel the creek. As expected, there was a vast clearing in the midst of the woods on their own western side of the south-running creek.

But their plan was short-lived. Jaz spotted two people as they popped up on a makeshift platform around the top of a grain silo. She didn't remember that platform being there before, and the people wore black uniforms. Arab invaders, then. Shots rang out, but the wagon was moving quickly and these particular soldiers weren't great shots, or their weapons weren't maintained well, or both. Either way, heading further north was out. To the south lay two miles of dense forest, as she recalled.

"Buddha guide us, we will have to take the creek," Choony shouted, and in response Jaz grabbed onto the wagon as tightly as she could. She hoped her friend's god or whatever was listening.

The horses sprinted toward the creek as Choony guided them, shaking the reins in the time-honored signal to speed up. The horses went from a gallop to a dead run, and Jaz said her own prayer then. If they made it across, they'd be clear all the way to Brickerville. If not, they'd be sitting ducks until after they ran across a hundred yards of wide open terrain, and she didn't like those odds at all.

"Oh, shit—" she whispered as the horses plunged into the creek, which ran narrow and rapid at that point.

The wagon went airborne. All Jaz could do was hang on for dear life and try not to fall off. Then the wagon hit the creekbed hard, bounced again into the air as the horses continued their headlong rush, tilted crazily to the left and threatened to overturn. Before that could happen, they struck the ground on the other side with a bone-jarring crash, and the wagon righted itself, keeping to its wheels. She heard a terrible cracking noise then, as of timber splitting, and Jaz prayed the wagon wouldn't fall apart under them— and it didn't. Instead, they settled firmly onto all four wheels, though now the rear of the wagon tilted to the right, and the wagon kept shuddering as it tried to pull hard to that side. The horses slowed as they had to almost drag that right rear wheel through the soft earth. But at least they'd made it across and the wagon hadn't disintegrated.

Past the farm with its new invader hosts they ran, hidden now by riverside trees on the other side of the creek, and turned onto a small road that ran eastward. In only a few minutes they were careening toward the wooden walls and iron gate of Brickerville, and Jaz hoped the people there wouldn't open fire on them. Fortune was on her side, though, and the gate swung open to allow the wagon to pass. Choony didn't pull the reins to slow down until they were well inside the walls of the tiny survivor village of Brickerville. The exhausted horses slowed to a stop, blowing hard, muzzles foam-flecked and heads drooping.

As the gates swung closed behind them, Jaz looked around with a wild grin on her face. The village of

Brickerville had never looked so beautiful.

* * *

1300 HOURS - ZERO DAY +145

Jaz picked at her constant stew, a courtesy of the village survivors. It was actually pretty tasty, but she totally never wanted to eat the stuff again. She'd had way too much this winter at Clanholme and would no doubt continue to have way too much of it, because constant stew was the single most efficient way to get nutrients and calories from food. With extra vegetables, leftover meat, and other bits and pieces thrown into the pot while it stayed on the fire at a slow cook, nothing went to waste. She'd learned that every culture had a version of constant stew, whether they called it hunter's pot or mulligan stew or any of dozens of other names. It didn't mean she wasn't sick of it. To her, it was constant stew because she had a constant problem eating it, a thought that made her hide a reluctant smile.

Choony ate his without complaint or even appearing to hate it like she did. He never complained about anything, though, so he might really hate it and she would never know.

Jaz said, "I wish I'd known those Marines better. I really like them, maybe just because we were the ones who found them and led them to Peter. We wouldn't be free now if they hadn't happened along when they did, and now I gotta think, like, four of them are dead."

After he finished chewing his mouthful of stew, Choony said, "They didn't just happen along. Ethan pulled off a minor miracle and contacted them, sent them our way. The timing reaffirms my belief in Karma, though. Anyway, there is nothing we can do about them, so it's pointless to make yourself suffer over it. Things are what they are. But I suppose they could be okay. We don't know for a fact they died. Maybe it was their radio that got killed."

Jaz took the last few bites of stew and pushed her bowl away from her. "It's been, like, over two hours. If they were alive, they'd have radioed in by now or caught up with us, dude. Anyway, someone is making a bee-line for us, so I guess it's show time."

Sure enough, the woman approaching walked right up to Jaz and Choony, stopped, and looked somewhat awkward. "So, I'm supposed to take you to our leader now," the young woman said. She couldn't be any older than Jaz herself, she figured, so of course she wasn't the leader. Just like they didn't let Jaz be on the Council, which irritated her to no end. Though after Cassy said nothing about her crashing their little get-together, she wasn't sure where she stood with the other Council people. Maybe you just had to believe you belonged there.

Jaz smiled at the girl, hoping to put her at ease. "Super! We've been all, like, on pins and needles waiting. Thanks."

She stood, followed by Choony who, she noticed, always seemed to want to walk behind her, though she was too used to that from people to even notice most of the time. They were led toward the town's center. It was a large lot that sold storage sheds before the war and now housed most of their supplies. It was fenced off, but the ramshackle fencing showed that it was a recent addition. The mayor's office was set in what was once the sales office.

Before entering, Jaz looked across the street—Highway 322—and gazed in wonder at the acres of greenhouses clustered there. "I wonder why they didn't put the mayor over there with all the food," she whispered to Choony, who only grinned. They'd met the mayor before, and he was on the portly side.

Then they both stepped inside. The office was lit with

several bright storm lamps of the sort that the Clan relied on. The base contained liquid fuel while an adjustable wick held a flame contained by a small glass chimney. They got damn hot and were a terrible fire hazard, but they didn't get snuffed out by the slightest breeze like candles and they were harder to tip over as well.

Sitting behind a rather plain-looking IKEA-style desk was the man Jaz recognized as the mayor of Brickerville. He looked a lot more tired than the last time she'd seen him, during a visit to Clanholme. She smiled at him winsomely and said, "Hi, Josh. How's tricks?"

Josh managed to smile back, but though his goateed lips made the motions, no joy seemed to reach his baggy brown eyes. "We're alive, thanks. Jaz, right? Surprised you remembered my name. Flattered, but surprised. Sorry for my appearance. None of us have slept in a couple days, since the invaders moved into the area."

That got Jaz's attention pronto. Maybe Brickerville had intel on their numbers or something. "How many, and when?"

Josh waved his assistant away and once she left, closing the door behind her, he closed his eyes and took a deep breath. Then he said, "We know of a platoon of Arabs. They're running around in five-man teams causing havoc. A trader was passing through at the time, and he said he'd seen the tactic before to the east of us. They come in, kill a bunch of homesteaders to cause a panic, and once everyone has mostly fled to a camp like ours, they move in trucks and loot the area before moving on. Like locusts. They're leaving all the seeds behind, though."

Choony nodded. "Yes, that makes sense. Now that they can't ship in supplies anymore, they have to eat just like we do. If they take the seeds, there won't be anything to plunder after next year's harvest."

Jaz's lip curled into a snarl. "I bet those bastards wish now they hadn't hit Lancaster with that haze crap," she said. That brown goo stuck to everything, killing plants and animals in hours. People, too. But it had to be applied by plane, and that wasn't an option anymore. Even the old crop dusters had electronics to control the chemical spray, so they couldn't commandeer and use those. At least, not for gas attacks. Not yet. "They're just looters now. At Clanholme we shoot them when we can."

"They hit us yesterday and we haven't slept since," Josh replied. "Everyone's pulling double shifts on the walls until the Rabs leave the area." His people called the Arabic invaders "Rabs," Jaz recalled from Josh's visit to Clanholme. Short for "Arab"? Maybe for "Rabble"?

The mayor continued, "I'm surprised you made it through, with half a dozen of their little terror teams running around between us and you guys."

Choony shrugged. "I'm surprised, too. I think we might only have made it here because our lost guards tore into the first team that spotted us. That's a guess, but we saw a reflection on a hill, and these days it pays to assume the worst, so we fled. Our guards went to check it out, and then we heard a firefight from that direction. Haven't seen our people since. And then we ran into some more at that farm and almost lost our wagon, fording the creek at a run. Our horses are exhausted."

Josh raised an eyebrow, then said, "My condolences for your loss of the Marines. We've all lost people, but it still sucks every damn time it happens. So where are you headed, if we let you out of here?"

Jaz slammed her foot to the floor. "What do you mean, 'if' you let us out? Thought we were allies."

"Calm down, you're not a prisoner here. But I won't open my gate again until I know it's safe for my people. Right? I have scouts out, and they should return by nightfall if they didn't get themselves killed."

Jaz grimaced. "What have your scouts got to do with us?"

"Well, depending on what they say, I might open the gate to let you folks get on with whatever it is you're out here to do. It will be getting dark, and a good time for you to slip out. Maybe you should take a nap or something and get rested before then... I don't recommend camping out within ten miles of us. If you're fast and lucky, they won't catch your trail in the snow. If they do, you're in for a rough time out there. Are you sure you don't want to stay awhile?"

Choony grinned. "The snow's a lot lighter around here because all the trees either blocked it or caught it. At least it's been a lot easier going than I thought it would have been, and once we're in the woods I imagine there won't be much at all."

The faint sounds of gunfire came through the open window. In response to Jaz's inquisitive look, Josh said, "Don't worry about that. It's the Rabs taking potshots at us. They can't starve us out, because we grow most everything we need in the greenhouses across the street. It used to be a nursery and garden center. But they can try to trick us into using all our ammo, and then they'd waltz right in. I ordered our people not to shoot back unless they get a clear shot, so those are just Rab shots you hear."

Jaz whistled. "Damn. With all that going on, I'm almost surprised you opened up for us. I couldn't have blamed you if you left us out there in the snow."

Josh grinned, a real smile this time, and his eyes lit up for a moment before exhaustion again overtook enthusiasm. "You aren't Rabs, so I couldn't leave you out there to die. Not when we'd have you safely outgunned if you were up to no good. But, seeing that you're Clan, I'm sure glad I did. And of course, I'd never turn down a beautiful chick in distress," he grinned again, jokingly, and added a lascivious wink.

"Perv," Jaz said and batted her eyelashes super melodramatically. "But thanks. Real talk. You didn't have to let us in, but you did. Cassy was right about you peeps."

"After what happened with White Stag, if the tales are true, I'll take that as a compliment. So tell me where you're headed, and I can maybe give you the best route. Given that you had to cross the creek, I imagine you got sidetracked a bit."

Choony said, "Definitely. We were going north to the game lands forest, then we were going to skirt around it to the west, ending up in the Falconry. Cornwall, they used to call it."

"Oh yeah, you got sidetracked alright. I don't recommend going back the way you came, but it's up to you. Since you're here, though, there's a way right through the woods. Take the highway west out of town, north to Boyd Road. To get there you gotta cross the Turnpike, but at night it shouldn't be too dangerous. You'll also have to creep by the weirdos in the compound across the Turnpike. It's a Christian group, but not like most Christians."

"What do you mean?" Choony asked. "The Christians I know are all good people."

"Well, these ones aren't good people. They think this is the Tribulation, and all the good people are already dead. They're trying to earn a trip to Heaven, doing God's work by killing anyone they run across, figuring anyone still here is evil and needs to go to Hell, but God just forgot about them. Or something. They'll kill you and take your stuff as a tithe, if they see you. Thankfully, they go to bed at dusk every night. Early to bed, early to rise."

"Holy crap. For real?" Jaz exclaimed. "They're nothing like our Christians, then. Ours are full-on 'turn the other cheek' types, but good people. Forgiving people."

"Nothing like ours, either, me included. But whatever the case, don't wake them up when you go by. Anyway, turn right on Boyd Road then and it takes you right to the heart of Cornwall."

"The Falconry." Jaz grinned.

"Whatever. What do they got that you Clanspeople need?"

"We're not sure," Choony interrupted before Jaz could speak. "Cassy heard rumors from a trader. Maybe the same trader came through your town. We didn't know about them, so Jaz and I are going to say hello and see what's up."

Josh had one eyebrow raised, but nodded. "Cool... I don't know much about them, except they consider themselves the guardians of the game lands. They sit on the only road going through the forest, shaving days off the trip for people on foot. For which they take a tax, but I haven't heard of them being bandits or sleazy. They do earn their little fees."

"Good to know," Jaz said with a smile. "Thanks for having people fix our wagon, too. I figured we broke something bouncing across the creek, but I didn't know what."

"Just a busted shock absorber, from what my folks say. Quick fix. We'll have it done before the scouts return. Tell Cassy we said hello, but don't forget to tell her we helped out. And I know radios are scarce and we're a small group, but we're strategically located. Will you let Cassy know we'd like to have a radio, so we can keep in touch with all you friendly settlements?"

Jaz and Choony agreed, said goodbye, shook hands—did all the expected socializing—and then went out to find a nice place for a nap. It would be a few hours before the sun went down.

* * *

Back at Clanholme, Cassy busied herself rubbing down a horse, just returned by a scout who had been riding the Clan's border all day. The late afternoon sun, low on the winter horizon, cast faint, speckled light into the barn. Nearby stood the real reason for Cassy's interest in the horse —the new guy, Nestor, was busy mucking stalls with a shovel and wheelbarrow. The manure would go straight to the composting pits that, by virtue of being dug into the ground, never got too cold or wet from leachate.

To Cassy's satisfaction, a Marine guard stood within view as well, unobtrusively. Michael had made sure Cassy's instructions to have Nestor watched at all times were followed. Cassy hoped they'd catch him doing something wrong, justifying her mistrust of the swarthy man. Something about him set off her survivor alarms. She still couldn't put her finger on just why she didn't want him in the Clan, and wished Choony were there to talk to. He had a way of asking questions that led Cassy to a deeper understanding of herself and her motivations, all without seeming to or getting preachy.

Nor could she talk to her mom about it, though usually Grandma Mandy was a great person to bounce things around with. She was a very perceptive woman. But Cassy knew exactly what her mom would say, down to the disapproving tone of her voice as she browbeat Cassy for being too distrustful, the man earned his place, he'd saved the kids, he'd done nothing wrong, he was doing his share of work, blah blah. Maybe Cassy didn't understand her own mistrust, but she had learned the hard way to believe in her instincts— they could be wrong sometimes, as they had been when Choony arrived, but they'd been right much more often.

Maybe she needed to talk to someone else. Choony and Grandma Mandy might not be options, but Ethan was, and the hacker shared her suspicion of strangers. She finished rubbing down the horse, put the bristle brush on its shelf, and left the barn by way of the back doors to avoid passing Nestor, mucking stalls. She went to the main bunker entrance inside her house and followed the dark tunnel from the hidden entrance in the shelved canned goods pantry under her stairwell. Two knocks on the heavy metal hatch at the end of the tunnel and it swung open to reveal the LED-lit interior of the bunker. Ethan stood at the door and, when he saw who was there, he smiled.

"Come on in, Cassy. I'm surprised to see you here. What's up?"

"Just wanted to bounce some thoughts off a fellow conspiracy theorist. Do you have a few minutes?"

"Sure thing. But you aren't a conspiracy theorist, really. Not by my standards. You just have a healthy understanding of what assholes people generally are when the mask comes off."

"Maybe. I hope that's not true about most people, but I'm afraid it probably is. People really are terrible, it's not just my imagination. Even good people do terrible things these days, just to survive. Which is what I wanted to talk to you about. Have you spent any time with the new arrival, Nestor?"

"A bit, yeah. Mostly out of curiosity. I know you don't trust him, so I wanted to see what the fuss was about."

"So what did you think? Am I just being paranoid?" Cassy scratched her nose, a reminder of how much the dry air of the bunker always bothered her skin. Maybe a humidifier was in order for him and Amber, if the scrounge team found one.

"Probably. He's quiet and intense, but that's not a sin these days. I guess he could be a spy, but if so he has already learned everything he's going to. I don't think he could learn anything that would harm us. Quite the opposite—if he is a spy, he'll report how strong our defenses are and his people will find a different target. But my gut says he isn't scouting us out for anything."

"So you think he really is just a wandering survivor who was in the right place and time to save the girls?"

"I have no reason to think otherwise. I think maybe you're just—"

Ethan was interrupted as the inner hatch to the bunk room opened, and Amber stepped out wearing a nighty. Ethan grinned and said, "Did you have a good nap, hon?"

Amber nodded, and smiled at Cassy. "Hey girl. How's our fearless leader?"

Cassy suppressed a smile. It was obvious Amber hadn't been sleeping, and her disheveled appearance had a different cause. "I'm good. Just had to bounce an idea off Ethan, nothing big. Are you two going to have the weekly report done on time, or do you need another couple days?" It was an irrelevant question, meant to change the subject. Ethan's reports were always on time.

"We'll have it in time for you tomorrow as usual, of course," Ethan said, feigning a hurt look on his face. "But I do have to get back to the terminals. If there's nothing else…"

Cassy scratched her nose again. "No, that was it. See you two at dinner, yeah? Let me know if anything important comes up."

She turned around and left the bunker, still feeling unresolved about Nestor. But at least now she could be reasonably sure it was her own issues, not anything Nestor had done, that set off her warning bells. If Ethan didn't mind someone, they were probably decent enough. He didn't like most people, after all, to the point of being almost reclusive. Cassy climbed the ladder back into her house with her nervousness somewhat calmed.

* * *

Choony got the wagon across the Pennsylvania Turnpike without incident and into the dense woods on the far side. He'd scouted on foot before bringing the wagon, looking for a place in the woods with enough clearance for both wagon and horses, so they could scout ahead on foot without leaving the horses too far behind. He had no intention of blindly riding past the compound of some death-cult religious nutjobs.

Then he and Jaz moved out on foot, gliding between the trees, parallel to Highway 322 but on the side opposite to where the compound was said to be. And just as Josh had told them, the complex was a quarter mile ahead on the west side of the road. He squatted behind a fallen log and peered at the scattered low buildings.

Jaz joined him a second later and nudged his arm with her elbow playfully. "Anyone awake in Nutty Land?"

Choony shook his head. "Doesn't look like it. I don't see any candles or lights on, anyway. Let's just sit here for ten minutes or so. Look for anything that moves. If there's movement, then people are awake and we have a new problem."

Jaz said, "I'm going to go scout around to the north, see how the path ahead looks. It'd suck if we got past the compound but, like, the road was torn up or something. We'd have to go back, prolly. Be right back."

Fifteen minutes later, Jaz returned. Choony had stayed in place so that she'd know where to find him in the dark. Choony whispered, "How does it look?"

Jaz grinned wide enough for him to see even in the dark of the forested night. "Looks good. There's a tree that leans all crazy over the roadway, but doesn't block it. I rigged a surprise in case we need to get out of Dodge quickly when we bring the wagon past the nutjobs. Let's go."

They made their way to the wagon, and Choony got the horses moving again. They kept to the road's right shoulder, as riding down the middle of the paved road would have made a racket with all the horse-hoof clopping and the wagon's wheels creaking. The softer dirt of the shoulder helped a bit with noise from both. They went slowly, without speaking. On their left, the compound—once a church and various smaller buildings, now walled with stacked dead cars —remained dark.

All went well until they were roughly parallel to the compound's gate. The entrance to the compound, the road, and the wagon were suddenly lit up as though in daylight. Choony realized they were being lit up by spotlights, and a bolt of fear washed over him. There was no point fighting, as they'd be greatly outnumbered and he wouldn't harm another person, so he snapped the reins and the wagon lurched forward.

Choony kept waiting for the sounds of gunfire, and he saw Jaz in the seat next to him with her shotgun pointing in the general direction of the gate. A moment later, Choony saw the tree Jaz had mentioned, which tilted crazily over the road.

Jaz shouted, "Watch this!" She leaned over the right side of the wagon and now had a knife in her right hand. She held her arm out as far as it would go, and then Choony saw a rope strung from the tree to the ground. He didn't have time to wonder about it, however, as they sped past it in an instant. Choony kept the horses at a full run until they were well around the next corner, and still no sounds of gunfire could be heard.

The horses began to slow, and in a couple of minutes they were back at a brisk walk. The noise of their hell ride faded to the muffled sounds of hooves and wheels in soft dirt.

As the adrenaline wore off, Choony said, "May I please ask just what you had planned? You mentioned a surprise at the tree, but I must have been too busy watching the road because I saw nothing special happen."

Jaz had her jaw set and eyes narrowed, and she looked pretty angry. "Screw you, Choony. You know damn well you didn't miss it. Nothing happened. My stupid idea didn't work, that's all. You don't need to tease me about it."

Choony suppressed a grin. Now that the danger seemed to have passed, her petulance was kind of cute. "So I see." After a minute of silence, he ventured to say, "So what should have happened?"

Jaz said nothing in return, and for long minutes they rode in silence. Finally, he heard her take a deep breath. "So, I tied our rope to the tilted tree. The other end, I fed around another tree, and the loose end was tied to a young tree. The rope was tight enough to pull the sapling almost over. I wanted to cut the rope, sending the sapling snapping out over the road. In an old movie, it knocked a cowboy's pursuers off their horses and let the hero escape, laughing."

Choony did laugh then, a hearty belly laugh. Jaz flushed red and pointedly looked away from him. When he caught his breath, he said, "I'm sorry for laughing, Jaz. I didn't wish to hurt your feelings. I just couldn't help it. If you'd actually cut that rope, the sapling would have hit us, not our pursuers. And of course, there was no one behind us. I think those lights were on batteries, motion-activated. And lastly, trying to cut a rope on a wagon with horses at a dead run seems a little... risky. The idea might have worked if we'd stopped after passing the tree and adjusted things. I didn't want to stop just then. Did you?"

Jaz made a weird face, and Choony wondered if she was about to yell at him, but then she began laughing, too. It sounded like she was trying to resist, which only made it come out harder once the first snort had forced its way out. Catching her breath, she said, "Yeah. No. Well, it worked in the movie. I guess it was pretty silly." She wore a winning, embarrassed smile, and it was infectious. Choony grinned back at her.

The journey became much more pleasant after that. And Choony realized that, although the idea hadn't worked, it was creative and showed forethought. It would also have probably been non-lethal. The girl was stronger and smarter than he had given her credit for, and he had no doubt that her next scheme would be much more carefully thought out.

* * *

0330 HOURS - ZERO DAY +146

Taggart stood in his command post, in the makeshift "radio room" under the street, while Eagan sat at the desk with half a dozen hand-held radios set up on it. They would intermittently squawk some bit of information from one of his units in the field, and Eagan responded without being told what to say or do. He was a great staff sergeant, even if he refused to wear any rank insignia. Private Eagan was now more his name than his rank, and Taggart's troops all knew it.

"Are we about ready for *Operation Screw the 20s*, Eagan?"

Eagan grinned, but didn't turn to look at his C.O. "Is that what we're calling it now? You really should ask for collateral input from the troops before making such important decisions, sir. Mission nomenclature is vitally important for troop morale, you know."

"Answer my question, shitbird. Are we all in position?

Our mark is in thirty mikes. You-know-who will be watching. Stop fucking around."

"Sorry, sir. Yes, we're in position. Per General Houle's orders, by way of the 20s, by way of Dark Ryder, by way—"

"For fuck's sake, Eagan."

The enlisted man, whom Taggart now thought of as a little brother, or even his son, made a great show of letting out a deep sigh. Taggart grit his teeth but didn't say anything —it would only slow down the process to get into their usual banter right now.

"Major, sir, yessir. Your troops, who are in the field while we sit here sipping delicious, freshly brewed coffee at this fine IKEA desk, are in position. We'll hit General Ree's positions in four places. Our ordnance was put in place an hour ago without incident or hostile contact, and should still be a go."

Taggart nodded and took a sip of his half-burned, tarry coffee—slurping at it, to make damn sure Eagan heard him doing it. Messing with the young man was one of Taggart's few pleasures in life these days. Then he glanced at the hand-sketched map his people had compiled from recon reports.

The 20s were sure to be watching from their drones, which they'd promised to send in as support for the mission, support that Dark Ryder had clandestinely informed him would not be coming. He had no damn clue why the 20s would try to send him on such a suicide mission, but Dark Ryder had assured him he was trying to find out. Without the 20s' armed drones, and without the promised offensives elsewhere to draw off Ree's troops beforehand as the mission orders had promised, they would have marched into a lethal ambush.

"May the Flying Spaghetti Monster bless you and keep you, sir," Eagan said, breaking into Taggart's thoughts. "May you be touched by his noodly appendages." He snorted, and his shoulders shook in silent laughter.

"What the hell are you laughing at, numbnuts? Pay attention to the radios."

"Yes, sir," came Eagan's reply, and Taggart suppressed a grin at the sound of Eagan's voice. Bless him, he was at least trying not to laugh out loud.

"Alright. So three mikes from actual contact, flash-bangs in building windows en route are rigged to go off one second before our emplaced demolitions go off in buildings opposite those windows, yes?"

"Correct, sir. With any luck, the drones will believe they have tanks or maybe field guns emplaced in cover within those flash-banged buildings. Our troops—sorry, your troops—will then retrograde the hell out of there when faced with 'tanks' and will exfiltrate via subway and sewer tunnel entrances, obscuring 20s intel on where they're going. They'll then rendezvous here in our Batcave."

"Our HQ"

"As you wish, sir. Our Bat HQ"

Taggart had to smile. "Hm. So, what do you think are the odds we'll get away with this little charade without alerting our mysterious overlords, Eagan?"

"Flip a coin, sir. If we pull it off, don't forget you promised me a shot of your rotgut bourbon."

Taggart grinned. "Yeah, if we get away with this I'll even give you two shots. And how many times must I tell you, Wild Turkey is—"

"...the finest mass-produced bourbon in America, yes sir. The C.O. is always right, of course."

"Don't forget it, either. Alright... It's showtime."

- 5 -

0500 HOURS - ZERO DAY +146

NESTOR SAT BOLT upright in his cot, drenched in sweat and shivering at the same time. Breathing hard, trying to catch his breath, he noticed that he could see his breath cloud when he exhaled. So it was cold, but he was damp with sweat.

The nightmare's remnants still rampaged through his mind, but part of him recognized the danger his evaporating sweat put him in. He quickly wrapped his thick woolen blanket over his head and around his shoulders like a parka. Hypothermia wasn't something he needed in his life just then. He glanced at the woodstove and saw that it had died during the night. He'd get that going again once his pulse slowed and his mind cleared away sleep's cobwebs. Let the others, still sleeping, wake up later in a warmed space.

As he waited for his body and mind to calm, he tried to piece together whatever he could of that night's dreams. Writing them in his journal would have been his next step, normally, transferring the terrible scenes from his mind onto paper where they couldn't bother him anymore. Cathartic, that was the word. But just like his old life in Scranton, the journal was gone—burned up during events that had been at least as terrifying as Nestor's dream-visitors. Nestor was reduced to mock-writing in the air as though it were his journal. Better this half-measure than to be visited by the Other again. He shuddered at the thought, and shoved it away in his mind. To think about the Other was to invite him to come, and no one needed that right now. Least of all Nestor.

No. Already too late. Damn. He felt the Other clawing at the edges of his mind as he sat in the darkness one minute after the next, trembling and again sweating from the exertion, but slowly he pushed the Other back. Back into the dark recesses of his subconscious. Soon, he'd forgotten all about that foul being. He'd buried it well, and now his mind was again as smooth as glass. Untouched. Unbroken. Serene.

Nestor looked around in confusion for a second as he emerged from struggling with the Other, then realized he was still cold and the woodstove still unlit. He climbed off of his cot and padded over to light it. His body clock suggested that dawn was still an hour or two away, so it was almost time for his pre-breakfast morning chores anyway. No point going back to sleep. Hopefully breakfast today would be eggs and sausage rather than the "constant stew" that seemed to make up half of these people's meals. The stew wasn't great, but it wasn't terrible either, plus it was always available and it beat going hungry. His pa's burgoo had been a tasteless porridge, while the Clan's constant stew had meat and vegetables and such. It had taste. Accept the blessing, he chided himself.

After lighting the fire for the others to wake up to, he slipped on his shoes and headed toward the Clan's kitchen—which was outdoors, of all places—to find something useful to do before breakfast.

***

Two hours later, Nestor polished off his breakfast. A hearty bowl of stew and some fresh bread that tasted like nothing he'd had before. He was ravenous from helping move cattle out to pasture before breakfast, but the Clan gave him as much stew as he wanted. They really were good people, even if they had harder eyes than the people he'd known in Scranton. No one still alive had gotten through the last few months unscathed, but these people had been through more problems than anyone had a right to suffer and had still come out on top with their basic decency in place.

"What's with the bread?" he asked with a smile, speaking to the man next to him. They all ate at communal tables, sitting on benches, so conversation was lively at meal times. The bread was sort of sweet, a flatbread that was almost like dense pancakes.

The other man grunted, then said, "It's cattails. Or the pollen, anyway."

"What, like those swamp weeds?" That didn't make any sense, but from what little Nestor had seen so far, a lot about how this farm ran didn't make sense to him. Their ways seemed to work, though.

"Yeah. We have about an acre of them, total, at our retainer ponds. I heard we get about three tons of pollen a year from just that one acre, and we cut our flour with it. Healthier than flour by itself, and you get way more food value out of cattails than just about any other crop I ever heard of. More than potatoes, even. Crazy, huh?"

Nestor tilted his head to the side. "Three tons, huh? Is that a normal conversation around here?" He then scooped up what remained in his bowl with his last slice of bread. He was full, but he'd never let food go to waste. Not ever again. He'd known real hunger, and it changed his view on food altogether.

"Yep," the man replied. "Cassy set this place up as a permaculture farm, which I hadn't heard of before I came here. It's completely different than any farm I ever did see before, but can't argue with results. Everybody wants to learn how it works." The man, done with breakfast, said a friendly goodbye and left the table.

Nestor looked out over the breakfast crowd, feeling comfortably full, and took the time to watch how these people interacted with each other. There were no public arguments or fights as there had been daily in Scranton. He could see there were people who didn't like each other, just like anywhere else, but here in Clanholme they just seemed to stay out of each other's way. Almost like they respected each other even if they weren't friends. All eating cattail swamp weeds together. It made his head spin some—but it obviously worked.

He spotted Cassy and a couple of the others he had identified as Clan leaders. They always ate with everyone else, usually not even at their own table but scattered about, talking to other people. And although the people seemed to give them a lot of respect, there wasn't any sign of fear. They weren't afraid of their dictators... Maybe they weren't dictators at all. That would be a nice change from what he'd been used to. Every place he'd seen so far had a dictator. Some person with more power than anyone else. They didn't call themselves dictators but that's what they were, sure enough.

One of the girls he'd saved from the dogs, the older one, walked through his view with a bowl and sat at a table with other teenagers, and Nestor smiled at the memory of the girls' look of gratitude when he saved them. It made a man feel good to—

A vision superimposed itself over the entire scene. The

light was suddenly red, full of ominous shadows promising doom. The girl, Kaitlyn, was covered in cuts. Cuts, and blood. Everywhere, blood. Just like his nightmares, he suddenly recalled. When had he had those dreams? He couldn't tell, but knew that he'd dreamed this before.

Kaitlyn looked a lot like his daughter now. No—she suddenly *was* his daughter. She screamed and cried. There was a demon inside her, poisoning her soul. Nestor clutched the hilt of his knife, tucked in his belt. There was only one way to get the demons out of people. Cuts and blood. His heart began to race, singing joy at the thought of the good thing he would do. The thing no one else could do, because no one else could see the problem. Hell was real, and here.

Nestor felt a hand on his shoulder, and jerked in surprise. Abruptly, the demonic scene was gone, the vision fading in an instant. He looked up and saw Michael standing next to him, hand on his shoulder. Beyond Michael, Cassy watched, eyes narrowed and staring. They couldn't see the demons, he realized. No one else could.

Michael's mouth moved, but all Nestor heard was a buzzing noise.

"What? Sorry, I… What?"

Michael frowned. "I said, what's going on? Don't much like how you're looking at people, stranger."

Nestor realized he had his hand on his knife. When had that happened? He hastily moved his hand to the tabletop where the Marine could see it and felt Michael's grip loosen. Nestor tried to remember what he'd been looking at, but it was like grasping at a dream that fades faster the harder you try. Something about a dream? No…

"Sorry, I was just remembering the dogs attacking those girls." That had to be it, he knew, though he didn't remember looking at anyone. "Lost in thought, you know? I'd never want anything bad to happen to kids, girls especially. I didn't mean to freak anyone out."

Michael nodded once. "Just be more careful, friend. One might misunderstand your intention, and my reflexes sometimes make me do things before I think it through. Understand me?"

Nestor nodded and realized he'd finished his breakfast. "Yeah, I get it. I understand. Thank Cassy for the breakfast for me, will you?"

Michael pursed his lips but nodded, then walked away. Cassy turned away from him and back to whatever conversations she'd been having.

As Nestor stood, he glanced around the room. These sure were nice people. Hard, but nice. He saw Kaitlyn nearby, one of the girls he'd saved from the wolves, and got a sense of déjà vu. It was confusing, since he didn't remember her coming in.

Abruptly, the daylight seemed to get brighter. Some weird memory faded from his mind before he could grab onto it. Well, whatever it was, it couldn't be that important if he'd forgotten about it already. He took his bowl to the dishes barrel—a 55-gallon drum everyone put their dirties into after eating—and walked toward the cattle enclosure for his after-breakfast chores. It was a pretty day for being midwinter, and he whistled happily as he went. This sure was a nice place, and he hoped they'd let him stay.

* * *

Eagan ducked down, chips of cement raining down over him and Taggart both. "Dammit, Eagan," shouted Taggart over the din of small arms fire all around them, "keep your fool head down." Damned idiot was pulling hostile fire their way.

"I don't get it, sir," Eagan shouted back. "The OpFor is twice what our intel reported!"

Taggart clicked his radio, ordering his north flank to pull back toward a rubbled building for better cover—they'd provide suppression fire to help the rest of the unit when they pulled back. "We keep running into that. Operation Backdraft didn't do much to help, did it?"

"Seems that way." Eagan popped his head over the cement barricade they were using as cover and fired two bursts before ducking down again. "I thought our revenge EMPs would level the playing field."

The radio crackled, reporting the north units had fallen back and were in place. Taggart confirmed, then ordered his other units to begin falling back. "I wish we knew where they were getting their supplies. We're struggling not to starve, and they're making it tougher now for us to just take some from them. They're wising up to us."

Eagan grunted. "Makes me miss dealing with the gangers, earlier in the war."

Taggart had to agree with that. The gangers were the biggest threat, early on, but they'd also been the biggest help. Now most of them were gone, blended into the populace or dead.

The south flank reported in. They'd reached their fallback emplacements. Taggart then shouted orders to the other soldiers with him in the center of their crumbling line. They bugged out, and the lines crumbled completely.

An hour later, the headcount showed they'd lost half a dozen soldiers. Debriefing suggested they'd given the invaders as many as two dozen casualties but Taggart still counted the encounter as a loss—his men couldn't be replaced, and the enemy seemed to have an unlimited supply of troops. Yeah, a tactical loss. Especially since they didn't get the supplies they'd gone out for.

"We can't keep this up, Eagan," Taggart said when they got back to the privacy of his "office."

Eagan, face still dirty from battle, nodded. "We're on the ropes, sir. We need a miracle. But either way, we can't keep raiding for supplies like this. We need a new plan."

Definitely a staff sergeant's comment—and confidence. Taggart realized they were now firmly in the role of guerrillas and it felt foreign to him. How did Eagan swing so easily into thinking like a guerrilla? He'd have to ask. Meanwhile, Eagan had become something like Taggart's reality tester. He wondered when he'd slipped through that particular looking glass.

* * *

Ethan decrypted the latest intel from the 20s and tried to reconcile that with the information he had from his contacts in the field. Survivalists, preppers, lucky groups, militias, guerrillas. He had dozens of such contacts, none of which he had shared with the 20s. He had never fully trusted the secretive group, and after the debacle with Taggart and his troops in New York City, he was pretty damn glad he'd kept the information to himself.

He wished Amber was there with him in the bunker. He just felt more centered, more functional with her around. Although she and her daughter, Kaitlyn, slept in the bunker, they spent much of their day aboveground doing chores or socializing, unless Ethan needed to divert them to the bunker during a crisis. Ethan himself emerged only at meal time, most days. He'd like to take his meals in the bunker, at his terminals, but Amber insisted he at least come out for meals so the others "can see you're still alive and kicking."

She had a point. In a small survival-based group like theirs, integrating with the group was an essential survival strategy.

His monitor beeped, and the last of the reports came in.

It was Taggart, via the back channel the two had set up some time ago. Taggart never went through normal channels anymore, not since the 20s had basically set him up for a slaughter—he now let Ethan filter that info for him first. It made sense but Ethan felt like he'd turned into some kind of spymaster. It felt weird. Well, somebody had to make sense of the welter of channels, where he had somehow wormed his way to the center, and he knew he was good at it. It felt familiar, like he'd practiced his whole life for it. Okay, back to work.

After decrypting the last few files, the big picture did become a lot clearer. Everywhere, the invaders were solidifying their territories into cantonments, self-sufficient enclaves that were more or less secure. The Americans still held most of the territory they'd had at the start of winter because the invaders hadn't tried to expand much since then, but those increasingly secure cantonments were becoming impossible to raid effectively. It had begun to shift into bloody guerrilla warfare, focusing on those who submitted to the invaders' yoke or, worse, actively supported them. As always, civilians were the easier targets. Anyway, those who submitted or actively supported the invaders weren't really noncombatants, not in the larger scheme of things. Mao and Ho Chi Minh had known that. Taggart—and the dozen or so other survival groups he coordinated without the 20s knowledge—clearly realized it, too.

Back in the bunker, Ethan's heart went out to the victims in the middle of this conflict. And since the invaders had sent out swarms of small units as "death squads" throughout the Eastern Seaboard and even into central Pennsylvania—close to where the Clan was—those innocent victims were no longer in some faraway place like Virginia. Some of them were altogether too close to home now. Reports had been coming in for days of isolated homesteads being razed, and small, nearby settlements getting raided. Maybe there was some way to set up better comms with all the nearby settlements that wouldn't use up the Clan's last few precious radios. Daily riders, or fire signals, or something. He added it to his To-Do List to bring up at the next Council meeting, to get some more ideas.

Updating his map left Ethan with one inescapable conclusion. Operation Backdraft, in which America had sent out EMPs to virtually every place on Earth—including North America, to neutralize the invading forces—was only a minor success even if you squinted your eyes.

And for what? By this time next year, over six billion of the seven billion people on the planet would likely be dead. And Ethan himself had been instrumental in enabling it. The worst mass-murder in human history rested squarely on his own shoulders, and it was little consolation that he'd only been following orders. That was the cry of most every villain throughout history. It was why some philosopher had once called evil "banal."

And in the end, it hadn't saved America like they'd planned. It wasn't entirely for nothing, as the Mountain and the Empire had found the breathing room they needed to solidify as well, but by any rational accounting the ends hadn't justified the cost. Not even close.

As he looked at his maps, a terrifying thought occurred to him. All those invader death squads on his map were probably just the opening moves toward renewed conquest come spring. Softening up the opposition. The pattern was clearly focused on the remaining food production areas and railheads. Why railheads? None of the locomotives worked. Oh, shit—horses could draw cargo on them. A few cargo cars at a time, the invaders could get the railways working again. They could move whole armies at light cavalry speeds, hitting in force throughout the agriculture beltway of

America. Nobody would be ready for that.

That map fully exposed the futility of Operation Backdraft, and as he considered the billions who would die because of what he'd helped to do, for the first time in years, Ethan wept.

* * *

The woman carefully tucked her blonde hair back up under her white knit wool cap and crawled up to the crest of the snow-patched, low-rise hill. In the distance she could see the community her fellow scouts had found, the one she and her team of slaves were sent to investigate.

At the crest, she pulled out a small pair of binoculars and peered out. It was nerve-wracking, because she didn't like being this close to the ancillaries without a weapon in hand, but there was nothing for it. She was probably safe enough, though—if they came back without her, or didn't come back at all, each of these men had families that would not survive the betrayal. The overlords were thorough that way. You obeyed or you died.

Below, the target community stretched north to south, although it looked fairly square. The north and south edges were extended by forest with dense undergrowth. The east and west edges contained large ponds, thick with cattails that would have no problem surviving the winter. Weeds, but like a razor wire fence they would make crossing the ponds difficult, especially under the watchful eye of the guard in the tower. The dwellings were interesting—one was a traditional rectangular house, but next to it lay a huge group of dome-shaped buildings, with a thick wall surrounding it that probably had an opening on the side opposite to her, facing the more traditional house. That would present a problem...

"I count thirty-two people, but with them going in and

out of those buildings, there could easily be twice that number." She turned her head to the man next to her and commanded, "Notation: thirty-two confirmed, recommend planning for twice that number. End."

The man didn't reply, but dutifully wrote in his little notebook.

Another of the four ancillaries with her said, "This plum looks ripe. Must we follow protocol? There's lots of kids down there."

The woman gritted her teeth. "It is what it is. No one likes what we must do, Ancillary. If our sketches and intel can convince the overlords it's too tough a nut, it may be referred to the Diplomacy Department instead and turned into allies. So ease your mind, and remember your family. They need you to stay strong for them."

The man grunted in acknowledgement, and the scribe began his sketching as she murmured observations to the note-taking ancillary. An hour later, the group crept back down to their waiting horses and rode west.

- 6 -

1600 HOURS - ZERO DAY +146

IN THE DISTANCE, Cassy, working as usual in the outdoor kitchen, heard gunfire. An instant later, the salvaged air horn on the guard tower wailed into life, its piercing shriek echoing off buildings and trees, alerting the Clan to immediate danger just as Cassy's radio crackled to life.

Ethan's voice came through the tinny speaker from his monitoring station in the bunker: "Charlie One, this is Bravo One. Romeo November reports hostile contact with tango times five, small arms only."

"Roger, Bravo One. Dispatch Romeo September to rendezvous with November."

So, the Recon North team—which today included Michael—was engaged by five unknown people. It could be a feint, or a spearhead, or even just trigger-happy survivors. The Recon South team was on their way now, but the fight would likely be over one way or the other before they found the battle site.

Cassy spent the next three minutes organizing the Clan's defenses, ensuring everyone was at their assigned posts. These days, the entire Clan could be in position faster than the time it took an enemy to close the distance from either food forest to the Complex. Emerging from the outdoor kitchen enclosure, Cassy made sure to clap people on the shoulder or arm as they went by, offering encouragement and bolstering confidence for every person with whom she crossed paths. A well-oiled machine had kicked into action.

The next five minutes seemed to drag on forever. Waiting was the hardest part, but Cassy no longer fretted or fidgeted during such times. Instead, she strode openly from one fighting position to the next, making sure everyone had their weapons and ammunition, that no one remained hiding inside. Then she checked on the children clustered inside the Complex, hidden away from flying bullets, overseen and tended to by two armed guardians.

Quickly, all was as prepared as it could be until they learned more. Only then did she take up her own position in the upper window of her house, with rifle and radio at hand.

Tick tock... Cassy became acutely aware of the sound from the seconds hand on her wind-up watch and counted them out as she waited. The north scouts' exact location wasn't known, so there was nothing to do but wait and pray they made it back unharmed. She had to wait almost ten more minutes before Ethan came through on her radio again and the sudden noise made her jump.

"Bravo One to Charlie One. Romeo November has reported in. I've notified Romeo September to return to their op area. Tangos neutralized, and one has been secured. November en route to Charlie."

Outstanding news, and Cassy felt her heart leap for joy at the confirmation that Michael was okay. The fact that they had one enemy survivor alive and secured was just gravy as far as she was concerned. She felt a little foolish for worrying so much about Michael and the Marines who were with him. They were Marines, after all... Not that it made them bulletproof, but they did seem to have a certain luck in combat, if luck was the word for it.

"Charlie One to Bravo One. Roger that. Advise Romeo November to meet me at the north smokehouse immediately on their return. Tell no one else what's going on, how copy?" No sense feeding the "what happened?" rumors no doubt already circulating among the Clanners.

Ethan confirmed he understood, and Cassy put on her jacket and knit cap before heading out the door. Turning there, she walked toward the north end of the farm and one of their two smokehouses. The northern smokehouse was isolated and not much in use this time of year, since the southern one was closer to the Complex and the animal pens and there wasn't much meat still left to smoke for the winter. She wanted privacy from the rest of the Clan until after she spoke to Michael and decided what her next steps must be.

* * *

1700 HOURS - ZERO DAY +146

Cassy sat in a chair in the corner of the enclosure, the shoulder-high wood fence that extended five yards out from the smokehouse entry. When meat was being smoked, it kept animals out but left enough space near the structure for people to work comfortably. Now, however, it would allow a different sort of work, the kind of work that no one involved would find comfortable.

Michael had bound the woman's wrists with sturdy rope and, after tossing it over the meat hook that hung from a cross beam that protruded from the front of the smokehouse, pulled on it hand-over-hand until the woman barely stood on her tippy-toes. He tied off the end securely and nodded to Cassy. "She's secured," he said as he wiped his hands on his jeans.

Cassy nodded, then stood. She looked the woman over carefully, in silence. The prisoner was tall, maybe five-foot-ten, and thin. Everyone was thin these days, of course, but her skin had the fresh, tight look of someone who hadn't lost much weight in the past few terrible months. Her blonde hair was tied in a ponytail, which hung over her right shoulder and went down below her breast in front. Like the rest of her, it was now wet and clung to her.

She wore black fatigues, or BDUs as Michael called them. The Arab invaders wore a similar uniform, but tailored them much differently. These were probably from a military surplus store. Her jacket had been removed, but was also black and cut in a military style.

The prisoner had thin lips and frown lines already, though she couldn't be more than twenty-five. She was a plain-looking woman, but the faint wrinkles in her face and especially around her eyes were, Cassy believed, a sign that this was a stern, cold-hearted woman. They were obviously not smile lines.

"Throw some water on her. I'm glad she wasn't wounded—we're not on a short timeline with this one."

Michael tossed the winter-cold water from a nearby bucket over the prisoner's head, and she awoke sputtering and coughing. "I'll get a fire going. No use killing her with hypothermia after sparing her from a bullet. Twenty bucks says you can't make this one smile."

Cassy smiled at him and said, "I think we still have some twenties in the outhouses, unless all the cash has already been used." Money was more useful as toilet paper these days or so the joke went. Funny because it was funny, and because it was true.

The prisoner finally coughed out the last of the water, and sucked air. "What the fuck? Where am I?"

Cassy raised one corner of her mouth, smirking. "Do you kiss your mom with that dirty mouth?"

"Fuck you." She spat into the dirt by Cassy's feet. "You have no idea how bad a mistake you've just made."

Michael stepped between Cassy and the prisoner, and stared into her eyes. Abruptly, his fist lashed out, a blur that ended with a resounding *crack* as it connected with the woman's jaw. "I'm sorry, miss. I don't like doing that but don't you dare threaten my friend again."

A faint bruise was already forming where Michael had punched her. Say what you will, the man was good at violence. That bruise would probably be purple and ugly in a few minutes. "Michael," Cassy said, forcing as much iron into her voice as she could, "do you remember the White Stag scout we once captured, and what we did with him to protect ourselves?"

"I do. I think it was a Tuesday."

"You're a cold man," Cassy said with a glance toward the prisoner. The entire conversation was pretty much a mind game meant for the prisoner—she knew how much Michael was still bothered by what he'd done to that prisoner, before the White Stag invasion. It woke him up in the middle of the night even now, she recalled hearing. And yet he'd done it and would do it again if necessary. In that way, he really was a cold man. Maybe it would be kinder just to say he never backed away from what he saw as necessary.

"Well," Cassy continued, "she doesn't know it yet, but she already screwed up. She's said one thing, just one, and she already screwed herself. Not too bright, this one."

The prisoner glared at Cassy. That was something. She clearly didn't like being called out on her stupidity. Tough luck.

Michael said, "I'll get to asking her some questions, I guess. You shouldn't be here for this—no point in both of us getting our hands dirty. Why don't you head back and keep everyone away from here. I prefer not to be interrupted while we tango."

"Dance. Heh. I'll have Mueller check in with you, see if you need anything for your dance recital." Mueller was a Marine, and technically outranked Michael, but had placed himself and his two Marines under Michael's command until the war was over, or until he got some valid orders to the contrary. She paused at the doorway. "Get what you can from her and then end it mercifully."

Cassy walked out of the enclosure and headed back toward the houses. She heard Michael's voice, though not what he was saying. She didn't hear the woman, yet. That would no doubt begin soon enough. She felt sympathy for the woman start to rise and resolutely pushed it back down. Safety of the Clan, she repeated to herself. Safety of the Clan.

* * *

2000 HOURS - ZERO DAY +146

Grandma Mandy came into the house looking relaxed, like this was a casual visit, but Cassy knew her own mother too well to fall for that. Mandy almost paced, but stopped herself. Reached up to twirl her hair, which she did when she was stressed out, but stopped herself. Cassy watched the display for a few seconds, then spared Mandy the awkwardness of bringing up a difficult subject.

"Mom, I know you have something on your mind. Just spit it out, and I promise not to get any angrier than I need to be, okay? You know you can talk to me about anything."

"Maybe. But times are different now. You're the Clan's leader before you're my daughter." Mandy wasn't able to stop her nervous habit this time and twirled her hair unconsciously.

"If this is a personal matter, I don't have time right now. If it's a Clan issue, then spit it out. I want to go to bed soon. I'm not trying to be rude, I swear. Really. Just exhausted."

Mandy pulled her finger from her twirled hair and set it on her hip. "You're tired because you're the Clan leader, and despite having all these people who rely on you, I think you need sleep more than you need to do everything yourself. But," Mandy said, and watched Cassy from the corner of her eye, "I do wonder how you can sleep at all, these days. I sure couldn't if I spent my days making the kinds of decisions you have to make."

Cassy felt a flush of guilt wash over her, but it quickly turned to irritation. How dare her own mother judge her? Or was she judging? Maybe she only meant exactly what she'd said and was speaking not as a mother, but a concerned Clanner. Cassy clenched her jaw, turned away from Mandy, and picked up a dirty plate, which she began to wash.

"Every decision I make is for the good of us all, Mom. But if there is a decision to make, I have to make it—I don't put it on someone else to decide. Part of my job is doing what's needful, so others don't have to. Someone has to bear that burden."

"I do know that, sweetie. And you're a good leader. Who would have guessed that six months ago?"

"All of us have learned a lot about ourselves since the EMPs. Unfortunately, our high-tech society coddled us for too long. Survival now means making tough choices, the kinds of choices that aren't acceptable in 'polite society.' But they've become matters of life and death now."

"Indeed," Mandy replied. With a glance, Cassy saw that her mom was looking at her with the intense gaze of someone who was studying an opponent.

"What now? Dammit, Mom, why are you always looking

down on me? What did I do this time? How have I disappointed you now?"

"You make it sound like I'm always looking down on you. You know darn well that I've never treated you badly, and I don't look down on you. Quite the opposite. I love you. You are and will always be my daughter."

"You didn't like my choice of colleges. You didn't like my choice of husband. You didn't think I should have a child until we got married, back before Brianna surprised us all. But just because I don't have the strong faith you do, that doesn't mean I wanted to rush off and have an abortion—so I didn't. Sorry I embarrassed you in front of your friends by daring to give birth outside marriage—"

"Oh, posh," Mandy snapped. "Yes, I thought it was reckless to try to start a family before getting married, but bless you, I never once thought you should have—"

"Why not? You disagreed with just about everything I ever did, so why wouldn't you want to sweep your embarrassing granddaughter under the rug?"

"First of all, don't talk to me like that. You may be the Clan leader, but I'm still your mother. Secondly, she's no embarrassment, and I'll thank you not to say that again. Some of the clucking hens at church had snide comments, but I'll be damned if I let some socially backward gossips affect me or my family."

Cassy sat in awe, as her mother *never* swore unless she had her temper dialed up to "10." Maybe Cassy had been thinking about this the wrong way all this time. "Mom, I'm —"

Mandy cut her off again, face red with anger. "I liked my son-in-law just fine, Cassy. I only said that I thought you shouldn't get married so young. Women these days wait until they're thirty all the time, so what was the rush? But you were *happy* with him, and I was heartbroken when the cancer took him. Your choice of colleges took you away from me, and I wasn't ready to let go yet, but I got over that, too. So are you fine, now? Can you get over your own hurt feelings and get back to the Clan? Because if you don't get your head on right, then my granddaughter is in danger, and so is Aidan, and so is the Clan. So which kind of leader are you, Cassy? You can be self-absorbed or you can get the job done, and Momma didn't raise no divas."

The combination of her mom's anger, her stony stare as she chewed Cassy out, and her admission of being insecure about some things when Cassy was younger—Grandma Mandy, insecure!?—and that last hilarious statement (with no understanding that it *was* funny) made Cassy's anger flow away. In its place, it left a moment of shame followed quickly by a renewed focus on the Clan's problems. She stifled a laugh that would only piss her mom off.

Mandy saw Cassy try not to smile, and after a long moment she released a long breath. Then, resigned, she smiled wanly. "You may have been young, sweetie, but I was young when I had you. Did you ever wonder where your middle name came from?"

Cassy eyed her mother warily. A joke at a time like this. Fine, she'd play along. Plus, she was curious. "Yeah, actually. 'Elenore' is not a family name that I know of."

"I named you after a song your dad used to sing to me when we were practicing to make you. Ask Ethan to find the lyrics to *Elenore* by The Turtles, and try not to look too grossed out. You owe your life to that song."

Cassy allowed a faint smile. "Sure, Mom. I'm dying of curiosity, now."

Cassy was about to ask another question, when Mandy said, "So the point of this conversation—you need to sleep, and you need to delegate. More importantly, you need to do whatever needs doing to keep Brianna safe, no matter how distasteful the tasks may be. You're struggling with something, but you need to knock that off. Make the right decision and then just get it done." Then Mandy spun on her heels and walked away.

What the hell was that all about? Cassy didn't have time to wrap her head around everything her mother had just said. There was an interrogation going on, and she needed to check up on their guest and Michael.

* * *

A guard showed Choony and Jaz into the waiting room of an office building on Main Street and politely asked them to have a seat and wait. Despite the late hour, the mayor wanted to see them immediately. Or rather, Head Falconer Stringfield, as the guard had referred to her, wanted to see them. An odd name, but what did that matter in these times?

Choony diverted his mind by casually studying their guard. He wore the BDUs, or cammies, that everyone seemed so fond of these days. Around his waist, he wore a duty belt laden with items including a rather large pistol. Normally—if you could call anything about the last few months "normal"— everyone wanted to carry a rifle, so the guard's pistol was a bit of a puzzle. An affectation, maybe. Everything about the man shouted that he had been either a soldier or a police officer in the good old days. Or maybe he watched cop movies a lot.

Then a pin on the guard's collar caught Choony's attention—a rank insignia usually went there, if the Clan's Marines were any indication. Instead of stripes or stars, their guard wore a pin the size of a nickel with a stylized black falcon on a white background. These people sure took their bird motif all the way. It might be amusing, but it would be improper to show it struck him so. It would only hurt the guard's feelings, possibly earning them an enemy but definitely earning bad Karma.

Some ten minutes later, just as Jaz began to squirm with impatience—so full of life, that one!—the double doors to the right of the lobby opened. The guard showed no emotion on his face as he told them to please enter and be seated. Jaz practically bolted out of her chair and buzzed toward those doors, evidently relieved after having to sit still even for a short while.

Choony felt a brief moment of near-panic. What if it was an ambush? As he walked toward the door at a slower pace, he chastised himself for his foolishness. If they'd wanted to kill him and Jaz, they would have done it outside the town when they'd met up with their perimeter guards. He followed Jaz in, keeping his face carefully neutral.

When he turned the corner, Jaz was smiling and shaking hands with the woman who was their leader, who also smiled. But when she saw Choony's face, her smile disappeared like flash paper in a fire, and her expression turned just as black. Uh oh…

"Hello, Head Falconer Stringfield," Choony said with hastily summoned calm, so that she would hear his American accent and nonthreatening tone before snapping to any rash decisions. He'd dealt with raw hatred for his race more than once since those from his family's homeland had come with EMPs and death for so many Americans. "I am Chihun Ghim, but everyone just calls me 'Choony.' Thank you so much for taking time to meet with us as spokespersons for the Clan."

Stringfield blinked a few times and clenched her jaw. Her nostrils flared once, and then she seemed to recover her politician skills. She shook his hand, but if her smile was forced, it was still an improvement over that black hostility.

"Please, call me Delorse, or Delo if you prefer. The

honored guests from Clanholme are welcome here." Still that rigid, plastic-looking smile. But when she turned to Jaz, her eyes crinkled as her smile became genuine. Probably genuine. "So, Jasmine, I assume Clanholme has business to discuss or they wouldn't have sent you two out in the dead of winter, much less just the two of you."

Jaz smiled again, and motioned toward the chairs with a raised eyebrow. Delorse nodded and sat, and Jaz and Choony quickly followed suit.

"You're not wrong," Jaz answered. "It's not urgent—not yet—but it is something our Clan leader feels is best handled well before springtime."

Choony added, "But they didn't actually send us out alone. We had four of our warriors with us for protection, but we got separated when we ran into an unknown number of invaders. The ones who wear the black uniforms."

Delorse leaned back in her chair. "Do you know if they are alive? I don't mean to be so brash about it, but if they live then I will let my guardsmen know to look for them during their patrols, and at the gate."

Jaz frowned. "No, we don't know. We got separated when they ran a diversion for us. But they were professional warriors before all this started. They're totally scary when they fight."

"Speaking of fighting, I'm told you came in with a shotgun," Delorse said and then turned toward Choony, "but that you came in without a weapon. Did you drop it when you were running?"

Choony thought he heard judgment in her question, though she was probably not trying to show it. Strike two...

"No, Head Falconer, it wasn't dropped. I will not carry weapons. Violence on my part would damage my chakras. My balance of Karma, if you will."

Abruptly, and surprisingly, Delorse grinned ear-to-ear.

"Oh ho! A Buddhist. Here I thought you might just be... Well, Korean and a coward at the same time, chosen for this mission? I was prepared to dismiss the Clan. But now I see they've accepted you despite your heritage and your pacifism. *Om swasti asu*, Choony." She then dipped her head.

Choony's jaw dropped. American Buddhists, besides generally being condescending without meaning to, seemed to have some religious fervor for saying *Namaste*, which had irritated him as a child. She had used a term barely known outside of Asia, or the Asian community. "*Om swasti asu*, Delorse. Are you then Buddhist?"

Delorse shook her head, and Choony let go of the disappointment he felt. Not healthy or productive—she was what she was.

"I ask because you use a proper greeting, which few here know. Where did you learn it? I am honored."

"My sister is Buddhist, but she's not your typical Yoga Buddhist. She studied in Thailand for several years. I picked it up from her. I respect her beliefs, because they were acquired through diligence instead of YouTube. She's a great girl. Or was, perhaps."

Choony saw the flash of pain in Delorse's eyes and decided this was not the time to discuss the differences between northern and southern Buddhism. "I regret asking, and causing you pain. Please forgive me. But I honor your respect for your sister and her beliefs."

"Nothing to forgive, Choony. I don't share her beliefs, but I know she was—is—happy with her life. What could be more deserving of respect? Don't apologize. The loss is mine, not yours, and I'm sure we've all lost people this year. And she may yet live. She was in Seattle when the lights went out, and I know they have a huge monastery there. I could never pronounce it—the 'atayamana' temple?"

Choony nodded. This was good news for her sister. Most of the Seattle monasteries were small and in densely-packed neighborhoods. "The Atammayataram. It's in Woodinville, actually, and the area is almost rural. My parents took me to visit it a few years ago when we drove across the country to see as many great monasteries as time allowed. Funny how such a drive irritated me then, but I miss it now."

Jaz looked bored, but only because Choony knew her so well. She smiled, nodded, made "mm hmm" noises at all the right places. She shouldn't have looked so bored, in Choony's opinion—the discussion was welcome, certainly, but it also revealed much about their host and what kind of person she was. Useful information in a negotiation.

"I feel the same. Thank you for that information. You've given me a reason to hope that, even if I never see her again, she'll be all right out there. But we've important things to discuss, I imagine. What does Clanholme want from us?"

Jaz said, "We had a trader come by recently. An honest-to-goodness traveling merchant. Cassy, our leader, says that's a great thing because it means America is starting to level out, and because with good trade going on, two communities that lack something vital can trade for what they need. It's the difference between two groups dying off or making it through this. The trader mentioned the Falconry in positive ways."

Delorse raised an eyebrow. "I see. And do you happen to recall his name?"

Choony said, "His name was Terry, and he had a muscle-bound sidekick he named as 'Lump,' if you can believe it."

"Do you remember those two?" Jaz asked.

"I should hope so. They're Falconry people. Scouts, we call them. They'll be back in spring, having scoured the region for survivor groups like ourselves, with notes on how they're doing, what sort of government they put up, what they need, what they have. We don't produce a lot locally, other than just enough food for ourselves, so we're setting ourselves up as a trading post. With the big cities of Reading and Harrisburg to our east and west, we'll be the only big gateway between central and southern Pennsylvania, and a good waypoint on any trade between east and west."

"We could certainly use a friendly trading partner," Choony replied, "as we don't produce much except food at the moment. What happens if one of those settlements decides to take what your scouts have," Choony said, careful not to call them spies, "or just kills them? Not all the survivor settlements out there are nice places to visit anymore."

"True. That happened at Hershey to our first scout team, right before the second round of EMPs hit. Now the team is actually three people—one stays hidden, following at a safe distance. They all meet up shortly after leaving a settlement, to give the follower all the scout notes and some fresh supplies."

"So if Terry doesn't come out, the follower makes a beeline home with all the notes?"

"That's the plan. We haven't had to use it yet, as Terry is pretty good at his job. He was a car salesman back in the real world and in the Army before that."

"I see. Smartly done," Choony said with a grin. "So, I formally invite you to send two or three people to us any time you wish to trade. We were rather proactive about requisitioning supplies from our neighbors who no longer needed them, to our disappointment. Farming implements and grains are what we have the most of. Oh, and more apple cider than we could ever drink in the coming year. But also some vegetables we've canned. We'll need most of that to last us through to next harvest, but we can spare some."

Delorse got a faraway look in her eyes. Unfocused as though calculating things, which she probably was. Choony waited patiently while Jaz looked back and forth between the two, fighting not to fidget. Then Delorse snapped out of wherever she'd gone and looked at her two visitors. "Maybe we could use the cider. We get fresh produce year-round with our array of greenhouses, but there isn't much to spare. Grains, we have precious little of."

So the negotiations had begun, Choony recognized. He wasn't much of a trader, but Jaz was. She'd been negotiating with people her whole life, usually to get out of bad situations.

Jaz straightened, smiled, and spoke up. "Fresh veggies would totally be nice, but I'm afraid it's not something we really need. Then again, neither is the cider and grain. I'm told you do have something else we might be able to trade for."

Delorse wore a friendly expression that was no doubt meant to be disarming, reassuring. "Do tell. I'm always interested in a creative exchange."

* * *

2200 HOURS - ZERO DAY +146

The negotiations had gone well and Choony had no doubt the results would please Cassy. He grinned and said, "One gasifier now and another when spring rolls around. Well done, Jaz."

"Always with the compliments. You're a nice guy, Choony. I hope Cassy doesn't mind the cost. Five barrels of apple cider and two tons of wheat and oats, and two more when we harvest the winter wheat. I don't know about the other thing—leaving a radio here when we come through on our way back."

"That one's going to hurt, but I think Cassy will go along

for two reasons. First, we have enough to spare one, even if we might have to take one out of storage when we send out more scouts in spring. Two, it might secure an alliance with Falconry sooner, and I understand that we need all the allies we can get. Cassy's certainly pushing hard on everyone as far east as Ephrata to join her little confederation, and we'll need that to be in place when the Empire starts pushing on our borders. That'll happen as soon as the snows let up, I'm sure."

"Don't forget that even if we don't get an alliance with Falconry, Delo herself said she'd alert us to any danger coming the Clan's way, or going through the Gap," Jaz replied with just the right inflection to show she'd started thinking of that description as being its name.

"The Gap. It's as good a name as any for that road we took. Cuts straight through the forest. But on the other end of that road is our ally Brickerville, so if we're lucky we'd be able to alert them before they get hit if raiders take the Gap, and if Delo really did warn us."

"So are we going to Camp Whatsitsname, like Delo asked?"

Choony leaned back in his bed, one of two in the well-apportioned room they were given for their stay in Falconry. "Camp Lebanon. I'm surprised that one's hard for you to remember."

Jaz grinned. "I'm not even legal to drink yet, you ass. How is that supposed to be easy for me to remember? All that crap happened before I grew up."

"I'm only a few years older than you! And no, it wasn't all before you came along. It's been going on forever, and will go on forever. I mean, the bomb that blew up the Marine barracks was before your time, but it has been in the news ever since then, too."

"Really? Only a few years? I thought you were old, like,

twenty-eight or something."

Choony half-heartedly threw his pillow at her, and she feigned being knocked over to sprawl out on her bed. She sure was adorable. Maybe more than adorable... He quickly squashed those thoughts. She wasn't into him, certainly, or a young woman like her would have made her interest known. Choony suppressed a sigh.

"I think you'll live, you ham. But anyway, Lebanon. It's about the size of Lititz, from what Delorse said. They were remote enough, and enough people split town after the EMPs to go look for family, that the remaining people didn't starve too much. Enough remained to draw a line in the sand to their west and keep the hordes of starving Harrisburg refugees at bay. But they are low on food now, and they know Falconry has it."

"Hungry and bigger than Falconry. It's a bad combination. Delo said they tried to negotiate instead of invading, at least, so they aren't flat-out raiders."

Choony's lips pursed. "And they still are trying. Lebanon sends a new envoy about two times a week to trade for food. If they get hungry enough, Jaz, they will stop asking nicely. When children begin to starve, people will destroy their Karma with violence and looting."

Jaz poked her finger into the mattress and fidgeted with the blanket by tangling her finger into it and then untangling it. She always fidgeted when she was uncomfortable with the conversation, a quirk he found charming.

"Don't worry, Jaz. That's why Falconry wants to trade with the Clan for food, even though they have enough for themselves, if only barely. I'll ask Cassy if we can spare a pig to throw into the deal with our first delivery. Just to be neighborly, and assuage any doubts."

"Ass wage? What the hell is that?"

"No—'assuage.' It means to make unpleasant feelings

less intense. To calm someone's fears, for instance."

Jaz grinned. "Oh, got it. So you, like, totally ass-wage me, Choony. You have a knack for making me be all like, 'I'm okay and everything will be fine,' you know?" She plastered a silly grin on her face, turned her eyes to the ceiling and issued an ecstatically, dramatically happy sigh.

"You have a dirty mind," said Choony, knowing full well that the innuendo wasn't what she'd meant. It had the desired effect: she flashed that brilliant smile of hers and threw his pillow back at him.

"We're not far from Lebanon," she said thoughtfully once the shared laughter had subsided. "Maybe we should go there, then on the way back, pick up the gasifier and leave the radio. We could just go there on horseback. Faster and safer, yeah?"

"I'll ask if we can go to Lebanon when we check in with Ethan on the radio." He doubted Cassy would allow it, given how badly she wanted that gasifier from Falconry, and in any case Clanholme was buffered from Lebanon by distance, the Falconry, the forest, and Brickerville. Choony would have agreed with Cassy, but Jaz would go anyway if she really wanted to. Choony would never let a Clanner make that ride alone, especially a trouble magnet like Jaz, so he'd likely be going with her despite his reservations if that's where her path took her.

Jaz rolled her eyes melodramatically. "Well, duh. So get on the radio, dummy."

Choony went over to the small wooden chest on the room's only other furniture, a chrome-and-glass desk that probably came from Wally World, and opened it, exposing their mid-range radio. The extra reception range wasn't needed from here but the longer broadcast range made the radio's additional weight worth it, especially as they had traveled by wagon. It really was amazing how much weight a horse could pull compared to carrying it on their backs.

He set the antenna on the balcony and ran the connecting cable to the radio box, then plugged in the microphone and the headset. He turned the tuning dial—they never left it on the band the scouts used, so that if the radio were seized or stolen, whoever took it would not simply overhear the Clan's communications.

"Charlie One, Charlie One. This is Sam One, over."

Choony had to try a couple more times before he got a response. A sleepy sounding voice, not Ethan's, replied. "Sam One, this is Charlie Two. Nice weather we're having, eh?"

Choony answered the challenge code. "Charlie Two, at least it's not a hurricane."

"Sam One, go for traffic."

"Charlie Two, copy that. We're visiting Aunt Florence," Choony said, using the code name for the Falconry, "and I'm happy to report that she let us have one of her horses. She wants us to bring her a few things, and then she'll give us another horse."

The Clansman acknowledged their mission success in acquiring a gasifier—the "horse"—but Choony wasn't done yet. "Charlie Two, Aunt Florence has said that while we're in the area, we should talk to Aunt Lisa on November 6th"—the date was code for six miles north—"before coming home. She also asked if we could leave our radio here, and we'd like to oblige since she was more than generous to give us a spare horse. We need to know if we can be late for curfew to visit Aunt Lisa"—Camp Lebanon, that is—"and if Aunt Florence can borrow our radio in the meantime."

The code they used swapped out the direction with the name of a month and the date for the approximate distance in miles only when dealing with north and south. East and west simply got swapped with each other to confuse anyone listening. Choony thought it stupid to use a different system for north and south than for east and west, but so far no one had paid attention to his suggestion that they simply use animal names for each of the four directions. Anything consistent would be better than the current system.

"Sam One, this is Charlie Two. Mom says that's fine, except that you need to keep the radio with you until you come back through to pick up Aunt Florence's horse. How long until you get home?"

"Charlie Two, probably two or three days. If we're not back after that, we ran away to Spain. Please confirm, we aren't to leave our radio here while we visit Aunt Lisa?"

"Copy that, Sam One. Mom says it's a safety issue, and says she'll blister your butt if you leave it behind, until after you've seen Aunt Lisa. Be safe, hope to see you in a few days. Charlie Two out."

Choony took off the headset and turned to look at Jaz. "So, we got permission to leave the radio on our way back through here and to go looking for the survivor group in Lebanon that Delorse told us about, but we have to bring the radio with us when we go north. We can leave it behind when we come back through for the gasifier. We'll have to figure out how to get that thing securely onto a horse without hurting the animal."

Jaz yawned and stretched her arms over her head, and Choony for a second was caught by the sight of her. She looked beautiful like that. She always looked beautiful, but for a second she had looked like a model or maybe a tasteful, stunningly beautiful pin-up. When he realized he was staring, he quickly glanced away, flustered and hoping she hadn't noticed.

She glanced over at him, smiling. "Well, it's getting late. What do you say we crash, Choon Choon? We'll figure this crap out in the morning."

"You go ahead. I'm going to meditate for a while, maybe a half hour, before I go to sleep. I need to recharge my batteries."

Jaz was faintly snoring like a cute little hibernating grizzly cub in just moments, and Choony went about the process of centering his mind and energy so that he could slip into a meditative state. He'd learned long ago that if he took the time to prepare himself before beginning, he only needed to sleep four or five hours to wake completely refreshed and rested the next morning.

- 7 -

1100 HOURS - ZERO DAY +147

THE GATES OF Lebanon, Pennsylvania rose up before them. Still a half mile away, Jaz looked through their binoculars and let out a long, low whistle. "You won't believe this shit, dude." She spoke more to herself than to Choony, talking aloud out of habit.

"What is it that you see?" Choony's response sounded distracted, only half-interested.

As she looked through the binoculars, she imagined the man next to her in his usual pose, sitting properly upright with perfect posture... Ha. Properly perfect posture. How silly. She stifled a giggle. "Okay, the whole town is walled up with rubble, cars, telephone poles—anything they could move under manpower, it looks like. There's two grain silos facing each other across the road, but I got no idea how they moved *those* monsters to there. They gotta be thirty feet high! And they got an honest-to-god drawbridge. Can you believe it? It's like something out of Thunderdome, but without the totally sick battle cars."

Choony grunted, letting her know he'd heard. He was supercool like that, always listening. A good listener, and a good friend. She hoped the locals wouldn't be total bigots or something—Choony didn't need that kind of grief.

The wagon rolled on, meandering toward the walled town. Once they got closer, Jaz could make out the scene in more detail. The towers weren't actually grain silos, she saw, but earthbag towers, like what Cassy had made her house out of but without the mud "plaster." Only the roofs were from grain silos, and they reminded her of upside-down funnels.

The drawbridge consisted of tons of steel plates welded together to make bigger sheets, with thick wooden beams between the front and back sheets. Two chains went from the corners up through slots in the towers, probably to open or close the thing. It was currently closed, probably how they normally kept it.

When they were maybe one hundred yards away, arrows flew from both towers, one from each, and thunked into the dirt a few yards in front of them.

"That's stupid," she muttered to Choony. "Why wouldn't they wait 'til we were closer to shoot at us with arrows? And arrows... like, really? Honest-to-god arrows. Whaaaaat?" she said, the last word drawn out at a high pitch. She'd seen that in a movie once and took to it.

Choony drew on the reins, and the horses drew to a halt. "We should just wait here until they send someone out, or until they shoot at us with something more dangerous."

Jaz slid her rifle into her saddle holster. "Prolly best not to look all threatening, and I hope you're right that they won't just shoot us and take our stuff. That would totally suck."

"We either take our chances, and then figure out how to resolve the issue between them and the Falconry, or we kiss the Clan's trade deal goodbye. I'm just glad they will allow us to pick up the first gasifier on our way back, or these people here might be a lot more inclined to do as you suggested—kill us and take our possessions, or our horses and supplies."

"It really wasn't a suggestion," Jaz said, laughing. "More like a concern." Choony always had a way of saying funny things and didn't seem to notice he'd done so. That only made it funnier. It was good to have a friend who could make her laugh. There hadn't been a lot of that in her life even before the invasion. But now was not the time to start thinking again about whether friendship was all there was to their interactions. "I hope they hurry up and figure out whether to kill us or talk to us. I hate waiting."

Choony shrugged. "Waiting is part of life. Embrace it, and use the time for something productive. They'll come out when they're ready."

"More productive. Maybe contemplate my navel and hum 'ommmm' or something?"

"Jaz, you are a brat. But I like that part of you. It makes waiting less tedious and a smile come easily. My mother said smiling fluffs the liver so life weighs less."

Jaz laughed and glanced over at him, her eyes sparkling. Then they heard a faint, deep rumbling sound, and the massive gate began to open. The operation took a full minute to complete.

Choony climbed off his horse. "I wonder how long it takes to close that thing in an emergency." He then stepped a few paces away from his horse. "You should get down, too, so they don't think we're a risk of flight."

"Yeah? What if we want to flee, did you think about that?" Jaz got off her horse though and stepped away from it. She didn't want to, but she would totally never leave Choon Choon to die alone. It wasn't the Clan way—and that was a big part of what she loved about her new people. She'd never been a part of any group, just an outsider hanging with this clique or that, usually hated by the girls and lusted after by the guys.

Movement at the gate pulled Jaz back to reality. Five people on horseback, each with a rifle or maybe a shotgun, clip-clopped across the bridge and approached at an easy pace. They spread out, keeping quite a distance between them. They'd probably circle around to block escape—that's what Jaz would have done. And she was right. As the middle figure stopped about twenty feet away, the other four kept moving to either side until they had surrounded her and Choony, like the points on a star.

Jaz said nothing, waiting for them to speak first, and Choony didn't say anything either. Jaz had learned from a book she'd read—*Influence: The Psychology of Persuasion* by Robert Cialdini—that whoever spoke last had the advantage. She didn't have to wait long.

The figure in front of them stared at the two Clanners for an awkwardly long moment, definitely sizing them up, then said, "You don't look like raiders. State your names and what business you have in Lebanon."

Choony said, "Thank you for meeting with us. I'm Choony and this is Jaz. We are envoys from Clanholme, to the south on the other side of the forest behind us."

"Choony, huh? You look like one of the invaders, but you don't sound like one. Where are you from?"

"If it pleases you, I am from Scranton originally. I've been with the Clan since they took me in, shortly after they settled at Clanholme."

The man eyed Choony, but at last he nodded. "Very well. What is it you want with us? Don't make me ask you again."

Jaz watched Choony carefully, sizing up his body language. Calm and at ease, as usual. Cool. "Sir, we're sent by our leaders to contact other survivor groups and see if there's interest in trade and mutual protection. An alliance, really. Between the invaders and the raiders, she feels it's in our best interests to help one another and band together if trouble comes."

"Official envoys from Clanholme, we welcome you... for now. We will relieve you of your weapons as we enter Lebanon, and you'll get them back when you leave. This is not negotiable. If you agree, we'll escort you inside to await a decision by the mayor as to whether or not he can meet with you."

That was a no-brainer. "My gun's on the horse. Choony doesn't carry any weapons because he's a Buddhist. All that nonviolence stuff. But he's brave, and he's a good man."

"Pacifist. Interesting. Still going to have to pat you down like everyone else."

One of the men dismounted and Choony, with arms raised, allowed the pat-down. Jaz looked hesitantly at Choony, but decided she had no choice but to allow them to frisk her as well. Soon, it was over and the man nodded at his associate.

"Alright," the man said. "Looks like we're all good to go in. Welcome to Lebanon."

They were led through the gate, and then they got to see how fast the gate could close—there was a whirring noise from both towers, and the gate slammed shut with a deafening noise.

Choony grinned. "Pretty well done," he said to Jaz, and they continued along. Jaz could hear Choony muttering to himself, still in awe over what she thought was simply a gate. "If I had to guess," Choony said, voice quiet, "they have a ratchet system inside with weights or counterweights. When the ratchets are released, the gate closes quickly as the weights fall."

"Wow," Jaz said, her eyes rolling up slightly.

Choony continued, "The guard then spins a wheel or something to reopen the gate, which at the same time pulls the counterweights back into place to get the system ready for next time, kind of like cocking a crossbow. That's why it opens so slowly, but closes with a bang. I'd have to see inside to know for sure. It's an engineering feat, though."

The guard who had so far done all the talking, a tall, well-built man, turned around and said, "That gate will stop fifty-caliber rounds. And we needed a gate that closed faster than it opened and could be closed by just one person if they had to—engineers come in handy these days."

Jaz grinned at him, and it was infectious—the man grinned back. Men were always grinning at Jaz, and like so many times before in her life, she was thankful for her good looks. "That's totally genius. We'll have to tell our own engineer about this setup, maybe make one for ourselves."

"You have an engineer also?"

"Our engineer isn't really an engineer. We call him 'our redneck engineer' because he didn't have any training, but seems to just understand all this mechanical stuff."

"I see," said the guard, who nodded and continued. Then he pointed at a tall building that looked like an old manor house. "That's City Hall. We'll take you there to talk with our Honorable Mayor Ruben Brutus."

A couple minutes later, they rode up to the front of the building. Their guide dismounted and tied his horse to the hitching rail there, clearly a new addition to the parking lot. Jaz followed suit, as did Choony and the other four guards in the party, using a clove hitch knot. Frank had once told her that cowboys used that knot to secure their horses for good reason, so she'd taken the time to learn how to do it. She had to admit it was a secure knot, fast to tie and fast and easy to release even if the horse had pulled against it.

The lead guard returned and beckoned for her and Choony to follow him inside. Once they entered, it took a moment for her eyes to adjust to the lower light level. The place had no skylights, so as they walked deeper into the old building she could see they had hung old-style storm lanterns from the walls, which flickered with even the faintest breeze. The head guard told her and Choony to have a seat and wait.

It took fifteen minutes before a young woman who looked to be about Jaz's own age came out of one of the back rooms. "If you'll follow me, the mayor will see you now."

She led them back, followed by the guards, and held the door open for them. Jaz and Choony went inside while the guards stayed outside. Probably in case of any trouble, but it felt kinda like they were prisoners now if the mayor decided to keep the two of them there.

Jaz took a deep breath, stepped up to the desk, and held out her hand. "Thank you for seeing us, Mr. Mayor. I'm Jaz and this is my friend and fellow envoy, Choony."

The mayor, who looked like he was maybe in his midthirties, shook her hand and then Choony's, and smiled. "Please have a seat."

Jaz and Choony took the offered seats. It felt awesome to get off her feet, and to sit on something softer than a saddle. She glanced around the room, nodding with appreciation. It was decked out with cool furniture and some nice paintings. Jaz let out a low whistle. "I totally love the office. This stuff's gotta be some of the best loot in town, I bet."

The mayor stiffened for a moment, eying Jaz, but he must have decided she meant no offense because he only replied, "It's safer in here than scattered all over town. All the other really valuable things we've found, mostly on abandoned property, are in various empty houses for storage and safekeeping."

Jaz smiled. "Good idea."

"So tell me, what does the Clan want from Camp Lebanon? We haven't had any visits from you before, yet now we're in the middle of winter and here you are."

Choony raised an eyebrow, and Jaz kinda felt like how Choony looked—the mayor's directness was surprising for a politician.

Choony confirmed that his thoughts were running along the same lines as hers when he said, "How long have you been the Honorable Mayor of the town? It must have been a big responsibility, getting all this set up and running smoothly."

"As smoothly as it can. I've been the mayor since about a month after the power died. The old mayor tried to keep things together, keep the town running and alive. Unfortunately, when typhus swept through town he lost his wife and daughter to it and killed himself a few days later. I always figured disease would come if the system crashed, but no one had any idea it would happen so fast."

Jaz pursed her lips, trying to show just the right amount of sympathy. Then she said, "You're doing better than Mastersonville. The flood of people came down Highway 283 and brought something with them. The little village was doing all right, holding off the hordes, until everyone started to get sick. Most of them died, as did the refugees. Now there's a few thousand rotting corpses there, and nothing else. Anyone who survived fled to places like this and Elizabethtown."

"Our scouts have been to both those places. Elizabethtown is where we heard of the Clan, but we weren't able to send anyone out to contact you before winter hit. We needed everyone we had, for a while, fending off the horde. It was heartbreaking sometimes, all those desperate, people with their hollow-eyed starving children. Same story here as at Mastersonville when the disease hit except that here, after the old mayor shot himself, someone had to step up. So I did, setting up quarantine zones and organizing our supplies. We had to kill or drive off anyone who tried to hoard or wasn't with the program, because we all *needed those supplies* to survive. Almost everyone pitched in, thank God." He paused, frowning at some memory, then almost visibly came back to them. "That's when we started work on our wall. It was a huge undertaking but worth every man-hour we spent on it."

Jaz saw something like sorrow flash across the mayor's face at the mention of killing or driving out hoarders. It was startling at first but she hadn't been here. She'd learned the hard way that tough times need tough people and organized action to survive. Well, the mayor probably needed to hear one of the envoys say so, so she spoke up.

"I don't know if I might have done the same with the hoarders if I was in your situation, but it looks like you were the right choice to take over. Our own leader, Cassy, says that if you don't do the necessary when you see it, you're likely to pay hard penalties."

"Maybe," the mayor replied. "I'd rather be chilling at the sports bar drinking beer and eating nachos, but someone had to get things going or we'd have all died by now. We're better off than Mastersonville, yeah, but we're also better off than New York, so I think we're doing better than most, actually. Maybe we can learn from the Clan and share a few things we've learned by living through this mess."

Choony perked up at the mention of the City and seemed pretty excited, surprising Jaz. Choony didn't get excited about anything, as far as she knew. He was the calmest man she'd ever met.

"You have word from the City?" Choony blurted. "You have to tell me what you know—is anyone left alive? Are they still under the invaders, like rumor says? I have family there. Not my parents, they're in Scranton, but a lot of aunts and uncles and such."

The mayor clenched his jaw, but nodded. "Alright. The truth, then. A lot of this is just pieced together, but figure twenty-five million people to begin with. A minimum of two-point-five million dead from diseases, both because of weakened immune systems and because of millions of bodies lying around. That's just for starters."

Choony's shoulders tensed. "Why is that the minimum? That's ten percent of what it started with."

"We talk to people from New York who pass through, and traveling merchants. Ten percent seems to be the average number everywhere, and a city as dense as New York has to be even worse, but we wanted to be conservative."

Choony took in a deep breath and let it out slowly. "Thank you for letting me rudely interrupt."

"It's quite all right, mister Choony. Anyway... Figure another million died from injuries, lack of medicine, the crazy neighbor with a shotgun, and so on. Again, that's about the average, from what we've learned. And then, some of the traders we've allowed in from the east say that about five million New Yorkers are enslaved by the gangs and by invaders camped out in the north end of the city. Can you believe that? Five million slaves..."

Jaz shuddered involuntarily and had to focus on slowing her breathing as vivid scenes of her own time enslaved to Jim, during the White Stag occupation, played through her mind.

The mayor paused, took sips of water, and when Jaz had regained her composure he continued without commenting. "So you have about seventeen-point-five million left. Each of them needs about seven hundred fifty calories per day to survive. That's thirteen *billion* calories daily, even after they used up what food was in the city when the EMPs hit.

"A human body averages about one hundred fifty pounds, half of it edible. Seventy-five pounds each. A pound of meat has twelve hundred calories, so one body has ninety-thousand calories on average. The daily calorie requirement divided by ninety-thousand is how many people must be eaten *per day* if there are no other food sources. We're told cannibalism has become common in the largest cities."

"That's one hundred forty-five thousand people," Choony muttered, jaw hanging and eyes wide.

"Per day, yes. Unimaginable. There's fewer people each day, so fewer must be eaten each day, it's on a decreasing curve. And there was some food in the beginning at stores and in people's houses. So we ran the numbers the whole way through, every day."

Jaz froze. She had not thought about this so methodically before. It made her heart hurt and that feeling was super uncomfy so she squashed it down, using her old street-kid survival trick, and didn't reply. Instead, she looked up at the vaulted ceiling and tuned everything out. Choony had a handle on this situation, he didn't need her for this. Not yet. But try as she might, the horrid conversation kept getting through her defenses. She wanted to scream.

Choony shifted uncomfortably in his seat and was silent for a moment. Finally, he said, "How many have been eaten, and how many people remain in New York City, do you think?"

"We compiled the numbers. I can only hope the New York numbers aren't on par with everywhere else, or maybe we made a mistake in our calculations. I pray to God that it's the latter, because if these numbers are right…"

Jaz couldn't take it. She had to get the conversation to stop, and the best way to do that was demand the answer Choony wanted. No matter how disgusting the answer, it would at least get this over with. "What are the numbers?" she demanded, as tears formed at the corners of her eyes.

"Eleven million people have died and most have been eaten by others in New York. Six-and-a-half million people are still alive. That's the best we could estimate. I doubt we'll ever know the real numbers, and I'm not sure it even matters now. However you look at it, it's been worse than the Black Plague was in Europe."

Jaz cried out, "How can you say it doesn't matter? What the hell is wrong with you?" Her hands shook. The bastard didn't give a shit about those people. How could that be? This mayor was a *monster*.

The mayor flinched but kept his voice even, as if he understood her emotional response. "The disgusting, sad truth is that cities can't raise much of their own food, especially not now that the infrastructure is destroyed. They can't even get city water. It would have taken a government-level effort and government-level resources to change city society that dramatically and nobody wanted to... Almost all of the people who still live in urban areas will eventually die now. Nor can they just escape. Just like us, with the flood of people fleeing from Harrisburg and Hershey, people in the areas around the cities will kill to protect what little they have left. *It's already too late for the refugees.* By the start of summer, there will be under two million left in New York. By this time next year, accounting for harvesting whatever they could by farming in the parks and such—more a question of finding seeds than farmable space, by then—we estimate only three hundred thousand will be left alive and they'll have eaten more than seventeen million of their neighbors. That's best-case."

Jaz felt something crack inside her. The thin veneer of armor she'd built up couldn't withstand the tragedy of what she'd just heard. She once had hope for her relatives and few friends, who all lived in cities just as she had. She'd hoped they could find a way to survive. And that hope had just been snuffed out. But unlike most people, who fall apart when the armor is cracked, Jaz didn't collapse. Instead, the coldness and apathy that had allowed her to survive life on the streets before the war flooded back into her, washed over her, and drowned the young woman she was becoming. At least for now, she needed those thick walls she'd thought were gone between her heart and her mind, or she'd come apart at the seams.

Choony looked at Jaz with concern, but so what? Getting close to him would only bring them both pain. There was no point, and she'd never let herself be that vulnerable again, she swore to herself.

Jaz's voice was monotone and dull, lifeless, when she replied. "I have just realized that none of that is important for why we're here, Mayor. People die, and will keep dying. So, let's change the subject and, if we may, let's just get down to business. You need food, and we need something a bit unusual from you. I think we can work out a deal that meets both of our needs."

The mayor looked startled at her change in tone. Well, she couldn't help that.

* * *

In the vacant hotel room they'd been given, Jaz drummed her fingers on the desk in frustration and clicked the radio button once again, though it would use some of their currently irreplaceable battery power. "Charlie One, Charlie One. This is Sam Two. Over."

It took a couple more tries before the radio finally showed signs of life—Ethan's voice said, "Sam Two, this is Charlie Two. Go ahead."

"We visited Aunt Lisa's place, and all seems well. She's a very practical woman, and she hears a lot of gossip from back east. I'll tell you all about that when we come home. She and Aunt Florence are again nice and friendly with one another, judging by our talk, so it was a good visit. We still need to drop off our radio and pick up a horse at Aunt Florence's on our way home. Over."

"Sam Two, I copy. Good job with Aunt Florence and Aunt Lisa. Stand by for update."

Jaz rolled her eyes, frustrated. It was Choony's idea that she should be familiar with working the Clan's larger, long-distance radio gear, but she didn't care for it at all. It was tedious, and it made her voice sound like Darth Vader. Nonetheless, he had a pretty good point, so she did her best not to complain.

A minute later, the radio crackled to life again. They went through the identity confirmation routine, and then Ethan asked whether they could speak openly. That was a terrible idea even if no one was eavesdropping here, because anyone could monitor the airwaves. But she confirmed that, on her end at least, no one else was nearby and listening.

"Sam Two, very well. You aren't going to like this. We have recent reports from friends that this entire region is lousy with squirrels," Ethan said, referring to invaders. "From north of you to south of us, small groups of squirrels are raiding the smaller trees and taking nuts from wherever they can. The weather is getting too bad for travel right now, Sam Two. You'll need to stay at Aunt Lisa's until the weather changes. How copy?"

Well, that was messed up. Invaders all over the place, maybe raiding compounds like the Clan's, and Cassy wanted her to sit here safe behind Lebanon's high walls? She looked over her shoulder at Choony. "No way. We can't abandon our people, right?" Of course Choony would understand! He just had to...

"Things are what they are, Jaz," Choony replied thoughtfully. "I think we should follow instructions, because we don't do any good to the Clan if we're dead, or worse, captured. And what if the invaders got hold of our radio?

They'd know not only that there are working radios out here, but they could monitor Clan traffic for at least a couple days, maybe more, before our people realized we were gone and switched channels."

Jaz could recognize truth when she heard it, even if she didn't like it. "And changing channels would mean sending riders out to all our allies to tell them about the updated protocols. I totally get it, but Choony—I'm still not staying here. We can smash the radio before we get taken, or better yet, you stay here with the radio to keep it safe, and I'll head back. With 'vaders all over, the Clan will be on double watch, double scouting rotations. Every pair of hands will matter."

Choony scrunched up his eyebrows and made the duckface with his lips. He clearly hated the idea of her leaving. That sucked, but it wouldn't stop Jaz from making her choice. She'd felt the wall go back up but that didn't mean she couldn't stand by her principles. She hoped Choony would stay behind with the radio and be safe, even though she'd totally miss his company. But he was right about keeping the radio safe. Plus he wouldn't fight, so he wouldn't be much use in a fight anyway unless the 'vaders attacked Clanholme in earnest. But she respected his scouting ability, and would likely miss that long before she got back to the Clan.

After taking thought, Choony replied, "Very well, Jaz. You go back to Clanholme, but I'm coming with you. I would never forgive myself if something happened to you out there."

Jaz hadn't thought of that. Maybe that was why Choony had looked so upset—not the radio, but *her*. She had mixed feelings about that. Okay, if she was honest, she liked that he cared about her. It was nice having a friend around who cared about people the way Choony did. "I can't stop you," she mumbled, unable to meet his gaze.

She picked up the radio handset. "Charlie Two, Charlie Two, this is Sam Two. Please advise Charlie One that we'll be home for the New Year's party. Wouldn't miss it. Sam Two out."

Before Ethan could respond, she reached out and turned the radio off. "Alright then, Choony. I guess it's time for another trip. I hope it doesn't turn into another Hell Ride."

- 8 -

1600 HOURS - ZERO DAY +147

CASSY WALKED WITH Michael toward the north Food Forest zone. He had said an attack would most likely come from the north, so now they were double-checking their lines of fire and their traps and adding some new traps where needed. Of course, he said the same about the White Stag invasion, yet their successful second attack had come from the south end.

"Yeah, but Cassy, they were amateurs. They got lucky, that's all. Luck matters more in battle than you'd think. Well, you've seen combat now. You know that. But the invaders are at least trained, so unless they're veteran or worse, elite, they'll follow a checklist. They're predictable."

"And if they're Rabs?" Cassy asked, using the word they picked up somewhere for the Arabic radicals who joined Korea and China for the invasion of America. "They're basically terrorists turned loose with limited oversight by their North Korean 'advisors,' right?"

Michael nodded. He bent down and buried one of their shotgun shell traps. "That's true, which is why we'll tighten up our defense of the south approach this time. Our Marines will spend the day emplacing a couple hundred traps along the far side of the hill and we've already added some sandbagged bunkers up there at the crest, scattered among the animal pens."

"They're not the only threat," Cassy said, adding, "Those scouts our people ran across? They were from the Empire out of Fort Wayne. Americans, not 'vaders. Any progress on your questioning?"

Cassy suppressed a shudder. She didn't like Michael's methods and knew Michael didn't either, but they seemed necessary in this new, more brutal world they lived in. Unlike the first time, just before the White Stag invasion, she was giving Michael her full support this time around. She had changed since the EMPs hit, as they all had, and though she didn't want the leadership role thrust upon her by circumstance, she was determined to carry out her duty as best she could. The vicious treatment Peter Ixin and his sadistic enforcer Jim had given her and the rest of the Clan during his brief occupation of Clanholme had hardened her, she knew. It had been a hard lesson for all the Clan's survivors.

"Some progress," Michael said. "We've relayed whatever intel I could entrust to Ethan to update his map, and he'll brief us all when time permits. He's kind of busy right now, like all of us. The scout questioning continues under Mueller even now, I'm afraid. We can't afford to give her time to recover her strength."

Cassy tied off a trap she had hung from an overhead branch, a coffee can full of glass, nails, small glass vials of precious gasoline, and Tannerite—an explosive that was easy to make out of ammonium nitrate and a bit of aluminum powder. It might damage the food forest if it got triggered, but it would certainly ruin the day of any attackers who tripped the wire. "So, are you sure the glass bottles will work?"

"Nope. I know the Tannerite we made will work and so will the shrapnel mine we put it in, but the explosion may or may not break the glass vials. I'm guessing it will, though. I need to ask Ethan how to make something like napalm, but I haven't had time. He's an evil genius with that sort of thing. Choony might be better, if his heart were in it, but you know."

Cassy grinned at the thought of the Clan's resident nerd as evil genius and pulled back some winter-killed ground cover to put in another shotgun shell trap as she replied, "He's a conspiracy theorist, you know? Can't believe those wackos. Nuts, all of them." That had become something of a running gag around the Clan since the second EMP round had been launched by Americans. It was Ethan who discovered the EMP retaliation was the work of a ruthless Army general in a bid for personal power.

For the Clan, the joke served two purposes. First, it kept people aware that sometimes the nutjobs are right. Second, it reminded everyone that Ethan was important, valuable—he had earned his place on the Council many times over and he knew things no one else did. Since he wasn't around to be seen that often, it helped him to stay integrated with the Clan and be seen as relevant when he did emerge from his 'cave.' People no longer snickered at the things he said, once reminded how often he had been proven right.

Michael smirked at the gag but said nothing more, and over the next two hours they finished planting dozens of new traps. They had also replaced some old traps that weren't in great shape anymore. When they finished, they headed toward the east retaining pond and guard tower, and started the process all over again.

* * *

2000 HOURS - ZERO DAY +147

After dinner, Frank hobbled along behind a line of children being led into a side entrance to the bunker just south of the house, the one that looked like some untrimmed bushes. They could blow that hidden tunnel if needed, but in the meantime it avoided telling everyone in the Clan where the bunker actually was. Most Clanners knew anyway by now, but it wouldn't do for outsiders to watch them go into the main entrance. Sometimes it pays not to advertise.

The kids looked a bit scared, but at the head of the line Grandma Mandy was busy reassuring each child as they entered the tunnel. She made it sound like a camp-out, rather than the emergency procedure it really was. They had reasoned that if invaders attacked and the kids stayed "upstairs," they'd become targets, distract their parents, and generally get in the way. So the kids got stashed in a large extra room in the underground bunker with a sign on the door declaring it the "Kidz Kastle." Directly across the tunnel in a room marked "Clinic," was a well-stocked extended medical treatment space.

It took almost half an hour before the last of the kids headed down into the bunker. Ethan and Amber awaited them there, with Ethan probably hoping the little rug rats wouldn't get loose in his computer room and comms center.

"Your turn, Grandma Mandy," said Frank, up above at the tunnel entrance. He no longer felt weird calling her that. It had become her name, for all intents and purposes, among the Clan members. She looked old now, and sickly, so Cassy had decided that her mother would be of best use helping with the kids. She had also decided Frank should go down there, which was irritating. He hadn't lost his aim just because he lost his foot to Peter, dammit.

Mandy put a gentle hand on his shoulder and looked into

his eyes. "Frank, you're a good man, and brave, but if the Clan needs to bug off or whatever Michael calls it, they can't slow down for you. They'd try, though, and people would die. Besides, we need an authority figure down there and Ethan, bless him, isn't one. He doesn't know how. You do, though, and the kids can see how much the Clan respects you."

Frank grimaced. "Yeah, I know. I do believe the reasoning, trust me. Plus, if invaders get into the tunnels somehow, Ethan will need another person who's a good shot and good with a knife."

"Definitely. Now get that flat mechanic's butt of yours down there. I'll close the lid."

"Hatch, Grandma Mandy."

"Whatever. Don't correct your elders, dear, or I'll have to think mean thoughts about you."

Frank, smiling, took one last look around, taking in the fading daylight—the last time he might ever see it, at least for a while—and with a deep breath began the climb down into darkness.

* * *

Cassy walked with Joe Ellings around the guard tower, checking for any needed last-minute fixes. The 'cage' at the top, where two guards stood watch, had been reinforced with sandbags and the structure reinforced with a lot of two-by-fours. It no longer had a somewhat rickety look, and the lookouts were much better protected now.

They had just finished testing the air siren, which was connected to a battery kept charged by the homestead's solar panels. The switch for the siren was mounted in the tower. The wires leading to the horn itself and to its battery power supply were in good shape. Cassy thought someone had scavenged the siren from a fire truck, but the Clanners who brought it back had insisted it was in a junk yard. There were no junk yards around the homestead, so Cassy had just smiled and thanked them.

Joe ran his hand through his thick mane of hair, shoving it out of his eyes. "Yes'm, I reckon we're solid for the tower. You reckon?"

Cassy smiled at Joe, as she always did when the man spoke. He was charming, laid back, easygoing, and had the thickest, most ridiculous cowboy accent ever, but somehow on him it just added to his charm. "I reckon so," Cassy said, and Joe didn't seem to notice the good-humored imitation. "You've done a good job with this, you and Dean. Traps are set, and mapped so we can get around them when this is over. For now, no one leaves the living areas without a guard escort and they all know where the traps are. I guess that's as safe as we can make them, all things considered."

"Yes'm, we're on top of that. Made sure all our people know about them traps, and told 'em to stay put."

Cassy walked toward the nearby outdoor kitchen—where the community meals were cooked and served—and she welcomed the warmth that radiated from the ground. Ducts led from the rocket stove exhaust down into branching, turning, buried tubes and then out an exhaust pipe for a chimney. The stoves thus heated the ground, making it the most comfortable outdoor place on the homestead in winter. In warm weather, they could bypass the tubes.

"Care for some cider? I'm parched," Cassy said with a grin.

"I don't suppose we got some of that hard cider, eh?"

"Not right now, we don't. Everyone's sober."

"Well dang, Cassy. You make it sound like a fellow can't hold his liquor. Takes more than a cup o' fancy wine to get me drunk." Joe laughed, but reached for the regular cider.

Of course he knew better than to use alcohol while under

attack. He was only pulling her chain. Cassy knew it and didn't think she had ever seen the man drunk, come to think of it. "Is everyone in place, Joe? We can't have any slip-ups. I know it's rough, being on lockdown with double shifts on guard, but with the Marines guarding our biggest entry points we didn't have much choice. At least we'll have plenty of notice if trouble comes around."

Joe took a sip of his cider and leaned back on the bench with his back against the table, elbows resting on top. "Trouble's always coming, Cassy. I reckon we're as ready as we can be. I'm hopin' that any of them invaders that sees us decides there's easier targets. We got local rumor on our side, too, making us out to be some sorta legends, and the woods make us look all dark and mysterious."

"Ominous, even," Cassy replied with a hollow voice, then smiled and sipped at her cider. "But on the other hand, we stock up stuff like this cider, attracting them. I'm not counting on them being too afraid to attack us. We only have about seventy people who can fight, and the rest are kids or disabled like Frank."

"Don't try to pass that off, Cassy," Joe said. He wore a smile, but it didn't show in his eyes. "My brother's got that bum leg of his when Peter had him hung upside down by it. He's out here with us anyway, doin' his duty."

"Joe, don't start on that, please. I guess I can tell you this, and you deserve to know. Frank's not down in the bunker because of his foot. That's just what I told him to get his stubborn ass down there. The truth is, I wanted a good fighter down there protecting the kids. My kids, and everyone else's. Your brother could've done that, but the kids already know and trust Frank."

Joe looked up into the sky and took a deep breath. He let it out slowly, then said, "Yes'm, I figure that makes a sort of sense. Sorry about that. Forgive me?"

"Nothing to forgive, my friend." Cassy put her hand on his shoulder. "We're all worried about the ones we love. There's no place safe, not anymore, and we worry. But I promise you that every decision I make is for the good of the Clan, as best I'm able. We're family now. We have to be, just to survive. Some day, America will rise again. It's too big and fine an idea to just die out. Until then, we'll have to make tough choices every day and pray it works out."

Joe nodded, and Cassy took her hand off his shoulder to reach for her cup of cider again. Then Joe said, "Speaking of tough choices, have we heard from Choony and Jaz? They've been out a mite longer than I expected."

"Actually, yes. They're disobeying my orders as we speak, heading back to Clanholme from some survivor group we made first contact with. It was unscheduled. The last we heard, they dropped their big portable off at another group we're negotiating with, for safekeeping, and they're on their way back. I'm worried about them. Two people on their own with all those soldiers running around... I don't like it."

Joe laughed, a real laugh that reached his belly, and Cassy raised her eyebrow at him, questioning. "That there is why I never figured on asking Jaz out. Never mind that she's into Choony, not that the poor bastard knows it. Heck, she might not know it herself. But the main thing is just that she's batshit crazy. A damn good woman, sure, but I like company that ain't so far off-kilter."

Cassy laughed, and they talked about smaller things for a while, then set out to make the rounds again, checking on their people at the guard posts.

* * *

0400 HOURS - ZERO DAY +148

After leaving through a hidden door and passageway through Lebanon's rubble wall, Jaz and Choony headed back south in the predawn hours. While the journey to Cornwall was only about five-and-a-half miles as the crow flies, they would have to take a circuitous route to avoid the roads. They also had to sidestep South Hills Park and the forest adjacent to it—they had been advised that it was infested with small groups of invader troops, and Jaz and Choony were lucky to have made it to Lebanon without encountering them. It would be best not to tempt Karma by going through there again on the return trip.

In fact, Choony thought the whole idea was terrible. They had received instructions to hold up in Lebanon, and if Ethan's intel suggested it was too dangerous to travel, then it probably was. "Last chance to stop, Jaz. We can still go back. I remind you that we do the Clan no good if we die or get captured before we reach home."

Jaz grunted, and was silent for a moment. Clip-clop, the muffled sound of horse hooves on dirt. Choony was about to repeat his comment, in case she hadn't heard, when she said, "Choony, I know it's dangerous, but I didn't take you for one who was afraid of dying."

Choony didn't like the edge in her voice, the clear judgment. In his mind, he knew he must simply let that go. Taking offense only upset his harmony, and replying in anger would only upset Jaz's further. It was odd that he cared so much about what Jaz thought, but he reconciled it by telling himself he valued her friendship. It was easy enough to believe, even, because it was also true. In a way. He was pretty sure that was all.

"I am not afraid of dying," he replied, keeping his voice calm and carefully nonchalant. "Death comes to all, and in the great cycle of life I am confident I won't be reincarnated into a lesser life than this one. But I'm also not eager to die needlessly, nor should you be. One more rifle won't make the difference if our home is invaded. You would be impossible to replace, and I feel responsible to keep you safe if I can."

Jaz sighed. "I know, Choony, but I could never live with myself if my Clan-family got killed or conquered while I waited it out in safety. No one has ever treated me like the Clan does, and I won't pay that back by being totally selfish."

"Very well, then. I get it, but I hope you know that I come with you because I care less for my own life than for yours or the Clan's."

"Maybe you don't care about your own life less than mine, Choony," Jaz snapped back, "but you'd put my life ahead of anyone else's, too. Even the Clan's." The words dripped with her harsh judgment and Choony jerked, as if she had slapped him.

Then Choony felt his rising anger flow away. Jaz's words were based on a misunderstanding. Why would it bother her if he would put her life ahead of the Clan's? She likely just wanted to hear him confirm it—to allay her fears that he would run, perhaps—but he wouldn't lie. Not to her or to anyone. No good came of lying.

"That's not so, Jaz. I'd place Cassy's life ahead of yours, for example. She is more necessary to the Clan than either of us, despite your very real value to us all, and the Clan keeps us all alive. In that way, helping Cassy would be the same as helping the Clan, and the same as helping myself and you and everyone I care about. Things are what they are, so please don't be offended that I'd put Cassy before you, but I don't want you holding a resentment about a false assumption. There's no need to upset your harmony."

Jaz growled—literally growled—at him. Choony decided that, since he didn't understand how he had made it worse, the best course was to simply accept the situation instead of resisting it. He was content to let the silence lay over them as they rode.

They kept to the low points, following the terrain on contour rather than the most direct route possible, in order to minimize their exposure. In this terrain, a sniper would have a field day. Then, in the distance, Choony spotted movement and checked through his binoculars. It was just regular people. Not invaders, at least not this time.

Following natural contours rather than moving in a straight line put them only halfway to the Falconry by the time the horizon began to grow lighter. This was unfortunate —he had hoped they would make it to the settlement by dawn so they could spend some of the daylight hours going through the woods south of Falconry, heading to Brickerville, but they couldn't make it. Nor did he want to set camp to wait for dusk, not out there in the open. "We'll have to risk—"

"Yep."

"You don't know what I was going to say," Choony said, bemused. He kept his voice light though, so Jaz wouldn't think he was snapping at her, or that he found her amusing. It wouldn't help anything to upset her.

Jaz let out a long, loud breath. Choony could practically see her eyes rolling, even through the back of her head. She finished huffing and said, "You were going to say we have to make the forest before we camp, even if it means moving out here during daylight. I know, Choony."

At least she didn't sound angry, but rather, sort of empty —flat and lifeless. "Yes, unless you have a different point of view?" He raised his voice at the end, making it into a clear question.

"No, that's fine. I don't want to spend all day out in the open either. Listen, I'm sorry I snapped at you. I've been thinking about it, and about us—"

"Shh!" Choony hissed at her. Ahead, as they came around the side of a low hill, there were five riders traveling in a long row, winding northward through the low-lying areas just as he and Jaz were. He whispered, "People ahead."

Jaz reined her horse to a halt and looked through her binoculars. Hers were smaller than Choony's field glasses, but at this shorter range she could probably see well enough. "Yeah, there's like, five of them with AK-style rifles. They're not in black, though. Woodland cammies. They're headed our way."

Choony took a second to calm his mind. Things were what they were. Don't resist, but adjust. "Have they seen us?"

Jaz paused to look through her binoculars again. "I don't think so. They're moving slowly, still all in a row."

That was good news. He doubted Jaz could fight them off by herself. But if she was going to make it through this alive, they would have to move quickly. "Okay, to the east," Choony said as he wheeled his horse to the left.

He put spurs to his horse, and they rode as fast as their horses would take them, following the contours between the gently rolling hills, staying in the gap. Their path soon meandered to the northeast. At the next opportunity, they followed a gap into a more direct easterly direction. Soon, Choony was half-mesmerized by the rhythmic thudding of hooves, and he found himself in an almost meditative state.

The next mile went by in a blur, and once the back of his mind decided they were likely far enough east to avoid the five mounted people, he came out of his state—feeling refreshed and alert, marveling once again at how one could be meditating *and* stay almost hyper-aware of their surroundings.

A copse of trees lay ahead, and they made a beeline for it. Only once past the tree line did he pull out his binoculars again, and in a few seconds he found the other group.

Thankfully, they hadn't apparently noticed him or Jaz, and at the moment they were continuing their path northward. "Seems like we made it. We had best stay here a bit, to make sure they aren't circling around, but I think we're clear of them."

Jaz dismounted and took out her water bottle. After a long sip, she finally looked at Choony. "I'm sorry about earlier. I don't know why I got so angry."

Choony smiled and nodded, then got his own water bottle. He sat close to Jaz, but not directly next to her. Best to respect her space until he was sure Jaz was over it. He was content to simply sit with her in a comfortable silence.

After a minute, Jaz turned her head to look at Choony. When he looked back, she said, "I have sort of a question for you."

"Is it sort of a question? I may have a sort of answer." Choony grinned and waggled his eyebrows like an Asian Groucho Marx, and Jaz smiled back. Maybe a little awkwardly, but Choony was glad to see her reaction was positive. For some reason he felt nervous.

"You sometimes mention reincarnation, like coming back as a cockroach or something. Or as a rich person. Do you really believe in that stuff? Buddhists, I mean."

Choony thought about the question for a moment. It was a difficult one to answer, because the answer was only "sort of" yes. And sort of no. "Not exactly. I know that most people think that's what we believe, so I joke about it, or use it for emphasis. Sometimes I even think it when I'm zoned out, but maybe it's more of an allegory than a literal truth."

He looked into her eyes to see if Jaz understood what he had said and she didn't look confused, just open minded, so he continued. "The reality is that most Buddhists believe we are different people from moment to moment. *You* are only *you* in this exact moment—you'll never be precisely there again. Part of the wonder is that moments are too short of measure. Karma is the totality of your words, thoughts, and actions through all your moments. Good Karma in this moment allows you to be reborn in a more positive energy in the *next* moment. There are several stages of human development ranging from simple beast to Buddha himself."

Jaz said, "That makes sense. Send good out into the universe, and good comes back." Choony nodded in reply. "So, what about when you die? Where does your soul go? If not into a cockroach or a rich person—or whatever—then where do you go?"

"That's the part that's hard to explain. You understand the idea of Karma, right? But you probably have the wrong idea about what Buddhists believe. Karma isn't Fate, but rather it's your personal energy, your place in the universe, your attributes and character and everything that means you are *you*. That's what determines what stage of development you'll spend your next moment-self. Buddha taught us to meditate to help us realize ourselves as whole beings in a peaceful state without pain, and 'pain' doesn't mean what you feel when you stub your toe, either. It all gets pretty abstract the deeper you get into it."

"I never heard that idea before. I thought it was, like, all the things that happen to you are because of your Karma."

"Every person has the freedom to choose what they put into the universe. Some people put evil out there. A lot of bad things that happen to people aren't because of their own Karma, but someone else's. How you react to it is what counts for your own Karma. That's the part you can choose. But at the same time, if you put good out into the world, your Karma not only affects you, it also affects the people around you, just like their bad or good energy can affect you. It goes both ways."

"So what happens when you die? Do you carry your

Karma into the next life? You already said we don't really come back as a cockroach or a squirrel, so you come back as a person with your old Karma, right?"

"All things are illusion, temporary, and won't last. From the big universe down to little you, it all eventually passes by. Yet energy can't be destroyed, only transformed into something else. When you die, that which is *you* transforms back into various kinds of atoms."

"So you believe we don't have a soul? That this life is it for us, and when we die we're gone? I don't think I like that idea."

"That's because you hang on to the idea that things can have permanence. They can't. The 'you' who said that is already gone, transformed into the 'you' of right now, and that's gone again as I speak. It's a constant transformation. Your Karma, however, being energy can't be destroyed. It continues on when you die, settling on some other person being born. Good or bad, your Karma now sets the stage for the Karma someone else begins life with. So when you think, say, or do things that upset your balance—things that give you negative energy in your Karma—you'll make someone else start at a lower level of consciousness, with negative energy. To a Western mind that might seem like the next *you* but it's not, or not exactly. *Everyone* can overcome what they start with, through their own actions and choices, but you might say they start 'in the red' if the Karma they begin with is from a bad person. It's like starting out in debt."

"Grandma Mandy says that all children are good, because Jesus said Heaven is made up of 'ones such as these' or something. I don't like the idea that my life was affected by the bad things some dead guy did."

"Why not, Jaz? Your life is affected by the bad things living people do, but I understand most people have a hard time letting go of the notion that they can somehow live forever, that they have a permanent soul. I respect those beliefs, you know. When people try to actually live by Jesus' teachings, they do wonderful things. Even if they don't know they're following Jesus' teaching. I like to call it a conscience. You think that's God nudging you toward a more Christ-like existence, and I think the conscience is your Karma trying to gain harmony with the energy of the universe. The result is the same. Does it matter what you call it?"

"Oh, Choon Choon. Don't get me wrong, I'm not trying to bash your Buddha ideas. I think you're an amazing person. If the world had more people like you, it would be, like, such a better place."

Choony, feeling calmed by her and liking it, smiled. She was so sweet, and though she had clearly never really pondered these issues before, in her heart she was a naturally good person. One of the best, even. He realized he was still smiling. "Jaz, you do more good in this world than you give yourself credit for. The entire Clan does. This permaculture idea that Cassy lives by is, at its heart, just trying to get back in harmony with the Earth itself, and it's full of joy and good Karma. How do you all live together without many problems? That's Cassy's good Karma affecting the people around her. Yours, too."

Jaz giggled, and Choony raised an eyebrow. "Sorry," Jaz said, regaining her composure, and explained, "Ethan calls it the 'Founder's Principle,' where the one who starts a society has, like, a big impact on how everything goes down after that. Kinda the same idea, I guess." She giggled again. "Same idea but they sound so different—no wonder people get confused."

Choony stood and stretched his back, and Jaz followed his lead. "I guess it's safe to head out now. Yeah? Let's try to make it to the Falconry before they put away breakfast," Choony said and repacked his water bottle.

- 9 -

0800 HOURS - ZERO DAY +148

WELL, THAT WAS unexpected. Incoming message through the hacked satellite "back door" channel. That would be Taggart. Ethan set his cup of coffee on the desk next to his laptop and went through his usual routine. Set up the sandbox. Bounce around through VPNs—though much fewer of those were online since Operation Backdraft sent EMP strikes around the globe—and connect his USB toggle with the decryption/encryption program they used to scramble the chatter.

They used a variant of Cipher P-1776, the 20s encryption routine that required both parties to have the same edition of the same book to have any hope of decrypting it (it was otherwise a string of random numbers and letters), but Taggart was using a different source book—he had the actual book and Ethan had an ebook version that showed the paper version page numbers. To the 20s, if they intercepted it, the transmissions were nearly unbreakable because there was quite literally no pattern at all. It would take many transmissions and a lot of time for even a computer to find any pattern at all, and one could never know if the "key book" had changed. Ethan loved it. It was pretty damn impressive. Thanks for the idea, 20s...

"Hey, Amber, did you see this back-chan come in from New York City? When did you last check it?"

From down the hallway, in the next chamber of the bunker, Amber's angelic voice called back. Even when she was hollering back at him through the tunnels, she still mesmerized him like no other woman's voice ever had. "I checked it like twenty minutes ago. It was clear then."

Oh, thank goodness. That meant it was fresh and hadn't been sitting there all night. No need to chew her out and then sleep on the couch later. Phew. Ethan fed the received file through his custom program and watched as it spit out a string of letters that became words, then sentences, faster than he could keep up. It must be one helluva process on Taggart's end. The poor guy probably had to do all this by hand. The thought made Ethan cringe. Computers made life so much easier.

But then the thought stopped him in his tracks as he realized that it was computers, and humanity's reliance on them, that had led to the war. The EMPs. Mankind losing seven of its eight billion people by the end of next year. Man's reliance on computers was understandable, though— they did miraculous things, and let everyday people do things that would be indistinguishable from magic only a hundred years ago. Most of mankind ended up being the sacrifice to angry Technology Gods...

The computer beeped, alerting Ethan that decryption had been completed, and he leaned in a bit to get a better view of the screen.

>> *NYC1 to Dark Ryder*, it began, and Ethan grinned. That guy just couldn't seem to get the idea that HAMnet wasn't the same as talking on a CB. *NYC1*

direct. Attchd r Intel from prior 7 days. NK swrmng NYC w Death squads. My cmbt eff grtly reduced. 3 full plat.remain. Situ8n untenable. Must retrograde. Need instruct. Most urgnt. Over.

Well, the terrible writing was understandable when the poor guy had to encrypt by hand. Irritating, maybe, but the least of Ethan's problems.

So. New York City was swarming with North Korean—and probably Islamist—death squads, Taggart was down to a company, and had to bug out, but where to send him? He had the unsettling feeling that it would be best to send him some instructions now rather than later.

Ethan arose and stepped up to his wall map with all its many-colored pins. Where to send Taggart... It was a tough question. Everything depended on whether they could get the hell out of New York and through New Jersey alive, which was a big question mark in its own right. But if they did get through, then what?

Amber padded into the room, stood behind Ethan, and rubbed his shoulders a little. Something about her scent was like catnip to Ethan. "Something from that Taggart guy, I see. What's up?"

"Things are just too rough in New York and he decided he has to get out of Dodge. 'Retrograde,' he calls it. I'm looking at the map to see where I should send him. He can't go south because it's all urban down there, and the same with northeast. It has to be anything from west to north."

"You know, for a genius you sure can be dense sometimes."

"Uh huh. Love you too. But seriously, I don't know where to send him. I know there's a band of Militia out by Liberty, Pennsylvania, but I doubt they'll last the winter in that little town. I've heard there is enough infighting among them that their group will probably either split up or kill each other. Or both."

Amber tilted her head back, holding her nose with one hand, and snickered.

It was all very melodramatic, and kind of amusing, and Ethan couldn't stop himself from smiling. "Alright, drama queen, why don't you enlighten me? Where do you think I should send them, if you're so smart?"

"Why not bring them here? They need a home, everywhere east of us is screwed, everywhere west of us is either Empire or Mountain, we're in the middle and we need the help. We could use his troops and you've said he seems like an effective leader, loyal to the country and all."

"It'd be a minimum of five or six days' journey, longer if our own trip is any indication..." Ethan's voice trailed off as he considered her words. In fact he had thought of it, but immediately dismissed it simply because of the journey's length. Maybe a company of well-armed, veteran guerrilla soldiers stood a better than decent chance of coming through alive, however. Imagine someone like Taggart leading patrols through their nearby hills and woods...

Amber added, "And you could direct them to some critical hot spots along the way. Turn a couple tie games into home-team wins."

"You and your sports. I'm not a fan but I could watch a good game of football right about now."

Amber play-punched him in the arm. "You know damn well that we're in America, and here we call that so-called sport 'soccer,' not football. In *our* football, grown men don't pretend a slight brush against another player is the end of the world, falling down crying."

Ethan glowered at her, but of course she'd know he was just playing along. "Real football is the favorite of the entire world and requires skill and flawless tactics."

"It's one dude with a ball. What tactics?" she teased. "But anyway, we're getting sidetracked. Bringing Taggart here makes sense. For us, for him. And when springtime rolls around, we'll be awfully glad to have another thirty or so veteran warriors with mil-grade weapons on our side."

"What if they decide they want to be in charge? Amber, I'm not sure we could stop them. Even if we could, it would decimate both groups."

"Figure the odds of them attacking Americans, given what you know. Then, figure the odds of us needing thirty more soldiers come spring, given your intel. Both bringing them and not bringing them could have a really bad end for us, but which is more likely? Whatever you decide, I know you'll make the right recommendation to the Council."

Her grasp of gamesmanship always impressed him. She had even gone for the long-term win when he gave her the "prisoner's dilemma" puzzle. Taking this to the Council wasn't something he had thought of. Being a wingnut loner sometimes made it kind of hard to think of things like that, but Amber kept him on the right track and reminded him of things like chain of command, or like bringing a company of friendly soldiers to the Clan just before the spring offensives started flying.

Ethan sent a quick coded reply to Taggart that said more information would come shortly and to get out of the area in the meantime. Then he kissed Amber, and the two headed aboveground for a late breakfast.

* * *

Cassy sat with Michael in her living room. They were alone since she'd chased out the others. She took a deep breath and steeled herself, bracing for the guilt she felt. "So how did the questioning end? Did we get what we needed?"

Michael closed his eyes for a second, then nodded. "Yes, we got all we could out of her. She didn't really know much of strategic value. Confirmed she was from the Empire, or the Midwest Republic as they call it. She was the leader of a band of scouts called 'Ancillaries,' and they were out here just to map the area and do recon on survivor groups."

"That's it? All that... the things you had to do. Just for that?"

Michael shrugged. "She didn't know much. We got some information that will be useful, though."

"I hope it was worth it."

"Probably not," Michael replied. "However, it seems that the Empire sends envoys out to the stable survivor groups the scouts locate. They tell the groups they'd love to have them in the Empire. They explain the benefits. And then they say that the group must vote whether to join the Empire or not. If they vote to join, then they get a new ruler."

"And if they vote not to?" Cassy asked.

"They tell the groups that if they vote no, they'll be left in peace but will be barred from trade with the Empire and so on, but won't be harmed."

"People fall for that?"

"Yeah. Any group that refuses is forced to let its members leave for parts unknown in the Empire, and after they're gone, the Empire burns the rest to the ground. No survivors."

"Why would they tell people they have a choice, only to kill off the ones who choose not to join?"

Michael scratched his chin, where he had some stubble on his usually clean-shaven face. "My theory is that they do it just to get at the truth without coercion. Those who only joined because there was a rifle at their heads would probably be more trouble than they're worth down the road."

Cassy nodded slowly. "Good to know, Michael. At least

you didn't have to do all that for nothing. You did well, you and Mueller. I hope we don't have to do that ever again."

Michael nodded. "Me too. But you and I both know that we probably will. I've already had the Smoke House cleaned up for its next guest."

Cassy took a deep breath, but remained silent.

"Don't feel too guilty, Cassy. I know it's rough, but this is a warzone, and a different world than the one we used to know. We all do what we must to survive, and there's no guilt in that. Better us and our families live than them and theirs."

Cassy made a polite exit, then went for a walk to clear her head. Michael was right, but that didn't make it any easier. Deep inside, she hoped that sending people to the Smoke House *never* got easy. As long as it was hard, she was still human inside…

* * *

Jaz and Choony arrived back at the walls of Cornwall—the Falconry, now—and were invited inside. After seeing Lebanon's, the Falconry's less imposing walls looked almost peaceful until she remembered that they both had walls for a reason.

Before doing anything else, they stopped to get breakfast. The Falconry did theirs just like the Clan, with a communal outdoor kitchen, but they were totally smart about it and had a small greenhouse with picnic tables inside for their peeps to eat at. Way more comfy than the Clan's eating area, at least now in the middle of winter. Maybe they took it down in summer. Jaz would have to ask, but not right now. More important things first.

As she finished up the last of her breakfast and saw that Choony was already done, she stood to take her dishes to the barrel. "It's kinda weird they use the barrel system for dishes just like we do. Maybe it was in, like, some military manual."

"I imagine it is. Since we both do it, the idea had to come from somewhere. It's effective, but I imagine the kitchen people would give a lot to have a working commercial dishwasher. So where to next? We need to do the swap for the gasifier and get our wagon hooked up."

"Yep. Let's go see Delorse first. You know, she seems too nice to be the leader of a place like this."

"Nicer than Cassy?" Choony ran his fingers through his mop of hair.

It was nice how his hair looked so thick and healthy. Jaz would kill for hair like that. Not black, though. "Cassy's not nice. She's kind, but you weren't around during the White Stag thing. Cassy's made of steel and can make the tough calls."

Jaz shuddered at the memory of Cassy allowing that first White Stag scout to be skinned alive. She had almost left the Clan after that, just out of disgust. It was kind of hard to believe, now. Hard to believe how much she herself had toughened up, too. She had thought living on the streets had made her hard but compared to what Cassy had to do... She shuddered again. Anyway, leaving the Clan would have been stupid. Probably fatal.

"Funny, I had the same impression of Delorse," Choony said, breaking into her thoughts. "I think hard decisions are the reason they took her as leader. Not everyone could make those decisions. Now we'll see if she holds to her word like Cassy does."

They walked freely through the streets of the Falconry, and it was kind of eerie how quiet everything was these days. Towns should have, like, a background humming. Like pollution, but with noise. Clanholme felt *right* with that silence, like it belonged there with only the wind and the animals in its little valley, but this was a town built around cars, and power grids, and air conditioners. Silence felt weird here.

It took only a minute or two to walk to the City Hall building, an unassuming building like any other on that block. The guard outside didn't stop them from going inside, this time. One even nodded at them and smiled as they approached the door. Jaz was the first inside, and it took her eyes a second to adjust to the dim interior light. She called out for Delorse.

A door opened, and the Head Falconer entered the room. Jaz had to look up to see Delorse's eyes. Boy, she was tall. Even though the Falconry had no showers since the EMPs, the leader's blonde hair still looked somehow perfect. "I'm jealous of your hair," Jaz said as the two grinned hello at each other.

After sharing greetings all around, they sat at the desk and Delorse had the attendant bring tea. Jaz missed tea, not that she was ever super knowledgeable about it. There wasn't much to go around in Clanholme. Then the irritating need to talk about small things that didn't matter. Jaz pretty much hated small talk. Pointless, took up time, and plus she wasn't good at it. Thankfully, Choony was good at small talk and carried the conversation with courtesy.

Then Delorse said, "So how was your journey? Did they let you in to talk?"

It was about time she got to the point. Jaz flicked a bit of hair out of her eyes, then realized she was slouching and sat up straighter. Time for business. "Actually, they did. They wouldn't let us come close to the walls at first, though. We came up from the south, where I guess they haven't had too many problems because someone told us that if we had come up to the other gate, we'd have been shot for being refugees."

Delorse's lips twitched, the only hint that she was surprised by that. "Indeed. While I don't agree with that, I also don't live where they do. They must have good reason."

It wasn't really a question, but maybe best to answer it anyway... "They do. Lots of invader bands and hordes of refugees like locusts. I don't think they like turning people away, the way their leader described it—'hollow-eyed children,' he said—but they don't have much food for themselves. They can't feed all those people from the cities west of them."

Delorse seemed to relax then. Maybe. Jaz couldn't be sure. But she had done what she could to not start any new quarrel between Falconry and Lebanon. "What is the area like between us and them? We haven't sent any scouts that way for a while, preferring to keep them close to home. Early warning in case Lebanon decided to attack us."

"Um. Well, there are lots of small groups, invaders running around and stuff. We had to hide from them, once. They're moving in groups of five, just like at Brickerville on the other side of the forest south of you. I didn't see any refugees. The invaders take a lot of pot-shots at the guards on the wall, so everyone is all tensed up. They're tired from pulling double watches, and they're all a bit hungry."

Delorse grinned. "The invaders are tired and hungry? Great!"

Jaz felt her cheeks flush. Stupid cheeks. "No! Not them. Lebanon's people. Sorry. They gotta keep twice the normal guards up on the wall to see everything, and the 'vaders shoot at them. More like toward them. The Lebanon mayor thinks the 'vaders are trying to get the guards to use up all their ammo shooting back, but he caught on quick, so now the guards don't shoot back unless they have, like, a good solid target."

Delorse took a flinching sip of hot tea, then set the cup down. "So to the meat of the issue, shall we? Were they interested in a truce with us, or do we need to keep worrying about raids?"

Choony coughed, then said, "They are indeed interested. A truce would suit their needs, and they seem to be decent enough people, but they're hungry. The refugees stripped everything in the region bare. That's the only reason they raided you. I feel they have genuine remorse, Delo. They were kind to us once we convinced them we were not refugees or raiders, nor did they steal our supplies. Not that we brought much, but if they raided because they wanted to, rather than needed to, they would have taken ours. As it was, our supplies wouldn't help them much, and they left us and our supplies alone."

Delorse steepled her fingers in front of her face, elbows on the desk, and let out a deep breath. She was quiet for a minute or two and looked like she was seriously thinking about what Choo Choo had said. "Alright. They seem like ordinary people, then. Who wouldn't do whatever was needed to feed their children? So then, peace may be possible. In fact, it would be in both our interests to develop a relationship. They don't need another enemy on another flank, and we could use both the friendship and the trade. They also apparently are one reason we haven't been hit with floods of refugees so in a sense, we owe them. What did they say they need? Maybe it's something we can provide."

Jaz watched as Choony leaned forward, listening to Delorse's words, but his left hand was busy drumming fingers on the edge of his chair. She knew him well enough to recognize this as a tense or bored habit. Probably tense. He never really worried about things, but he always seemed to really care about things like people suffering. Especially kids.

Choony said, "What they need is something you yourselves can't provide, which is food. Yet you're trying to be a trade hub, right? It seems to me you might be able to arrange some trade agreements that let you set up a different deal with Lebanon, with you in the middle as maybe an escrow service. That puts you in a very useful position."

"Maybe... It's a fine idea, but is it practical? Brickerville has some food, but not enough to feed themselves, us, and Lebanon together. Our other trading partners are smaller still, homesteads mostly. They can't trade for much yet, and without working tractors and trucked-in fertilizers and pesticides, they're in a bind until they can get next year's crops in and figure out how to do this in a new way. Or rather, shift to some very old ways."

That got Jaz's attention. She felt rather foolish for not thinking of the idea herself, when she was actually in Lebanon, but Delorse had just given her a great idea.

"Interesting. I know we said you'd get us another gasifier in trade for some food, but we know where there is enough to feed all of Lebanon through the winter, at least."

Choony sat bolt upright. At least she had his attention now. What did a girl have to do to get his attention, anyway? Give away the store? Then she wondered why that thought had been so bitter, but shoved it aside for the moment.

"And what in return?" Delorse asked mildly. She leaned back in her chair, obviously trying not to look too interested, but Jaz knew right away when someone was interested in something she had. At some point they had slipped into negotiation mode, and Jaz knew she was damn good at that. Before the EMPs it had been a survival thing, learned through hard lessons with bad men. Life in the streets.

"We can always use a third gasifier. But there's more."

Delorse moved her hands away from her face and laid them on the desk. She hadn't flinched when Jaz mentioned a gasifier, so that was a yes, at least.

Jaz continued, "As you know, there are some survivor communities that aren't as nice as the Falconry and the Clan, or Lebanon or Brickerville for that matter, and the invaders also look like they're moving into our neighborhood. I'm sure you've heard of the Empire—they're coming, too, probably with the new spring, and they don't have any room for a free trade town anywhere near them. It's not in their plans."

"You want my Falconry to follow your war drum, is that it? Sorry, sweetie. Falcons don't fly in flocks. We won't join you in attacking the Empire, nor Adamstown. What else do you have?"

"You have it wrong," said Jaz, putting on her best smile, broadcasting cheerful amusement at the misunderstanding for all she was worth. This one could go south in a hurry if she messed it up. "We don't want you to join us. You're too useful as a trading hub. Essential, even. You have to stay neutral. Sorry to be so blunt, but since the invasion Clanholme doesn't have time or patience for old-school politics. I'm laying it all out here. You'll do what's right for your people, just like we will for ours, and like Lebanon will. But we've only just started to put it all together, you know?"

Yeah, that was a veiled threat buried in there, or maybe a warning—seriously consider what the Clan offers, or no deal and no food, and a hungry, pissed off Lebanon just north of you. "What we want is to give you the food you need to get you *and* Lebanon through the winter, at the price of Lebanon's alliance with Clanholme. And Brickerville. And Ephrata. And Liz Town. All of us in a confederation with the Falconry providing our essential, neutral trading center. Together we can clear a big area of the raiding refugees, invader death squads, and hopefully, even the Empire. You stay officially neutral as the trade hub. Heck, maybe you could even trade with the Empire. That'd be risky…"

Delorse looked thoughtful. "So we can even trade with the Empire for the stuff your confederation needs, if I read this right," Delorse replied. She smiled. "The Empire, and the nearest 'vader enclave too, maybe. Our brave new world…"

"That's right, maybe. And all the while passing us the info, the four-one-one. Spying. On our side in spirit and in passing us information, but not in public. Just good neighbors." Jaz glanced to Choony and saw that he watched her intently, but he looked calm. He was always more comfortable with truth, and what she said was the honest truth. Cross her heart, hope to die.

Delorse got up from her chair, and smiled. "It sounds like a workable plan, so long as we are the neutral ones. I just hope you aren't flying blind." Again with the bird references... "You've got the Clan's reputation on your side, which might work in your favor. I'll need time to clear it with my Falconeers, but I'd like to work with you on this."

Jaz grinned, then said, "Oh please. You're the Head Falconer. You don't run a democracy any more than the Clan does, probably for the very same reasons, but I understand if you need time to decide."

Delorse nodded, but remained silent.

Jaz continued, "How 'bout Choony and I go hook up our wagon, get the gasifier on it, and resupply at your market. We'll come by on our way out of town to get your decision. Whatever your answer, we're happy to honor the original deal. Five barrels of cider, two tons of grains, two more when spring arrives, all in exchange for a second gasifier on final delivery. Anything more can be a separate arrangement, but this will get us all through the winter and put our trading onto a solid footing." She liked that last bit—it sounded so mature.

Delorse shrugged. "I figured you would honor that deal either way—it's a good deal for both of us." A smile crept onto Delores's face. "One good turn deserves another—we have a surprise for you, waiting at your wagon."

"Oh really? Is it a pony? I always wanted a pony."

"Ha! No. Nothing that 'peachy keen,' my girl. You'll just

have to settle for your four troops that you got separated from. They followed your trail here and have been hanging around flirting with every attractive young man or woman who passes by. I'd appreciate it if you got them out of here before they get too comfortable and decide they don't want to leave."

Jaz grinned. She was obviously joking. Mostly joking, anyway. At least Delores had a sense of humor like her own— a bit rough and acidic. "Thank you, Delores. On behalf of the Clan, I appreciate you taking care of our lost sheepdogs. Maybe more like pit bulls, since they survived long enough to get here. If you decide to take us up on the other deal, I'll take it to Cassy, but I'm sure she'll be thrilled. I know I am."

Choony shook Delorse's hand and said, "The Buddha has said, 'Better than a thousand hollow words is one word that brings peace.' I hope your word is 'yes,' but know that my word is 'friend.' May we meet again, Delo." He bowed and then he and Jaz walked out into the dim winter sunlight to fetch their wagon. Jaz was still smiling.

* * *

Choony sat with Jaz on the wagon, quietly chatting about nothing much. Their reunion with the soldiers he had thought lost had been joyful but necessarily brief. As they left the Falconry and then Brickerville behind, two soldiers always rode ahead and one to either side of their precious gasifier load, all of them keeping it barely in view as they traveled. When Brickerville faded behind, Choony felt the bittersweet, mixed joy and sadness normal at the end of a risky but successful adventure. Almost home now, and Choony couldn't get the thought of a hot shower out of his mind. His physical discomfort was mostly irrelevant, but the hot water and the white noise of the water falling always helped him find his center again. His harmony would be enhanced, and that's what he so looked forward to.

Then Choony saw the two lead guards stopped in the middle of the trail before them. He nudged Jaz, and reined the horses to a gentle stop. After a couple minutes, one of the guards rode back toward the wagon.

Once within easy earshot, he called out to Choony, "Councilman, there is a large body of troops ahead, traveling the same direction as us—toward Clanholme." He looked tense, eyes narrowed and jaw clasped.

"Very well. Can we make out any details, and how far away are they?"

"Sir, there are at least fifteen of them. Enough for a raid or recon-in-force, but not for a frontal assault. Armed with rifles and mounted so they are highly mobile. They wear black battlefield dress. The rifles have the look of AK-forty-sevens."

This was distressing. The Clan might be caught unaware, unless they were alerted—and the Falconry had their radio. "How fast are the invaders traveling?"

"They're moving at a slow enough pace that they may be conserving their mounts for the raid, and to exfiltrate the op area afterward. Not slow, but definitely at a cavalry's walking speed."

Jaz said, "So we gotta go around them, right? Try to just go faster than them and get home before they do. It doesn't matter if our mounts get tired, they'll be home when we get there."

Choony shrugged. "If we get there first, that would be a good thing. Alright, let's go. Circle east and then continue south so we stay out of view." He looked to the guard. "Stay closer as we move. Don't lose us. We can't afford to lose this gasifier, either."

The miles passed quickly. The horses began to slow after

maybe half an hour, but the farm was close now. The scent of all the Clan's hundreds of kinds of plants gave the area around Clanholme a unique odor, and Choony caught whiff of it. He saw a familiar copse of trees ahead. "We overshot the farm," he shouted. "Turn west, we'll come up on the south edge of the farm, where the animals are penned. Mind the traps when we hit the woods! You all know where they are."

Choony shook the reins to signal the horses to give more speed, but he kept it light—enough to renew their energy for one last, long spurt.

They came to the hill and saw the animal pens at the crest. Somewhere up there was a sandbagged position, but the guards would recognize their own. They careened up to the base of the hill and lost some momentum as they began to climb. Simple physics, of course, but the hill didn't slow the horses too much.

Then a faint report from a rifle reached his ears, and then another. Buddha, they were too late to warn the Clan. He felt his inner harmony flee. "Guards, you are released. Go, go, go! Help them," he cried out.

Nothing was permanent, of course, and all things eventually passed. Even the mountains would someday be worn flat by the elements. The lives of these people meant little in the grand scheme of things, and their Karma would live on if they died, but even so, Choony's inner harmony wouldn't return. In this moment, his Karma was not good. In the next life, the next moment, he would begin in a troubled state. This, however, was no time for meditation or philosophy. Action was needed, though it always disturbed one's serenity.

Choony whipped the horses into as fast a pace as they could safely maintain while hitched to a wagon, and then they were over the crest. The southern food forest lay below them, between the Complex and him and Jaz. Momentum carried them now, as fast as the struggling horses had done but with much less effort for them. It was a serene thought, that their horses may be regaining their own harmony even as he and Jaz propelled them all down the hill toward danger.

"I take refuge in the Buddha, the Dharma, and the Sangha, never lies, never violent. All things pass. Karma and destiny..."

Her eyes wide, Jaz listened to Choony chant his peace and marveled at his calm tone as they rolled down the hill toward where the bullets flew.

- 10 -

1030 HOURS - ZERO DAY +148

CASSY VAULTED OVER her bed to reach the hand radio on her nightstand, which crackled as Ethan broadcast from the bunker's camera monitor station.

"Charlie One this is Bravo One. Tangos incoming from the north. They've avoided the traps. Unknown number. Over."

No kidding, Sherlock. The shooting had already begun... "Bravo One, Charlie One. Copy that, we're under fire! Get me a count and recall the scouts." Cassy cut off the talk without wasting time to close the radio conversation properly.

She slid back across her bed to the small, north-facing window where her rifle leaned against the wall and just barely peeked out the window. It would be unfortunate if someone got a lucky shot on her, but the odds of that dropped if she took deep breaths and moved slowly. Don't draw attention, she told herself in a patient hunter's mantra. As she peered out, her right hand found her rifle's burled black oak hand guard.

Cassy could hear intermittent firing, both from nearby and out within and beyond the Jungle. In the summer and fall, it would be hard to move through the dense growth of those intensive gardening beds, but they would also have blocked her view almost completely. Now, with most of the vegetation winter-dead and matted, the snow-covered Jungle looked like a dense series of small white hills. She could see people in cover behind those mounds, but only a few and only when they moved.

With the Clan's hard-earned reputation and the number of people she had at the ready, no one would be stupid enough to attack Clanholme with only a handful of people. There had to be more coming. Cassy picked up her rifle and was about to bring it up into a good shoulder weld, but stopped. Something Michael had said about his Recon days—which weren't nearly as far back as he pretended, but everyone else went along with his charade—something about sniping people from a window... People look *at*, not *inside*, a window for snipers. That was it. She grinned and wished Michael were there so she could thank him. She'd have to do that later.

Cassy took three steps back from the window and only then raised the rifle to her shoulder, planted her cheek on the stock, and peered through the scope. She imagined that she saw movement all over those little white hills. Opponents may have been moving, but she couldn't be certain. So, as in Michael's story, she froze in place still peering through the scope, waiting, not moving despite the little jump her heart gave every time a new barrage of fire was exchanged outside.

Whatever was happening, it was moving much slower than events had when Peter showed up with his White Stag "army." Or maybe it was she who was different. She'd been through a lot since then and didn't find herself all shaky on the inside like she had before all that happened, and—

There! That was definitely someone's head peering over one of those Jungle mounds, but it was hard to see because the head was splotchy white like the snow around it. Winter camouflage... Where would some random starving bandits get winter mil-gear? Irrelevant. Cassy shook her head and peered through the scope again. Now she saw the head more clearly, and others too, though they seemed to shift and whirr into the background when she looked directly at them. Hm. Have to get some of—*Bang!*—those herself. She noted that the eye-blurring white camouflage effect was now ruined by a broad spray of crimson, standing in stark relief against the snow. One down.

Cassy's radio chirped, and Ethan's voice came through. The voice rushed through the I.D. procedure and then said, "Cameras show about twenty that I could count, mostly north. All November Foxtrot, be advised, they are low crawling toward your positions. Stay frosty, they'll be set to banzai in one mike. September Foxtrots, I show six or maybe seven tangos advancing up the back side. They'll crest at the same time November gets hit. Be advised, they are wearing white camouflage and will be hard to spot. Bravo One out."

The radio went silent, and Cassy wished the southern foxholes well as she turned her attention back to the north window. The two Clanners in those southern foxholes, or four if everyone stuck to the defense plan, would be on their own. They had clear firing lanes all around, and the Clan had set wire traps, razor and barbed wire, and punji-stick pits all along the back face of that hill. Attackers would be funneled to where both foxholes had intersecting lanes of fire, as Michael called it. Lanes of fire. Fire lanes. That'll get you a ticket. Cassy grinned as the thought sped through her mind.

She pulled the trigger and her rifle kicked, but there was no satisfying spray of blood this time. Hitting a moving target was hard at the best of times, during training, much less in these conditions against camouflaged troops in a real firefight. She let it go, breathed calmly, and swept the rifle seeking a new target.

* * *

Nestor lay on the dirt floor of the shed by the pond. He had been returning a screwdriver when he heard the first shots, so he just dropped to the floor and stayed put. He was a nice guy and sure didn't deserve to get shot for these people, good as they had been to him. Standoffish maybe, but he was the outsider so he didn't blame them for that. They'd come around eventually, just like the people in Scranton had done, and unlike Scranton, these people didn't seem the sort to turn suddenly violent on one of their own.

So yeah, as long as he didn't get shot before then, the Clan would accept him, and why not? Plus, they were hard people. Good, but hard. They'd been through at least as much trauma as Nestor himself during these past few months, but unlike Scranton, they'd kept a good heart. He liked that. Maybe he could learn.

The *Other* would have a field day in a place like this, but Nestor was pretty sure *he* had been left behind in Scranton—if *he* was even real. Nestor hadn't thought so, but everyone else there had... He shook his head to clear unpleasant dream memories that were rising up. Memories of terror and chaos as they hunted Nestor, poor Nestor, who hadn't done anything wrong and why did they keep saying those things about him and he could never hurt anyone—

A brief, strobe-like vision imposed itself over everything, and his rising panic was driven out by the shock. It was just like his dreams. The other dreams, the ones that came true. Why couldn't people see that he was an oracle? He only *saw* terrible events, without being a part of them himself.

And here, again—the vision, red and bloody. A pause, and then again. Again. Faster and faster, bright lights, a strobe lighting up his brain. Gore and blood and crying and begging. And terror, overwhelming terror, but not from him. From who, then? The pain grew as the edges of his vision faded. Soon, he knew, he would pass out from the pain. The *Other* cometh... oh God... he crawled toward the door, but knew he would never make it. But where was this? It wasn't familiar. Some sort of shed. What was happening to him? What...?

All went black.

When *he* woke, he found himself sprawled on a dirt floor in some dirty shed. It wasn't any place he remembered in Scranton. His ears picked up a noise, and he grinned. Not noise—a symphony orchestra of life and death, and he was the audience. Gunfire, screaming. An explosion, maybe from a grenade. The music came from outside, then. It was a song he could play note for note. He was good at it.

Reaching for the door, the Other barely cracked it open, just enough to look outside. Ahead lay a string of homes, but outside of the nearest one, a man wearing snow cammies straddled another man in normal clothes lying on the ground. Cammie Man had a wicked knife and was using both hands to try to plunge it into the chest of the man beneath him. A life and death struggle—*his* own private movie. Fuckers never brought popcorn for the audience when they played this movie. Never.

The Other looked around, until he found what he sought. A weapon, a hand scythe with a polish on the blade that announced it would be sharp. He picked it up and then peered back outside. The Other spat, and cursed under his breath—Cammie Man was walking away, leaving behind the man he'd stabbed to lay twitching in the dirt. Motherfucker, first show in who knew how long, and he'd missed seeing it.

Anger rose—the bastard hadn't even made sure his victim was dead. A rank amateur. But the Other was no amateur. He tucked the scythe into his belt and then rushed out the cracked-open door and skid to a halt on his knees next to the stabbed man, who looked up at him with fear.

Did the Other know this pincushion? "Hey mister! Are you all right? How bad is it?" He made sure to widen his eyes because that's what frightened people always seemed to do. It worked, and the man's features morphed from fear into relief. The Other, master thespian!

"Nestor, drag me into that shed. You're gonna have to bandage this and keep pressure on it. I ain't no good for fighting, now."

The Other stopped the frown before it hit his face. Nestor? Why the hell did actors always seem to call him that? Sounding like they knew him? Goddamn diva actors. He was the director of this movie, and this was the part where the background track hit its crescendo. Well, that made it time to roll credits on this jerk.

"Yeah, man, that looks bad. Let me help you, before your shelf-life expires." The Other ignored the confused look on the disrespectful little shit's face and brought one leg up and over the man's body so that he ended up kneeling, straddling him just like Cammie Man had.

"Nestor? What are you doing, man? Get off my chest, it hurts!"

The man took a deep breath from the pain that spiked through his bloody shoulder as the Other settled on top of him, but he wasn't about to let "Nestor-Man" ad-lib his final lines by screaming. The Other's hands slithered up to the man's neck and wrapped lovingly around it. His pulse quickened as the grip tightened, and he licked his suddenly-dry lips. One, two, three—this would be nothing but a quick "paint-by-numbers" kind of performance because with the symphony playing all around them, he sensed that it would be best to make this a quick scene.

The Other's thumbs pressed into the actor's throat just below the Adam's apple. He hated those movies where they just squeezed for ten minutes. It was a sloppy performance, done that way. A real pro used two thumbs on the trachea—it was faster and much more certain.

Right on cue, the other man began playing his role to perfection. They always did. Face turned red, eyes bulged, hands clawed weakly at the Other's own hands. He wanted to shout with glee—See, fucker? With the right motivation even you can do this shit right!

As the last light left the man's eyes, the Other shuddered with ecstasy. A brilliant performance. The orchestra was still playing, however, so the Other rose to his feet, pulled out the scythe from behind his waistband, and moved to the wall of the building, intent on edging around to follow Cammie Man's tracks. That sloppy bastard was gonna make up for his limp-wristed attempt at doing what the Other had done easily with bare hands in almost no time at all. It was all the time the scene deserved, though he had helped the amateur grow into his role brilliantly at the end. And still the orchestra played.

He slid along the wall. Crouching low, he passed beneath a slit-shaped window in the house wall. The barrel of a rifle stuck out from the window, ratta-tat-tat. An M4, one of the Other's very favorite instruments. But whoever was shooting it was doing it wrong. You just couldn't pull the trigger that fast and still aim, and firing it without aiming was like bashing on drums with your fists. Loud, and fucking annoying. The Other reached up with his left hand to grab the rifle's barrel by the heat shield, and with his right hand he swung the scythe tip-first into the narrow window opening. There was a satisfying *thunk* of metal piercing bone and meat, and the Other pulled the rifle out through the window. He left to follow Cammie Man then and didn't bother to free the embedded scythe. Ha. Sucked to be that guy.

The Other came to the corner of the building and took a quick peek. Two men fired at one another from some twenty feet apart, both on their bellies in the dirt. Cammie Man was one of them, while the other wore more civilian-type clothes. He noted that the other man had a crew cut, military style, and fired the weapon one slow shot at a time. Methodical. A true actor, then—someone else who could hear the same music he did. If the Other didn't hurry, the guy would soon destroy Cammie Man, who fired seemingly at random in the general direction of crew-cut boy. The Other wanted to steal this scene for himself. He aimed the rifle, pulled the trigger—but nothing happened, and Cammie Man and Crew Cut continued their performances uninterrupted.

That wasn't fair. The Other had gone through all the trouble of getting that rifle, even losing his wicked-cool scythe in the process. And it was out of ammo? Guess what, fuckers—the M4 was the kind of instrument with two dangerous ends. Not as good as an AK in this method, but it would do for now.

The Other bolted out from behind cover, his rifle raised above his head, sprinting toward Cammie Man, who couldn't see him. With his back to the Other to face Crew Cut, Cammie Man saw what was about to happen and stopped firing. A shame, really, because he had played it so well, but the Other was safer without bullets coming in his direction by accident.

The Other reached his target in under two seconds and, using the momentum built up from sprinting, slammed the butt of his rifle into the exposed upper right side of Cammie Man's head. He then kicked the guy's rifle, striking it on the lower receiver and sending the whole AK-47 flying. Without missing a beat, he continued bashing his rifle butt into the man's head. After about the third strike, Cammie Man stopped twitching and blood oozed from his nose, ears, and mouth. A superb performance! And the orchestra played on...

The Other tossed his M4 and reached down to pick up the AK rifle, checked its ammo—still half a magazine and one in the chamber—then turned to face Crew Cut, who was grinning at him. Now there was a man who understood the symphony going on all around them. A fellow director, not some B-list wannabe. He smiled at the other man.

Crew Cut stood and faced him, and lowered his rifle's barrel. "A-one job, newbie. I think the Complex is cleared out. Let's head north and reinforce against the Jungle." Whatever that meant. Crew Cut turned to leave, and the Other was content to follow. Hey, the guy clearly knew where the party was. Things were looking up.

Over his shoulder, Crew Cut said, "Thanks, Nestor. You really surprised me back there. I owe you some of the good cider tonight."

Fucking Nestor again! Who was this asshole, Nestor? One thing was clear: if the Other ever found Nestor-face, he'd make sure his dance card would be full with playing mean. Nestor was a stupid name anyway. But for now, Crew Cut was the one he was pissed at. They never got his goddamn name right. Never even asked it.

Bang! The Other almost casually squeezed off a round, striking Crew Cut dead center in the back. It was hilarious how the man's arms went flailing like limp noodles as he fell, skidding to a stop on his *face*! Epic. What was it the kids these days called that? A "Kodak moment" sounded right. That's what this was. Get the camera, honey, this one's on the money. He did a little jiggly dance step.

Then the Other's view flickered. What the hell? He didn't know where he went when he blacked out, but it always happened after a kill or two. What a pisser. He was gonna miss out on seeing this guy release himself when he died. Jeez, all that work, what's the point?

Here it came again... he hated this...

The normally red-shaded world flickered in and out, alternating with black-and-white views, then images superimposed over everything around him. Images that looked the same, but they had garish, disgusting shades of... something that wasn't red. Different. Colors? Yeah, that was the word. Goddamn colors. Then a field of blackness formed over everything in view, and it rushed toward him. He always tried to turn away, to run, but every time, it hit him at the speed of light and felt like a ton of bricks in a burlap sack smacking him in the face.

As his head exploded in a cacophony of lights and colors, pain and sound, the darkness struck him and *he* knew no more...

Light. And pain, oh the pain! His head throbbed worse than any hangover had. He looked around as he sat up. The noise of the battle was still all around, but less intense than it had been. That was good—it meant these people had fought off whatever bandits had attacked them. To one side lay the bloody corpse of a man wearing snow-pattern camouflage, and to the other side, closer, lay the body of a Clan soldier. One of their recently added Marines. A hole in his back still smoked from where a large-caliber round had struck him. Then Nestor realized he held an AK-47 in his hand. When had he picked that up?

A bolt of fear slashed through him then, every nerve from his toes to the top of his scalp tingling with adrenaline —the barrel of his own rifle was still smoking. Had he shot the Marine in the back? No way. No! No, not again. The *Other* couldn't possibly have found him way out here, so far from Scranton! Whoever that shadowy entity was, his coming always spelled disaster, and—

The Marine stirred, and let out a low, tense moan. It sounded like he was saying Nestor's name. As terrified and confused as he was, Nestor couldn't let the man die in the dirt like that, not when the Clan had been so good to him. He staggered toward the man then sank again to his knees. Mueller, that was the guy's name. The Clan soldiers, or Marines, always went by their last names like it was a badge of pride or something. And maybe it was, if it was true what people said about Marines.

"Mueller, I'm so sorry—"

Mueller coughed once and then held up his hand for silence. "Shut your pie hole, Nestor. You scared off that sniper, and I'd sure as shit be bagged up if it weren't for you. Can't believe my MoTaV stopped an AK like that, but I still won't be in this fight."

Nestor stared dumbly at Mueller. "Notaff?" was all he could stammer. Could it really be that Mueller didn't think Nestor had shot him? Everywhere he went, people blamed him for the nasty things that happen in this world, so this would be a first. These people were fair.

"MoTaV. Modular tactical… Never mind. Body armor. Help me get to the Hospital." That was the designated rally point for combat wounded, which was really Cassy's lower floor the rest of the time.

Nestor struggled under Mueller's weight, especially with the armor thing on. It had to weigh a ton. How did that guy wear it? Did his sidekick Sturm wear one of these bulky things? He wrapped Mueller's left arm around his shoulder, and put his own right arm around Mueller's waist, and together they hobbled toward the "Hospital."

* * *

Ahead of them, and now only slightly below, lay the Complex. Most of the attackers were hard to see, but appeared to be clustering for an assault that would lead them directly around and under the guard tower. Jaz hollered, "If they go through the tower they'll get hit hard by the guards up there, but none of the Complex people will be able to hit them until they've passed the tower."

"They will be nearly on top of the homestead by then," Choony replied, then grunted as he struggled to keep the horses moving at full speed *toward* the shooting.

In the back of her mind, Jaz mused how similar the horses and Choony were—both useful in battle for reasons other than the shooting, and both hating every minute of it. And both headed toward the fighting anyway, not away from it. Choony was brave, in his weird way. She didn't completely get it, but she respected it. Anyway, she'd shoot for both of them.

She had a sudden thought. "We gotta aim for the mass of them," she yelled, "try to hit them just when they swarm around the tower. If we can disrupt their charge, we'll give the Clan time to react!"

Choony turned the horses a bit to the right, eastward, drawing out the distance to time their arrival at the tower. He was listening to her. For some reason that felt kind of exciting and she leaned forward, eyes bright. She wondered why he didn't just slow the horses for a moment, but didn't ask. He'd have a good reason, she didn't doubt.

* * *

Cassy took another shot, but her target ducked back down too soon. She swapped out for a fresh magazine, as there could only have been a couple rounds left in the old one. Her ears told her the battle was petering out—the back-and-forth gunfire sounding less feverish, winding down. Instead of feeling thrilled for victory, however, she worried. Once before, they had been caught off guard by attackers who had only shifted forces to launch a new thrust elsewhere. Until they scouted and found the region clear, she wouldn't let her guard down.

Into the radio, she said, "Bravo One, this is Charlie One. I need a SITREP, ASAP." As goofy as all that had once sounded, mil-speak saved time and sometimes lives in battle. She still hated using it, though. It made her feel like a cartoon character.

"Charlie One, copy that. Stand by." A few seconds later, Ethan continued, "Surveillance shows the OpFor is falling back, but they are disorganized. They've moved mostly off-camera but I see movement in the corner of the camera facing Golf Tango. OpFor may be massing for a new thrust from the northeast."

Great. That would make sense for the invaders. The guard tower would be overrun if Ethan was right—and why call it the Golf Tango, anyway—but the enemy would then have a massed, fixed location. If saving the two guards at the top seemed impossible, at least the Clan would gain an excellent target of opportunity for crossfire. Silently, she cursed herself for thinking in such cold-hearted terms, but this was survival. These days, everything was survival. No wonder those cartoon soldiers from World War II always looked so weary. She shook off the thought—now wasn't the time.

"Bravo One, copy that. Charlie One to all units, continue to engage at will. Ready pineapples, but await orders to use them. All Frank units, remain in place. Romeo, Romeo—shift November Echo, remain in cover but get eyes on Golf Tango. How copy?"

As Cassy listened to mobile, roaming fire teams—Romeo

units—check in affirming they understood, she watched from the window. Just as she had ordered, the foxhole defenders stayed in place while the five Romeo teams moved cover-to-cover to get into position looking out at the guard tower.

In less than half a minute, all the units had checked in to report they were in place. Cassy could see the Romeo One team from her window. They wouldn't have much of a fire lane until the enemy had passed beyond the tower and the foliage around the pond, but they'd have an outstanding crossfire position afterward, just before the OpFor hit the Clan's line and the fertilizer hit the windmill. She spared a half-smile at the image she had overheard Ethan using months before. No time. Back to business.

To her left, the few remaining enemies along the first line of attack were firing away like crazy, probably making noise to seem bigger than they were and mask the fact that the rest of them had gone elsewhere. She frowned. This seemed practiced. Disciplined.

Even without a clear firing lane, Romeo One could lob the unit's two grenades toward the tower if needed, over the tall grasses and foxtails that grew around the east retainer pond. Everything was set, and now she had only to wait. Cassy hated that part more than being shot at, sometimes. She breathed slowly, got calm. C'mon, fertilizer, get it over with...

She didn't have long to wait. A shrill, piercing noise rose, probably from a whistle, and then a great roar of angry voices. The enemy was coming, screaming like Huns. They burst out from behind the pond foliage and swarmed at the tower just as she had expected. But they didn't just keep coming toward the main Clan line. And while they were so close to the tower, the guards above couldn't get a shot at them, nor could the crossfire begin until they emerged beyond the tower and foliage.

To Cassy's horror, she saw tiny flames blaze up from among the assembled mob. They had bottles in their hands, most of them, and pulled back to throw them at the Clan's line. They couldn't know that Cassy had amassed her people along that line, that she had known they would come and had prepared for them, but her tactic had only given them a densely packed target now. No no no no...

Through her radio, she cried, "Now! Fire now, throw now! Pineapples!"

Before the firing could begin, flaming bottles started arcing through the air toward her Clanners, at first just a couple—

Movement to her right caught her eye. A horse-drawn wagon careened along the thin path between the pond and the Complex, the horses moving at a sprint right at the attacker's position. Oh lord, it was Jaz. The other must be Choony driving. It looked insane! Where the hell did they come from, and what were they doing? "Belay the pineapples!" she screamed into the radio, just hoping she was in time.

The enemy hadn't thrown even a third of their bottles yet when they caught sight of the wagon bearing down at them. A couple bottles flew at Jaz and Choony but landed where the wagon had been, not where it was. Too bad for them, they hadn't had their rifles ready. Only a couple shots rang out from their position before the wagon mowed into them. The horses in front, weighing many times what a person did and with the added mass and momentum of the wagon behind, didn't even slow down. Bodies flew everywhere. One of their Molotov cocktails exploded right in their midst. Figures spouting flames ran, screaming.

And then the wagon was past, flying onward and away. The Clan opened fire and grenades weren't needed. Thank God no one had thrown before the wagon arrived...

As the attackers fell beneath a hail of bullets from the now slightly repositioned Clanners, Cassy smiled a real smile, though she knew it must look bloodthirsty. A victory smile. She reached for the radio and clicked the button. "That's it, folks. Finish them off, and get a bucket brigade going before the tower burns down," she called into it. Her voice was all business, but her heart soared to see their attackers being mowed down now like so much wheat at harvest time. The bloodthirsty smile came back to her scarred face.

* * *

After swinging the wagon around, Choony slowed to a halt and surveyed the carnage beneath the guard tower. Fifteen or so dead attackers, no wounded survived the Clan's counter-attack, and only a couple were seen to have escaped. The entire thing was tragically pointless. Nothing had changed except that people had died and now hate and anger would grow. And not just among the Clan, either—these dead people had husbands, wives, children too…

He heard Cassy's voice, calm and clear as she walked up, asking, "How many of our own were casualties?"

Michael, carrying a clipboard, replied, "Two dead, four injured. Both of our fatalities were the result of one enemy who got into the Complex, and one of our wounded is from him as well. The other three are a bullet wound we think will heal and two burn victims. One is expected not to make it, and I told Sturm to notify her husband and child."

Choony got off the wagon and helped Jaz down, then approached Cassy. She was busy making sure the fire was put out, the wounded moved, and other leaderly duties, but then she took a deep breath and turned to Choony and Jaz.

"That was reckless beyond measure, you know. You

risked your lives, our horses, and the cargo. A second later and you would have run into our grenades. I'd already given the order to throw them."

Jaz ran her fingers through her disheveled hair and said, "It seemed like the thing to do at the time." She did not look apologetic.

Cassy snorted, and grinned. "Might have saved a life or two, since it worked out. I just want you to think about how badly that could have gone off the rails, that's all."

Choony bowed slightly. She had a point, of course, but there hadn't been time to think it through. "I suppose you're right, but I think in the heat of the moment we would make the same choice again. We all live or die together, but the Clan lives on even if one of us does not. The family abides. Such a death has honor and no small amount of Karma."

"I guess. Anyway, it was brave. And insane. So did you get the gasifier device? Did they show you how to work it?"

Jaz grinned, grabbed the tarp in the wagon, and ripped it off. "Ta da! One hundred percent grade-A power, in a miniature package that's, like, small enough to fit in a wagon. For the low, low price of one working radio."

Choony smiled crookedly at that, then added to Cassy, "Yes, it's fairly simple. We fill the small barrel with wood, put on the lid, then put it into the larger barrel. Fill that with wood and ignite it. The heat and lack of oxygen in the inner chamber causes its wood to outgas. It flows out the cooker through the tube to an old car radiator to cool it, making the gas denser and so the energy more compact. Not the right word, but you get the idea. Then that outflow is directed into any engine's air intake, somehow ignited, and then it just acts like a natural gas-powered engine." He paused to refer to a small pocket notepad. "It'll get up to five hundred miles on a cord of wood, or half that on what you can fit in a pickup truck bed with other travel gear. That's what they said. I took notes I can give you when things calm down. I haven't had a chance to completely figure out the details."

Michael, staring at the gasifier, said thoughtfully, "I'll get Dean Jepson to look at it and figure out how to make another car work with it. He'll probably figure out how to make our own before long and improve the design while he's at it." He turned to Cassy. "While Dean's figuring out the car, we can use this one to generate a lot of power for Clanholme. No more rationing, and maybe we can get some working electric water pumps so we aren't at the mercy of the wind so much. And keep the battery bank charged for storms."

Jaz commented, "If he makes it better, I bet we can trade the design to the Falconers for a lot of whatever we need. They got themselves set up as a trading hub."

Choony automatically glanced at the windmill that drew water from the ponds into the uphill cisterns. They wouldn't last forever, and the more they could be used as Plan B for power instead of the *only* plan aside from manpower, the better. "We have one more cooker coming from our new friends in the spring. We traded supplies and stuff for that, you'll remember, from that traveling medieval merchant."

Michael replied, "Okay, but March is a long way away and we'll be dealing with the Empire by then, too, if these damned invaders haven't overwhelmed us all by then. I don't like how organized and strategic they were. So we need more of everything now, not later. I need real cars working to do real recon at a distance."

Cassy put a hand on Michael's shoulder, gently. "You're right, of course. But now we have a new ally, with a radio, and they know people we don't. We need to work on alliances, and *this* gasifier is earmarked for our diplomats to go forth and make new friends. Nothing beats a face-to-face meeting for building trust and reliable alliances. I think Choony here found that out when he spoke to the Falconry's leader."

"Delorse, yes," Choony answered. "I doubt she would have put herself on the line for strangers she had never met, never looked in the eyes. She's sharp, and she spent the entire time evaluating us. It was probably Jaz who won her over with smart trading. She took us more seriously after that."

"That was good trading, yes," Cassy said. "It's why we let you two go. You didn't disappoint us. Given how well that worked out, don't plan on getting too settled in, you two. Jaz, Choony, you'll probably be out there again sooner rather than later."

Choony shrugged. "Whatever is necessary." To think Cassy had almost chased off both him and Jaz, at one point or another. What a mistake that would have been... Maybe she should take another look at Nestor, too. He decided to bring that up later, as there was too much to do at the moment.

Michael made his excuses and left, moving the wagon toward the far shed where Dean seemed to do his best "redneck engineering," and Jaz wandered off to help deal with the messy aftermath of battle, leaving Choony alone with Cassy for a moment.

"I think Jaz and I should talk with you and the rest of your council and go over everything we learned. You'll have some planning to do after that."

"Of course. But for now, go to my house and help at the Hospital while I get things situated with this mess," Cassy said, motioning toward the mass of bodies, "and I'll meet you there later with the Council."

Choony nodded and headed toward the only real house on the property, the one that predated the EMPs, as he pondered what the Clan's next moves would be. Soon, the lights inside wouldn't be dim LEDs or lanterns but real lights with actual bulbs. It was a nice thought. But they would have to stay mindful. The better off they looked, the more they'd attract outsiders who would want what they had.

As he walked, he chanted under his breath, "*om ami deva hrih*," happily dedicating some of his Karma to the deceased in the hopes they might find the Pure Land rather than continuing their cycle of life and death. He knew it wasn't right to do so, but he still said the chant twice for the Clan's own dead.

- 11 -

1800 HOURS - ZERO DAY +148

NESTOR SAT AT the outdoor table, shivering cold, staring blankly at his food. Another bowl of "constant stew," as they called it here. At least he had a carrot and bread to go with it, and real butter even. It didn't much matter, though—his appetite was playing hide-and-seek with him. These random images of the Other—were they real? Had he blacked out, been possessed? And did that mean he really did what they said he did, back in Scranton?

He felt like he was in shock and wondered if he could live with knowing it was real, if in fact that's what had really happened. He always thought he just had some sort of psychic connection to the evil bastard, but maybe the Other was... him. Hiding inside him. Watching him squirm. All that blood, all those other times... Please, God, don't let this be real.

"Oh, it's real alright," said a voice behind him, startling him. Nestor turned and saw Cassy, who carried a trencher loaded with a stew bowl and bread. She sat down opposite Nestor and slid her tray, centered in front of her. "And it's healthy, so eat up. Do you always talk to yourself?"

"I didn't realize I said that aloud," Nestor replied weakly. "I just don't have much of an appetite right now, I guess."

Cassy's gaze was direct, never wavering from Nestor's eyes, but her tone was friendly enough as she said, "You need to eat. Keep up your strength. You don't have anything to fret over, that I can tell. We lost good people today and killed other human beings who were probably decent folks, other than being rash enough to attack us like that. What have you lost that makes you lose your appetite? Or maybe you just don't like the food. There's a Foster's Freeze about ten minutes' drive from here. Maybe you'd prefer a cheeseburger and deep-fried mushrooms?"

"That's a nice speech, Cassy." He blinked at her. "I didn't know you'd care whether I ate or not." When her eyes narrowed he added hurriedly, "You're a good leader from everything I've seen, you really are, you just don't strike me as the sensitive type to coddle strangers who suddenly turn into finicky eaters." He looked up at her placidly.

Her eyes remained narrowed, but at least she didn't lose her smile. Maybe antagonizing her wasn't the best move he could have made, but dammit, he was tired of her mistrust. Then it hit him that maybe she was right not to trust him. The realization struck him like a hammer between the eyes, leaving him with a faint, throbbing headache. He looked down and rubbed his temples. He felt bewildered.

"I'm not, really," Cassy answered. "Not anymore. But whether you stay or leave, I don't want you dying off just because you can't stomach some forever-stew. There's few enough people left whole as it is." She sat by him on the bench. "Maybe you're wondering why I'm sitting with you? Why I care?"

Nestor's stomach sank, but he tried to mask it by picking up a slice of thick, fresh-baked bread and nibbling at it. He forced a smile and said, "See? I'm eating. I did wonder why you're here, but I guess you'll tell me in your own good time."

Cassy crunched on a carrot, chewed it slowly, and finally swallowed it—all the while gazing thoughtfully at Nestor's face. Measuring, probably. He hoped he measured up.

"Well, I guess I'll get to the point. I have some questions for you about the battle. Mueller—the Marine you saved, who got shot in the back—says you must have scared off whoever shot him. I wonder, did you see anyone else? This sniper, I mean. Did you see anyone else there when Mueller got shot, and maybe you could tell me why they didn't just shoot you, too—those are questions in my mind. Where was that sniper?"

Nestor shifted in his seat. The rough-hewn bench he sat on felt suddenly hard and uncomfortable. Unwelcoming. "Other than the attacker I killed, the one Mueller was shooting back and forth with, I didn't see anyone else. Maybe they took a shot and ran. I'm glad he was wearing armor."

Cassy nodded, and smiled. "Maybe. That's probably what happened. Everything was completely chaotic, after all. I'm just surprised you didn't see them. It turns out there's a bit of powder burn around the bullet hole in Mueller's flak jacket, or whatever they call those things these days. So, the sniper had to be close enough that you would have seen him. Or her." She frowned, shook her head. "That's how it seems."

A chill washed over Nestor, across his scalp and down his spine. She couldn't know anything or he would be dead already, right? She was only fishing. Had to be. "Nope. Didn't see anybody. I saw him fall and thought he was dead, but I didn't see anyone when I turned around." He realized he was starting to babble and went back to his half-hearted eating.

Cassy shrugged and downed half a slice of buttered bread in one bite. After taking a sip of water, she said, "Well, given that we had two Clanners get killed right around the corner from where you killed the enemy for Mueller, maybe you saw what happened to them?"

"No, I didn't."

"But you did check on the guy who got strangled, right?"

Nestor sensed a trap. His thinking was clouded with fear, so he decided honesty was the best policy. Half-honest, anyway. "I did, yeah. But he was dead. I grabbed his rifle, but when I tried to shoot the camo guy it was empty. That's why I had to beat him with it instead of just shooting him."

"No, Nestor—not the guy hanging out the window with a farm tool stuck into his skull. That's the rifle you grabbed."

"Was it? I didn't see him. He must have dropped it outside the window, I guess. Anyway, I thought it was from the guy I checked on."

Cassy's eyes reminded him of a snake's now, with that poised, eager glow they got right before they struck. "Hm. That must be it. I do kind of wonder why the soldier strangled that poor Clanner, instead of just shooting him. He still had ammo after all, since he was shooting at Mueller when you found them. Maybe he was just some kind of sick bastard who got off on killing him up close and personal. Or maybe something else happened. We may never know, right? Fog of war and all that." She finished the other half of the bread and then stood. "Well, thanks for the clarification. I appreciate your time, but Nestor, you should get back to eating. Whatever's bothering you, don't let it starve you on top of everything else."

Cassy turned to wave to one of the Council members—her mother, if he remembered correctly—and left the table with a friendly nod at Nestor. Finally he relaxed, but only a bit. It felt like there were eyes on him coming from all directions. As much as he didn't want to eat, he forced himself to peck at his food. Getting up just then would have looked guilty.

As he nibbled at his stew without enthusiasm, he wished

for nothing more than to be away from there, from those good people who didn't deserve more trouble. Away from himself, if that were possible. But no, wherever he went, there he'd be.

He had to leave. And he wanted to scream.

* * *

0600 HOURS - ZERO DAY +149

Ethan lay on his back, one arm pinned beneath Amber's head, and rubbed his eyes with the other hand. He let out a groan. "Is it that time already?" he managed to croak, but the words came out hoarse and garbled. He'd been awake all of five seconds. Then he realized his left arm wasn't waking up with the rest of him, blood deprivation from Amber resting her head on it keeping it "asleep" longer than the rest of him. He groaned again.

"Shut up." She moaned theatrically and whined, "Five more minutes, Mom, I'll get up, honest." Amber half-smiled, but even she couldn't quite chuckle at her little joke. Too damn early for that.

"Maybe if we just stay here, no one will notice we're missing," Ethan muttered. "We can skip all the New Year's stuff." It'd be great if Amber agreed, but he knew she wouldn't. Still, it was worth a try. "Why celebrate anyway? It's just an arbitrary date that three caveman chiefs in Europe or somewhere agreed on. Like Christmas, when they needed to co-opt a pagan holiday."

"Ethan, my love, seriously—shut up." He could hear the laughter hiding under her stern voice.

He grinned at her. "One chief said hey, these days are really short, let's make the shortest one the start of a new year, and then everyone will have to celebrate on that day forever and get in trouble with their wives. Then later, the Pope lost track of what day was the shortest, but we still had to party. All because of some Type-A caveman jerks sitting around the fire they just invented. That's all it was. Let's skip it."

"Conspiracies don't exist until after at least three cups of coffee." Amber propped herself up on one elbow, facing Ethan, which took the weight off his arm. Her sleepy grin was just lovely.

He tried to move the arm, but it wasn't ready for that just yet. Oh joy, the pins and needles would begin any moment as the blood rushed back into his arm... "But babe, we're rationed to one cup a day, each, and you sure aren't giving me yours."

"Then you can talk about it *after* coffee, and only once every three days," she grinned.

Ethan grinned right back. It was a running thing between them, his "conspiracy theories"—which were true, dammit... well, mostly—and her willful ignorance. Or her common sense, if one listened to Amber's version. "Fine, wear those blinders if you must. I'm getting some coffee, speaking of that. We went without yesterday, right? We get two cups today."

"Yep, and I can't wait. Although I wish we could use sugar. Pollenpowder isn't the same."

Ethan staggered his way around the bed and headed toward the door. Over his shoulder he said, "Pollenpowder, huh? Is that what we're calling that cattail dust these days?" The door was only a privacy curtain, really. "We need bees. Honey would do fine." He stretched. "More than sugar, I wish we had T.V. I'd love to watch the ball come down in Times Square at midnight."

Amber didn't reply, but she might not have heard him. It wasn't important anyway, so instead of repeating himself, he poured them each a cup of black heaven, added cream to his —Amber didn't like cream in her coffee—and then with a grimace, he used the tiny spoon to shovel in a bit of cattail pollen. It added a weird taste, but at least it covered the coffee's bitterness with a touch of sweet. They had tons of the damn stuff, and he doubted they'd ever use it all, even cutting their flour with it to make the flour go farther.

Cups in hands, he walked back to the makeshift bedroom and ducked inside, careful not to spill their cups on the curtain. Inside, he nearly missed a step. Amber sat with her back against the wall, knees pulled up to her chin, her arms wrapped around her legs. Her unhappy, vacant stare showed she was somewhere else, lost in thought.

"Honey? Earth to Amber, come in." He sat on the bed next to her and when she looked over, he handed her a cup. "Something's on your mind. Did I say something wrong?" The truth was, he rarely knew when he had stirred something up so it had become a habit to ask.

Amber took the cup, sniffed it once, then took a sip. "No, sorry. Nothing you said. Well, it was, but you didn't do anything wrong. I'm just thinking about the ball in Times Square. Like, it's really gone and done. For real. None of this is a terrible dream, it's just a terrible new reality, right? No New Year's ball dropping, no really old guy stiff with Botox, mangling his lines for the camera. No people standing out in the cold, kissing, wearing ridiculous sunglasses and yelling 'Happy New Year!' when the ball hits the sidewalk, not ever again."

Ethan froze. What a terrible, morbid thought for starting the day. A kind of quiet sadness filled him. That world was dead, yesterday's dream, replaced by this dark world. "I wonder if the people in New York will figure out a way to make the ball drop anyway, even without electricity."

Amber's jaw clenched and her nose wrinkled a bit, while

her face flushed red. He recognized that look... "What people, Ethan? What people are even left there?"

"Not everyone there is dead, sweetie. Someone's alive, someone who could do it. They could! If they really wanted to, they could get together and figure out a way to lower the ball themselves." He practically shouted it. In the back of his mind, he wondered why that thought suddenly felt so very important. In fact, he felt kind of frantic and closed in. The bunker, his safety cave, the comfortable place where reality couldn't find him and every game was his to win, took on a dark atmosphere as he looked around. It felt oppressive in this moment, even prison-like.

Then he felt something on his arm and looked down to find Amber's hand lightly resting on him. He looked up at her face and saw her concerned look.

"Ethan, it's okay, I swear. Take a deep breath. I know just what you're feeling, okay? That's why I was all curled up when you came in, remember? Deep breaths. They help."

Ethan forced a smile. "I should be comforting you, not the other way around."

"Maybe. But the truth is that all of this—the dying, the hunger, the violence, all of it—is too much for anyone to just be fine with it, not all the time. It's overwhelming. But the numbers I saw about New York? They're beyond simply being overwhelming. All those people..."

Ethan swallowed, knowing what she had to say next, and his throat was so dry that it hurt to swallow.

Amber paused, then said what he knew she'd been thinking. "There were ten million people in New York City and all that surrounding urban sprawl. Two million of those got taken to god-knows-where by the invaders to do god-knows-what. A million died right after the EMPs, within a few weeks. One million people, Ethan! If your intel is right—and it usually is—*another five million people have been eaten* since then. So let's celebrate?!" She was openly crying now.

"You're right, and it's tragic," he said, keeping his voice low, soothing her. "More than tragic—I don't have the words to describe such a horror. But what can we do?" He realized his own voice had been rising and he paused to breathe for a moment. "It bothers me, you know. I have nightmares about it, ever since I got that intel. But it's not like it happened here. We're alive and we're not eating people."

"Don't say that. We had our run-ins with cannibals, or did you forget the Red Locusts? But in New York... by now, for every man, woman, and child still alive in that city, two or three left their bones littering the streets. Can you imagine that? Imagine what those survivors must be like now. Hardly even people anymore. They gave up their humanity to survive, and for what?"

Ethan coughed. She was right, but not for the reason she thought. He would do whatever he had to for Amber and her family to eat, to stay warm, to stay alive. That included eating the hell out of strangers, dogs, cats, pigeons, rats... No, she was right because by this time next year there'd be only a few thousand people left in New York City. The rest would either figure out how to get out, die trying, or get eaten, until what they could grow in the parks or catch in the rivers balanced the population. "We are alive, Amber. That's victory, these days. Everyone alive by next Christmas will have won the damn lottery-of-life. It's a big win. Don't you see?"

"That's my point. Big win. So happy fucking New Year, we won—and that's why we have to go out there today with the others, and dance and sing, and drink our faces off with hard apple cider and moonshine. Not a Pope losing track of the calendar, just us. Up there, out of this bunker with the Clan, *our people*. Because we *are* still alive. Really alive. Safe, sort of, and with enough to eat. Enough extra to have someone teaching our children instead of working the fields. And we all know we might not be so lucky by next New Year. Live while we can, as much as we can, and damn the rest of it. For one night, Ethan, just screw all of that other garbage. The fear, the hunger, all of it. Tonight we are alive, and maybe if we go up there and party with the rest, we'll finally feel that way. Even if only for a moment."

Damn. In the space of one cup of coffee, Amber had worked her way around from despair to as good a reality as anyone could have, these days. Amazing, good—really good—woman. As much as he hated to leave the bunker, he knew she was right. But he still didn't want to go. Maybe that was all the more reason to do it, though. So that the winning lottery number he picked up wasn't wasted. Someone out there deserved to live more than he did, surely, but had already died cold, hungry, and alone except for the nightmarish people who killed him like lions on a gazelle. A shitty way to die. For that person, then. It would be a total travesty to waste the life he'd been given, when so many better people hadn't made it, or soon wouldn't be more than a gnawed leg bone on the street.

Ethan sighed. "Fine, I'll go. Sometimes I just need a swift kick in the ass. Besides, we won't have much safe time to celebrate after this, not with Indiana coming our way."

"Fort Wayne? The so-called republic we call the Empire? We don't need to worry about them. Not tonight, and not until spring. I figure maybe May, even, because they won't come until spring planting is done or they won't have enough to eat next winter."

"I'm not betting my life on that timeline, Amber. It's fine to be optimistic, but let's prepare for less-than-perfect timing. Remember, George Washington attacked on Christmas and the Brits were too drunk to fight back. The Fort Wayne bosses could have set up a slave-based agricultural system for all we know. They sure had enough people to pick from, out of all those thousands of starving people who must have flooded them from every direction—Chicago, Detroit, Toledo, Indianapolis..."

"Shut up and drink your coffee, Dark Ryder," Amber said in her 'I'm teasing you' voice. "We need to go help set up the party."

* * *

1300 HOURS - ZERO DAY +149

Amber's daughter Kaitlyn had spent the lunch hour with her older teenaged friend Brianna. The two had grown even closer after they barely escaped some attacking dogs, and now Kaitlyn had an idea to share.

"Grandma Mandy says people need to be recognized for the good things they do, right?" she asked Brianna, who nodded. "Well, this was like twice that Jaz and Choony came in at the last minute and helped the Clan drive off invaders. And everybody treats them like, yawn, yeah, thanks, good job, what's for dinner. And that's not right."

Kaitlyn was obviously as sure as any early adolescent could be about right and wrong, and Brianna kind of agreed that what Choony and Jaz had pulled off deserved special mention. From the advanced age of fourteen, she could see that it would be good for Kaitlyn and her to do something special for the two older crazies, too. Young people need encouragement, Brianna told herself wisely.

Plus, it was kinda ravey. A pacifist Buddhist and a Philly street girl jumping into battles together like that... Who knew such a pair could be, like, almost superheroes! "They're having an assembly after dinner so Mom can tell everybody what the whole battle seemed like from the boss point of view," Brianna said thoughtfully. "I bet we could do something special for them then, like an announcement." She saw Kaitlyn looking at her from the corner of her eyes—yeah, her young friend was definitely up to something. "What? Why are you looking at me like that?"

Kaitlyn grinned. "I wrote a song about them."

"What? You can write music?" she whooped, grinning.

"No, not really. But I wrote some words to a tune my dad used to sing when he had too much beer. Mom didn't like the song, said it was crude, but I thought it was pretty funny."

"Let's hear it!" As Kaitlyn's eyes widened, she added, "The Jaz and Choony song, silly, not your dad's beer song."

Kaitlyn shook her head no. "Not here. People will listen, and it has to be a surprise. And anyway, we need something more. We need to give them something. Medals, maybe."

Brianna frowned. "How can we get medals?" Kaitlyn was onto something with this idea, for sure, but she hoped the little kid knew where to get them and wasn't just hoping Brianna would know where to get some.

"I bet Mr. Jepson has some. He seems like an old soldier."

Brianna laughed. "You're going to ask that grumpy old farmer? He always just scares the little kids away when they try to watch what he's doing. Half of the younger ones think he bites." Oh, that would be perfectly funny, wouldn't it?

"He never chases me away. I spend a lot of time learning cool stuff from him," Kaitlyn answered defensively. "He can make anything! He's a genius. I like him."

Brianna tilted her head at her younger friend. "Really? Let's go over and see what he says."

* * *

As usual, Dean Jepson was working on some project at the small forge when the two girls arrived. He had set up his "shop" at the southern tool shed, where there weren't too many people around. He had a nasty way with a sharp word and no patience for anything that struck him as foolish, which was most of the time, so people simply stayed away from him. It wasn't worth the grief to take his insults if you could do something for yourself instead, and that suited Jepson just fine. Being the crusty old man felt like wearing comfortable old shoes. They could look sharper, maybe, but they never pinched your toes.

When he heard footsteps approaching from behind, he whirled around, ready to blast someone with grouchy words, but then he saw it was Kaitlyn and broke into a broad smile. He liked that kid, but he'd never admit it to anybody.

"Well howdy, Kait! Hi, Brianna. What are you two fine belles doing out and about in the cold?" As he talked, his hands never stopped working to fit pieces of metal together. The reputation he had as the world's best redneck engineer was well deserved, though he himself paid it no mind.

"We have a problem, Mr. Jepson," Brianna said. "Do you know how to make a medal?"

Jepson pursed his lips. "I don't hold with playing war, if that's what you're up to. It don't do any good for people to go at each other like that, and we have enough of it here for real. Nope, no medals to play war with. Won't do it."

"No, no," Kaitlyn objected. "We want to give some recognition to Jaz and Choony for the way they keep coming back by surprise and saving our lives and stuff."

Brianna added, "Kaitlyn wrote a song for them but we want to make some sort of medal to go with it." The younger girl grinned at Brianna's use of "we," Dean noticed, probably assuming that with Brianna on board they could pull it off.

Kaitlyn continued, "I still have some red and blue

ribbons in my sewing kit, so if we had a medal, we could hang it around their necks, like a medal of honor, you know?"

Jepson's pursed lips had disappeared and a slow, wide smile had spread in its place. Mostly for the girls' benefit, of course, because ol' Dean didn't want to hurt little girls' feelings if he could avoid it. "I reckon. When do you need 'em?" he asked.

"At the party tonight," Brianna said. "It starts with dinner."

"No problem, I have some tin sheets we can work with if you two will help," Jepson told the two girls. "Shouldn't be too hard."

Kaitlyn, eyes bright, nodded her head enthusiastically and Brianna grinned. Rubbing his hands together, Jepson asked, "What kind of medal?"

Kaitlyn frowned, puzzled, and asked, "What do you mean? Just a medal." She cocked her head and looked over to Brianna, who looked equally lost, Jepson realized.

"Well... most medals are for something particular that somebody did, and it was usually something brave," he explained. "Or something stupid and fatal, more'n likely. So what're these medals for?"

Kaitlyn broke in. "Last time, I heard they came charging over the hill in the wagon and completely broke up the raiders by the guard tower before they could throw fire bottles at us. It was awesome!"

Jepson nodded. "Why'd they have a wagon, not horses? What was in it, that wood generator thing they traded for?" He'd been working on the wood generator set for several hours now, fiddling with improvements, and thinking about the idea ever since the trader had come through, so he knew perfectly well that was what they'd brought back.

But this was the girls' idea. Let them direct things. He

wasn't gonna do everything for 'em, they had to do some of it. Hey Dean, can you do this? Can you do that? He got sick of it. He almost growled at the girls, but remembered in time that it was little Kaity. Couldn't growl at her, scared little thing that she was, with not even a real father, just that idiot tunnel geek. He cleared his throat and waited with his version of great patience, tapping his boot on the hard ground only a little as the girls whispered back and forth for a couple of minutes.

Finally Kaitlyn spoke up. "They were bringing back some food and that generator thing for driving a car. Can we make a medal with a wagon and a generator on it, or something like that?"

"Well..." Jepson said, "you gotta keep it simple because you don't have a lot of space on a medal. Wagons are complicated. Wheels, and tongues, and leather braces and all. But we could do up a couple of little cylinders with a little buckle thing on top for the ribbon. Might take a half hour, I bet. But we need a design to go by. I don't suppose either of your moms taught you anything useful, like how to draw?"

Brianna nodded toward Kaitlyn. "It's her idea, and she's good at drawing. I'll just sit back and watch and learn, while you two make a couple Medals of Generator."

Jepson smiled at her label and nodded to Kaitlyn. Cassy's girl, she was okay for a teenager, letting her younger friend take it over like that. Cassy wasn't all bad, he supposed, for raising a girl like that.

"Okay, Miss Kaitlyn, let's get to work if you want 'em by dinner," he said, gruff-toned. Brianna grinned as Kaitlyn jumped around like a little kid. Which she was, after all. Jepson smiled to himself. He always did try to take a minute when the kids wanted help with things. The good kids, anyway, and especially the little ones, the girls, and the few that had missing parents. Dean knew how rough that road was, though it was a long time ago.

He walked over to paw around in his junk metal pile, looking for some light tin sheets he remembered tossing onto the pile, and called to Brianna. "You know what goes with medals? Uniforms. One of you could go talk to Mr. Michael, see if he'd bring some of them Marines to line up and salute or something."

"Great idea," Kaitlyn said and looked over at Brianna. "Can you go tell him what we're gonna do? I have to work here with Mr. Jepson. You could tell your mom, too. No! Keep it a secret. Just tell Michael."

* * *

Brianna laughed at the way Kaitlyn bustled around, taking charge. "Yes, ma'am!" she shouted and gave what she thought was a pretty snappy salute, but the younger girl had already turned back to rattle around the metal pile with Mr. Jepson. Soon the two of them were in a huddle, talking about dimensions and incisions or something. Brianna left to find Michael.

When she saw Kaitlyn again an hour or so later, the girl already had two Clanholme Generator medals in hand, small tin shields onto which two tiny cylindrical "generators" were soldered. Punched-in lettering proclaimed: "Clanholme Bravery." A slot on top held a loop of ribbon for draping around a hero's neck. Nice work, and Dean must have helped her. He wasn't as grumpy as everyone said.

"Those are great," Brianna told her. "Michael says it's a fine idea. He says for you to go see him ASAP to work out a 'presentation ceremony.' He's gonna round up some Marines and tell 'em to put on their best uniforms. They'll march up and stand at attention or something."

"Cool," Kaitlyn squealed. "Where's Michael?" Brianna

pointed toward the guard tower, and off Kaitlyn ran, leaping over things in her way, jumping effortlessly over them like a young deer.

And Brianna suddenly realized that what she was feeling right now was joy. She'd almost forgotten how that felt.

- 12 -

1800 HOURS - ZERO DAY +149

DINNER WAS DONE, and Cassy stood beside Tiffany, Michael's wife, finishing the last of the dishes. Cassy always made sure people saw her doing her part to help out around Clanholme, even though no one expected her to, because it helped morale and let the Clan know what was expected of their people. Leaders included. "Let me know when you're ready to get started on the party dishes after the clock ticks over, okay?"

Tiffany smiled, acknowledging her, and then hung up her apron to wander off and join the fun. There were a bunch of games set up, old-timey ones that didn't need batteries. Bobbing for apples, pie eating contests, a horseshoe toss, the works. Tiffany's favorite was horseshoes, and she excelled at the game. Cassy knew that before the night was done, some poor sap would probably be stuck with Tiffany's post-party dishes duty. And maybe her chores for the next week, too... The thought made Cassy smile.

Cassy turned to survey the games, deciding which one to lose at first, when she heard a rider coming in from the north with their mount at a dead run. The rider wasn't blowing an airhorn, the scout signal for "battlestations," but it still couldn't bode well.

"Dammit, what now," Cassy muttered. Couldn't they have one day without complications? But she took off her apron, hung it up, and walked out toward the rider to meet her away from the festivities. There was no point alarming everyone when the horn hadn't been sounded.

The rider approached and reined in her horse, then got off to talk to Cassy. She was young, though it was hard to tell people's age these days, and her jaw was set tightly. Cassy couldn't remember her name, only that she'd been with the Clan since shortly after they'd thrown off the yoke of slavery put on them by Peter and his White Stag people. Bad memories, those, but today was a day of celebration so she shoved the thoughts away. "Report, scout," she greeted the youngster.

"Yes, ma'am. I'm to relay this message to you: 'We have two dozen refugees halted at the food forest north. They request asylum. Armed but not hostile. Awaiting your orders.' That was from Michael himself," she said with a note of pride, her back ramrod-straight.

Cassy restrained a smile. Many of the younger adults and older teens craved "action" and vied to join Michael's scout teams. Feeding chickens got boring after a while, so she couldn't blame them. This young scout clearly felt like she'd joined an elite and loved it. Cassy replied in a formal voice, knowing it would make this youngster's day. "Very well, scout, return and advise him that I am en route. Do not allow access to Clanholme before I arrive."

Without waiting for a response, Cassy turned on her heels—pretending not to see the rushed salute the girl gave her—and headed toward the small stable near the Complex with her ever-present rifle. The Clan always kept a few fresh horses close-in to the houses for situations like this, and no one ever went completely unarmed at Clanholme. Most wore pistols when they were busy around the homestead, though. Rifles and shotguns got in the way.

Cassy didn't bother with a saddle. Untying one of the horses, she simply swung up onto its back. The animal grunted at Cassy's weight, then moved about a bit, eager for the command to move out, maybe even to run and stretch out a bit.

These days everyone who had regular access to a horse rode it like an extension of themselves, but it still amazed Cassy that six months ago she could barely get on top of one of those things. Now it felt like the only natural way to get around for any distance and she swung on bareback as easily as any sixteen-year-old. When the kids rode, they seemed as natural as if they were centaurs, putting her own skills to shame, but that was okay. A privilege of age.

The kids always let the older grownups—the few people older than about thirty-five who still lived—win their playful ad-hoc races and would swear with the utmost sincerity that they'd lost fair and square. It was like a game to them, showing such fine horsemanship that their beasts didn't mind coming in behind. Nobody minded playing along with them.

Damn, how far society had changed in a few months... Maybe if the world had been full of people like this, then the EMPs—

Enough of that. Cassy shook her thoughts clear and turned the horse north. She stopped only long enough to tell a passing Clanner to arm the adults and stay put. Then at a gallop, the rifle slung over her back, she rode hard only a few minutes before she saw Michael and some other scouts up ahead, through the trees. She passed through the last few meters of forest and then stopped ten feet away from Michael, keeping a stern look on her face but her hands away from the rifle. It was best not to start a problem with strangers where none existed, by seeming too aggressive, especially since almost everyone everywhere went armed these days...

Michael saluted her as she approached, which was a bit odd but she saluted back anyway. Maybe he was putting on a show for the refugees. Or for his scouts. And there were indeed a couple dozen refugees, maybe thirty counting some children. All of them were dirty and thin. A couple adults wore old, dirty bandages. These people had been through hell and back, that much was clear. Some looked dazed, on their last legs maybe. Desperate people could be unpredictable...

"Hello," Cassy called out, trying to mimic Michael's quiet-yet-loud military bark. She hadn't quite gotten it down yet but the volume at least pulled their attention. "You are on Clan territory without invitation. Can someone explain to me what your business is with Clanholme?" She kept a faint smile on her face, trying not to look like an immediate threat or even hostile, but not a sucker to mess with, either.

Beside her, Michael looked relaxed, but Cassy knew him well enough to tell that he was coiled like a snake, ready to strike if the need suddenly arose.

A tall man stepped forward, dirty as the rest, with sagging skin that showed he'd once been a lot heavier and eyes dulled by thirst or hunger, or both. She watched him carefully. From beneath his shaggy black hair, his brown eyes revealed the hardness of a man who had seen and done too many difficult things just to survive. That was a common look these days, but it told Cassy she wasn't dealing with some hermit who had only emerged from hiding when the food ran out. These were people who had simply survived any way they could, for far too long. They were worth being wary around.

The man said, "Hello. We didn't know it belonged to anyone. We saw the fruit trees and hoped to glean some scraps for the kids, or maybe some mealworms. Lizards. Whatever. Pretty amazing place—whoever planted these made 'em almost all fruit and nut trees. Must be nice..."

Cassy saw his eyes narrow, and they got a gleam to them. The starving man thinking about food, just lying on the ground or hanging in trees everywhere... Clanholme must seem like Shangri-La to those people. The Big Rock Candy Mountain, where the bluebird sings by the lemonade springs. Unfortunately, that fantasy could raise the odds of a violent end to this, so it was a good thing she had thought to get the others ready before she left the party.

"Been picked clean, friend," she told the man. "What we didn't gather, we let fall for the pigs to forage. This little holding keeps a balance that we have to honor or we'll all go hungry. We got enough to give you a meal and all the clean water you want, but if you're looking for a superman you've come to the wrong place. No one saw this coming—no one has enough food to go around." Cassy readied herself for an outburst, or worse.

Instead, the man's eyes lit up as he grinned. "Oh Lord, thank you! Just a meal, one good meal, put some energy back in these kids. They're starving too... I swear, if you can't find room for us with your people, we'll move on. We aren't looking for trouble and we aren't raiders, but no one wants to watch their kid starve. You're doing a fine thing for us, Miss..."

"Cassy. You can call me Cassy."

"Miss Cassy. Thank you. I'm Barry, and these people, we were all neighbors on a nice little cul-de-sac. Good place for kids. When the EMP hit, we stuck together as neighbors and rode out the worst, did what we had to do to protect ourselves. Shared our food, too. I had a couple year's worth for my family, others had arms or tools to contribute, so we all lived through it, but when food ran out we had to take our chances out here. It hasn't been easy. We can't get much further on our own, I'm afraid."

"Where are you coming from then, Barry?" Cassy tried to make the question sound friendly enough, casual even, but it was anything but.

"We're from Rhineholds, north of Adamstown. We tried to check out Ephrata because they have people and working farms and everything, but they thought we were Adamstown spies. We've dealt with those Adamstown raiders ourselves, so I can't blame them, but the kids were just confused. Asked why they won't help us just because we're from another town. We never told the kids about the hundreds of people we turned away ourselves." He looked down, frowning.

At the word 'Adamstown,' Cassy's ears perked, and Barry had noticed—he couldn't hide his surprise, maybe—but he'd kept talking like nothing was amiss. As he finished his story, her mind had been whirring. At first with suspicion, but hell, if they really were Adamstown spies they sure wouldn't say they were from over that way. But it didn't pay to be trusting, not anymore.

"Barry, I feel for you. Don't be hard on Ephrata. They're good people, but they're on the front lines with Adamstown, and those raiders have been cozying up with the invaders lately if rumors are believed. I believe it. They've suddenly become much more active, and they're raiding deep into our side of the Interstate. So where are you headed?"

A small child, maybe six years old, ran up and wrapped her arms around Barry's leg. He patted her hair with a smile. "Anywhere this one can have a chance, really. East is all invaders and bandits, from what we've heard, so it was 'go west, young man' and see what we can see. Crappy plan, not really a plan at all. But staying just wasn't an option anymore."

"You might try Liz Town, or sorry, Elizabethtown. They're a rowdy bunch, but good enough people, and it's an open city. You work, you eat. They'd probably draft anyone fit and over fifteen as soldiers, though. I don't know if you've heard about Hershey and Harrisburg, but Liz Town has their hands full with them. You'd be welcome there, probably. They need more folks. Barbarians at the gate and all."

Barry snarled his lip. "Oh yeah, we heard the rumors. Not much different than a lot of other places, though. Liz Town sounds great..."

Cassy caught the edge on his voice. "But?"

"Our kind isn't welcome in Elizabethtown, from what we've heard from more than one person. Plus, the guards at Ephrata told us the same."

Dammit, this guy was seriously making it hard to help him. Cassy wondered if he was one of those "yeah but..." people who always had a reason not to do things, always ready with an excuse dressed up as a reason. Most of those types were dead by now, of course, if they weren't already in a community by pure luck, but anything was possible. She let out a long, frustrated breath.

"Alright, I'll bite. What is 'your kind' and why won't the Lizzies let you in? Think about how you answer this, please. It's rather important." She shifted so that she faced him directly, looking him square in the eyes. Liz Town were allies, and she wouldn't abide a bunch of strangers stirring up trouble.

Barry nodded. His nose didn't wrinkle, eyes didn't widen... no indication he'd taken offense. So it must have been a question he was used to, and that was alarming in its own right. "Oh, I understand how important it is. They're friendly with you, and friends mean more than Friday barbeques now. I promise, it's nothing against them. But the thing is…" His voice trailed off. Cassy waited patiently while he gathered up how he wanted to say whatever was on his mind.

"The thing is, Miss Cassy, you may not have noticed but we're not white, black, brown, or yellow. We're more what they might call 'sandy,' in a manner of speaking."

Cassy stared at the man, mouth open. Just because they were Indian? Or maybe Pakistani. "Why would they have problems? You're Indian, right? Or Pakistani?"

"Indian, but only by heritage. All of our grandparents came over at the end of World War Two, and we were all born and raised here. We worked in Adamstown for a company owned by a really nice Indian immigrant. He didn't make it after the EMPs without his heart medications. It was a sad day for us all. He used to pay random employee medical bills, or rent, and even helped with a kid's college tuition once. All without ever mentioning it, but we all knew who did it. A good man."

"And what's that got to do with Liz Town? Your race or your boss? They aren't very important anymore, I would think. We're all mongrels here. No offense."

Barry smiled wanly. "None taken. Being offended at the truth is low on my list of give-a-damns these days, miss. But rumor has it they kicked out anyone with a, shall we say, swarthy complexion. Didn't want light brown people around."

Cassy bit down, clenching her jaw, and turned to look at Michael with one eyebrow raised. He only responded by giving her a single curt nod, and Cassy's heart sank. How could that be? These days, wasn't racism low on the list of people's priorities? Of course, she'd done it herself with Choony because he looked like the invaders did…. Damn. Better look in the mirror, exalted leader. She sighed.

"I guess I can't very well blame them," Cassy replied. "As

much as I'd like to, you do look a lot like invaders to most local folks. Life is pretty fragile right now. Too fragile to take chances, especially if you have a family."

Barry pursed his lips, nodded, but added, "I understand that, but it's a logical fallacy. You don't hold their racist views, yet you said they were good people. How good can they be if just hating Arabs isn't racist enough for their tastes —they have to extend that to everyone with a 'sandy' complexion? Our ancestors were Hindus and Sikhs and Buddhists and a dozen other religions. Why on Earth would I put our children anywhere near people who hate them simply because they look 'only a little not the same' as the locals who are already in place?"

Cassy found herself looking away from his steely eyes, staring at the ground. Not only was he right—Liz Town was indeed an ally, and now this?—but the memory of how she'd reacted to Choony when he first arrived felt like a neon sign that put her to the same shame as them. She wished she'd brought Choony or Jaz along, or both of them. They'd throw some perspective out for people who needed it—like herself and this Barry guy, clearly the leader of his group. She had a sense they should be friends, and neither of them was all that racist, yet race questions were trying to come between them anyway.

Thankfully, Michael intervened without missing a beat, diverting attention from her for the moment while she collected herself. "First of all, we didn't know they were banishing anyone the wrong shade of brown or pink, nor are we responsible for their actions. Secondly, they are good people despite that. They aren't cannibals, they don't raid other survivors, they work hard. They share what they produce and they trade with others, just as we all do. They stand with us against those who do awful things, sometimes at the cost of their own lives. Those are people's friends and brothers, children and sisters, dying to protect not just themselves but all of us in these parts. So please, I would appreciate it if you could be a bit less judgmental of them and us both. We're all just figuring out how to survive as we go. People make mistakes."

Michael stopped abruptly and simply stood there looking Barry in the eyes, neither challenging nor apologizing, but just waiting. Cassy felt that his nonchalance was almost eerie.

Before Barry could respond, Cassy raised a hand placatingly, palm toward Barry. "Okay, okay, no sense getting mad at each other. Thank you for letting us know about that, Barry, and if we see any more people like yourselves we won't be telling them to go to Elizabethtown. But that leaves a question that's more important than whether Liz Town is being fair to strangers who haven't fought and bled alongside them—what will you do now?"

"You've already said we can't stay here. We wouldn't take it by force even if we could. We aren't stupid, or lazy, or greedy. Just hungry."

"Barry's an odd name for an Indian." Cassy grinned. She turned to Michael and said, "Have some people bring a meal out to these folks, and refill their water bottles." Michael nodded and motioned to his young messenger scout.

Barry shrugged. "My name is really Barid, which means 'cloud,' but everyone in school called me Barry. I just sort of adopted it. Thanks for the meal. I guess in the morning we'll move on and out of your territory. Some may be angry about it, but I understand and appreciate what help you could give us."

Michael's head snapped toward Barry, and he stared for a moment before finally saying, "Hey, Barry. I see you have weapons, which is a needful thing these days, but are you willing to use them?"

Cassy eyed Michael cautiously. What the heck was he up to? She trusted him though, so she kept silent and waited.

"We've had to before, to my regret. Yes, we've used them to protect ourselves and our neighbors, or the friendly ones at least. But that can't be a surprise—anyone alive and not in a bunker has had to do things they didn't like in order to survive this far."

Michael glanced to Cassy, and then said to Barry, "You know, there are a lot of empty homesteads and farms just west of Clanholme. Their owners were killed, or moved, or teamed up with friends elsewhere while things shook out. There are enough empty farms for you all to find one and maybe beef up its defenses, raise food and animals this spring. Good neighbors raise everyone's property values." Michael chuckled. "If you did that, we could advise you on how we do things, and you see how well it works out by looking at that forest. You should see it in the spring and summer. It's a wonderful stretch of something, not a farm, exactly, but it supports all of us. We don't go hungry. Believe me when I say that we've had to protect it, but we've always had the people we needed to do that. And we're making alliances as fast as we can with people like you, people who don't think they have a license to raid and are willing to trade with us and protect each other."

For a moment, Cassy was irritated that Michael would suggest something like that without talking to her about it first, but then she stopped. This was the perfect timing to talk about such a thing, while the refugees were still hungry and looking forward to food. And still grateful. Her gut told her these people were decent enough. Everyone would do whatever it took to keep their kids from starving—that was something she'd seen often enough that her old notion of what it took to be basically good had long since gone out the window—but they seemed only to do what was necessary.

That was important.

Her gut also told her they weren't the Raider type, and Michael must have had the same sense. Not to mention the fact that having them to the west as allies would put a buffer between the Clan and the unknown out west of the farm, in an area that was currently devoid of people, which made sense of Michael's questions about using those rifles they had. She read a book once where the characters said the only questions you should ask an ally is whether they have guns and would they shoot them at an enemy. Michael was setting a higher bar than that, which was good. He wanted neighbors. Very well, she'd give these people a shot.

Cassy said, "Absolutely. You need a home and seem like better neighbors than the cannibal gangs we had to clear out from these parts. Talk about it amongst yourselves, and you and I can get together on it tomorrow. For now, I think I hear your food coming."

As the food arrived and the refugees swarmed the Clan servers with hungry hands and grateful nods and smiles, Cassy looked to Michael, and he gave her one curt nod. He didn't need to be told to keep an eye on these people tonight. Just in case.

* * *

It was shortly after midnight and the cheers and kissing were over. While no ball had dropped in Times Square on T.V., it was amazing how much fun everyone had with no T.V., drinking moonshine or hard cider, and bundled up like polar explorers against the biting cold. The festive mood continued and the party didn't look like it'd slow any time soon—almost everyone was still there, except those on guard duty. Enough people had volunteered to stay sober for watches that they had shifts covered for the night, actually half-shifts so the volunteer guardians could at least enjoy one half or the other of the winter celebration. In the wake of their recent victory over yet another invading force, the celebrating was intense. Spontaneous hilarity could be seen breaking out all over the Complex whenever Cassy looked around.

As Cassy refilled her cider—not the hard cider, she was staying sober what with so many unknown people encamped only minutes from the Complex—she caught movement from the corner of her eye. Turning, she saw that Michael was marching half a dozen of their former-military troops into the common area. Something was up. She was concerned at first, but then she noticed that Michael held little Kaitlyn's hand as they marched, and she wore a huge, anxious grin. This should be good, whatever this was…

Michael called cadence as the troops marched into the clearing, and they stopped adjacent to the common area. The other Clanners quickly gathered to see what was happening. Michael cried an order and the "unit" turned smartly at once to face everyone. With his stern military voice on full-Marine mode, he called out, "We have a special presentation this evening." He paused, then bellowed, "Jaz and Choony, front and center!"

Those two had been watching from the sidelines with Grandma Mandy and were obviously surprised when Michael boomed out their names. But the sight of little Kaitlyn standing there with Michael, a grin on her face, told Jaz that whatever was going on, they didn't need to hide. Jaz grabbed Choony's hand and dragged him out to face Michael, Choony visibly resisting as the crowd called out encouragement and a few whistled at Jaz or made general catcalls at the two of them. Jaz waved to her admirers, but never stopped dragging Choony forward.

Michael then escorted Kaitlyn to face them. "Atten-hut!" he barked to his Marines, who went into the "position of attention" with snap and pop from their heeled boots, standing ramrod-straight, rifles at their right sides. Then he addressed the crowd.

"Our fellow Clanner Kaitlyn has a special request this evening. In the Marines, we consider it a responsibility to recognize heroic deeds in song and ceremony, and Kaitlyn here has reminded us of that duty. With Dean Jepson, the famous and admired Redneck's Own Engineer, she has prepared appropriate medals of valor. These are the first Clanholme valor awards ever. And to go with what Kaitlyn has named the Clanholme Medals of Generator, she has prepared a commemorative song about our victory over the Adamstown raiders and the daring deeds of these two brave, young heroes."

Predictably, the Clanners cheered at this. And drank some more.

Michael turned to the little girl and crouched so that he spoke quietly to her, face to face. "Ready, sweetie?"

Kaitlyn nodded, standing as tall as her small child's frame allowed, and speaking loudly enough for all to hear, she announced with a high-pitched, cracking voice, "I am proud to present Jaz and Choony with the very first two Clan awards of valor—the Clanholme Medal of Generator!" Her voice may have quaked with stage fright, but she grinned like the Cheshire Cat when the Clan began to cheer her.

Cassy watched, smiling, as Jaz broke into a chortle and Choony laughed in his quiet way, but as Kaitlyn put one of the ribbon loops around Jaz's neck, those close enough could see one little tear rolling down her cheek. Choony was grinning as widely as anyone had seen in the time he'd been with the Clan as he straightened up after receiving his own, fingering the neat little medal Kaitlyn had awarded him.

Michael then broke into the crowd's noisy cheers, his disciplined military voice easily piercing the din. "And now may we present The Ballad of Jaz and Choony." The crowd yelled its approval as Kaitlyn, practically bouncing now with excitement, turned to face them. Cassy could see her visibly gulp with nervousness as the crowd quieted and attention focused on her, but the brave kid didn't falter. Then her suddenly strong, sweet voice burst out of that tiny body, surprising everyone with its strength as she began to sing—

Here's Jaz and Choony, they'll save the day!
Coming in fast, driving goons all away
And everyone here will jump up just to say
Jaz and Choony! They're saving the day!

At the end of the first verse, the Marines stomped their feet once and then stood to attention again, brought their rifles from their sides up across their bodies to hold with two hands, then up to their right shoulders. They then brought their left hands across their bodies to touch the rifles with fingertips, just at shoulder levels. It was neat, in unison, and made a popping noise. Cassy hadn't seen the Marines salute with rifles before, or whatever they were doing. It looked fantastic, and Kaitlyn beamed with pride.

The process then reversed itself, until they stood again with rifles resting by their right foot. The laughing crowd shouted encouragement as Kaitlyn went into the second verse.

Choony and Jaz are coming with gunny sacks
Full of trade goods and hardware they bear on their backs
The goonies they see them and run, making tracks
Jaz and Choony! They're saving the day!

On the final words this time, the crowd joined in, shouting "saving the day" with more enthusiasm than talent.

The Marines in formation then barked their bark and shouted "Ooh-rah!" in unison, going to Present Arms with their rifles again, then back to attention.

The audience roared. Jaz stood and bowed to them, grinning, while Choony just looked painfully shy about the whole thing, but he wore a smile. The two of them turned to leave, and Choony put Kaitlyn up on his shoulders to march over and greet Grandma Mandy while their Marine honor guard fanned out to rejoin the fun and the merrymaking. The mood Kaitlyn and the Marines had set for them made the crowd boisterously happy for the rest of the night, as people talked and traded stories and celebrated the miracle of just being alive.

Cassy marveled at the intense sense of community all around her, a feeling she had sought all her life. Just maybe, the loss of the old society would someday be looked back on as a blessing after the turmoil ran its course.

Kaitlyn refused to be removed from Choony's shoulders for the next hour, and no one tried very hard to make her until she started falling asleep and Grandma Mandy took over, walking with her to her mother and Ethan. Choony had worn a faint smile the whole time he carried Kaitlyn. Neither he nor Jaz took off their handmade Clanholme Generator medals until they finally had to go to sleep as the sun began to rise.

It had turned into the type of great celebration that lasts at full roar until dawn, all noise and laughter and energy, and no fights at all. Later, it became known as the First New Years, and people would tell First New Year's tales for years afterward.

They were alive and fed and they felt safe for now. It was enough.

- 13 -

1000 HOURS - ZERO DAY +151

CASSY SAT ON the recliner in her living room, elbows on her knees, leaning forward as she listened to the chatter. These informal meetings included representatives from various surrounding holdings who had managed to hold on without raiding others. Originally, Cassy had intended the meetings as a way to reach out to others though early attendance was sparse, to say the least—only someone from Ephrata had come to the first one, three months before, shortly after Clanholme had defeated Peter and his "goons." Cassy had to smile at the way Kaitlyn's "Jaz and Choony" song had entered their local lingo.

Since that first meeting, the group had grown. Their individual names weren't important but their titles were—each was there to represent their survivor group, at the invitation and request of the Clan. Soon it would be time to build someplace that could hold these meetings more comfortably as attendance grew, which it was sure to do as word of them continued to spread.

For this third survivors' meeting, the living room, small as it was, had begun to feel crowded. Frank sat in the other recliner, acting as the Clan's rep. Cassy was present only as a neutral arbiter and meeting coordinator, her duty as the host. She had made Frank the Clan's rep both to distance herself from any unpopular demands the Clan might make and to showcase Frank's missing foot, which raised sympathy and reminded people of the Clan's toughness—as did her own prominent facial scars. It amounted to a show of will and power. Plus, Frank's easy, non-threatening, people-savvy ways made him a natural choice.

On the couch, sipping tea, sat three reps, one each from Ephrata, Brickerville, and Liz Town. Brickerville's rep had concluded the town's status report, sharing what they had, what they needed, and what their current challenges were. It was the last status report of the evening, thank heavens. All the challenges had seemed difficult but surmountable, a blessing for everyone. Ephrata was fending off bandits and invaders but had the manpower to do it. Liz Town was holding fine against Harrisburg now, and rumor had it that plague was running through that evil place. Brickerville had the toughest challenge now as migrating teams of invader troops brought violence into their area. Things had gotten so bad that the town, lacking Ephrata's manpower, found itself essentially under siege.

"...so we're mostly cut off from the Falconry and the supplies they trade. I need to know if Clanholme would be willing to put up both our merchants and theirs, along with the goods we bring, and offer us protection in your territory so we can trade in peace. Other groups trade with us too, with our greenhouses growing surplus food the way they do. Without help, we could be in real trouble before too much longer."

Frank nodded as he used his cane to scratch at his leg stump. "Of course we're happy to host traders. But we can't guarantee their safety coming or going from here, just to be clear. That'd have to be up to the participants. And if trading sessions between you and the Falconry work out here, I bet they'll grow. Setting up an open marketplace to everybody, inside Clanholme, needs more discussion. Maybe a better place would be along the border with our new neighbors to the west? It'll take some thought. But for now, I don't see why not."

"Thank you. That will take some pressure off of our northern flank, not having to run interference for wagon convoys coming in. Or whatever they're called."

The visitors having finished, Cassy watched as Frank took his turn.

"Pardon me for not rising to speak, but my leg is bothersome in this cold. The fact is, we're doing well enough on our southern border. Mostly, now, the people down there are either in tiny settlements or are dead or dying off. There just was too much ruined by the 'vader's gas attacks—with Lancaster wiped off the map and it's people killed outright, we haven't had to deal with floods of starving refugees like you all deal with from outside."

The Liz Town rep set down her tea cup and said, "I hear you have some new neighbors. Anything you need help with, or are they friendlies?"

"Yeah, we helped them set up on an empty farm to our west, or southwest rather. They were refugees looking for a handout when we met them and they turned out to be well behaved and hard-working. They're respected now in our territory, once we introduced them around. We're helping them set up with permaculture there, in the Clan fashion. Come spring, they should get completely self-sufficient, for food anyway. They were cul-de-sac neighbors in the suburbs who held together, kind of like we did out in the woods when the EMP came. They'll buffer our western border, and Liz Town's southern flank too." Frank nodded to Cassy, indicating that he was done.

Cassy had watched the other reps' faces while Frank spoke and saw envy but no indignation. They were all friends here, and it seemed that would continue. A very good thing. She set her cup down, rapped her knuckles on the wood T.V. dinner tray that served as her recliner end table, and smiled around at the group. "Now that we're all caught up and the general plans are in place, I'd like to discuss the reason the Clan invited you here again to talk instead of setting up a radio conference."

When everyone looked at her and none objected, Cassy continued. "In one of the nearby deserted farms, we found a small stack of printouts showing a roadmap of the area. Based on the information we got from you and our scouts, we've added the little survivor groups we know about and I added the new ones you reported this morning. It'll give us a good strategic map. We put other things on the map as well, anything we thought might be important, such as areas where we've heard about invaders looting."

The Clanner handling refills of tea and muffins went around the group with printouts, each with hand-drawn additions that wouldn't reveal that the Clan had computers and satellite access and other such working tech-world goodies. No way Cassy wanted that information just floating around out there, tempting the wrong parties.

Frank added, "We sent a single copy to the Falconry—old Cornwall—even though they're officially neutral, to help them send their wandering traders out. As you see, we've added almost two dozen dots for different survivor groups, with rough estimates of population. We also sent an envoy with a blank map to Lebanon, hoping to get information from their side of the world and maybe get them to join our meeting here starting next month."

Brickerville's rep frowned. "You didn't ask us how we felt

about talking to Lebanon. Or Falconry either." His body stayed relaxed, Cassy noted, so hopefully he didn't feel insulted or threatened and just wanted to make a point—they were allies, not subjects. Allies need to be consulted on the "big" moves.

Frank spoke up then, in his role as the Clan representative. "No, we didn't ask. But we've dealt with the people of Lebanon before. They're a lot like Liz Town in many ways, and they're holding off the bad guys from our north. They're out there mostly all alone and could use any help we give them. Also, they helped Clan envoys headed elsewhere when they didn't have to. But as the meeting coordinator told us, the map we sent them didn't have all these details on it. Better to receive info than hand it away, right? Unless they join us."

Cassy continued as though there had been no interruption, still with a pleasant smile. "As you can see, we added a bunch of notes too, from the information we got while our people were at the Falconry. The Clan hopes to get the same kind of information out of Lebanon. That puts the total of other groups at twenty-seven so far, plus all of us. We all have radios, but they don't. What I'd like is for each of us to invite a half-dozen or so of these little groups to report regularly to one of us, whoever is closest, and for us to pass useful information to them. Get them used to us, and used to working with us. The idea is, they'll share their information if we share ours, and it'll benefit everyone."

Cassy waited for anyone to speak up with questions or objections, but the other reps stayed quiet, waiting attentively. Of course they'd figure she still had more to discuss, or they wouldn't have been invited to attend in-person meetings. Ethan would just have coordinated secured radio talks.

Finally she continued, "I see there aren't any questions

yet. Then it's onward to the main reason I asked you all here, beyond just being time we got together again. First, we have all this new information about other small survivor groups but no plan for dealing with them. Right now, we're all in the "divided we fall" category, and we should be using them as canaries in the coal mine. That means helping them survive while they can. They can be recruited as our forward observers, and our buffers. Most of them, being survivors, will be hard-working, no-nonsense people. And we do know they aren't raiders, or we'd have heard about or dealt with them already. It's likely many or most of them would be eager to set up deals with us."

A murmur arose around the coffee table, until the Liz Town representative spoke up and said, "It seems to me, if we can make them friendly and they want to keep to themselves, more power to them. Seems to me they'll trade for our goods, diffuse any attacking forces, and yeah, be our early warning canary. Makes perfect sense, yeah?"

Ephrata stood, taking the speaking position. "And just who gets to deal with these small survivor groups? They're a valuable resource and Ephrata, being bigger, needs more resources. But they'll be a burden, too, if they're in bad shape. Your odd smallholding farming methods are spreading fast, but not everyone knows about them yet. People are hungry out there." He sat down.

The others, she noted thankfully, remained silent and waited to see how Cassy would react. "I see your point, but haven't we had enough in this world of the strong taking the most benefit? No, the survivors should set up first with whichever of us is closest, if only because it's safer, and we should favor those who have fewer resources. Isn't that what's best for us as well as for those survivors? We need to consider what's best for them if we're going to bring them into our fold. We can handle any imbalances between us like we do now."

Brickerville then stood, looking at Ephrata. Cassy noted his jaw wasn't clenched, eyes weren't narrow, so she expected Ephrata would probably go along...

"Frankly, Brickerville would be willing to donate—voluntarily, mind you—a share of our excess to go to whichever of our nearby towns need it most," the Brickerville rep told the group. "That includes these small settlements," he said with a fingertip tapping at the map in his hand. "What goes around comes around, we used to say. We help them, they'll help us. But only with our surpluses. None of us are going hungry to help people who have never helped us."

It was Liz Town's rep who first responded, snapping, "Yeah? And who decides what's best, or what the priorities are going to be?"

Cassy felt her heart leap. She had hoped for just this sort of opportunity, and it was the real reason she had called them all together. She wasn't surprised that it had been Liz Town's rep to bring it up. Those people were direct and to the point, a byproduct of their environment and the "Founder's Principle" at work in that community. Keeping her face a mask of pleasant unconcern, Cassy stood and the others sat or turned to better look at her.

"You know," Cassy said, allowing her face to transition into concerned-mom mode, "this touches on something else I wanted to discuss. It all goes hand in hand. Remember that Ephrata young man who took liberties with a visiting Brickerville girl? We need a way to handle that kind of behavior, and it seems like the same solution could deal with Liz Town's concern at the same time. It'll get more important, too, if we set up an open market somewhere."

She saw the representatives lean forward unconsciously, listening carefully, and fought the urge to grin. Her idea for a confederation could find fertile ground here. She prepared herself to launch into the idea of forming into a confederation of states with rules and penalties, sharing benefits and responsibilities. She'd let Ephrata pick the name if it would help secure their raw excess manpower for the whole group's use.

What appealed most to Cassy was that they'd all keep their independence and their identities in a confederation—no one wanted a central government anymore, not until the U.S.A. came back to life. But a UN-like council at the top could distribute extra resources or manpower, handle intergroup conflicts, and collectively bargain with outsiders. And here they were, the start of the all-groups council they'd require.

There was strength in such an arrangement, strength they'd all need to avoid being gobbled up whole by more organized, militaristic groups like the Empire. Cassy intended that the Clan would avoid that fate, which meant lining up the Clan's neighbors and allies. Right here, right now, they had a fine start.

The meeting wound on long into the night as they discussed ideas and details.

* * *

The general paced the short length between the walls of his pavilion tent, hands gripped tightly behind his back. "You are certain this Spyder was killed?"

Gen. Ree's latest aide, whatever his name was, stood stiff and out of the way of Ree's pacing as he replied, "Several sources all state that Spyder was killed immediately after the Americans launched their own EMPs, my leader. It is said that the American terrorist, Major Taggart, is the one who ended both Spyder and his psychotic crony, Sebastian, and the bodies were strung up on street lamps to prove to all that they were indeed dead. For the soft Americans, it was enough to ensure the remaining citizens do not turn against him. I understand some now regard him as a hero."

"Then who is it being such a thorn in our side? I know when Taggart strikes because he leaves his calling cards and our intelligence is good, but someone else is operating out there now. Taggart is too useful to simply destroy. He keeps order while we pursue other ends. Otherwise I'd simply kill or seize his men and question them more thoroughly. As it is, we must rely on our spies to answer our questions."

The aide nodded. He lowered his eyes and said, "Forgive my ignorance, my leader, but is it not possible that destroying Taggart would be beneficial? We could end his threat and secure the information you seek, all at once."

Ree looked over at the aide for the first time during this conversation, evaluating. Was there a hint of too much ambition in this man? But his aide's eyes were properly averted and his slumped shoulders showed he had the proper level of fear when addressing him, General Ree, the Great Leader of New York State until such time as communications were once again possible with Korea. Fear was good; it meant the man must feel strongly about what he suggested. He might be wrong, but he was being honest, not ambitious. You couldn't always tell who to trust in these difficult days.

Ree adjusted the already-meticulously placed lapels on his field uniform. "Well, your opinion is noted. I will give it the consideration it warrants."

Ree pretended not to notice the aide's faint smile. Such a statement was high praise, coming from Ree. The aide would likely brag about it over American beer and cards after his shift, but let him. There was little enough to be happy about in this forsaken, miserable country, even before the Americans paid the whole world back for the righteous crusade of a few. Ree had never been one who thought America would just die peacefully in its sleep, anyway, so their occasionally fierce points of resistance were not much of a surprise, nor was the EMP retaliation. He had taken what preparations he could and left the bigger morality questions to the Great Leader. May the missing communications be reestablished soon!

Ree sent his aide out for refreshments and welcomed his last visitor before lunch, the commanding officer of his production department, Major Pak Kim. "Welcome, Kim. Come in and be at peace."

Kim had the slightly oval eyes of one of the tainted, those unfortunate families that had suffered certain abusive liberties at the hands of Western troops during the Great War. Though the North had defeated giant America, winning had come at great cost...

"*Annyeonghaseyo.* Thanks to my older brother for his hospitality, my General."

Ree was clearly not related but he admired Kim's friendly greeting, offered with such style and humility. Kim was a good officer. "My younger brother is welcome in this house," Ree replied, formalizing the exchange. It let the officer know he was welcome and fondly received, but not so fondly as to be casual in Ree's presence.

Kim bowed. "I have the reports the general requested. Firstly, the numbers for New York. The population is reduced almost precisely as planned. There remain only some six-point-four million living residents, according to our data. This of course does not include the two million blessed ones of the People's Worker Army in New Jersey," he said, the state's name sounding clumsy on his Korean tongue.

"As expected. Your words fall like rain most welcome. But tell me, how are our P.W.A. lesser brethren going to meet their goals? I assume my little brother has these things well in hand. Forgive an older brother for asking."

The last thing Ree wanted was to irritate the major to the point of disrupting finely laid plans, and the man was known to be prickly. He could be replaced, but he was brilliant at his current post and replacing him would risk disruptions. Better to offer honey than vinegar, as the Americans said—at least, better when here in private.

Kim stood tall and snapped his booted heels together, standing at attention. That boded well, Ree mused. It likely meant he was proud, and that meant he had succeeded in meeting the goals supposedly handed down through Ree by the Great Leader himself...

"General, it may please the Leader to hear from you this glorious news. Our requisitioning efforts have stripped the supplies of all who do not side with you to a radius of twenty-five kilometers. We now have enough food to last ourselves and the Worker Army until more can be harvested, and we had greater success than we had planned for in terms of harvesting fish and other foods from the ocean. Fish density must be rising, which was not factored in. Please, Big Brother, do not punish those below me for this failure. The mistake was mine, and I beg the forgiveness of family."

Ree felt irritation, but of course no expression of emotion ever crossed his face unless he willed it so. Discipline such as that was the reason Korea stood in triumph at the end of the last great war with America and why it would do so again when this mess was over. It was indeed a failure to not factor in reduced human population on the quantity of fish and such, though. Had Ree known, more people could have been saved—and thus used—through the People's Worker Army. Still, it would have been much worse to overestimate supplies.

Ree said gently, "Many civilians will starve needlessly now, outside of the warm embrace of the Worker's Army, because of your failure. Yet it is done and there is nothing for it. War is chaotic and not all can be foreseen. Strive harder now for the Great Leader and his plan, that you may atone for this error in the eyes of your ancestors and descendants."

The remainder of the conversation went more or less as expected. Ree had ordered the creation of many small slave labor camps, scattered all over the area just outside of the urban sprawl, to demolish and clear away whatever buildings would interfere with the upcoming spring plantings. It had worked well, despite the raw manpower required to set it up. His soldiers guarding the workers could now focus on the region's perimeter to keep starving people out, New Yorkers bottled in, and a few small central bases spaced regularly throughout the interior to keep the workers in fear enough to motivate their work efforts. Such "castellation" had worked in ancient Korea and even medieval Europe, and it was working again here. Ree allowed himself a small frisson of satisfaction, but of course he didn't allow it to show on his face.

After the briefing, with the appropriate formal bows, Kim left Ree's quarters. His aide returned with lunch shortly after, somewhat cooled as the aide waited politely outside for Kim to leave. Fish, rice, and some odd American vegetables. Ree, of course, had all the soy sauce he wanted to cover any unfamiliar tastes.

While he and his aide ate, they chatted about unit positions and other strategic concerns, it being Ree's duty to help his minion's skills grow so that he might be of more use for the Great Leader's plan here. Between dishes, Ree said, "I have considered your earlier suggestion and have decided that the terrorist Taggart's uses outweigh the risk he poses. Can you perhaps guess what my thinking is on the matter?"

The aide was silent for a moment, thinking before he spoke, which was a fine quality in an aide. Then he said, "My general, I am not qualified to have an opinion, but may I ask questions and see whether my logic is sound?"

Ree nodded once. "Little Brother is wiser than he knows. By all means, let us share our knowledge with each other."

"Could it perhaps be because you are able to guard his targets with those troops who have doubtful loyalty to the Great Leader's plan and to your authority in his name?"

"Yes, that is one reason, and a large one. I usually know when and where this bandit will attack, so I can remove the most valuable supplies and guard what remains with traitors and the lazy. Sloth is greed, and is also thus treason."

The aide nodded at the old saying by sheer habit. Everyone knew that it was each person's responsibility give their all for the state, so it could in turn use those efforts for the benefit of all. "Then there must be more to it or you would be pleased with my question, General. Is it because his forces, terrorists that they are, take supplies from the people to care only for themselves? It seems to me that he can only take what the stealth of the greedy allowed us to miss. By leaving the American terrorist in place, they take those supplies, which makes the People more loyal than ever to our benevolent guidance. By coincidence, it also punishes those who disobeyed anti-hoarding edicts meant for the good of all."

Ree again nodded. "From a philosophical standpoint, that is correct. I allow the Americans themselves to punish those who are traitors to their fellow citizens. Many of those hoarders die in those supply raids, and such traitors do not deserve to live. I use the Americans to punish Americans and no anger rises toward us. The irony pleases the Great Leader."

"I am sorry, Big Brother. I can think of no other questions to ask." The aide lowered his head and looked at the floor, showing his submission to the general's superior knowledge and wisdom.

Ree then smiled warmly, looking for all the world as though he was greatly pleased. In truth he was pleased, but such outward displays were by design, and never spontaneous. "There is another reason, though not as important as those you already asked about. If I attack him and his cells where they hide like the roaches they are, I would kill most of them but probably not all, and I would no longer know their whereabouts and intentions."

"So as things stand, my general, if you wish to stop a terrorist raid then you have only to reinforce the guards at that target, and they scurry away to find easier targets?"

Inwardly, Ree grinned. What a find, this aide! He may be only a lieutenant now, but that would soon change if he did nothing to betray Ree's trust and confidence. And he hadn't guessed Ree's ulterior motive: Taggart must never be allowed to leave the city. Hemmed in here in the city, he was useful. Out there, he could be a genuine threat to Ree's plans.

The rest of lunch was quite pleasant.

- 14 -

1800 HOURS - ZERO DAY +154

THE RADIO CRACKLED, startling Ethan mid-bite. He scrambled to set his dinner plate down and get to the damnable thing to throw on the headphone mic, dancing to correct as his food slid toward the edge of his plate and dropping his fork to the floor in the process. He cursed as he put on the headphones, and heard, "...do you read me? Bravo One to Charlie One, come in."

That would be Brickerville, trying to contact the Clan directly. He had a sinking feeling in his stomach. "Bravo One, this is Charlie Two. Say again."

"Heya, Ethan. This is Josh direct. We have a problem. Break for copy."

"Go ahead."

"We're under attack by 'vaders. I thought Charlie One would like to know. We're completely surrounded by them. We figure at least a hundred, mostly small arms and a couple RPGs, but they haven't used them yet. Seems pretty low-intensity for an assault. Any ideas?"

Ethan had plenty of ideas, but needed more information before he could take it to Michael or offer advice. "Copy, surrounded and under attack. Low intensity doesn't sound like they're trying to roll over you, though. How are they arranged, what side are they on rather?"

A slight pause, and then: "They're on all sides. Same five-man teams they've been using lately, just scattered all around us. Every time a sentry sticks their head up, they take heavy fire. We've extinguished the wall torches, but that means we have to double up the guard to make sure no one creeps over the walls. We're already run ragged, so this isn't the most welcome news. It's like a siege laid by an armed Boy Scout troop. Doesn't make much sense."

Ethan took a deep breath and realized he had clenched his fists. He relaxed them, then rolled his shoulders to release tension. Okay, this was better than a full-on assault, but it could be a preamble to much worse. Something just felt *different* about this, though, maybe from the tone of Josh's voice but maybe his intuition had got onto something...

"Hey Josh, risk some people to take a gander with those NVGs we sent back with your ambassador, the ones our redneck engineer made up. Take a close look at a few different ones and then give me every detail—what are they carrying, how are they dressed, what gear can you see with them. The works. I may have an idea."

"Scout with night goggles. Copy that. I'll get back to you."

The air went dead, and Ethan took off the "earmuffs." He swiveled over to the nearest laptop, set up his sandbox and the other usual security protections, and linked up to one of the birds through his back door. A glance told him one precious satellite was overhead. One was enough. There was no way he'd divert one unless everyone's survival depended on it, so he said a quick prayer of thanks upstairs. Not that he really believed in God, but living with Mandy these past several months had given him cause to doubt his belief in no belief. She was tenacious and made a lot of sense, so maybe there was something to what she said... anyway, they were all in a foxhole these days so it was okay to call on God, even if it made him feel a tad embarrassed.

Ah! He was in. Without adjusting the camera, so as to avoid detection if the Mountain's people were watching, he went into the software and started sorting through the high-res images. That took a while—the files were huge, and the connection had the lag that satellite comms always did.

Then he found the one he was looking for, a shot of the Brickerville region, and began the download. Between the limited bandwidth and the sluggishness of sending data back and forth through his filters and multiple sandboxes, whatever, it would take at least a couple of minutes. Fortunately, the satellite wouldn't go out of view before he was finished. *Thanks*, he thought again, looking up, then looked back down, feeling silly. An opportunistic believer, that was him. He shook his head and shrugged.

Getting up, he stretched his legs and went to get another cold soda. Those were a huge luxury, but hell, if the fox guarding the henhouse couldn't take a chicken once in a while, what was the point? Amber would disagree, of course, but she was above-ground doing family stuff with other families. She'd never know so it couldn't hurt.

When he got back from the cold locker, the image had finished downloading. He terminated comms with the satellite and, scanning as he went, he pulled it out of the remote sandbox, transferred it to the isolated bunker PC, and loaded it into the rather odd program used with that satellite's file format. It was a sluggish, bloated beast of an application, embodying everything he had come to expect from multi-million dollar code-monkey projects developed by Uncle Sam. Hairball garbage coding, of course, but the app worked and he had it, so...

There. He zoomed in on Brickerville and noted the timestamp. Only twenty minutes old. After it finished re-rendering at the zoom he needed, he saw a much clearer picture of the situation—no pun intended. Damn, sometimes it sucked to be right. For every couple of teams camped out, there was a horse-drawn covered wagon, with kids and people in civilian-looking clothes. Cooking fires, wooden outhouses at each camp's periphery, the works. This wasn't an attack, it was a migration, and Brickerville was right in the swarm's way.

Ethan began furiously writing notes about the images he was seeing and waited for Josh to get back on the radio.

* * *

2100 HOURS - ZERO DAY +154

Cassy watched over Ethan's shoulder as the hacker went through his meticulous notes and images while Michael stood watching over his other shoulder. She was glad Michael had been free when Ethan asked her to come down there—they'd need Michael's more experienced take on the information.

Michael's face was unreadable as he looked at the images and notes Ethan had made. "Yes, those are mostly invaders, but with families. This isn't an attack formation like anything I've seen before. Women, children, wagons... I agree with you, Ethan. They're moving in to stay."

Cassy let out a deep breath, full of frustration and fatigue. Why did these idiots have to invade a settlement when there were so many empty farms around? They didn't act wild, like the earlier cannibal raiders had. Did these problems never stop? But of course they didn't. The world had been sent back to the dark ages, and they were indeed dark.

"Fine, I agree," she said. "I don't want to, but it seems clear it's hostile. An invasion. But you said 'mostly' they were invaders. What do you mean?"

Michael looked to Ethan, who gave him a nod, and Michael said, "The 'vader uniforms are different from ours. I'd expect every fighter, male or female, to be in a uniform. Barring that, any women not in uniform should be in traditional garb. Burkas, veils, whatever was their local custom. But here we have women in pants and shirts, but not in uniform. Plus, I figure there aren't too many blonde Arabs or Koreans."

Ethan added, "It could be assimilation of the locals. Both the Romans and the Huns did that as policy."

"Or they could be slaves the invaders brought along. The early U.S. did that, too," Michael commented.

Sure enough, Cassy noted, the image did show a few blonde women, or at least women with very light hair. So the invaders had traitors or slaves with them and that, too, suggested they intended to stay. "And right now they have Brickerville surrounded," she commented. "But they're not approaching and not going far around the town. Given your experience, what does that tell us, Michael?"

"Either their destination is close or they're in too much hurry to give Brickerville a wide berth, so they plan to roll over them, I imagine."

Cassy said, "Ethan, you said there's been increasing activity lately, and Brickerville was already under a low-intensity siege when Jaz and Choony went there last time. Their ambassador said the same thing. They aren't in a rush or they'd have moved on by now. Process of elimination..."

Michael said, "It could be they're just loitering in the area, waiting for something. Some surprise they know is coming. Damn."

Ethan set down his notes and rubbed his chin. "That sounds ominous. What could they be waiting for? And should we be getting ready for it, too?"

Cassy rubbed her neck with one hand, feeling the stress build in her neck and shoulders. The unknown was pretty terrifying when everything and anything could kill you, and too much of it actively wanted to. She'd have bet ten bucks that Adamstown joined the invaders. They'd come from the east, so they had to go through Adamstown to get here, and Adamstown collaborators might explain the civilians traveling with them better than the idea of bringing slaves with them on a migration. Maybe Adamstown quislings were running the wagons for them and such.

"We should definitely get ready for something, Ethan," Cassy said. "This isn't just random. Let's get an inventory done, and give me a list of who we should bring down into the bunker if things go sideways on us."

* * *

0700 HOURS - ZERO DAY +155

Ethan was just finishing his first cup of coffee for the morning, made with yesterday's coffee grounds. Soon there wouldn't be any coffee left, and he'd be stuck drinking some weird concoction made with ground-up walnut shells and cattail pollen or something. That would be a sad day.

The radio buzzed, alerting Ethan to incoming chatter, and he set down his mug to pick up the mic, waiting. "Bravo One to Charlie One, are you there?"

Ethan figured it would be Josh over in Brickerville, hopefully with the results of his little intel-gathering mission, suggested by Ethan after the briefing with Cassy last night. "Charlie Two here, go ahead."

"We sent a scout team over the wall last night with those night-vision goggles you people made. Our guys got back an hour ago and we just finished debriefing them."

"No casualties, I hope. So what's the verdict?"

"The 'vaders wiped out that little religious nutjob compound north of us in the woods. Your people had to sneak around it—I'm sure you remember it from their report when they got back with the gasifier. Those people were no loss. Anyway, they're all dead. The 'vaders left that area, though, because the house and one of the garages got burned down during the fight. Their storage barn was cleaned out, but the 'vaders never found their underground storage."

"I take it your scouts did?"

"Of course. Turns out those wackos had a whole armory in there. Nothing too spectacular, but a couple of nifty toys. My advisors and I came up with a plan, but we'll need Clanholme's help to pull it off."

* * *

Just after breakfast, Cassy put her dishes in the first water-filled 55-gallon drum, which was kept at a slow simmer by means of a rocket stove built into a Dakota fire-hole. It wasn't the most efficient rocket stove setup, but far better than just setting the drum over a normal fire. Not that the Clan lacked wood, but heat was a resource. Why be wasteful?

Looking up from the drum, she spotted Ethan approaching the Clan's outdoor kitchen area. He saw her and walked briskly toward her. She hoped it would be good news this time. Last night's revelations about the invaders moving into the area like hostile settlers were unsettling.

As he drew up to her, Ethan smiled. "So, Brickerville has a plan, and I think you and Michael will like it, but they need our help."

"Walk with me," Cassy said, and turned toward her house, their headquarters during the daytime.

Ethan fell into step beside her. "You remember that religious compound Jaz and Choony had to sneak by on their way to the Falconry? Well, the 'vaders wiped them out and burned most of it to the ground. Brickerville used some of those NVGs we sent them for their scouts to check it out and they found the compound's armory. Get this—it was loaded. They found five Soviet-made RPGs with a couple dozen rounds, which is great, but without working enemy tanks it's not crucial. Better yet, they found crates of dynamite with all the fixin's. They can string up tripwires, daisychain homemade mines, whatever. But I'm saving the best for last."

Cassy grinned. That was fantastic news for Brickerville! What to do with all that? Knowing Josh, their leader, Brickerville probably already had ideas. The problem with the way the invaders were arranged was that you couldn't just attack them. They were too spread out, but could respond in force pretty quickly if anyone attacked their perimeter. Only a major, concerted attack could hurt them, and in that event they were well set up to just scatter and melt away into the woods or whatever. "So what's the best part?"

Reaching the front door to Cassy's house, Ethan opened it and held the door for her before replying. As they went inside, he said, "Drones. They had two dozen good-sized drones still in the packaging down there in the underground armory. The kind that can carry about a kilogram each. They have cameras on them that feed back to a display on the controllers. They sound like the 3DR Solo quad drones, pretty much the best prosumer drones around. Too bad they didn't get a bunch of 3DR's Pixhawk boxes. They can run off GPS, which is still working, and they could have programmed all those drones from the compound and just sent them on their way."

"Wow, you are such a geek, Ethan," she laughed. But that had definitely gotten Cassy's attention. An amazing find that presented some new challenges. "So, they either have to sneak out two dozen people to use the drones from the compound, or sneak all that material back into Brickerville through the scattered camps. Either way could invite a disaster. Michael says it would be all but impossible to sneak through the invader positions with the way they're set up, at least not with cargo or so many people."

"Yep. But Josh has a plan to deal with that, and he needs our help. He wants us to raid all along their southern and western perimeter, hard enough to draw away squads from elsewhere. Then Josh will send out half a dozen people with small human-pulled wagons, like rickshaws, and load them up for retrieval back to Brickerville."

"Not a bad idea," Cassy said. "At least it sounds workable. But Michael will have to give the final word on it. I should think we can spare about a dozen people for that, probably send our Marines out. They've been acting restless lately and it's right up their alley. I don't think that'll open the window wide enough for the operation Josh described, though. Let's call in Michael."

Ethan sat on the couch and ran his hand through his mop of hair. She'd have to talk to him about keeping up appearances later, but now wasn't the time. "I suppose we could radio Ephrata for some people. If they aren't getting hit too hard right now by Hershey, they could maybe spare a squad of trained fighters."

"Yep. They won't want the invaders to take out Brickerville any more than we do, and they'll be eager to get that trade route to Falconry open again. After we talk to Michael, you can radio them and see what they can send our way. I think we'll also send word to Taj Mahal and see what they can spare. Time to earn their keep, I'm thinking."

Ethan grinned, and it was that infectious, boyish grin he used to show so much. Cassy loved it. "Cassy, you're really calling it Taj Mahal? I suppose it works. Those Indians we settled out there did seem plenty willing to be a part of this thing we're setting up."

Cassy shrugged. "If they hadn't, we wouldn't have settled them near us. We'd have sent them on their way to wherever. But I have to consider the good of the entire alliance we've started, not just our own good, so having them buffer both us and Liz Town just made sense, strategically."

"I don't know how it fell on *you* to be the leader of this motley alliance, but hey, it works. Either way, they're smart enough to see that their survival depends on the goodwill they'll earn, and anyway they kind of owe us. Barry will get the rest to go along. Remind 'em of how it was before they cadged a meal off us and so on."

If they didn't go along to get along Cassy would drop all assistance to them, which would probably wipe those suburbanites right out. But she wasn't about to tell Ethan that. There was no way she would allow even neutral groups to live so close to Clanholme. But she believed it wouldn't be a problem. Their leader Barry seemed like a practical man and they were heavily, emotionally invested in their new farm by now. This was a debt—Barry would see that they paid it. Just another example of how one-time everyday decisions had become matters of life and death, even if you didn't realize it right away.

* * *

1030 HOURS - ZERO DAY +155

Taggart sat hunched over his "desk" with its two oil lamps providing light as he read this week's Intel briefings—dozens of slips of paper from all over the city and a couple of typed pages of analysis from the Defense Intelligence enlisted man. Taggart couldn't remember the kid's name, but he had been in Third Company until his Intel training came to light and he had been transferred to Taggart's HQ immediately.

The majority of the sheets were clipped together into one stack, the SALUTE reports—an acronym that stood for Size, Activity, Location, Unit identification, Time, and Equipment —which had been sent in both by his battalion and by their many informers throughout the city. Organized with the most recent reports on top, he knew his Intel trooper would have the priority details put together on one of the typed sheets that accompanied today's stack.

All in all, between the SALUTEs and other intel they'd put together, the data painted an ugly picture. He grabbed the summary sheet he had set aside and flipped to page two, where there was a handwritten note that read—

525,000 Vaders (425,000 ISNA / 100,000 NKor)
300,000 Gangsters (280,000 Loy'st / 20,000 Vadist)
200,000 Militia/stragglers (175,000 Loy'st / 25,000 Vadist)

Vadists: 570,000 - Unified cmd, organized minions
Loyalists: 455,000 - Coalitions, disorganized

He didn't need the notes with the numbers. Every week the numbers grew more accurate as data was compiled, and on paper those numbers didn't look all that unpromising. His forces trailed by only one hundred thousand, and he didn't have to secure an entire base of operations large enough to manage a force that size.

In addition, most of the remaining locals were downright partisan in supporting them. Mao, Fidel, and many other guerrilla war leaders had recognized that support by the populace is always critically important for success at the guerrilla warfare that Taggart was now caught in.

But Taggart knew the numbers were misleading, mainly for the fact that nearly all the enemy were actual soldiers in a unified command structure while his own forces were scattered over the entire city. Most were either undisciplined gang members or retired and former military who were self-organized into something much like the cells of an insurrection.

Hell, they *were* the insurrectionists now. It was a good thing he had spent so much time in the Sandbox of Iraq and Afghanistan because he had gotten to see how insurrectionists did things. It was a completely different way of thinking. He smiled to remember that, in the 1700s, American colonists had fired at marching Redcoats from behind trees and rock walls, sparking British complaints about ungentlemanly behavior. Mao and Fidel didn't invent guerrilla warfare. Still, continually figuring out how to deal with the enemy in Afghanistan had taught him what not to do, here and now…

A rap at the door brought him back from his musings. "Enter."

Eagan opened the door and came in, closing it behind him and not bothering to salute here in the privacy of Taggart's office. "I brought you coffee. I also wanted to talk to you again, now that you've had a minute."

"I've been awake since oh-dark-thirty. Thanks for the coffee."

After a moment, Eagan asked for permission to speak freely, and Taggart nodded. Eagan said, "Sir, I see the movement orders you give out to the other units in our little confederation of survivor groups. I'm pretty sure I know what you're up to."

Taggart raised an eyebrow, but frankly, it wasn't much of a surprise. Of course that smart little shit would figure this out before anyone else. That was one of the things that made him a great staff sergeant, because the shitbird didn't need to have his hand held when Taggart passed him orders. "You don't approve." It was a statement, not a question.

Eagan shrugged. "What do I know? I'm not paid all this money to think, sir. But I'm still a glorified monkey, and I got that monkey curiosity. Like, why are we pushing to leave the island? We're getting stronger all the time now that we've got all these assets under us. A lot of them are going to die if your draft orders get finalized and sent, and without you coordinating all this there's a chance the resistance in the Big Apple's gonna fall apart again."

Taggart, mug in hand, stood and strolled to the large NYC wall map. The thing was littered with pushpins that had little paper labels like flags, all color-coded and with details written on them. They showed the locations of all known units, friendly or otherwise, plus a lot of caches, enemy strong points, and other Areas of Interest, or AOIs. For a moment he only stared at it, sipping his coffee. It was important to say this right so Eagan would be on board—not that he'd disobey, because behind his mouthy act he had discipline, and he trusted Taggart's judgment, but it was still better to have one of your best men pushing, not following.

Taggart said, "We know Ree is getting supplies from the mainland. If we get to the mainland, we can intercept those supplies. Our friend Dark Ryder has shown us the casualty projections for New York and as you'll recall, within six months most of New York will have eaten one another. Our people are getting enough supplies from our raids that we haven't had to do that yet, which no doubt accounts for a lot of their loyalty, but we will eventually see cannibalism here if we stay, probably starting with the gangbangers. They make up the bulk of our Manhattan army and they're the least reliable, most untrained military force possible. Loyal to themselves and no one else. Plus, they're ruthless from living in the streets. If they get hungry, they know where some of the other units are and *that makes the resistance itself* the easy prey. Things will fall apart fast after that. We don't want to be here."

Taggart watched as Eagan stared at him, unblinking and pretty clearly holding his breath. It was terrible having to shock him like that, but the force of those words would do wonders to motivate the young aide, who was also the Army's most reluctant acting staff sergeant. After a pause for it all to sink in, Taggart continued. "Moreover, I have intel that suggests the area to the northwest of us has been depopulated of survivors. It's a form of low-intensity guerrilla warfare with the practical effect of genocide or migration away by the natives. Settlers always follow migrations of that sort."

Eagan slowly nodded. His wheels were turning. "So, Ree was smart to do that because those migrants cause chaos and even more stress on all the regions surrounding us. It prevents them from organizing and trying to push through to the City center. And the now-vacated area can be easily resettled with the slaves Ree took from the city before the American EMPs happened. Almost like he knew our side would eventually be able to use EMPs in retaliation."

"Yes, almost like he knew it was all coming. Makes you think, doesn't it? The militia support that never turned up. We'd have been wiped out without Dark Ryder's warning. And Ree has set himself up now with a food production center within reach of the City, supplying his Island fortress.

Once the City's people eat each other down to a sustainable population level, nothing stands between Ree and his controlling the entire Eastern Seaboard by autumn's harvest time."

"So you want us to get out before things fall apart. And you're willing to sacrifice a lot of our forces to do it." Eagan didn't look disgusted or judgmental, but his blank expression didn't look friendly. Then again, Eagan was utterly practical. He'd heckle Taggart for it here and there, in private, but it wouldn't affect his drive or energy for the task if he bought into the need for it. Much like the kid brother Taggart usually thought of him as, he'd probably seem rebellious until the chips were down. Then he'd be fierce.

"They're dead anyway when things fall apart completely, or they will be. This way they win us some room to maneuver. Dark Ryder's analysis matches my own—he says there will be barely over half a million people left in all of New York City by next winter. I'll take as many of the trained Militia and ex-military assets with us as my analysis shows we can support in the field while still staying in command. So far it's turning out to be a surprisingly large number. We can all do better without worrying about what the street thugs get themselves into. I've had enough of them anyway."

"So what then? What will we do once we break out of this prison Ree put us in, if we manage to not die trying?"

Taggart grinned then, a wolfish expression. "The same dispersal of his assets that makes it easy to control that region on the mainland will make it easy for us to strike hard and deep, and keep them squealin' from the feelin'. Every little fortress we take gives us more guns and all its slaves. They'll be motivated partisans once they're free and fed, I'll bet my huge paycheck on it. We can start a cancer that spreads way too fast for Ree to deal with."

Taggart looked at the map again. It was a great plan, if

he could keep it secret from Ree. Eagan commented, "That means not telling anyone outside this unit about your plans. That Intel guy says he's pretty damn sure our resistance is riddled with double agents."

Taggart nodded and replied, "We don't have to tell any of them the whole truth to arrange for the militia units we trust the most to be close enough to come with us when we cross to the mainland."

Eagan nodded thoughtfully. He'd been steadily losing that "no expression" look, and Taggart knew that meant he was buying into the whole idea.

To make this work, Taggart would use the identified double agents to his own advantage by feeding them false information. When he and Eagan were done, no one would know what the hell was going on until it was a done deal and much too late to stop it. He'd be deep into Hackensack, New Jersey territory by the time Ree could organize well enough to close the window of opportunity. With luck. He had to remember that no plan ever survives the first encounter with the enemy. But you had to plan.

"We'll turn the tables on him, Eagan. Happy New Year, Ree, you little bastard. You got some big misery coming."

Eagan was grinning now. Yeah. The two of them could pull this off.

- 15 -

1100 HOURS - ZERO DAY +159

ETHAN SAT AT his computer and stared at the screen with a sly, sloppy grin. He'd been asked not to use his satellites to track Taggart's activities or the area in and around New York, but not the reason for it. He hadn't asked, and for the one satellite that had been in perfect position he simply put it into a long series of diagnostics. That would make the bird inefficient for anyone else to use, but more importantly it gave Dark Ryder the alibi he'd need to cover his own intentional negligence if the 20s should happen to wonder why Ethan hadn't alerted them to Taggart going "off the reservation" and ignoring orders.

Now he saw just why Taggart had sent the request a few days back. He called Amber in, and she padded into the "room," looking over Ethan's shoulder.

"Taggart's report—sent through our back-channel comms route—explains why he asked me to hang up the reports. Just after I told him the bird was taken care of, he got busier than a hyperactive squirrel on caffeine and meth!"

Amber snickered, and read over his shoulder. "So, first thing Taggart did was give the order to launch something he'd obviously spent some time planning, simultaneous attacks on a couple *dozen* 'vader supply stations all across the west end of the City? It couldn't be coincidence that his gangbanging cells were tasked to hit the places with tons of food awaiting transit to Ree's base on the other end of the island. He says that most of those locations ended up being guarded by 'vader forces several times the size his intel said, just as he said he suspected they might."

"Yeah. That can only mean one thing: Taggart has enemy spies in his units, *and he knew it*. He set them up for failure, and to cause a huge ruckus while they were at it. And here's the part I love—while the gangbangers held Ree's attention, a lot of his best ex-military troops attacked unimportant sites near the Hudson River using a quieter commando style. Maybe a couple *thousand* military-grade fighters. All far away from the biggest noise."

Amber grinned and said, "I get it. Let me guess—once all hell broke loose, he crossed the Hudson with his best peeps?"

"Yep. Crossed the Hudson with few thousand experienced troops. Pushed straight through to the Hackensack Meadowlands Conservation and Wildlife Area and vanished for a while."

Amber said, "I can only imagine how rough it would be to try to get through that swamp with gear and rations and whatever loot they could carry."

"Not to mention the looks on the faces of people he left behind when they figure out what he did. As for the gangbangers in that southern group, he must have been so sorry to lose those guys..."

Amber snorted and Ethan grinned up at her. They both knew the gangbangers had caused trouble for Taggart more than once. But Taggart had been smart to set up his short-range radio to skip over to another radio, still in New York, rigged as a repeater. Anyone tracking his signal would likely think he was still in the City, or at least be mighty confused about where he really was. The ruse wouldn't last forever, of course, but long enough. Or so he hoped, and crossed his fingers for Taggart. More superstition, he knew, but he did it anyway.

Amber sat in the chair next to him and started going through the messages in earnest. Ethan rose and went to get something to eat while she read, then sat and watched episodes of *iZombie* from his stash of downloaded shows and movies while he ate. Toward the end of the second episode, he heard Amber finally getting up to stretch. Well, it had been a lot of data to sift through. She came into the room and sat next to him, and he paused Episode 2. He watched her with a half-smile, waiting for the moment when all that data assembled itself in her mind into a good picture of Taggart's activities. Yes! There is was. He grinned up at her.

Amber cleared her throat and then said, "Okay. In the past two days, organized teams of his new army—his elite, really—burst out from the Wildlife area in all directions, but especially north, and with Ree's decentralized structure the 'vaders didn't have anything that could stop them. His people pushed far north into the Hackensack area and discovered some of the slave labor camps you mentioned before. He also found some of Ree's little fortified areas, one of the notes said. I guess Ree used them to project power in the region without actually having to guard everything. But they did have pretty good armories, which Taggart's people seized."

"Right," Ethan said. "Taggart freed thousands of slaves and let Ree arm them for him. Taggart probably left thank-you notes to Ree just to rub it in. I would have, anyway. Then he sent those newly freed slaves out on fresh raids elsewhere in the area. I kind of picture it like, a creeping flood of blue dots overwhelming red dots, turning them blue as well, releasing and arming more slaves kinda like zombies spreading. Or like a nuclear chain reaction, growing exponentially. Ree won't be able to stop it now that it's started." He grinned at the thought.

Amber was giggling. "Zombies? Really? That's what you came up with... You are just the cutest geek ever." She reached over to pinch his cheek.

"Hey," Ethan protested as he dodged away, his tone sounding wounded but still wearing a grin. Then a thought struck him. "That's a pretty good description, actually, because everything they didn't use, take over, or take with them, they burned. Everything's lit up now across the whole urban sprawl from Hoboken in the south to Garfield in the north, and his report says it turned into a firestorm. So it's spreading and growing all by itself now. I doubt it'll burn out until everything between the Hudson and Passaic rivers is toast. Ree won't be able to reclaim it anytime soon."

Amber frowned. Of course it was sad to burn whole cities like that, but with the fire and the chaos, the invaders couldn't even react directly to Taggart's assault—they had to clear out and salvage what gear and supplies they could if they wanted to survive the winter, and that left no time for hunting guerrillas. Brutal, maybe, but he bet the freed slaves cheered at the sight.

"Smile, honey," Ethan crowed. "That sumbitch Ree is going to realize pretty soon that it's no guerrilla operation—it's Taggart off the island. It's a mirror image of the way the 'vaders are doing it now around Brickerville. Wouldn't you just love to be a fly on Ree's wall when they figure that one out?"

A beep from the computer area interrupted their conversation and Ethan got up to check, leaving Amber in the other room. When he got to the computer, however, he saw it was a chat request from Watcher One, whom Ethan figured was his "handler" for the 20s, and through them, for General Houle back west at the Mountain. He let out a frustrated breath. They couldn't have waited twenty minutes for him to finish watching *iZombie*?

He hollered out that he'd be a minute, and went through the authentication and decoding routines. Then the window finally popped up—

Watcher1 >> *Dark Ryder, respond...*

Ethan gritted his teeth. Ugh. That guy just got on his nerves for some reason.

D.Ryder >> *Go ahead*
Watcher1 >> *Need SITREP on NYC status ASAP pls*
D.Ryder >> *Aff. What's up?*
Watcher1 >> *SITREP please. We've noticed some concerning chatter.*

Well. That was interesting news. It meant that the 20s had at least some minimal way of checking radio and maybe Net traffic from New York even though Watcher One was, to Ethan's best guess, somewhere down in Virginia. Another player? Maybe a secret channel into Ree's HQ?

D.Ryder >> *Copy. I'll write up and send ASAP, but basically he vanished. You-Know-Who did some big op while I wasn't looking w/no warning, then went 2 ground. Still trying 2 piece it 2gether.*
Watcher1 >> *Neg. A friend hacked a bird! Haxxor teh wurld, ikr? Says New Jersey's burning. Got another shortwave radiohead in the City who sez r guy is broadcasting from in-city. Not sure what 2 make of all that. C'mon, Ryder, ur slippin! I win!*

Ethan caught himself just in time to not reply to the taunting. Old hacker competition was a habit that died hard. Yet that was interesting information by itself; the 20s had access to at least one satellite—though right now there were two that could be taking snapshots, including his main-use one—and he'd have to be much more careful to cover his tracks in the future. What Watcher One said about a HAM operator in New York *could* be true, conceivably, but that seemed unlikely. The Big Apple had gone silent after the second wave of EMPs, so far as Ethan had seen. It was probably all disinformation from start to end, so let it go...

> ***D.Ryder*** >> *Enuf lolz, u cant beat me! I'll figure it out b4 u do and send teh report. Weird about that fire tho, tell me if u hear more. Dark Ryder out.*

Ethan frowned, then stood and took a deep breath. Putting a smile on his face, he walked back into the other room to finish watching his show with Amber. She wasn't down in the bunker with him nearly as much as he'd have liked because she had responsibilities and a child who needed her as much as he did and who had "dibs" on her main attention. So he was determined to spend what time he had with her well. Especially, he would not hunch over his computer with his back turned to her for hours again. He would not, *would not*, risk driving her away.

* * *

0400 HOURS - ZERO DAY +160

Cassy walked with Michael as he inspected their "troops." For some, such as the full squad of his Marines assigned to this mission, the title of "troop" was apt. For the others, well, everyone still alive probably knew how to use a rifle. Anyone who didn't have enough discipline to follow orders was either dead or still hiding in isolation somewhere Out There, she mused. Her Clanners were tough as nails by now, and every one of them combat veterans, so the dozen going with the Marines were capable in their own right. They'd all been issued one of the Clan's irreplaceable M4 rifles for the mission.

The twenty-two Clanner troops were joined by eight men and women from Taj Mahal. Their leader, Barry, wasn't in the group, but Cassy hadn't needed to pressure him to send people for this. The man clearly understood that they were either party to the region's affairs or they wouldn't be welcome or supported there—a practical man indeed.

Michael and the thirty-something troops were about to head out in the predawn hours, through freezing temperatures and some lingering icy snow, to meet up with however many people Liz Town had sent for this Op. Liz Town's numbers would depend on how much pressure they were under at the moment from the monsters out of Hershey, but it could range anywhere from a four-man team to twice what the Clan had mustered. Cassy was hopeful they'd send more rather than fewer, because Hershey was rumored now to be plague-stricken and had more pressing business than making life difficult for everyone else in their neighborhood.

As they walked, apart from the troops, Cassy said to Michael, "So you won't know your exact tactics until the meet-up and you see what people and gear Liz Town sent?"

"That's about the size of it, but the general plan stays the same. Only the details are up in the air." To the assembled troops he said, in that loud but not-really-yelling command voice of his that carried so effortlessly, "Double-check your ammo, then check your neighbor's pack—I'm not losing anyone tonight because someone was too stupid to put an assault bag on right!"

"Wish I could get that tone right. It doesn't seem like it should carry so far, but we hear you even over the noise of battle."

Michael shrugged. "Just something you eventually pick up when you're trying to herd a bunch of cats in a firefight. That's what it feels like in battle—cat-herding."

"Just think, no one will ever look that video up on YouTube again. Or see a commercial, for that matter. I miss the Super Bowl."

Michael didn't reply for a moment, while they all walked toward the northern edge of Clanholme, but finally he said, "Just between us, if it looks too hairy, I'm pulling out. I'm not going to sacrifice all of us to save Brickerville if it would only be a futile gesture. Wish us luck, and if I don't come back, make sure Tiffany never gets remarried."

Cassy smirked along with him at the sad little joke. The danger of not coming back was very real. "I swear they'll be taken care of for as long as there is a Clanholme, Michael. But come back, okay? We don't have to destroy the invaders —we only have to let Brickerville get those supplies and smuggle out as many fighters as they've decided they can spare. They do no good holed up behind those walls. Once we get them out, that's when we'll plan the battle that'll deal with this enemy properly."

* * *

Nestor walked with Michael and Mueller through the morning haze. They headed northwest, keeping off Highway 72. It would have been easier going on the roadway, but also easier to snipe at if any 'vaders were creeping around. "I've never been to the Pennsylvania Ren Faire," Nestor said, imagining castles and people in pantaloons.

"Don't get your hopes up," Michael said. "I saw one accidentally in California when I was stationed at Pendleton, got dragged into it actually, and it was pretty silly. Cardboard castles and people trying not to use the word 'cellphone' when telling some other geek in tights to set their phone to silent." Michael grinned at the memory.

Well, that was a bit disappointing. Nestor asked, "So why are we going there, again?"

"It's where Liz Town wanted us to rendezvous with the unit they're sending. I guess there's a survivor group there that's a new ally to the Lizzies, one of the groups Cassy just added to the master map. Ethan wouldn't tell me much about the group, but he was grinning like an idiot when he told me where we'd meet up. All he said was that it would probably be weird for a guy like me. I'm trying not to imagine dudes with swords wearing feathered caps or some crap. If I hear one guy try to ask about my rifle in fake medieval gibberish, I'm going to have to pop him in the mouth. And shoot his friends."

Nestor chuckled. Of course Michael wouldn't do that, but the image was hilarious. "I doubt anyone has time for weird geek hobbies like that anymore. Maybe someday."

Michael gave Nestor an odd look, then grinned. "Not much farther now, Nestlé."

"Ha! Nestlé... Funny guy. Is that my Ren Faire name, then? That would make you what, 'Melchior'?"

Michael gave him a playful punch to the shoulder, and they kept walking. So far, Nestor figured Michael to be just about the nicest, kindest Clanner he'd met. Most of them were nice, but Michael never had a hint of judgment or doubt. He just seemed self-assured enough to take people as they were and had no use for suspicion when he could probably kill almost any man he met, one-on-one.

Maybe half an hour later, they converged with Highway 72—Lebanon Road—and a smaller crossroad at the edge of what looked like a vast forest. The terrain had been growing woodier as they'd traveled, so that wasn't a surprise. Ahead, on the far side of the highway, stood a large white building with a cross on the roof, some sort of church. Across from the church was a car dealership. Nestor frowned at that— millions of dollars in inventory that would never work again, for a civilization now gone. They might as well have been alien artifacts. Future archeologists would ponder the circuit boards and conclude they were religious icons of some sort. Maybe they'd be right... in a way.

Michael called for the unit to gather, abandoning their traveling pattern of keeping strung out in twos and threes. When they'd all rallied, he told them quietly, "Alright, people, we're to meet up at that white building, which was a Mennonite church before all this. It's been fortified, so I want weapon discipline all around—keep your rifles slung and pointed *away* from them. Intel says these guys are trigger-happy because they get raided a lot. That building is this survivor group's southern outpost, guarding the road that goes through the AOI. Form up in a column, three even lines, and we'll march in. I want to impress them."

The ten Marines stood at the front of each line, in perfect order like this was second nature to them. Nestor found himself toward the front of the first line in the column, behind the four Marines who led it, near where Michael stood off to the side calling, "Forward! March!"

It took only a few minutes for the column—precise in the front, more ragged in the rear—to march to the road and then follow it the last hundred yards to the church. They turned "left oblique," making a sort of half-turn, and marched into the church's parking lot. Michael called a halt. After that, they stood in line and waited for those inside to figure out what they were going to do next.

Shortly after, a tall woman came out of the building, followed by a man a little shorter than her. They both wore the distinctive leather jackets spray-painted blue that had become the hallmark of Liz Town's warriors. Nestor had never seen a Liz Towner come through Clanholme who hadn't been wearing one, actually. As she approached, Nestor watched as Michael approached her and her partner, and when they met, they shook hands. The three talked amongst themselves, but Nestor couldn't hear anything they were saying. Still, the woman smiled, so that was promising. From everything he'd heard about the Lizzies, it could be a crapshoot whether they'd be openly friendly or not. They were a weird bunch, he'd heard.

Then Michael came back to the column and dismissed everyone from formation. "Our Lizzie friends say we'll be led into the relative security of the settlement, which they call the 'Barony of Renfar,' and we'll spend the rest of the day either taking care of gear or getting to know the Liz Town unit. They're already settled inside."

They were led further down Lebanon Road and Nestor saw that the edge of the giant forest he'd seen was really just a thin band of trees, like a windbreak that stretched away to the east to join what looked like a real, and denser, natural forest. So it was really kind of a privacy screen, too. Smart to have left those trees alone when they cut firewood.

As they walked deeper into Barony territory he saw that to the left of the road, the actual forest stretched away unbroken—only a building along the side of the road broke it up visually. The building looked like a large pole barn with an attached wooden tower, obviously built pre-EMP, but he could see that the many windows up the side of the tower had been sandbagged. The large street sign outside proclaimed to be the "Divine Swine Authentic BBQ." Their guide told them that it was now where traders doing business with the Barony were welcomed, but that the rest of the Barony's territory was more or less off-limits to visitors unless they had a good reason to come in.

The Clan, of course, had good reason, and so they were led over to the right of the road. Vast open, snowy fields lay between the road and a cluster of buildings that had once been some sort of winery. Now it looked to have been turned over to farming uses, with everything stacked and ready for sowing in the spring.

Their Barony and Lizzie hosts led them past the winery and into the grounds of the Pennsylvania Renaissance Faire proper. Nestor was thrilled to see an old-style castle wall on the right, complete with stone towers that now had sandbagged positions at the top, and he noted that they were manned. Ahead on the left lay a fortified manor house, or rather, someone's interpretation of a medieval manor. It looked grand, on a small scale.

Their guide said, "That's where the Baron lives, and holds court. Michael, after you get your people settled in, he would like to meet you. Just find your way back here and someone will let you in."

The little roadway then turned slightly to the right, where they saw a massive double-door gateway with stone walls stretching off to either side. The gate was open but the wall didn't enclose anything. It would have been simple enough to just go around it. How disappointing, thought Nestor. They went through the gate and followed a trail to the right. There, a long row of faux-medieval houses and shops lined the pathway. "These are now our homes, so if you ever visit one of our gentry you'd likely be staying with them in one of those."

The branching trail they followed next led to the north and ended amidst more shops-turned-houses. Except here, many had been turned into actual shops for woodworking or forging, and others looked like the group used them for storage.

"Okay people, you are welcome to wander around and just basically make yourself at home. There are merchants here selling meals, the going rate is one bullet for a drink, five for a meal, or whatever else you can barter. Knock before you go inside, but nothing is really off-limits here except the Baron's manor itself."

The nearby sign proclaimed in medieval script that this was the "Queen's Market Square." Nestor glanced around and saw Michael making rounds, talking to clusters of Clanners, Indians, and Lizzies. Once he'd talked to everyone he left, heading back toward the manor.

Nothing to do now but pass time, Nestor figured, but heck, he could kill a couple hours at least just wandering around and gaping at the scenery, looking for geeks in tights. Not many of those left by now, he'd bet, but if they were anywhere, they'd be here.

He was only a little disappointed that all the people he saw wore normal clothes and guns, not Ren Faire garb and swords. Sad—just another victim of the end of the world.

* * *

0545 HOURS - ZERO DAY +161

Nestor crouched in the early morning damp and chill, nearly shoulder-to-shoulder with the two people he'd been teamed with: a Taj Mahal woman and one of the Lizzies' men. He wished he'd been teamed with one of the Marines, but he understood Michael's decision to put them in their own units —the Marines were taking the more difficult targets and they were trained for this. Mixing up units with other groups' people was dangerous, but it would also spread the risk if one unit got wiped out. And it'd teach the groups to trust one another. Like a joint military exercise.

All three of them held coffee cans with what looked like battery terminals tack-welded to the lids. His was the one with ball bearings and glass—the "shrappenator," as he thought of it. For the other two, one held a can that would produce a huge quantity of smoke and the other one, he'd been told, would make a large cloud of some kind of poison gas. Chlorine, perhaps. Thin wires extended to spools behind them. Each team had been tasked with creeping in and emplacing the explosives, not directly within a 'vader camp but fifty or so yards away. Close enough to be dangerous work, far enough to encourage some optimism. They could do it.

Five teams including Nestor's were running emplacements. He crawled on his belly, only half-dressed to reduce noise. This really sucked... But the wind was a perfect two or three miles per hour toward an encampment just east of him, and the gas was likely to be the most effective. The smoke would cause chaos and limit visibility while the Killer Teams, as he thought of them, would roam the battlefield slaughtering everyone they found. When the gas hit one or two of these little encampments it would create major coughing confusion, but it would dissipate before it hit Brickerville itself, he realized, and checked that worry off his mind.

The Lizzies had only brought a dozen fighters, bringing the force's total up to about forty-five including Michael and the Lizzie leader, but they'd also brought a damn wagonload of these "IEDs," or improvised explosive devices. His shrappenator was the hardest to emplace, as it had to be aimed—the end opposite the terminals needed to be pointed at the encampment, like a big shotgun shell.

Yards behind him, the Indian woman finished setting her canister and gave the thumbs-up. "Hurry up, Clanner," the Liz Town man whispered.

Nestor didn't reply but simply focused on finishing the task right. This was his third emplacement, and each time he'd taken the longest. Well, if they didn't like it then let *them* implant the shrappenators. He double-checked the wire connections and nodded. "Done, let's get out of here," he whispered.

The three of them once again crawled on their bellies away from this latest 'vader camp. It took quite a while to get back to his unit's rally point, out of view behind a low, gently sloped hill, and once back, he made a beeline for his clothes and gear. He'd probably have hypothermia from this little outing, but someone had to do it and he'd had to learn to sneak around back when those townspeople had been chasing him. Now, if they got caught, it would start the fight before the alliance was ready. But they'd gotten away clean. Like Michael said, always pick the time and place for a fight if you can. Well, they'd done that in spades. He wore a grim little smile on his face as he put on warmer clothing, the team's emplacements finished.

Soon the 'vader troops would start to rouse and wander out and about. It was in that first early morning confusion, when camp noises picked up but people weren't yet awake enough to find their shoes, much less react quickly to an attack, that they would set off their devices and the Marines would begin their open assault of some choice 'vader camps that hadn't gotten their own IEDs, while the civilian squads dealt with gassed, half-blind people in camps hit by the shrappenators and the clouds of smoke and gas. They all had gas masks from some Clan stockpile, too. It seemed like the Clan always had a handful of whatever was needed. Whoever set it up had prepared for the end of the world, it seemed, though he took care never to ask about it since the Clan obviously wanted to keep it hidden. He didn't blame them. No sense advertising what they had.

It felt like only ten minutes later when, still shivering, Nestor noticed an increase of activity in the camps where they'd planted IEDs. He picked up his M4 and met up with his two teammates, and the groups rallied around Michael for a quick, final battle briefing.

Once everyone was in place, with the Marines taking a knee in front of him in perfect order, Michael cleared his throat. "Alright, listen up. I'll lay this out in terms you'll all understand. We're about to attack the enemy. We're organized in teams of three, except the jarheads. They'll take the south flank. We aren't here for the civilians! Don't kill them, but don't let your guard down, either. They're aiding the enemy, remember that! No, our only objective, besides to kill as many of these invading sonsabitches as possible, is to pose enough of an obvious, real threat to draw them away from Brickerville's west side. That should be no problem with the toys Liz Town brought," he said with a nod to the Lizzie leader.

Michael continued, "You must remember to *fire and move*. Don't just stand there shooting. It's dark out and your muzzle flashes will give these assholes a target, so once you shoot, whether you hit anything or not, quickly move at least ten feet away—and for God's sake, *not* right to where your teammate was standing. Clear a camp before moving on if you can, but if they get their shit together before you kill them all then move along to the next—strike and fade, then strike and fade. We're greatly outnumbered so *do not slug it out*." He looked around at each group, to drive in that point, before he continued.

"Next up—when you hear the whistles coming from behind you, that means it's time to fall back to your individual retreat rally points, which we'll give out before we attack. Any questions, yet?"

No one spoke up, so Michael began to call out the units and assign their first targets and tell which fallback point they were to rally at. Once rallied, they would all hightail it into the woods north of them and get the hell out of the area. Brickerville's available troops would meet up with two of the Marines somewhere else and then find their way to the unit, assuming anyone lived through this.

Nestor nodded, but had other thoughts running through his mind. It would be a shame to die now, after surviving all this time despite the Other always messing up a good thing and all the bad things that had happened to him since the EMPs.

Finally almost warm again, Nestor and his two teammates double-checked their weapons and ammunition, then moved to their insertion point. Nestor had no doubt it would be impossible to miss the go signal, not with the Liz Town toys starting the party. They settled in and waited, and nervous sweat dampened his forehead. He just wasn't wired for combat...

Boom... Nestor felt the thump in his chest a split-second before he saw the cause. Along hundreds of yards on the front "line," such as it was, brilliant flares of light lit up the night. At this distance the brightest points were small but the tiny points still burnt into his eyes, leaving a ghostlike after-effect. A dozen screams from the front line encampments announced that the shrappenators had done their evil work quite well, and in an instant more screams from deeper within the enemy-held territory surprised him. Nestor took a moment to realize that all that shrapnel didn't just stop just because it missed the nearest target.

He wished the Marines were there with him, but the thought was fleeting. Then he was moving, rushing forward in a low crouch with his rifle welded to his shoulder, eyes sweeping in the dark looking for *prey*. His two companions were with him, and all along the line a dozen other teams like his would be rushing into the night with killing on their minds.

He felt frightened, but not like he thought he would—nothing like the terror that crippled him when he hid in the toolshed during the Adamstown raid... No, now he felt like... a wolf among sheep. That was how it felt. The feeling confused him but he shoved it away.

Move forward... Well duh, he was already doing that. His eyes swept back and forth, held wide open to try to gather as much light as they could, looking for a sheep, a human sheep. Ahead of him, the masses of thick smoke, visible for being blacker than the black of night, were moving in the same direction at about the same speed he and the others were moving. In a moment they were washing over the 'vader tents, preventing the enemy from seeing the wolves rushing toward them.

He heard a sick noise from about twenty feet ahead, and as the smoke wall continued to advance it left behind three figures—two men on their hands and knees, and what was left of a woman. Her entire head down to her left arm were just *gone*, clearly having taken a direct hit from someone's shrappenator. The two men were coughing, but it was a wet, bubbling noise like nothing he'd heard before—it must have been the gas attack that had done that...

Good. Fuck them up, now. What the hell? Where had the voice come from? Well, it was right. Nestor fired one round into the first man's head and he collapsed. The Indian woman beside him took out the other. They ran into the encampment and didn't slow down. Another opportunity would be revealed ahead somewhere.

More sheep to hunt. Nestor's head snapped left, then

right, looking for whoever was talking, but there was no one. He kept running, staying near his partners, and the cloud drifted ahead of them. *It's always darkest before I fucking kill you...*

"Shut up!" rasped Nestor without thinking. He glanced at the Indian woman, who was closest to him, but she hadn't seemed to notice. *Nice ass on that one.*

Damn that voice. The very tone of it, ringing in his head, made him shiver with contempt. It was evil, he could hear the devil in it, and if he saw who said it, he'd gladly kill them. No one who sounded like that could deserve to live.

There! Left! Party time, man.

Nestor looked and barely made out the brief glint of something metal. He swung his barrel that way and double-tapped—a cry of pain with the first shot, cut short with the second. The Lizzie on his other side firing, his shots dropping another 'vader emerging from their tent.

Where's the third little piggy? No time to deal with that. Nestor wouldn't let himself be distracted.

Movement just ahead to the left caught his eye, but his rifle was pointed to his right. In the almost non-existent night light he saw a man rushing at him. He had a long beard and a knife, and Nestor didn't notice anything about him but those two things. A wave of panic-driven pins and needles swept from the base of his spine to his scalp—there was no way he would get a shot off before the man got to him.

As Nestor opened his mouth to scream, a pure reflex, the scene abruptly slid to the right and back, like a camera shutter snapping open then closed. Suddenly, everything was covered in a sheen of blood. The man, his knife, the ground, the faint moon that hung in the sky behind him—all bloody.

The next thing he noticed was his body moving on its own, a marionette with strings held by someone else. Instead of turning as he had tried to do, he ran straight at the invader. As the man tried to slash at him, Nestor did something he hadn't even considered. He used his right hand to thrust the butt of his rifle forward while his left hand moved the barrel up and back, and the rifle butt thrust forward like a piston, smashing into the Arab man's face with a sickening crunch.

The Arab had momentum, but the rifle butt stopped him, so his feet flew out from under him and he landed with an audible *thump* onto the ground.

Now kill him, pansy-ass.

Nestor's vision did the funny camera-shutter thing again, and the haze of blood over everything vanished. He realized he could control his movements again. The Arab's right hand thrashed around seeking the knife he'd dropped, but Nestor wasn't about to let him find it.

Two shots, just to make sure.

Nestor fired off two rounds, ending the threat. "Not because you told me to."

Twenty-six left in the mag. Don't just stand there stroking your ego, fucking move it.

Nestor heard the sound of bullets whizzing by, with the bang of being fired coming right behind them. He ducked and ran, heading north to put a low, rolling hill between him and the shooter. On the other side he found an already-cleared camp, five bodies sprawled out, so he kept running. He angled slightly easterly to head deeper into 'vader territory.

Keeping the hill on his right, he rounded it and ahead of him sat a large wagon and three small tents. All was silent, and no invaders were around—must be one of the civilian wagons. He came to a stop, listened for a moment, then crept into the camp, keeping his rifle ready.

Maybe we can find another actor for our show. Check the tents. Better yet, an actress.

Nestor checked the smallest tent, but it was empty. Likewise with the 3-person dome tent. That left only a 5-person tent, and the door flap was closed.

If you just stick your head in there, you'll be the actor. Don't be stupid.

"I wasn't," Nestor muttered. He circled the tent, considering whether to just tell anyone inside to come out, but that probably wouldn't work. Civilians inside wouldn't answer, and 'vaders would shoot at his voice—not that they'd be hiding in a tent anyway, but you never knew.

Click, the camera shutter again, and the scene looked like something from a horror movie. Blood drenched everything. Damn the Other! Nestor felt something pushing at the edges of his mind, gently at first but then with greater force. He shook from the effort of keeping the Other at bay, but it kept whispering in his mind to let go, let him handle it... Which was tempting...

The instant he thought it, he felt a *whoosh* in his mind, and knew he'd just lost the battle. Nestor was again a passenger in his own body with the Other at the wheel. To the Other, Nestor thought, *Why do I know you're here now? Before, your time was just a bunch of blank spots in my memory.*

Nestor watched in horror as the Other raised the rifle and fired into the tent with one smooth motion, and there was a scream from inside. Keeping the rifle to his shoulder, the Other slid to the right, toward the door, probably in case they shot back...

"Come out now or I burn you alive in there. Get the fuck out. Five... Four..."

From inside the tent came a woman's sob, and a man said, "Wait! We're coming out, I swear." The voice was perfect regional American English.

The Other backed up but his aim never wavered.

"Three." Obviously he wasn't going to give the occupants time to think of something stupid to try, Nestor noted.

The zipper rose and the flaps opened. With their hands up came out three women and a man—inside was the corpse of another man, blood on his chest. The four survivors filed out and looked scared. They were dirty and bruised. One of the women had a black eye, and another had a split lip, obviously where someone had struck her hard.

Of course they're scared, Nestor thought to the Other. *They have to be slaves. Free them.*

"Shut up."

The American man, hands up, drained of color. "I didn't say anything, I swear," he said, voice cracking with fear.

Nestor realized the Other was about to shoot the man and thrashed out, trying to regain control of his own body. The Other abruptly froze, and for a second their body shook as he resisted Nestor.

Not going... to let you... do this!

Click-click. The camera shutter snapped again, and Nestor found himself once again in control of his body while the Other howled in rage in his mind, practically drowning out the noise of everything going on around him, but a second later he quieted.

You gotta sleep sometime, asshole.

Nestor ignored the voice. "Who are you people and why are you here with them?"

One of the women dropped to her knees and put her face into her hands. Sobbing, she said, "They caught us outside Adamstown. Those... bastards, they *use* us for their... For their entertainment. And to carry their stuff. We're captives. For the love of God, don't kill us, please. We'll help you!"

Nestor watched them all closely, but they made no hostile moves. They were frozen like statues, no doubt eager to hear whether they'd live or die.

"Damn. If I leave you here, you're going to get yourselves killed. The 'vaders will think you're collaborators, or a risk at the very least. Grab your gear and let's get the hell out of here. I know a safe place."

Nestor paused, but they didn't move. "Did I stutter? Freakin' *move it!* We have to get out of here. Their whole damn army is coming this way." That was, after all, the entire reason for this raid, but they'd shoot the hell out of any Americans they saw.

"To the right... that's it. Now forward. See those trees way out there north of us? Head there. If you try anything or startle me, I apologize now for what I'll do to you then. Understand?"

The people muttered agreements, and moved out. Nestor told them to move faster, and they did. He trailed some twenty yards behind, a safe distance if one turned on him. They hadn't carried anything with them except for one backpack, which the man wore, so they wouldn't have a problem keeping that pace until they reached relative safety.

But what the heck would he do with them? They were kind of his responsibility now.

Kill them and get back to the script, you diva.

"Shut up. You're not welcome here." The Other was the cause of all his pain, the reason people always turned against him throughout his whole life. The reason he'd been locked up in that big building for years over a crime he didn't commit—because he *had*. It just hadn't been *him* doing it.

Now that he knew the Other was there, maybe it could be useful. Somehow he had gained an upper hand over the Other. But the Other was better suited much of the time, here in this "dark new world," as Cassy put it. Could he ever go back to the Clan, knowing what he now knew? The Other could escape at any moment, and what would happen then? The Clanners were good people and didn't deserve to have a time bomb among them. And Cassy would want to help, but would she? She'd either let him stay, which would be moral but foolish, or she'd kill him to protect the Clan. That'd be the smart move, as far as Nestor was concerned. Maybe it was time for a new plan.

- 16 -

1145 HOURS - ZERO DAY +163

LTC TAGGART WIPED some of the grime off his face with his sleeve and stretched his back. Eagan was going from body to body, finishing off any who survived. They'd bury or burn the bodies later, to help control the battlefield stench. He hadn't expected to get hit by 'vaders here in his field HQ, and it had been a bloody affair. Of the platoon with him, most of whom were used as runners to bring orders to the units down below during the battle, maybe twenty still lived. That was bad, but finally they'd taken out almost every one of the attackers, some forty of the bastards.

"Eagan, you shitbird, stop slacking and get on that radio. We got privates for that."

"I *am* a private, Sir, Sergeant Lieutenant Colonel General, Sir."

Taggart let the wiseass remark go. Eagan was his staff sergeant whether he wanted to wear the insignia or not. "I need updates to adjust the map," Taggart said with a motion toward the wooden picnic table. The map laid out on it was held down by dozens of colored bits of wood that represented various units. It was about as old-school as you could get, but in this day and age it still worked. "So get runners out to the units without radios."

Taggart looked back toward the map, then down to the city below, visualizing the details on the map as they would look in the real city it represented. The Battle of Hackensack was brutal, no doubt about it, and had lasted a full day and a half. Comm problems had jeopardized the whole battle in the first few hours, but he had adapted on the fly and come up with the runners. Reinventing basic command skills of a century past was rough, especially when any mistake could be deadly. It would have been nice to go through OCS for the bits of history that officer training would have given him, but his "field promotions" hadn't allowed for that. Necessity, meet invention.

Eagan sat back at the radio station and fumbled with the headset. "Once we liberate the slaves in this city, you'll be a Full Bird. Who would have thought you'd be a colonel someday? Not me. Sir."

"Nor me, believe that. Uncle Sam doesn't care what rank we want, though. Isn't that right, Staff Sergeant? Let me know when we're all caught up."

All joking aside, Taggart didn't much care for the rank-inflating effect this war had on him. Life was a lot simpler as an NCO, but someone had to command and, until he found someone better, the job was his out of necessity. He had managed to keep this show running without any of the tools that were considered critical only six months ago, when the world was nice and bad things happened *somewhere else*. He had once defended a nation that had the luxury of debating whether the military was really necessary and had taken pride in standing between them and the bad things in that world so they'd have the privilege of chattering about such topics over lattes and croissants.

Taggart let out a long, frustrated breath. While Eagan

was coordinating runners and getting everything updated, Taggart went to look at the map again to work on planning an attack on the slave compound. Three thousand slaves were down there waiting for liberation. By recent experience, he figured half would join him, doubling his command to two brigades. Almost a division. Half of the rest would wander off in twos and threes to go guerrilla, and probably sink into banditry, but he could worry about that later. The remainder would either want to go try to find lost loved ones, were too afraid to leave, or were too worn out to be of use even to themselves. And then there were the sick and the dying left untreated by the invaders. It was a moral headache he had come to dread, and he felt like a mass murderer after every conquest when he had to order his units to move out. He couldn't leave much food behind—combat effectiveness was his first priority—so those hundreds, the lost and the lame, would likely die, a fact that invaded his dreams many nights.

He suddenly noticed Eagan standing beside him, silently. When Taggart raised an eyebrow, Eagan said, "All updated. We'll have the map updated shortly but it's moot. The enemy is on the run, and we're seizing their assets faster than the IRS. Our boys and girls are having a party splitting up the loot." Taggart felt Eagan's hand on his shoulder. "The only knot of real resistance left is the one you're standing there dreading, my friend."

"I should be more careful about being so easy to read," Taggart muttered, his unfocused gaze still on the map. "Bad for morale."

"Screw that," Eagan said. "You're still just human like the rest of us. But don't worry, the others don't know that and can't read you like I can, sir. We've been fighting together too long." Eagan shifted his weight. "Command has got to suck. I know I hate the stripes that have been forced upon me but I do the job because somebody has to do it. And guess what?

You aren't a special snowflake. You're in the same boat. But you do your best."

"I'm unique like everybody else but I'd be an awfully dark snowflake, Eagan. Bad simile."

"That's a metaphor, sir. Why they put you in charge, I'll never know."

"You want the job, shitbird?"

Eagan only laughed, and Taggart watched the kid turn and walk back to the radio.

I'd trade places with you if you'd let me, Taggart thought. I'm barely keeping this together, and we're going nowhere but uphill any time soon.

* * *

1300 HOURS - ZERO DAY +165

Jaz closed the door to the Clan's HQ—Cassy's house—and made her way to the outdoor kitchen for lunch, having delivered the reports Cassy had asked for. Still no sign of Nestor and one of the Lizzies from the raid a couple days prior, and Jaz was pretty sure there would never again be any sign of them. Their absence didn't much bother her. People died all the time and if they weren't close then crying over them was a waste of perfectly good angst. Save that crap for the peeps you know.

She ducked into the pavilion with one of the wood trenchers the Clan used for plates, loaded up with a bowl of stew and some fresh bread. An indoor kitchen would be nice this time of year, but it wasn't so bad since they'd found a huge military surplus tent to eat in. More like a pavilion, really. And the kitchen's rocket stoves vented through "earth tubes," flexible piping buried just below the surface that snaked back and forth from the rocket stove exhaust on one end of the new mess hall to the vent stack on the other end, rather than straight up a chimney. The earth around the tubes got nicely warm and radiated heat up into the pavilion, so whereas it was in the low thirties outside, it was probably fifty-five degrees inside. Maybe sixty. Most toasty, compared to eating outside like they had been doing.

Spotting Choony, she sat next to him and when he smiled at her, she smiled back. "What's up, Choon Choon?"

"Nothing much. Contemplating how I can dislike this Constant Stew so much when there are so many people out there who would kill their brother for what I'm going to leave in my bowl when I'm done."

"Dude. Morbid. Just eat it and try to imagine you've had something else to eat in the last six months. Like, Mac and Cheese with hot dogs."

"I think I'd prefer the stew—"

"Shut up!" Jaz laughed. "I love this tent thing, and the rocket pipes."

Choony grinned again, and of course he was gonna make fun of her somehow. He just *loved* making fun of her. Probably must be like when sixth graders throw the dodgeball at some girl they like. The Choony-Monk version of it.

"You refer to the corrugated tubing that ventilates the rocket stoves and emits radiant heat into the soil to warm the interior of the Army-surplus vinyl 'Tent, Medium, General Purpose'?" Choony asked without a trace of humor, his eyebrows raised in disapproval. "Nomenclature, Jaz!" he lectured. "Learn the nomenclature." He stacked a frown onto his disapproval.

"I hate your face," she said, grinning, and punched his shoulder. Not hard, because he was a Buddhist and wouldn't play back. It wouldn't be fair. "Ready for the meeting tonight?"

Choony shrugged and set his spoon down, turned to look at her more directly, and let out a long breath. "Not really. I've barely gotten my bones warmed up since spending the last two days out there in the snow dodging invaders and bandits with you, playing Special Envoy to all those new survivor groups we didn't even know about a week ago."

"Yeah, but the whole point was to get them here, right? Have the Grand Poobah meetup, kiss hands and shake babies, do Cassy's politician thang…"

"Yes, of course. I'm not complaining—that wouldn't change anything—but I wonder if it was worth the effort and the man-hours we spent on this. Some of their diplomats aren't very…" He paused.

"Diplomatic?" Jaz finished for him. Her friend Choon Choon was too polite sometimes, and truth was truth. Of the half-dozen who'd already made it to Clanholme for the meeting that night, half were definitely not the sort of people she'd want living with the Clan. Good thing they were *out there* instead of here, or there would definitely be a 'diplomatic incident' with a couple of those goons. She'd bet searching some of them would recover half the Clan's flatware and more than a few of the Clan's supplies. Clanners were too trusting for their own good, she figured.

* * *

Cassy stood behind a simple lightweight podium they'd looted from a church somewhere and looked around the big military surplus tent. She was grateful to have it, and not just for a much more comfortable place to eat than the great outdoors. Having so many people in her own tiny living room would have been very unpleasant, assuming they could even fit in there. There were representatives from Ephrata, Brickerville, Liz Town, Taj Mahal, and Lititz, of course, but they were the only familiar faces. Newly-allied Lebanon sent a representative, and his story about the journey to Clanholme was pretty strong stuff. It hadn't been easy, and one of his small entourage hadn't survived the trip.

In addition, there were seventeen others who showed up. They'd been invited by Clanholme and the other alliance members, each dealing only with the newfound survivor groups assigned to them in the last alliance meeting. The division of responsibilities had worked out pretty well, and this meeting came together much faster than it would have if Cassy hadn't delegated responsibility among the other alliance leaders.

Granted, many groups hadn't sent representatives. That was a problem for another time, though. The dozen or so missing groups would either abide by the alliance's decisions or they'd be cut off from both help and trade. No one had enough resources to just hand them out to people who weren't on the same team—you helped yourself and your own first, if you wanted to survive these days. The dying time wasn't over yet and they all knew it.

Cassy cleared her throat, and the faint conversations died down. Then she introduced herself and the Clan, talked briefly about what Clanholme was all about, and the challenges she and her people faced. In a corner, two transcriptionists from among the Clanners took shorthand notes. Then she had the other representatives all come up front and do the same, one at a time—all twenty-three of them. In size, their groups ranged from an isolated family of five to a farming group of fifty or so. Some had weird names like RetCon or the Barony of Renfar but most took their names from the tiny places where they lived, like Colebrook.

Almost universally, the smaller ones had the biggest problems with food. Security came in second, but the five original alliance members—Clanholme, Ephrata, Liz Town,

Lititz, and Brickerville—had been pretty good at clearing out bandits in the last few months, something many of the new groups hadn't realized. They'd assumed the bandits were dying off, but hunger was only part of the reason for the disappearing raiders. Cassy noted that their features relaxed a bit as they heard about all the alliance team had unintentionally done for them.

The next part of the meeting was spent talking—not lecturing, but a conversation with the group—about specific issues they each faced, about how those could be resolved with the resources of the group, and about how that help could be repaid. Clanholme needed bearings for a new windmill for their client and friend, Taj Mahal. Colebrook had extra bearings but needed two huge stones moved, and Cassy offered the use of the Clan's two working vehicles to pull them out of the way. It was a typical bargain of the night, people bartering their groups' time, services, and goods for goods and services they themselves needed. Cassy figured they would all come out the better for tonight's meeting—and that was exactly what she had hoped for.

The conversations lasted well into the night, and only one major hiccup threatened to tear apart the amity. Renfar had a closely allied survivor group, the RetCon people, but Liz Town had demanded the ally come under their control since Renfar was itself under the wing of Liz Town. Without the Lizzies' sacrifices holding off Hershey, the whole area would have been overrun, and they felt entitled to claim their area's primary loyalty. But Renfar had spent its own time and come to the aid of the smaller RetCon group several times and felt it was their relationship, not Liz Town's.

Cassy was a master diplomat, there. Her time working in the Marketing Department before the EMPs paid off when she applied her office-politics skills to the issue. In the end, Renfar kept their primary standing with RetCon while increasing their participation in Liz Town's efforts to hold off Hershey—which is what Liz Town had really been after in the first place. The dispute could have been a disaster that ripped away the entire western area of the alliance, especially since RetCon didn't *want* to be "under" Liz Town. She'd turned it into a compromise that made everyone stronger and built on Cassy's unspoken but well-earned credibility and authority.

Late in the night, Cassy came to her last talking point, and she was at the top of her game as she laid out her vision for the near future of the region, a Confederation. The groups would continue to manage their own affairs internally—no one would be asked to submit to some authority that had no idea of their developing culture, their immediate needs, their problems.

Instead, the Confederation would exist to handle issues between the member groups—a neutral arbiter that would hear both sides in any complaint and either negotiate a solution or issue a verdict that both sides would be honor-bound to follow. They'd follow it even if they had no honor, though, because to do otherwise would get them cut off from the Confederation's resources, including trade and mutual aid.

The Confederation would also coordinate a unified system to defend the groups as a whole against outside aggressors and would provide the supplies needed for that. Only on this issue, where the larger groups would provide the bulk of the fighters, would size matter. The six largest groups—the original five, plus Lebanon—would determine the overall strategy and select a leader to get a given job done, and the smaller groups would have to go along with it. But the smaller outfits didn't resist, since they wouldn't need to provide much materiel or manpower to the effort, at least not when compared to the bigger settlements. So they went along with it to get the one thing everyone wanted and only the Clan knew where to get in abundance. *Food.* By the time they all had their own farms delivering enough to support themselves, they'd be used to the arrangement, or so Cassy hoped.

And if deeper problems developed, the six larger allies would allow any of their "client" survivor settlements to choose another group. If Renfar didn't think Liz Town was being fair to them, for example, then at the start of any season they could put themselves under Lititz's protection and guidance.

It was messy, and it would need constant refinement as time went on, but it did the one thing Cassy knew they'd need to survive when spring came around—it established the basics of a *nation*. Despite the current 'vader threat to Brickerville, she reminded the assembly, *the Empire was still coming*. They had to be ready to deal with it from strength.

Only with the foundation laid tonight could the patchwork allies stand against someone like the Empire— organized, evil, and they didn't give a damn if you wanted to give them your food or not. Alone, the allies would submit or die. With their efforts as part of a confederation of interests, there was a chance they'd survive until next winter without becoming just so many more Empire slaves.

A slender thread of chance, perhaps, but it was better than none.

* * *

2310 HOURS - ZERO DAY +165

Nestor looked at his group of survivors and tried not to grin. The three women and the man he'd first rescued, another two men shortly after, and two more men plus another woman he'd saved from 'vaders, who were about to put them down rather than leave them unattended while they went off to fight. They had one more guy, but the next day he had tried to take over control of the group while Nestor slept, and the Other put an end to him. Guess he should have tried while Nestor was at the helm. No one gave Nestor any lip after that, though he tried not to act like a tin-pot dictator. He was in charge here, but they could leave at any time—without the group's supplies, of course.

Nestor was still piecing together what had happened with the man who tried to take over, since his memory wasn't perfect once he handed the reins to the Other and he didn't want to tell them about his mental hitchhiker. But he'd experimented a bit since the battle and found he could just sort of let the Other come up for air without letting him loose. Especially if he was scared or nervous—as he had been during the running gun battles they'd had with the 'vaders—and he found he could control the bastard in his head. Okay, not control. But he could let him take over only when needful and then jam him back down into the genie's bottle, so to speak. With Nestor at the helm, he had the upper hand and was learning to use the Other like a tool, brought out when needed and put away afterward. The Other hated it, of course, but now that Nestor had won a few tough mental battles for control, the Other stopped trying so relentlessly to take over.

Anyway, that left him nine people in his "survivor group," as Cassy called the little settlements all around, and all were now armed with the enemy's AK-47s. He also had two Russian fragmentation grenades after searching a dead invader—though how they got Russian grenades, he didn't know. The group had stolen a wagon loaded with food, water, some blankets, and other supplies. All in all, he was doing just fine at the moment. They'd spent a day finding a good place to shelter near some running water, made a quick encampment, and inventoried everything.

Natalie, the pretty young woman who'd broken down and cried during his first rescue, said, "So why don't we just go to your Clanholme place, then?"

It was a good question. There were glances between the others, who were probably just as interested to know the answer.

Nestor replied, "There's no way to get there right now. Not from here. Everything south of us is 'vader territory, unless you think you can creep through ten miles of occupied territory. That will clear up soon, but certainly not tomorrow."

"Then why not go back to Adamstown? You wouldn't even have to come with us. There's nothing to eat there anyway, but nobody wants us Adamstown people. We had some nasty people ruling us and some of them were friendly with the 'vaders. Any of them will kill us for escaping if they catch us. We were better off where we were!"

One of the men, Randy, cut her off. "Shut up, Natalie. You know damn well they started killing their slaves after the battle started. We'd have been shot, too. It's the damn Clan that did this to us, and you want us to go kiss their asses?" Then he nervously glanced to Nestor. "I know you're not really a Clan member, but no thanks."

Nestor nodded, only half-listening. He'd told them he was from Scranton, and how he'd just sort of ended up at Clanholme without any intention of doing so—captured after helping some Clan children avoid getting eaten by feral dogs. None of them counted him a Clanner. That was good enough for now, but it bothered him. These people didn't understand anything at all.

Then Natalie let out a tiny growl. She sounded

frustrated, and Nestor couldn't blame her. She said, "I don't want to go to the Clan anyway. They almost killed Nestor here, and he saved all our asses. He wouldn't have had to if the Clan had left the Rabs well enough alone. Why'd they have to go and kick up the hornet's nest, anyway?"

Nestor poked the fire coals—they kept it to only coals, in a Dakota fire hole, to avoid making a bunch of smoke—and said, "The invaders have Brickerville surrounded. I was told the attack was to allow at least some of the residents to escape before the invaders level the place."

Randy spit into the dirt with sudden violence, and Nestor eyed him warily until he said, "Screw Brickerville. I hope those bastards get what's coming to them. And Ephrata, too, after what they did."

Nestor raised an eyebrow, now very interested in the conversation. "Really? What did they do? The way they tell it, Adamstown is full of raiders, cannibals, and degenerates."

Natalie was the first to reply. "That's not true! A week after the lights went out, we went out to scavenge what we could. The food had already run out. There were a couple Mormons in town with lots of food, which we took and distributed—selfish pricks—but what's a lot for a family of Mormons isn't much for a town full of people. Reading is east from here, and believe me, you *do not* want to go that direction."

"Why not south, then?" Nestor asked, trying to picture the layout in his mind. It was mostly farms down that way, if he remembered right.

Natalie replied, "The Rabs used some sort of brown gas on just about everything south, killing all the plants and most of the people, so no food there. We went west but between the two of them, Ephrata and Brickerville had already looted just about everything we could have used. The people in some other small towns, Denver and Reamstown, tried to fight for it, but they got mopped up good by Brickerville's war party. The only good thing the Rabs did was gas Swartzville, or they'd probably have used us for dinner by now. As it turned out, their survivors joined us."

Randy interrupted before Nestor could respond, "And as for the north, there's a band of forest for miles, but running along that band is all the Reading suburbs. Hell, we'd have been *their* dinner if we hadn't set up raiders all through those woods. The suburb folks would come through, get whacked, and well, somewhere along the way some of them got eaten."

Nestor felt his stomach churn. "Oh come on. You can't just say that no one wondered where the meat came from. People didn't just get accidentally barbequed."

"People came back with mounds of cooked meat for us all to eat. We didn't think to ask where they got it. Figured it for deer or a goat or something. It was only afterward that we found out what it really was." Randy looked uneasy and hesitated a moment before he continued, "The thing is, we kept starving and they just kept coming, so... Do the math."

Nestor frowned as his stomach flopped and threatened to heave. "Why'd you kill them, then? Why not just let them pass, if you're trying to tell me you weren't hunting people for food."

"We couldn't just let them come to Adamstown, either," Randy said. "Nothing for them to eat but us, and they would if they could. So we don't just hold them off, we kill the shit out of them when they come through those woods."

All of that made a certain sense, actually. Ruthless, and the cannibalism was a stomach-churner, but could Nestor say he'd do differently if the meat was already there and he was about to die from hunger? Probably not. He summarized, "And the raiding is both payback and to keep Ephrata from getting too brave about coming into your territory."

"More or less," Natalie said. "We're not bad people, Nestor. Just not as lucky as those assholes west of us in their safe little farms. You don't know how many of us died from starvation. Some still do. Adamstown is barely hanging on, and we can't go anywhere but west to forage."

Randy added, "It is what it is. So yeah, let's not go back to Adamstown. And I don't figure we'll be welcome in Clanholme. So this wagon of food is great and all, but I think it's just delaying the inevitable. We're going to die, and everyone's going to die, and then the world will belong to the rats and the cockroaches. People just haven't figured that out yet. Maybe the rats and cockroaches will do a better job of it."

Nestor, looking thoughtful, took another bite of rice and beans, the staple foods in the wagon. "I don't think I care to go back, either. At least out here I'm free." That wasn't the whole truth, but it wasn't a lie, either. "You know, it occurs to me that the 'vaders have all the supplies we need. What you don't know about guerrilla fighting, I can teach it to anyone who feels like staying. I'd rather eat invader food than what you all were eating, and they have an army's worth of it out there waiting to be taken." At least, the Other could teach them all they needed to know...

And that meant it would be the Other doing the guerrilla stuff, not him, which made it an easy decision. At Clanholme he was a danger to all those good people. Out here, with these people who actually *liked him*, he was only a danger to the assholes invading the country and the people with him— Adamstown cannibals and raiders and collaborators.

Nestor almost smiled—he could use the darkness within him to fight the darkness out here, and maybe someday he could feel like he redeemed himself for all the gruesome things people said he'd done before the war. Maybe that was why he'd been cursed with this Other his whole life, though he didn't know it until a few days ago—he was put here for this time, for this purpose, and the only thing that really mattered was what he chose to do with that dark curse now. And he felt ready, maybe for the first time in his life.

- 17 -

0745 HOURS - ZERO DAY +166

JUST BEFORE HEADING to breakfast, Cassy heard two brief blasts of the guard tower's air horn. She frowned as she slid the supplies ledger back into its place on her bookshelf—two blasts meant the return of last night's raiding party, and she never knew whether the news would be good or tragic when a party returned. She took a deep breath, closed her eyes briefly, then headed out the door to meet the incoming coalition fighters.

As she approached the guard tower, the fighters filed out from the Jungle, the Clan's intensive gardening area when it wasn't midwinter. Mueller led them, she saw, and her heart lurched at first, until she remembered that Michael hadn't led last night's raid.

Mueller saluted and grinned as they approached. So it would be good news after all. A wave of relief washed through her and she smiled back at the Marine.

"Good morning, ma'am," he said, still grinning. "Got a whole squad of Rabs last night, and the ambush went perfectly. No surprises this time, except one on the way back. We lost the new guy, Nestor. We didn't find his body, though, so there is a good chance he's still alive. We'll send out scouts to look around for him."

Cassy frowned. "Maybe he ran off during the battle, or got wounded and crawled away before dying. Have the scouts search the area around the battle first to rule that out."

Mueller then turned around toward the rest of his men coming out of the Jungle and waved at Sturm as she emerged. She nodded and headed toward them. She had company. Bound by the wrists, and with a makeshift hood from a Marine's shemaugh, was a prisoner.

"That's interesting," Cassy said. "Is it a Rab?" She would chew their asses if it was, but knew they wouldn't break the order to never again reveal Clanholme's location to an invader.

"Nope. Adamstown scum," Mueller replied. "Said he has a message for the Clan and then he requested asylum. Hope he brought his own food."

Cassy didn't respond right away, but understood the sentiment. Never mind that he was from an enemy group, food was getting scarce. The Clan had lots of grain, having squirreled away the rare silos of the stuff they had found and looted in the fall, but everything else was hard to come by. She had already decided to consult with Brickerville about putting up a greenhouse at Clanholme in the coming year, if they could find enough glass to make it practical, or maybe using reclaimed windows. For now, though... she shrugged. At least they were all fed.

Once Sturm got close enough, Cassy answered, "Take him to the Smoke House. You know where."

Sturm stayed expressionless as she nodded and turned to go with the prisoner, grabbing a second Marine to go with her. The Smoke House would never again be used to preserve food, not with so much human blood and misery seeped into its very walls.

Cassy glanced at Mueller and then watched Sturm lead the prisoner away. Mueller was quiet, but then he was always the silent type. Finally, he said, "Well I better go get Michael. I'll have a report to you before lunch, ma'am."

Cassy nodded her consent. Mueller wasn't happy about this situation, but neither was she. No one was. She had overheard Mueller talking to Sturm once about the questioning Michael had done there and knew that he understood the need even if he didn't like it. Hopefully this guy was legit and really did have a message for the Clan. Otherwise, it would get very ugly for him until the truth came out or he died protecting it.

She was suddenly not very hungry, so instead of going to breakfast she went back to the house, grabbed her outer coat, and headed toward the Smoke House, far north of the Jungle. Almost to the food forest, even. Best to just get it over with instead of avoiding it. Nothing unpleasant got more pleasant by putting it off.

When she arrived, the prisoner was sitting on a rock, still hooded and tied at the wrists. Cassy said nothing, but waited for Michael to come along. The man shifted around in his seat, probably nervous. Who could blame him? She was curious to hear what he had to say, but she doubted it could be good news. Adamstown was a den of cannibals and raiders, had been from the early days of the collapse. The worst sort of human beings. She'd kill them all if she could. Someday she might just get that chance, and she looked forward to it.

A scuffle of dirt behind her told her Michael had arrived. He walked up behind her and touched her on the shoulder before approaching the prisoner. He nodded to Sturm, and she looked relieved at Michael's arrival. She couldn't get out of there fast enough, accompanied by the other guard. Only

Michael and Cassy remained with the hooded man. He wasted no words or time before grabbing the hook and chain that hung from a pulley on the cross beam extending out from the front of the smokehouse, slid the hook under the rope binding the prisoner's hands, and then went to pull on the chain. In moments the man was forced standing, just barely able to rest on his feet.

Michael paced in front of the man, making no effort to be silent but not speaking to him, either. She once asked him about why he did that, and he had said it was both to unnerve the prisoner and to steady his own nerves and prepare himself mentally to do the necessary.

The prisoner had no leverage to try anything and no way to escape from that position. Yet he didn't make a sound. That struck Cassy as odd, but she didn't interfere. This was Michael's place, not hers, and she'd leave if it got too uncomfortable for her.

Michael didn't have that luxury, but he always did the needful and suffered the nightmares on his own time, the poor man. She would think less of him if she thought he enjoyed it.

She hoped he'd be compliant quickly because then the whole nightmare could stop—Michael was somehow a good interrogator and spotted truth when he saw it. People lied under that kind of questioning. Michael, however, had an uncanny ability to piece together different bits of truth to get at the big-picture truth—compliant or not, they always gave away their secrets in the end, to one degree or another.

Finally, just as she knew Michael intended, the prisoner broke the silence. "Listen, man, I really am just here looking for asylum, and I got a message for the Clan leader. I could just give you the message and you could pass it on, and maybe let me get something to eat. I'm not here to mess with you. I walked up and turned myself in. Really, man. Ask your guard."

Michael didn't respond. Instead, he slowly walked behind the man, boots crunching in the gravel, and then he stopped. He stood only inches behind the man, and Cassy could see that Michael was tense. He stayed silent for half a minute and then leaned forward to whisper in his ear, "Maybe you're the food. That makes it hard to feed you, I think. I guess I could feed you your own foot. You'd live, and have a full stomach."

Cassy felt a cold shiver of fear and loathing streak up her spine. The words were bad enough, but the *way* Michael said it was so... believable. Evil incarnate. Add one to the nightmare files.

In a more casual, chatty voice Michael continued, "Scum like you did that to a friend of mine, not so long ago. You didn't know them, but I suppose one cannibal bandit is like the next, eh? We got sour cream to go with your foot. You'll love it because we make our own sour cream, you know. It's a great recipe, tangy and a bit thinner than what you used to buy in the store for your baked potatoes. Tell me that doesn't sound delicious."

Cassy had enough now and was about to leave when the man began to laugh. What the hell? It was not the expected response. Not a bit.

Michael's jaw dropped for a moment, then he snapped it shut and stood stock-still, fists clenched at his sides. Cassy had never seen him surprised like that before, and as the man laughed himself out, Michael seemed frozen. This had probably never happened to him before, not in the Sandbox of endless Gulf war and not here.

The prisoner finally caught his breath and, panting, said, "Oh, man, sorry, I tried not to laugh—"

Michael snapped, "Are you out of your damn mind?" Then he snapped his fist forward, driving it into the man's back. The prisoner's legs buckled, and he screamed out in pain.

Cassy half-rose from her seat and then froze in shock. If that was a kidney shot... There weren't any hospitals anymore. Then she reminded herself that this was an Adamstown man, a cannibal, a rapist, a bandit...

The man staggered to get his feet back under him and whimpered at the effort. "*Dammit!* You asshole! Why'd you do that, man," he said, voice quivering. "I just laughed because everyone knows the Clan don't eat people. Oh damn... My damn legs don't work."

Michael slapped the man on the back of his head. "Shut up. Don't cry, it'll embarrass me, and I don't like to be embarrassed. You don't know us. We could very well eat you. Cut you up and toss you in our forever stew, and no one would ever know you weren't a deer."

"No, you won't. You guys are a bunch of selfish bastards, but you aren't like them people at Adamstown. You'd kill me quick or skin me alive if you thought it'd help anything, but you wouldn't do it for kicks, and you sure don't eat long pig. Everyone knows that."

"Everyone knows we're selfish bastards?" Michael asked with narrowed eyes.

"That too, yeah. Look, Adamstown is just people, man. Not bogeymen, not trolls under the bridge. Just fucking people tryin' to stay alive. If you and your friends hadn't looted every damn inch of ground between here and Adamstown, we might not had to do what we done. It sure ain't because we woke up one day and thought, gee, the cops are gone, let's go get some McNeighbor Meals for the kids."

Michael clenched his jaw, but to Cassy's relief he didn't hit him again. Not yet. She wasn't sure why that was such a relief, but she found herself hoping this would take a sudden turn in a different direction. This wasn't going the way she had thought it would.

"You still kill people for meat," Michael said through tightly clenched teeth. "People who might have made it, except you figured your one life was worth more than all the people you ate to stay alive."

"Fuck 'worth,' man, it's just staying alive. Everyone will do what they got to, whether they're worth it or not. You're no different, you're just luckier. And screw that other garbage, man, we don't kill people for meat."

Michael said, "Everyone knows that you do. I've seen the evidence myself—bodies with the meat carved off, the rest just left to rot."

"I don't know whose Kool-Aid you been drinking, or who you're talking about, but it's bullshit," the man exclaimed. "Yeah, we didn't let it go to waste when we got five-year-old little girls starving to death, not when there's a perfectly good piece of meat just laying there bleeding out after they tried to come up on us. They attacked us and afterward, we chose not to starve. It was meat, and they weren't using it anymore." The man took a ragged breath and continued in a calmer tone. "You'd have done the same if your kids was starving. You make it sound like we set up 'Free Meals Ahead' signs along the roads or some shit to pack 'em in. We got attacked, we defended ourselves. Dammit, man, where the hell did you hear rumors like we were the same as them assholes in the red bandanas?"

Cassy stood suddenly and held her hand up to Michael to stop. This was getting nowhere and was besides the point. It had to end.

Michael took a deep breath, held it, then let it out. He gave Cassy one curt nod, then said, "We can discuss your diet later, if we decide to give you a trial instead of just killing you and fertilizing our forests with your corpse. You know what? I need to call you something. And since your name isn't that important, I'm just going to call you 'Fritz.' You said you had a message, Fritz. Well, let's hear it."

Fritz paused for a couple seconds, and Cassy figured he was trying to collect his thoughts. The last couple of minutes had to have rattled him. Then he said, "Yeah, that's why I found you guys and turned myself in to your patrol. Did you notice I didn't fight? Just remember that I'm the messenger, not the message."

"Perhaps. We'll see. I do hope you convince me you are telling the truth. I have other things to do today than to pull your teeth out one by one, so please, let's have it straight."

Fritz nodded inside his hood. "Awesome. So, here's the deal—Adamstown flipped."

Michael looked down at the ground for a moment, then back up at Fritz. "What exactly does that mean, Fritz? You aren't dazzling me with your message. You came all this way and went through all this, just to tell us they 'flipped'? Like what, went crazy?"

"As far as I'm concerned they're crazy, but no, man, I mean they *changed sides*. Decided to join the winning team and went 'vader. Aid and comfort to the enemy and all that. The whole nine yards. The whole damn town took a vote and it was, like, ten-to-one in favor. Anyone who voted against being traitors got the boot. I guess we're lucky they didn't just eat us. I mean, Jesus, if you'll join the people who killed America, you'll do any damn thing, so when they said get out, you're damn right I got the hell out like my tail was on fire. Came right over to warn you, turned myself in like any good citizen."

Cassy raised an eyebrow. That was actually pretty important news. She stood up—all the way, this time—and walked until she stood directly in front of Fritz. "I am Cassandra Shores," she said with a steady, strong voice. "I lead Clanholme, as you may know. And if what you just told us is true, we may not just kill you when this is all over."

"It's true. I swear," he said, and Cassy caught a note of uneasiness there, something new. Perhaps her name carried such a reputation there that he feared it more than he did Michael. "I'd love to just be let go, because all this is your doing. Not ours. Not mine."

Michael smacked Fritz in the back of his head again. "What does that mean, cannibal? I'd speak up if I were you."

"I mean that the Clan and your whole damn alliance look after yourselves first and screw everyone else, right? You attacked their unit, killed a bunch of them. Freed their slaves. So they were on their way west, when—"

"Stop," Cassy broke in. "Why were they going west, and how do you know what they were going to do?" Something about that statement had triggered her intuition. It was more important than this guy realized, maybe. "Everything you know about it, no matter how small."

Cassy couldn't see his face, but noticed his shoulders drew back. She hoped that meant he would bank on her leniency if it was good information.

"There's some sort of group, like a new Republic or something, out of Indiana. The Rabs think they're spreading fast and might be a threat soon, so they sent a unit out to spend the winter doing recon. Like, if they could attack now and nip it in the bud then they would, but if not, they were gonna spend the winter scouting all the stuff they could find out about this new group. We got a whole battalion in our own area, but they sent out two others, with each one going a different way. I think a battalion is like three companies or something—anyway it's a lot of people with guns."

Cassy fought the urge to curse. This was terrible news. It meant several things at once, none of which would be good for the Clan. First, it meant the invaders had some idea of what was going on hundreds of miles away, and that was scary because how did they know? Somebody was telling them.

Second, it meant the 'vaders could afford to station—she did the math in her head—just shy of four hundred troops to go scout... something. They weren't even sure what, but it *might* be a threat to them later. So they sent out hundreds of troops to look. *Hundreds.* What chance did that leave the Clan, even with the Confederation?

And third, because of the raiding party they had sent to help get Brickerville's fighters out of the besieged town— which now seemed like it hadn't really been the target at all— the rest of an entire combat battalion was now making friendly and "kicking it real," as Jaz would say, over at Adamstown. From the battle reports, that left at least three hundred 'vaders hanging out on the Confederation's eastern border, now allied to the Clan's longstanding enemies over at Adamstown.

On the bright side, they had hurt the invaders enough with that raid to derail their plans, else why had they fallen back to Adamstown? The mission itself had been a success, too. Not only did Brickerville's fighters get out, so they could be of some actual use in this fight, they also smuggled in those drones and other supplies from that defunct nutjob compound. Brickerville's plan for the drones was no less than brilliant, though she'd have rather had a few of them for the Clan. Maybe this whole situation could be turned to the Confederation's advantage somehow.

One last thing was nagging at her, though. "Fritz, tell me something. Why did Adamstown suddenly throw the gates open now, instead of when the invaders rolled into the area going west in the first place?"

"Because we figured they'd just attack us, passing by, so we got our defenses up the best we could, but they never did. They just kept right on rolling west, but first they raided us, caught a boatload of our people, and made them into slaves. They never tried to occupy our place. You saw the slaves they grabbed when you attacked them, I'm sure. They just needed some of us to free up their troops for combat, I figure. I got the impression they didn't think they'd need slaves when they left wherever they came from, New Jersey I think. Or they weren't allowed to bring the ones they had, or their slaves ran away or something. Either way, they decided getting some along the way from us sounded fantastic."

"Then why give in to them when they came back? You were ready to fight them the first time, so I have to wonder about your story, Fritz."

Cassy saw his hands clench up and assumed that was a frustration response. It meant his next words would likely be honest, or at least the truth he knew.

"Like I said, some of us still didn't want to knuckle under to them. But the first time they came through, we didn't really know how many there were. Then we counted them going by. Plus, when they came back they had slaves. They still had about a hundred of us, whichever ones you hadn't freed in the fight. They lined them up outside and said they'd shoot the slaves if we didn't negotiate a surrender. Those were our friends, our families, you know? They had caught almost a fifth of us when they raided us the first time, so everyone in town had a son or a brother, whatever, out there, lined up and waiting to die right in front of us. So, we voted to open up. Not me, but most did."

Cassy had gotten the information she wanted and it seemed consistent. She nodded to Michael. "Anything else you want to know?"

Michael frowned, the wheels in his head obviously turning. Finally, he said, "Why didn't they give you to the 'vaders as slaves, those who voted no?"

"I couldn't say. Maybe we weren't handed over because

we have friends and family there, even if we voted no. My wife helped get me out, and nobody was really eager to try to stop people from sneaking us out of town. As I said, we're exiled now."

"And why would they bother to send the Clan a message, warning us about what was happening?" Michael's expression was pensive.

"They asked me to risk coming to you to let you know and ask if maybe you can help us. You or some of the other places you trade with. We're not really raiders the way you think we are. We're just trying to survive, and we're willing to work for food and a place to stay."

"Didn't you think your reputation would work against you?"

"Listen—not everyone in Adamstown is evil. Some wanted to warn you because we're all Americans, despite the town opening its gates to the 'vaders for survival."

Michael nodded. "I imagine that's true. So did you vote for them to open up the gates to those bastards?"

"No way. I didn't want to open up to them, and I don't want them winning. And I figured coming here to tell you everything I know might earn me a spot at your table. Hell, work me as hard as you want, if that's your thing, but give me a chance. I promise you won't regret it, man. Some of us were just there because our luck sucked."

Well, that was probably the truest thing he had said. Cassy wondered what she'd do if Brianna and Aidan were starving and someone dropped a plate of hot, seasoned barbeque on the table. Would she ask questions first? She didn't really care for the answer she got when she thought about it. She'd probably try to hide the truth from the kids, but she'd feed them. How could she not?

"Michael, ship his ass to Liz Town and tell them he's a refugee from back east. It isn't a lie, exactly, and they'll probably catch him out quick enough anyway, but at least he will have a shot at making it. They always need more people who can work."

"Yes, ma'am," Michael said with a nod. He was so closed up emotionally, from expecting to have to be a lot rougher in questioning this guy, that she couldn't read his feelings the way she usually did, but she trusted that if he had a problem with it, he'd tell her before sending Fritz away. In the meantime, she felt better about what had happened here, and her appetite returned with a vengeance, reminding her that she missed breakfast again.

* * *

In a safely held area of upstate New Jersey, Ree rode in the passenger seat of the old American muscle car, a war trophy —old enough that it still worked, despite the EMPs. There were still a few such pre-digital vehicles around, although it was becoming a challenge to find gasoline that had not yet gone bad. Without a refinery, there soon wouldn't be any more gasoline that worked, and then he'd be without a car. Of course, no refineries still functioned. Nor were there working tankers to get the oil from the well to the refinery. And no working wells to fill the tankers, for that matter. No, that world was dying, and in a year it would be gone entirely.

Ree's empire, however, would last much longer than that if he could only deal with the terrorists who bled him to death with a thousand tiny cuts. Beheading the Arab officers who had allowed Taggart to escape New York City had made him feel only slightly better, because he'd had a feeling in his gut about what was going to happen next. He had known he must prevent it if he could—and he had been right. Taggart had figured out Ree's master plan: the large farms to the west, run by the People's Worker Army, with defenses set up to deal with the kind of low-intensity conflicts he had expected. Still, Taggart's cancer hadn't spread all that far, not yet.

"This situation is growing beyond our ability to control it," Major Kim said as he drove slowly along the raised earthen embankment. "Rather, it is beyond my ability, Leader."

Ree didn't look at him. It would be rude to so obviously watch the man squirm at his own poor choice of words, and he'd corrected himself after all. He kept his voice calm, to reassure the younger officer. "The incompetence of the Islamists has allowed a finely balanced game with Taggart to tip in his favor, but the incompetents have been dealt with. In the future, those ignorant sandy officers will drive their barbarian soldiers harder to succeed, if they will wish to avoid the same fate. The only way to motivate these disgusting savages is through chopping off heads, it seems. I detest having to stoop to their level to get the point across, but what can one expect from such a people? It's all they understand."

"Of course, Leader. It was wise and necessary to make the point in a way they would understand, even if distasteful and uncivilized. Still, we are left with the problem they created. The American terrorist, Taggart, runs amok and spreads his treason wherever he goes, yet we cannot divert troops to deal with him right now. The City is bubbling with activity as the other American rats fight amongst themselves and with us to build their own dying empires. Fools."

Ree nodded, finding himself in agreement with Kim. "True. Nor can we divert our frontier troops, because only they keep the dying hordes of Americans from ravaging our cantonment's food areas here in New Jersey. I had hoped the American leadership's leftovers wouldn't be *yong-ui mauseu*, but they achieved their aims despite being the mouse to our cat. I have a plan to correct this situation."

"Yes, Leader. I have ordered ten of our People's Centers, close to Taggart's advance, to gather the People's Worker Army under their care as you instructed. They await orders from your runners."

The car pulled into one of the "People's Centers," a military base that controlled a portion of land around it for the purposes of clearing and eventual spring farming. It had been Ree's great idea to recreate the ancient feudal system here in America, with his officers as the lords, and his troops the mounted knights enforcing the lords' rule over the American serfs. Of course, it was couched in terms of working for the People. Ha! The People. When did the people ever know anything? They needed the guidance of a Great Leader, so they could align their hearts and minds toward being productive for the common good. Otherwise, they only drank and begged. Even here in America, it was the same.

His car stopped in front of the bunker-like fortress standing well away from the cluster of buildings used by the P.W.A. Ree climbed out, dusting off his trousers. "Get the scribe, or take notes yourself, Little Brother. We will need a record."

Of course Kim wasn't going to be a secretary, so he got a lieutenant, using a blank pad of paper.

Ree told the man, "Write this out, then write out ten more copies. I will keep one, and Major Kim will be honored to tell you where to send the other ten. My title is to go at the top, and I will sign them after lunch." When the man was ready, Ree nodded in approval and said, "Take this note:

> The American terrorist comes. All those who aid or join his cause are already dead; our Great Leader has foreseen this, and so there can be no mistake. He has determined that your base is not tenable. All units are to withdraw to Base A-1A immediately,

so that your lives may again be useful as we battle the American false ideals and the World Evil they spread.

You will retrieve all items of military or other value and bring them with you, so their value will not pass to the American terrorist when he comes seeking to destroy your glorious People's Worker Army.

However, the Worker Army is not needed. Their lives have more value as a message to the terrorist, so that other lives can be saved. Nor can we leave them to be taken, lest their new honor, found in work for the People instead of for themselves, be tarnished through treason.

It is therefore unfortunate but necessary that their lives be spent in delivering a message from the People to this terrorist. They cannot be brought, nor can they be left behind, and so their Next Highest Value is in delivering this message.

Accordingly, assemble the Worker Army under your care, and in the timeliest method possible, using the least amount of useful materiel, you are to permanently deny their use to the enemy under General Orders 5A dated June 4th, 2016, in the General Orders Log provided to you by the Great Leader. The Log itself is to accompany you on your journey, but the page for General Orders 5A shall be affixed to a prominent building of no military value.

All other assets that exceed what you can bring with you will likewise be denied to the enemy, burned so he is left only ashes.

"Did you get all that?"

The officer saluted smartly. "Yes, my leader!"

Ree watched the man leave to make the transcriptions. He had shown no outward emotion on hearing such a terrible, tragic order, and Ree inwardly smiled at the officer's discipline. Such orders were necessary in war, as was the need to follow such orders. It required discipline.

Ree turned to Kim. He brushed off his lapels and said, "It is sad, this loss of life, but no more sad than any other, and this will serve far greater purpose than most. And when

Taggart finds so many thousands dead, their assets burned, he will know two things. First, we will leave him nothing further to survive from. Like a flea on a dog, he is sucking the very life from the glorious future of the new America."

"And the second, Big Brother? You said there were two lessons for the terrorist."

Ree frowned his carefully rehearsed expression and said, "He will know that there is no liberation from the People's Worker Army. His misguided attempts to save his Americans from their glorious future will result only in their having no future at all. Let him contemplate that truth and see if he continues his course. A wise man would leave his fellows to their future and find some other region to plague. Let him bother General Park in Pennsylvania or General Yi in Virginia or Maryland, since they have refused my offers to lead them."

Major Kim bowed slightly, hesitantly.

Ree let out a frustrated breath. "What troubles you?"

Kim paused and then said, "Leader, this action came about after a message was received from an unknown American. I don't know how this was accomplished, but I surmise the two events are connected."

Ree clamped down on any expression. He was fairly certain no hint showed on his face that he had very nearly struck the Major down on the spot. His pulse raced and his anger seethed. How dare he question... No. Killing Kim wouldn't have value, he was a useful officer who shouldn't be squandered. Ree of all people felt that emotion had no place in making decisions. Still, this called for a correction.

Ree knew the correct course. He smiled, appearing for all the world like the friendly Big Brother Kim thought him to be. "Some burdens are for me alone, Major. But I suspect that what we are doing here today will motivate Taggart to follow his own orders more scrupulously. Americans are undisciplined, but I think we align his desires with his orders through this sacrifice we make for the greater good. How very astute of you to draw the correct conclusions, Major."

Maybe too astute. Ree made a mental note to find out who leaked that information, and their death would be slow and painful, held during his officer corps' evening chow, if he had anything to say about it. Then Ree smiled... He was the only one who did have a say in it, and that was as it should be.

* * *

1945 HOURS - ZERO DAY +166

Taggart crouched near a low fire set next to a now derelict 'vader vehicle, something like a crude Humvee. It acted as a shield against the faint breeze, hid the fire's glow from at least one direction, and reflected heat back to the group. Eagan was trying to get their HAMnet up, whatever that was, so they could again communicate with Dark Ryder and get any information or instructions the 20s had passed to him since they left New York City. The 20s would be angry by now, he reflected, and shrugged as he picked at an MRE. He had taken it in order to let someone else have one of their precious few remaining real meals. Raiding 'vader bases often earned them real food, but fresh food didn't keep well between raids.

Eagan came into the fire's circle of light and nodded, but didn't salute. Taggart had given standing orders that no one was to salute while they were out there in the open, despite the patrols he had going. "Colonel, we had connection briefly, just long enough to get the back-chatter downloaded. I have it decoded."

Taggart took the thin stack of papers Eagan offered and

glanced through them. Several attempts to get them to send a SITREP, of course, which he had expected. He had a growing suspicion that the 20s somehow had been keeping an eye on him, probably through satellites. That was why he had asked Dark Ryder to keep the birds from watching him as he set up his breakout from the City, and it turned out to have been a wise idea. They were still asking, so they weren't sure.

"Think they have our location now that we've received these?" Taggart asked, flipping through the printouts one at a time.

"I doubt it, but it's possible," Eagan answered thoughtfully. "At most, they'll know we're outside of the City somewhere. But the fires will tell them where to start looking."

Taggart hoped they were still clueless. Even knowing he'd left Manhattan would be dangerous if his suspicions about certain things proved correct. Then his eyes froze on one transmission, looking at the header information. His mind raced to decipher what had caught his attention. Something about that one...

"Eagan, take a look at this message," he said urgently. "Check the headers. What do you see?"

Eagan stared hard at the offered sheet for the better part of a minute before one eyebrow went up. "Well—this could be nothing, but this one from Dark Ryder—the header isn't right. They usually end in five-seven-three, but this one ends in one-six-three. Transmissions from him from before and after this one have the usual header numbers. It's like his signature."

"Yeah, you're right. What's it mean?"

"Garbled IP addresses, I think," Eagan said, thinking as he went. "So he overrides them with a false IP address, but always uses the same false one even though it's probably a dynamic IP. That means this one isn't really from Dark Ryder."

Taggart nodded. It made sense. "It also wasn't encoded with our usual back-channel cypher. Normally we have to decode it using a book, right?"

"Yessir," Eagan replied. "It's a pretty ancient way to cipher, using two identical copies of the same book. Same edition, printing, everything. We have one, and he has the other, so his reports often come through as a series of garbage numbers and letters if he's encoding it again with the standard cipher before transmitting it. Getting clear copy usually takes two operations."

"He does that with important things, anyway. This particular message seems important enough to warrant that coding, yet it isn't coded that way."

"What does that tell you, if you don't mind sharing classified information with an enlisted man with no clearance or college education, Colonel General Sir?"

"You're such a shitbird, Eagan. Do you have to ask? We're not back at base shining shoes and prepping for locker inspection."

Eagan smiled and crouched down nearby within easy hearing distance as Taggart continued in a softer voice, "Listen, these are orders from General Houle, supposedly passed on through Dark Ryder via the 20s as usual. That's trouble. He knows something. The short version is that they're movement orders for a new mission. So somehow they know we're not in the Big Apple anymore. And they're pretending to be Dark Ryder because they're testing him. Or us. Who knows what Dark Ryder told them? We need to find out before we answer."

"I figured that much out," Eagan commented. "I thought they might have a satellite or something, checking up on us. Dark Ryder said something about another bird up there."

"Satellite? Maybe. Maybe a leak. Maybe something else. It doesn't matter. But the orders? They do matter. We are ordered by the Commander-in-Chief, under blah blah executive order authorizing him to yadda yadda, to relocate about one-hundred-sixty klicks west, near Allentown, Pennsylvania, and set up guerrilla resistance operations there—"

The sounds of shouting reached him, and Taggart cut himself off to listen, his hand reaching for his rifle. When it was clear they weren't under attack, he relaxed a little. "Eagan, go stop whatever's going on over there. I need to read this. Let me know what's up."

Eagan left while Taggart went over the mission orders again. They were pretty clear—this was a direct order from the Commander-in-Chief, or someone claiming that authority at least. The last he had heard, the President had died en route to some bunker, but there would of course be people lining up to be in charge of a country that no longer existed. Houle, probably.

Why would they be ordered west? He had reported all this food-producing slavery crap, with a loose description of the strategic and tactical situations—nothing that a leak could use against them, but enough to show how vital his operations were—and whoever received those on the other end couldn't possibly have any situation more important than this one. Taggart had the opportunity here to knock out an *entire theater of operations* for the enemy, and restore food and order to several states at once. A reborn America, or a good start, really. He had the equipment and manpower to do it here, the troops and loyalty to get it done, and a unique opportunity to finish Ree fast. Yet Houle, or someone else, wanted to short-circuit that opportunity. Why?

Eagan returned, cutting into his dark thoughts. "Sir, you'll want to see this. Private Johns!" he barked, and one of the liberated civilians who had joined his forces approached the fire. "This is Colonel Taggart himself, so show some respect, but tell him what you told me."

"Johns" looked nervous, but nodded and stepped forward. He tried to salute—awkwardly, like a civilian—but Eagan stopped him. "No saluting in the field. Snipers."

Pvt. Johns nodded again and then looked to Taggart with an expression akin to adoration. Taggart was almost a living legend in these parts by now, especially since he had released two hundred thousand slaves already and set up a guerrilla army one hundred thousand strong. They were rampaging against the enemy like no one had since the invasion began, fueled by rage at what had been done to them. The guy looked like he was going to shit himself in awe, for Christ's sake.

Taggart gentled his voice and said, "Go ahead, son. What do you have for me?"

"Thank you, sir. I'm... honored to meet you. Can I just say—"

"Son, I'm busy running a war. Just tell me what you have to say and then Eagan here will get you set up with chow and a spot to get some rest."

"Oh, um. Yes, sir. Well, we were scouting out a bunch of those enemy bases, the ones they use to keep the slaves in check and gather up supplies and stuff, and they're all dead, sir. All those civilian slaves, from at least five bases. Maybe more. The 'vaders took them, bashed their heads in, and slit their throats. They left thousands at each base, stacked up like cordwood. They burned everything else, but left a note at each base. They're all the same note, written in Korean."

Taggart froze in place, struggling to contain his anger. Those bastards... It couldn't be real, could it? But of course it could. They weren't human, not really. They'd do all sorts of inhumane things. They fried whole cities with gas, why not a few thousand slaves to leave a message? "Did anyone know enough Korean to translate these notes?"

"Sir, they're all the same note. Printed out and everything. We think they're, like, military documents from before the EMPs hit back."

"Again—did they get translated?" Taggart was angry, but he knew it wasn't this guy's fault. He just wanted to lash out, but best to do it to the right people. "It's important. We need to know what those notes said."

"Yessir, we got part of it translated. We have a guy who had Korean grandparents, like from Korea, and he knew some of it. I brought the copy we translated for you."

Taggart held out his hand, and Johns handed him a sheet of thick paper about half the size of printer paper, torn along one edge. The translator had done about half of it, his notes printed on the paper under each line of double-spaced, tiny printing. The text layout definitely had the look and feel of military orders, or maybe some sort of manual.

He froze stiff when he read it. "The fuck..." It was some sort of military General Order, a contingency plan dated from *before* the actual invasion even started, stating that if American forces—which they called "traitors to the New American Cause"—threatened to retake an occupied area, it was to be "rendered of no materiel or personnel value" to the re-occupying forces. It was a goddamn Scorched Earth policy that the commanding officers could institute at will.

"Johns, thank you, son. Go get chow." He turned and raised his voice as he said, "Eagan, show Johns where to go and then you're with me." Taggart's face was grave, and Eagan took only a minute to return.

"What is the terrible news, sir? You look about ready to kill someone."

"The North Koreans in charge of this side of the war left us a copy of contingency orders. From here on out, if they see us coming they'll kill every slave operating out of that base and torch whatever supplies, weapons, and food they can't run away with."

"Seriously?" Eagan now looked pale in the reddish light of the fire and as nauseated as Taggart himself felt.

"Thousands dead. I'll guess twenty thousand, maybe more, based on how many slaves we've been finding at these little 'vader bases." Taggart paused, then continued, "I got a question for you, Eagan."

"Yes, sir?"

"Talk to me like I was still your sergeant when you answer this. What do you think are the odds of getting orders from the 20s, which *pretend to but did not go through Dark Ryder*, telling us to move out of this region, right before the enemy begins Scorched Earth policies?"

Eagan clenched his jaw. "Given that we haven't even had time to mention this in our reports... You know, it struck me as odd that we didn't get a heads-up this was coming, back when the EMPs first hit. Something that big would get noticed. I mean, how many people in Korea and the Middle East had to know about this invasion to get something that big organized and executed? It had to be a lot. But nobody warned us."

"Don't forget the Russians in Alaska and the rest of the West Coast. And maybe the Chinese for all we know." Taggart spit into the fire, relishing the angry, violent hiss of moisture hitting the red coals. It fit his mood entirely too well.

"So what are we going to do, Sarge?" Eagan said in a dead voice.

Taggart knew that was his insubordinate way of saying he should think like an enlisted man serving his country, not an officer serving some distant general. Maybe he was right.

"I don't know yet, Eagan. We have orders to abandon

two million enslaved Americans. For now, we delay until I can decide on a long-term strategy. But I do know one thing —we're not in Hotel Company anymore. We stopped being in the Regular Army chain of command a long time ago. Today, we embrace the madness. We're going to start *being* what the troops and civvies have been calling us all along."

Eagan grinned, a vicious look. A predatory look. "Yes, sir. It's about time we started acting like it. Welcome to *Taggart's Titans*, sir. That's what the troops call us. We've been there for a while, waiting for you to join us."

* * *

Ethan decoded the message from the 20s by way of Watcher One, and when his computer chirped the alert that the operation was finished, he sorted through them. After skimming the ones he could decipher, he forwarded it to the outgoing cache to deliver to Taggart. Toward the end of those messages, one caught his attention.

"From the Commander-in-Chief to Taggart? I haven't seen that before." He skimmed further and a frown crept across his face. "It just says to hurry up and follow his move orders."

A chill settled across the room, and the hair on his arms stood up with goosebumps. Something was *not right* about that. Someone else was talking to Taggart, bypassing him, and he had no idea what those orders were... nor who sent them. Ethan felt a rising panic wash over him.

From behind him, arms around his chest, Amber said, "When did we pass along movement orders? Yesterday? I wasn't here, so—"

"That's the thing. He got orders some other way. *We never sent him move orders.*"

Amber froze briefly, and Ethan turned in her arms to

face her. Her eyes were wide and frightened-looking. "We got trouble in River City," he told her, his voice shaky.

She nodded. "We have to warn Taggart."

"Jesus," he breathed, thinking of the high-res satellite images of Clanholme they kept sending him. "They know where we live."

- 18 -

0930 HOURS - ZERO DAY +170

NESTOR LEANED AGAINST a tree and looked over his survivors. Three women and two men—including Natalie and Randy—remained from his original group, along with another half-dozen men and women he had liberated in the past few days who had chosen to follow him. His mind wandered to one of the followers who died earlier this morning, a young woman who looked a lot like Kaitlyn, the Clan child he had saved from dogs. It had been Kaitlyn really, who set him on this new path in life. For giving him the opportunity to redeem himself, he loved her almost like a daughter—like the daughter he lost long ago, whose death had set him on the path that led eventually to saving Kaitlyn and her older friend Brianna.

That long chain of events in his life stretched back behind him in his mind. He sensed a purpose now, some faint glimmering of a new destiny that now seemed to have guided every step he took. Every loss, every victory, the hardships and the blessings—all had led him inexorably here. This was where he was meant to be, where he was needed. Roaming the woods with a band of fellow lost souls, finding meaning through each other and through their mission of destroying the 'vaders so that others, less lost than they, could rest at ease.

He suspected they would all die soon, violently, one at a time or all at once. Whatever happened, their deaths would accomplish something greater than his life ever had in the years leading up to now. Was it God guiding him? Some other higher power with a higher purpose? He felt as though he could *almost* glimpse the threads that formed the web of events that defined his life, both the past and, less clearly, what would come. He recognized this as a holy moment, even if "epiphany" was too fancy a word for the likes of him.

You need me, Nestor. Cut the posturing. Let me free. This is my game to play, not yours.

"Shut up, Other. I let you out when I need you. You have a role to play in this destiny, too, or you wouldn't have afflicted me. You'd be in someone else, some other dead person. Gone with the rest of America, the rest of the Earth."

You're no poet, Nestor. Once, I ruled you, remember? It can happen again.

"You ruled when it was destined that you should. You killed my daughter, but it led me to the Facility. After the EMPs, you killed more, and I was stoned and barely escaped alive, but I *did* escape. Me, not you. And that set us both on this path."

Your "Great Destiny." Rubbish. You're a psycho and a killer, just like me. You are me. We dance the same Waltz to the same bloody music.

"Perhaps. But I recognize God's hand in this, and your time of taking me is done—because I'm here, where I am meant to be. We both serve the same destiny. Now it is His will that you serve me. Stop complaining. I let you out to dance your Waltz when needed."

When no answer came, and having lost the flavor of the

moment he had been savoring, Nestor rose and went to his followers. They knew he talked to himself, but no one said anything about it. He had saved their lives and given them a new purpose after they lost their families, their old lives, everything but the heart that beat in their chests—maybe the gods he talked to would save them, too, they probably supposed. Nestor knew they felt this and thanked God, or Destiny, for the gift of followers. They made his purpose easier.

And he had been achieving his purpose spectacularly since the battle separated him from the Clan and from Kaitlyn. In saving her from the feral dogs, he had become responsible for her life. She would probably never know the debt he owed her—she had given him purpose. Protect Kaitlyn. Protect her Clan. The Clan was destined for something great, and it was his own destiny to help them achieve theirs.

That was why he stayed to fight instead of fleeing when his group escaped the pursuing invaders after that battle. In the days that followed, how many Arabs and Koreans had he and his people killed? The invaders had lost many dozens to his band of guerrillas. Maybe more than a hundred, with half as many slaves now freed to live their own lives for however long they lasted in this grim new America. The cost of those victories had been losing five of his own group, but those who remained were hardened and were learning the Other's lessons fast. Some of the freed slaves always joined the group, too. And for the price of those five brave American fighters, he cost the invaders enough lives that they had been noticeably thinned out now. Fewer patrols, and they didn't venture as far from Adamstown as they once had.

They had a name for his group, now—*Night Ghosts*, a label he assumed lost something in translation. They feared him now. Nestor clenched his fist, rage building against them as the Other began scratching to get out. *They should fear us.* He couldn't tell if that last thought was his own or the Other's.

* * *

Taggart and his HQ encamped in the lee of a long, low hill, fighting the cold wind and the snow. His stomach rumbled, telling him with the precision of a watch that it was now lunchtime, but he put thoughts of food aside.

Eagan said, "Are you sure it's wise to stay offline completely? We might be missing vital orders and intel. Or a heads-up from your Dark Ryder..."

Taggart nodded, looking at a map of the area that was marked up in pencil with any information he thought might be useful. "Aff. The longer we can stay offline, the longer I can put off making a decision about our orders."

"They aren't my orders, sir. At least, that's how I will look at it, and I'm not alone."

"You'd disobey Houle's orders? Even if I left the area? That's pretty harsh." Taggart looked up from the map at Eagan, judging his aide's body language. Eagan didn't look confrontational or even angry, just... resigned, as he returned a level gaze without answering. Yes. He'd make the choice to fight even if it cost him everything. A good man, that one.

Taggart let out a long breath. "I tend to agree with you, Eagan. I haven't decided yet if I'm going to follow those orders, but the thought of leaving two million Americans to suffer doesn't sit well with me or with my Oath. The idea of splitting my command in half doesn't sit well, either. Division in the face of a superior enemy rarely works out well."

Eagan opened his mouth to reply, but then froze. Taggart felt a flash of panic—adrenaline kept people alive, these days

—and stopped to listen for whatever had set off Eagan. He heard—

There. Not distant, a low rumble. Then his hand, resting on the rock where his map lay, felt a vibration. The sensation brought a weird feeling of déjà vu, and part of him fought to remember whatever had triggered the feeling before.

Eagan croaked, "...Train..."

That was it! The rumble was just like a train's. But that was impossible—trains were dead... The rumble grew louder. It came from the far side of the hill. Taggart bolted for the hill and scrambled up the side, sliding a couple of times before getting to the top and flopping onto his belly to crawl the final yard to the crest. He peered carefully over the top.

"No fucking way." Eagan, beside him, stared down the far side of the hill.

Down there were train tracks, but what was amazing was the rumble, growing louder. Down the line, coming around the corner, train cars! One, two, three... But no engine. Then he noticed the cars were pulled by the largest horses he had ever seen. He hadn't seen many horses, but he knew enough to recognize these as *big damn horses*. A flag on the roof of the lead car showed a giant gold star over a red background. Those assholes were making the railways work again...

"Eagan, imagine what's so important to the enemy that they'd get the railways working again."

"Food, guns, or slaves, probably. More important, think of what could be so massive that moving it by rail with *horses* is easier than taking it by wagon? Whatever's in there, I think there's a lot of it."

"Must be," Taggart replied, and peered through binoculars but the car doors were closed. "Can't see anything but about a dozen guards and an eight-pack of big-ass horses."

"They don't come in packs, sir. But they're probably real

valuable to the 'vaders."

"Yep... Say, be a good boy and go get the troops ready. I think we got our lunchtime entertainment set. We got about five minutes, at the speed they're going."

Eagan slid away down the hill, and Taggart soon heard the rustle and commotion of troops getting ready for action. His heart beat faster in savage anticipation. Whatever happened next, twelve damn invaders wouldn't be getting back to barracks tonight and maybe Taggart's forces would have their own big-ass horses when this was over. More importantly, now he knew something important—the rails could work again. Why had he not thought of pulling railroad cars with horses? It was called a "road" for a reason.

If the 'vaders could do it, he could too. And if the trains were running, that meant train stations were back in use. It was enemy materiel on a grand scale. A chance to really hurt the bastards, get payback for thirty thousand enslaved, murdered Americans, and increase his own resources while he was at it.

Taggart knew better than to try to rein in his troops this time. For those 'vaders down there, the whirlwind was looming.

* * *

1530 HOURS - ZERO DAY +171

Cassy slammed her fist into the countertop, a long string of curses flowing out, and only the surprised looks on Michael's and Frank's faces made her stop. "So the invaders are pulling out of Adamstown?"

"That's right," answered Michael, shifting uncomfortably.

That shifting wasn't normal for him, but neither was her

cursing. The circumstances weren't normal. "And they did *what*, again?" She felt the anger rise, and she barely resisted the urge to hit something again. Or someone.

Michael clenched his jaw hard enough that Cassy worried he'd shatter a tooth. "Lined the civilians up and killed them all, one at a time. Cut their throats and left them where they fell, lined up along U.S. Two-Twenty-Two. They say the highway looks like they painted it red."

Frank said, "Then they burned the entire city, turned east, and they're burning everything along their way. They left a note in Korean. Choony translated it, then went out back to throw up."

Michael spit—inside her house, but she let it go—and said, "It's a contingency order issued before the invasion even started. If they are losing a territory, they are to kill everything and everyone, and burn everything they can. 'Deny them to the traitors and terrorists,' the page says."

"They were getting stretched too thin to hang on," Cassy said with savage glee. "Between Brickerville's revenge raiding with no quarter given, and these *Night Ghosts* we heard about slaughtering 'vaders anytime they venture out with less than a whole platoon, they're too weakened to hang on. So they're pulling back to regroup, and then they'll come back through here like a hammer instead of like locusts. But we can stop them when they do, I'm sure of it. Frank, have Ethan alert everyone, and I mean *everyone*. We all need to be ready when the 'vaders come back, and then we'll shove their hammer right up their backsides."

"You got it, Cassy," Frank said.

"Just keep your rifle with you. There'll be action enough for everyone when it happens."

Frank hobbled back out of the room on his crutch, and she didn't have the energy to spare appreciating how well he had recovered from having his foot cut off by an enraged

Peter.

"Michael," she said after Frank left, "these bastards must be moving pretty slowly. Loaded down with their goddamn blood-bought loot, hurt by everyone in the area who can hold a gun but feeling pretty fucking cocky after they murdered all the turncoats at Adamstown. Those people were bastards, but they were American bastards, and the damn Koreans and their ISNA lapdogs did this to them after they had already knuckled under."

"So you want me to gather the fighters, saddle fresh horses, and get ready to kill some bad guys... Aye aye," Michael said, snarling, and swept up his coat on one arm as he stormed out.

Cassy grabbed her coat, too, and headed to the bunker tunnel to tell Ethan what was happening. She practically had to order him to stay in the bunker to man the comms and spread the word when she told him, but he eventually saw reason. He had no place on a battlefield anymore, not with his vital skills. They'd all be crippled without him.

Then she headed back up topside, to the horses. Michael had all the Marines and thirty others, armed and already slinging their grab-bags onto their saddles. The bags had been Ethan's idea. One for everyone in the whole clan meant they could all leave on ten minutes' notice with a three-day supply of everything they needed. Cassy felt "grab-bag" sounded better than "but-out bag" but either way the bags were handy for a better reason.

"Ethan told Taj Mahal, and they're sending a half-dozen more people," she told Michael. "And he's getting Brickerville ready, too. They said they have a great surprise for us, and they'll bring some RPGs, too. We'll see what they have cooked up."

Michael nodded and mounted his horse. From somewhere in the back, a man shouted, "Regulators! Mount up!"

Cassy might normally have grinned at that Old West quote, but not today. She only got up on her horse facing the troops and, when everyone was ready, wheeled her horse around and into a run. Her makeshift army flowed out like water behind her. A flood of revenge was coming for those 'vader bastards—at least for *these* invaders. They had earned it.

Without the worry of 'vaders scattered everywhere, Cassy and her band made good time, arriving at Brickerville in only twenty minutes despite the rough terrain. Waiting there were another thirty or so troops, probably riding all the horses they had left. Most had odd boxes strapped to their horses' flanks like saddlebags; the remainder carried the RPGs they had recovered from the burnt-out nutjob compound. Words were short—there was no need and it wasn't a social visit. Five minutes later, Cassy began the real pursuit with almost eighty troops behind her. The enemy was on foot—they couldn't escape. The radios Ethan had insisted on giving to the outlying major allies despite her initial resistance had paid off in bloody spades.

The mass of troops rode fast, knowing this was not an endurance test. They needed to catch the bastards. Heading east on Highway 322, they galloped on the softer shoulder to save the horses' hooves until it swung southerly at Clay, where they left the road entirely and cantered cross-country directly east. They crossed old, abandoned farms and disused watering arms and useless tractors, past burnt-out houses and dead cars in empty yards. They ignored skeletons hanging from windows or strewn across patios—there would be time enough later to deal with the dead. Cassy imagined them cheering her party on and who knew? Maybe they were watching, vengeful ghosts still awaiting justice.

At Schoeneke Road they turned to follow it northeast as

it shot straight toward I-76 and the Pennsylvania Turnpike, trotting and cantering to eat up miles. She sensed her prey was close; it was that feeling she got when a deer was *about to* come into view, the instinctive part of her brain noting patterns for her unconscious mind to weave together as she looked around. She fought the urge to shout and whoop for bloody joy at what they were bringing the murderous invaders. No sense alerting them.

And then they were there, close ahead—the enemy. The invaders. They murdered two hundred or more unarmed people at Adamstown alone, and Cassy swore they'd lose twice that number this very day. There had been no justice in the past six months, but justice was about to come down on them like a hammer. She was only outnumbered five-to-one, but they were already bloodied, in full retreat, exhausted from carrying their blood-loot. Their greed would be their undoing.

"God," she prayed, her words whipped away by the wind as she kicked her horse into a sprint, "be my shield, and let me be thy rod..." She didn't know if there was a God, not the way her mom did, but right now she felt as though she wore divine armor and nothing could touch her. "...and make these fuckers burn in Hell tonight!" she added, not caring what her mother would say about such a prayer.

A cry rose from the invaders ahead, and they began to run. Most dropped what they were carrying except for their weapons, and a moment later, Cassy and the others were dodging backpacks full of looted gems and jewelry, even paintings the invaders had been carrying away. Cassy would be in shooting range in moments.

Then a sizable group split from the clustered invaders, sprinting northeast toward Schoeneke Church and the dense woods behind it. Cassy yelled, "Michael, go!"

He must have heard, because she saw him swing away

from the group, a dozen Marines riding with him. The other sixty-five Clanners and their allies stayed hard on the heels of the main group until the retreating 'vaders reached a huge limestone quarry to the left of the road, where they scattered like the roaches they were. They practically fought one another to get into positions behind the towering line of machines once used to process the limestone. The rest, for whom there was no room, fled into the quarry's interior. Cassy grinned like a wolf about to bring down a meal. There was no way back out of that quarry but the way they came in. Once the massed troops at the machinery by the entrance were dealt with, it would be time to go hunting for survivors. Those who survived this fight would die soon enough of hunger, having abandoned their bags at the beginning of the rout.

None would leave this place alive if she had anything to say about it. These people might have destroyed America and killed thousands without mercy, but there were still Americans here and Americans fight, she screamed in her mind. They were going to learn their mistake today, right here. Right now.

As she approached the quarry, Cassy saw that they had caught up too late to prevent a sizable group of invaders from taking cover behind the machines. She swerved east away from them, out of immediate gunshot range. The invaders scattered fire at the Clan army, but none hit, and Cassy continued away until the enemy stopped firing. Her frustrated army milled around her, chomping at the bit to get to the prey like a dog whining and barking at game they had treed. She screamed her own rage, like a hawk stooping to a kill, but held up her hand in the time-honored signal to stop.

"Spread out," she ordered. "If they try to escape, I want to see them drop!"

The unit stretched away north and south, forming a

semicircle facing toward the quarry and its machines. Cassy paced back and forth feeling as if she was about to lose her mind with frustration. She hadn't remembered that assembly line, and damn, she did not want to delay her gratification on this hunt. For it was, no mistake, a hunt, and sometimes the hunter had to wait. "We'll starve them out if we have to," she called to her troops, and swung down from her saddle.

After a moment, still struggling to control her frustration, she let out a long breath. To the Brickerville man next to her she said, "They won't get away. They'll starve in there. Hell, they'll drink the quarry water first, and that'll get them. And more of us are on the way—Ethan's spreading the word. This *will end* here."

The man, a stranger to Cassy, clenched his jaw and said, "Yes it will, and sooner than you think." His lips curled back as he said it, baring his teeth.

She paused mid-step. "What do you mean?"

"Those boxes we brought are the drones—"

Cassy cut him off. "Great, but what can the drones do against them?"

"Our leader, Josh, had this idea to use them on the 'vader encampments, but they left before we had them all ready. Then we found even more." He grinned again, "We have twenty set to go now, though, and they're special. Plus we brought some RPGs that they won't much like either."

"Yeah, so what did he come up with?" Cassy asked, trying to sound calm, but knew she was coming across as too eager. She took another deep breath. Damned adrenaline.

"We rigged the dynamite—we have stacks and stack of the stuff. You know the shotgun shell darts that kids make? Rubber cap for weight, nail sticking through—throw the shell and it lands, with the nail acting like a firing pin."

"Can you *please* get to the point?" Why do technician types always get so lost in the how-it-works?

"Right. Well, we rigged up dynamite to the darts and glued-on fins. We got boxes of them with us. We rigged cages on the drones we got, too—they'll hold the dynamite darts. Fly the drone up, tip it and the dynamite falls out, basically a small impact bomb like in the World War Two movies. A nice little nitro-and-sawdust hello to them." He was still grinning.

"But... with drones?"

"Yep. We may not even need the RPGs—just have everyone ready to rush in when things start blowing up. It's going to freak them out."

"Damn, that's brilliant. And it's dusk. They won't see the drones coming even if they hear them. Alright, now we're banging on bacon!"

The man looked confused so she added, "Permission to gloat, you guys earned it," and grinned at him. She'd explain her daughter's slang some other time, if she ever figured out what it meant herself.

Cassy walked down the line of fighters, passing on the news and the plan, and more than one laughed or cheered. It'd be like watching a movie, one commented.

Twenty minutes later it seemed dark enough to risk the drones, which had been laid out and prepared. Each carried four "dynamite bombs," and it was clear the Brickerville people with their controllers had practiced because they seemed confident their plan would work. They did seem to know what they were doing so she didn't interfere, but watched closely as they readied their air force. "Ha! The new Confederation Air Force." She laughed, and a few people nearby laughed with her.

When the drones launched into the air, they sounded like a swarm of bees. They took off cleanly, without any collisions, quickly gaining altitude and speed. Yes, the Brickerville people had practiced. She lost sight of them in the growing darkness but the controllers each had a monitor for the drones' cameras, and the pilots didn't seem concerned, so she turned back to watch whatever would happen next.

She didn't have long to wait. Although she could no longer see the drones, the effect they had was astounding. All along the 200-foot length of the lined-up machinery, some forty sticks of dynamite exploded within a few seconds of each other, on both sides of the line.

"Go, go, go!" Cassy screamed, and along with the others, she sprinted toward the enemy. The machinery was only just becoming visible amidst the fireballs as they got close enough to engage any survivors. The few surviving soldiers near the machinery fled toward the quarry itself, and those few already inside provided covering fire. In only a few minutes, Cassy and her army had taken the smoking wreckage of the quarry machinery and now faced across it toward the quarry opening, firing at the backs of the few straggling invaders.

All eyes turned to Cassy, awaiting the inevitable orders. To the two fighters next to her she said, "Spread the word—I want a third of our forces on that south embankment, for elevated coverage. Tell them to rally along the ridge and then fire at will until all the easy targets are dropped."

The two ran off to pass the order along, crouching to stay as low as they could. Cassy didn't blame them. These few invaders were in a defensible position, and it was almost a tragedy that the north rim of the quarry looked too unstable to put thousands of pounds of weight along it to get some crossfire. "It is what it is," she muttered, fuming. She wanted nothing more than to charge in there and exact blood revenge on these foreign troops who'd slaughtered so many of her fellow Americans.

Cassy's remaining troops were by and large gathered up behind the machinery with her, three deep because it wasn't long enough for everyone to have a spot. "Listen up," Cassy bellowed, and noticed that her 'command voice' was improving. Soon it would be as good as Michael's, she hoped. "When the ridge opens fire, we're going in. We're going to hunt these bastards down while the ridge keeps them pinned. Grab a buddy, and *stay with your buddy*. I see anyone wandering alone, they're not getting cake tonight for dessert!"

A cry went up, cheering her as her troops chomped at the bit every much as she did, psyching themselves up for the coming assault. As much as she wanted to go in and get her hands bloody, there was another reason for her to lead this charge—she had a mystique now among the allies, and the more she bolstered that image, the stronger the Confederation would be. With luck, it would survive after she was long gone, but the confederation needed time to solidify. She was going to have to risk her life for the Confederation to buy it time to gel so it would outlive her. Maybe if she slowed down mid-assault so her wave of soldiers made first contact? A catch-22, but it would be fine so long as she didn't die here. That would be tragic...

A couple of minutes later, the troops along the south ridge opened fire, and a few cries of pain rose from within the quarry. Her troops cheered. Then Cassy was up on her feet. She sprinted forward, waving the others to follow. As a wave, they rose up and charged after her, dozens of fighters running. They entered the mouth of the quarry, which would have been the Kill Zone had she not put troops on the ridge. As it was, resistance was minimal so far. A few 'vaders were struck down where they hid, surprised looks on their damn faces as they died.

Cassy slowed, and most of her troops flowed past and around her like a wave on a beach moving around some rock. As they ran by, Cassy grabbed two men near her. "Follow me," she shouted over the din. They moved from rocks to rocks, what little cover there was. She'd thought about following the spiral-cut walls, but there would be zero cover there. Instead, they skirted the northern wall.

Maybe she wasn't the first into battle, but there was enough fighting to go around, and she spotted movement. Ahead lay a pile of rubble large enough to hide a couple people, and she could just see the tip of a rifle extending above it. Someone on the ridge kept a steady beat of fire on the crest of that mound, keeping the enemies' heads down. *Boom*-one-two-three-*Boom* went the cycle. Cassy put her left hand out, restraining one fighter beside her.

She waited until the *two* count in her head before sprinting toward the pile, her two "buddies" to either side. They rounded the corner just after the next shot had struck the rubble and saw not two but five ISNA soldiers huddled there. They seemed to notice her group just as Cassy opened fire with her buddies, and two 'vaders went down bloody.

The other three, though, returned fire. The man to Cassy's left, a Liz Towner judging by his jacket, collapsed when a round struck him in the head, clearly dead. Cassy and her remaining companion both went down to the ground at the same time by pure reflex. As Michael had taught her, taking cover was just instinctive when rounds came at people. She used the butt of her M4 to slow her fall, but it was still rather painful. Marines did that over and over again during their training with Michael, she'd seen, and after being taught the move, she had a new respect for how easy they made it look. In reality, *that shit hurt!* Better than getting shot though, she realized as the whizz of bullets passed over her head.

She lay there exchanging fire with the enemy, but they'd taken a prone position behind their dead—Cassy and whoever was next to her were more exposed. She looked around seeking help, but all around her the scene was the same. Small knots of her people fighting clusters of the enemy.

A huge fireball appeared a hundred yards away, and the explosion's report washed over her, bouncing off the quarry walls, making her ears ring painfully—one of the drones, perhaps, had dropped another stick of dynamite on a pile of rubble that hid a particularly troublesome enemy strong point. For whatever reason, they'd dropped dynamite into the middle of this battle, and it sent a shower of pebbles and a bit of gore out over thirty yards, some raining down on her painfully. One struck the soft spot at the back of her left knee, and a bolt of pain shot from her knee to her groin. She bit her lip, but didn't cry out.

That did give her an idea, though. In the adrenaline, she forgot that she had two of the Clan's precious grenades. She pulled one off her "combat webbing," really just suspenders with bits of cloth sewn to it to mimic MOLLE gear. She pulled the pin, but kept the spoon compressed. To her remaining fighter she said, "On three, cover me and pour on the fire!"

The man nodded, aimed, and started the count.

One - the 'vader fired a burst at them, one round bouncing off the rubbled ground barely a foot from her face.

Two - she almost lost her grip on the grenade, her hands sweating as much as the rest of her, but she kept her grip. Her heart raced faster.

Three - the man beside her fired his rifle, an AK-style assault rifle, as fast as his finger would pull the trigger. *Bang, bang, bang, bang...* To Cassy's ear it sounded only a little slower than some actual automatics did, even though it was clearly only a semi-automatic weapon.

As the first shot rang out, Cassy rose to her uninjured right knee, with left foot flat on the ground in front of her, and hurled the grenade with all her might just as Michael had taught her—you couldn't throw it like a baseball or you'd tear up your elbow, he'd said, and the method he taught was painful and uncomfortable, but worked and didn't shred anyone's elbow. The grenade sailed through the air...

It would miss, she saw. It landed atop the rubble that protected her target from the troops on the ridge. She didn't have time to stare at it though, as the three remaining ISNA soldiers returned fire. One round whistled by her right ear, and she felt a streak of burning pain along her cheek. The trooper next to her cried out in pain, a terrible sound, and dropped his rifle to curl up in a ball. He clutched his left hip, the one that had been facing the enemy as the trooper lay prone. He was out of this fight, if he even lived. No time to help him, though, as all three enemy laid fire toward Cassy. She saw tufts of dirt and rock fly up, tracking along the ground toward her—puff, puff, puff.

Just before the tracking bullets found her, however, there was a terrible *whump* as her grenade went off, seeming to suck the air straight out of her lungs. Fortunately, she hadn't been looking at it when it went off. A new voice cried out from her enemies' position. One of the ISNA fighters staggered out of the smoke clutching his throat. His lifeblood spurt several feet from between his fingers, with every heartbeat. Cassy put him out of his misery with a bullet to his head, even as she rose to her feet. She sprinted toward the smoke and dust that nearly blocked any view of the enemy, firing as she went. As she entered the cloud, she saw two men, both flat on their backs but getting up. The closer one had black and blood and dirt stuck to his face, and blood dripped from his long beard. She pulled her trigger and two rounds struck him in his belly and chest, and he flopped over backwards without crying out.

The remaining ISNA fighter had risen and stood almost

next to her. He swung the butt of his rifle up, snapping it forward to strike the bottom of her barrel, and her own rifle flew from her hands.

Fear and adrenaline, her constant companions, shot through her and without pausing, she put her hands together as if gripping a baseball bat and swung at the enemy's head. He reared his head back just in time and she barely missed, even as he reflexively raised his rifle to protect himself. When Cassy missed, however, the momentum carried her around and her hands struck his rifle. It, too, went flying. She followed up with her right knee, planting it in his belly.

He let out an "oof" as the air was knocked from him, but he stood up like a piston rising, and his uppercut smashed into her chin; she flew backwards with a cry of pain and fear.

For a split second, her body refused to obey her commands and she only lay there. The ISNA soldier pulled his combat knife out from its sheath at his waist and bolted toward her.

Faced with this new threat, Cassy's body decided suddenly to work again. Her right foot shot out and connected with the man's knee. There was a sharp *crack* and he cried out, falling forward—landing right on top of her. Pressing her down into the rocky ground. A thousand little pebbles pressed painfully into her back and spine, and a thought bolted through her mind, completely out of place: I hate quarries...

Her enemy held his knife like an icepick and drove it down toward her face. Cassy reached up and caught his wrists with her own, stopping the blow, but he leaned into it, adding more and more of his body weight to the knife plunging toward her face and throat. Her left arm let out a quiver—soon it would collapse and she would die, and the Clan would die, and the Confederation. Houle would rule the world, Taggart would be given to the Koreans as a gift, her daughter would be killed or worse. And it would all be her fault. Why had she led this attack? Stupid, foolish... She had told herself that her image required it, the Confederation's future required it. But laying there, the knife an inch now from her left eyeball, she knew—it was pride, and hubris. She was now too important to do whatever the hell she wanted—and it was about to cost her life.

A tear ran down her cheek. "Please," she said through strained, gritted teeth, "I have... a daughter..."

The ISNA man only grinned, half his teeth broken and black. Her arms were weakening; the blade came down another inch. She closed her eyes and could feel just the tip of the blade on her left eyelid...

She heard the abrupt noise of gravel crunching, and the weight on her arms was suddenly gone as the sound of fighting reached her ears. She opened her eye and saw someone she didn't recognize struggling with her ISNA fighter in the dirt and rubble. More people she didn't recognize ran by, from right to left, heading into the quarry's interior. Holy crap! These people, these insane people, had *come down the north embankment* of the quarry! She saw another sliding down, seeming almost like he was surfing, but his hard landing proved it hadn't been intentional. More were coming down, as well. They weren't ISNA, but she didn't know who they were.

The newcomers ran on, but in the confusion, they left their one man still fighting on the ground with Cassy's ISNA warrior. They rolled around, the dust rose until it was hard to see who was on top. Then there was a cry of agony, cut short by a chopping, meaty, wet sound.

The ISNA fighter scrambled to his feet. "*Allahu 'akbar!*" he shouted, and the knife in his hand dripped blood. Cassy saw, however, that he was wounded—his foe had left a knife stuck in his shoulder.

Cassy wasted no time. She sprinted at him, ignoring the pain in her leg, and rammed into him from behind with her shoulder, arms wrapping around his waist, and they both fell forward into the dirt, while his knife flew away out of sight, spinning like a frisbee. Her enemy landed face-first, more or less *on* his face, while Cassy landed atop him. She straddled him and from her waistband, she whipped out her own knife.

The ISNA fighter bucked and struggled, nearly throwing Cassy off, but failing to do so. As she recovered, he spun around onto his back. Now the scene was reverse. Cassy plunged her knife downward toward him. He caught her wrists, and they struggled, the blade inching closer to his chest. Sweat again poured from them both as they struggled, but the blood he was losing from the knife stuck in his shoulder made this battle a foregone conclusion. With renewed energy and purpose, Cassy shoved even harder, baring her teeth at the man and hissing at him with every ragged breath.

"*Tabaet 'awamir,*" he screamed, fear-filled eyes wide as saucers.

"Fuck you," Cassy growled, and the knife went lower still —about a half-inch of the tip slowly slid into him.

Then he said over and over, begging, "*La 'astatie 'an 'amut huna...*"

Cassy gritted her teeth and put the last of her energy into pushing down on the knife, down on his arms. The man's arms quivered, and then gave out, and the blade slid an inch at a time into his chest until only the handle remained visible.

"*Allah 'anqadhnaa,*" he whispered, a tear rolling down one cheek.

As the light left his eyes, Cassy flopped down onto him, exhausted. She'd used every ounce of energy she had, and she knew that soon the pain would start as adrenaline left.

She'd probably vomit from the adrenaline crash, this time, as her stomach already felt queasy.

"Fuck your Aunt Quadnie," she said between ragged breaths. Probably not the man's actual dying words, but whatever. That's what it had sounded like.

Finally catching her breath, Cassy rose shakily to her feet and looked around as the Confederation "army" swarmed throughout the quarry, now in squads—hunter-killer teams that did their job with more enthusiasm than discipline, brutally slaughtering what enemy survivors remained. There weren't many.

Fifteen minutes later, there were none.

- 19 -

1000 HOURS - ZERO DAY +173

CASSY LEFT THE home of the second wounded Clanner, feeling rather bouncy about the score, despite the brace on her leg. Only two others were wounded among her people—a Marine and one of the Clanners who attacked the quarry—and two fatalities. Of the wounded, the Marine would be out for a month, probably, but he'd recover. Cassy herself would recover quickly, in all likelihood.

The thought that hundreds of ISNA fighters and their North Korean masters wouldn't be returning, ever, made the light of day seem brighter, and she didn't even mind the hazy, overcast sky. It had been night of celebration for her survivors, celebrating life. Mourning the dead would come soon enough. In these times of daily life-and-death decisions and events, it seemed people turned to celebrating their own survival before mourning their losses. Cassy wondered what future sociologists would say about that—

Her handheld radio crackled, and Ethan's voice squawked, "Cassy, Ethan. We just heard from Liz Town, and you'll want to hear this. Come on down when you get a chance."

"On my way, be there in a minute."

She limped her way to the tunnel and let herself in. Once in the bunker, she found Ethan at his computers, of course. "Hey there, what's up?" Cassy asked.

"Liz Town says a couple of people from out west were captured in their territory, but they turned out not to be Hershey spies. The couple said they were on their way to Clanholme and that they were representatives of the Republic. You know, the Empire?"

"Yeah? What do they want?" Cassy asked as she adjusted the brace over her knee.

"They're coming here to talk to you, personally, and they knew where we were. Gave directions and everything, just to prove they were who they said. Liz Town has a couple guards riding in with them and they'll be here in half an hour. You might want to get ready."

"Well, that was unexpected. Thanks for the heads-up."

She made her way back topside and got busy cleaning herself up and putting on some less travel-worn clothes. No point meeting Empire envoys in her farm work and fighting clothes. She brushed her hair and stuck it up under an Eagles ballcap she scavenged from a convenience store that had no food left, but lots of ballcaps. The hat was handy sometimes. Go Eagles!

A half hour later, two tall men wearing old western-style riding dusters and leading pretty little quarter horses came up to her home, hitched their horses outside, and entered with the two Liz Town guards and Frank.

"I am Cassy, leader of the Clan, and this is Frank, our general manager. Some tea, gentlemen?" she offered.

"No, thanks. I'm Oscar and this is Jason." The two sat on the couch where Cassy motioned them.

"Nice to get off your feet?"

"Yes, it is. I wonder if you might put us up for the night? We've been sleeping under the stars for quite a while," said

Oscar, who seemed to do all the talking so far.

"Doubtful. We don't let strangers stay with us. But we'll give you some supplies if you need them, and you can camp outside Clanholme. Under watch, of course," she said in as cool and neutral a voice as she could manage.

"Ah well. I had to ask. These days, no one remembers manners or even what they used to look like. We will be delighted to encamp outside of Clanholme, at least until our business here is done and we can get back to civilization."

Cassy forced a smile. Jerk-offs, leading with an insult like that. "As you wish, for now at least. I appreciate your instruction on being civilized and will give it all the consideration it deserves. So what does the Empire want with us?"

"Wow. Not even dinner first."

"We mostly eat dinner only with friends, and even then only if they offer something back. Food is a bit of a luxury item these days." Cassy adjusted her cap to mask a growing nervousness and anger.

"Well," Oscar said, "it is my delight and honor to let you know that you have been specially selected to win a fabulous prize. The *Republic* would like to be friends with you and your friends. Nice and friendly. I assure you, our friendship does offer plenty of something back."

"Great! We like friends, too, the more the merrier. So, what does the Empire offer as 'friendship' and of course, what does it require in return?"

Oscar let out a deep breath, a pained expression on his face. "You wound me. We're not an empire, Miss..."

"Shores."

"Miss Shores, we're not an empire. I mean it when I say that we're a republic. Every enclave that has joined us has done so of their own free will, after voting. We insist on that. Most are quite happy to join, of course, since we have food and medicine they often lack."

Frank replied before Cassy had a chance, saying, "I think I can speak for everyone here when I say that we're not really inspired by the Empire's democratic values. We do hear things, you know. Your reputation precedes you. We have enough, so that's not the carrot-on-a-string you seem to think it is. No offense."

"No offense taken, I assure you. I've heard worse, and they've mostly changed their minds later, but like you said, you aren't that hungry. That's a bit surprising. Your little corner of Pennsylvania managed to hang on for the most part."

Cassy said, "We've worked hard to get by and worked together to do it. Not a lot of trust for outsiders in these parts, though. We've been through a lot."

Oscar glanced at Jason, but the latter was still unreadable as far as Cassy could tell. Perhaps he was the enforcer, but given his average stature that seemed unlikely. Maybe a negotiator? It was weird that he hadn't spoken yet. "Well, that's another thing about these parts—never had a lot of subtlety even before the EMPs. You've had to work hard against extraordinary odds, so subtlety is expendable. You deserve praise, not threats, and we're not here to threaten you. We only want to talk, and I personally think it would be foolish not to at least talk. After all, we're your biggest neighbor, invaders included, and we're what, fifty miles from your doorstep? We want friendly neighbors who don't play the radio too loud until two in the morning on a Tuesday, if you see what I mean."

"Well, we invited you both in, Oscar. So we haven't forgotten how to be hospitable. Are you hungry? We have stew, but I'm afraid the bread won't be done until lunchtime." If they said yes, she'd be sure there was something extra added to their meals...

Jason spoke up for the first time, which Cassy found relieving, and said, "No, thank you. These days offering food is more than polite, and accepting when you're not hungry is more than rude."

Well that had been just the right thing to say. So she was right: not the muscle of the operation. "You're welcome. So Oscar, you haven't answered my first question."

Oscar said, "You asked what the Republic might want from you, that we would reach out to you. You also hinted at some rather unkind things. I'm not going to say we haven't had to send peacekeepers into some areas, those who couldn't help themselves and declined help otherwise, but we've only done that to save lives. You aren't in that position, clearly."

"We have already helped ourselves," Cassy replied, noting that Oscar was continuing to skirt around actually answering her question. "So what of the people you turned away to starve to death? Your hometown is mostly rural, surrounded by cities, and we've heard stories. People killed at your borders, stacked like cordwood. It's difficult to believe the helpful big brother projection, given that."

Oscar frowned, not even trying to hide it. "I'm sorry you see our own necessities that way, Miss Shores. How nice it must be from your position, where you've never, ever had to turn anyone away and have always had enough to take care of outsiders. We have not been that fortunate, but I ask you not to judge us too harshly. We weren't able to take care of half the people in three states by ourselves, no. But we never killed needlessly."

Cassy's jaw dropped, and she felt her cheeks flush. She couldn't tell if it was from anger or embarrassment, or both. "You sanctimonious—"

Frank cut her off, chopping the air with his hand, "No. We have not been that fortunate. We *have* had to turn people away. Nine of ten people will be dead in a year because there isn't enough to go around, and those who hand out all they have won't save everyone, they'll just be left without enough for themselves. I will not judge you for that, and neither will *Mrs*. Shores. Please accept our apology if we seemed to judge you. But there is a difference between turning people away and forcing them to take help they do not want."

Cassy's jaw snapped shut, and she remained quiet as she fought to regain her composure. To her, it sounded like these guys were carving up America's carcass and fighting over its bones—and winning, mostly—so they weren't the innocent helpers they portrayed themselves as. She watched Oscar intently for his reaction.

Oscar didn't seem flustered by Frank's comment at all. Instead, he smiled, a casual and friendly expression, and said, "Absolutely, Frank. And that difference is called 'saving the ones who can be saved.' It's like triage at a hospital. When there is not enough to save all, you save the ones you can. We've done that. They haven't been forced to join us, nor enslaved. Once they saw the benefits of joining us, they did so voluntarily. But please note that we have not yet asked you to join the Republic. To the contrary, we asked what it would take to be friends. If the Republic wants more than that from you, we have not said so. You have pre-judged us and you leaped to conclusions. Whether you're right about us or not is irrelevant so far because we've only talked about being friendly neighbors."

A lawyer, then, masking threats under a velvet glove...

"Well," Frank replied, "you got me there. I don't think you did ask us to join you. That's fantastic news, and I can't wait to tell our friends that you aren't interested in having us all join you. They're sure to ask, once word gets out that we received Empire guests, and now I'll have something good to tell them."

Hah! She had forgotten that Frank was in his home waters with people like this—he had worked with and around them for years. Sure enough, it was Oscar's turn to flush, though he kept his face carefully blank. "I didn't say that, either. I've said that the Republic wishes to be friends with you, but I have not said what that friendship means."

Frank didn't look perturbed at that. "Well, Mrs. Shores did ask, but I can't say you ever actually answered her rather direct question." Frank paused, then continued, "But we seem to be putting words into your mouth whether we say you do or do not want us to join the Republic. I fail to see a third choice in all this, but maybe you could enlighten us. I wouldn't want to put words into your mouth again."

Cassy froze, trying to mask her delight at Frank's handling of these men, and turned her head back to Oscar, one eyebrow raised. Much rode on Oscar's response, after all, so she made no effort not to openly stare, waiting for his reply. But it was Jason who spoke next.

"The third option is that Oscar and I are here to evaluate what sort of threat you present. Whether you'll be worth dealing with on our way to our real objective. And whether, in the long run, you'll be in the category of people we couldn't help, or people who needed our help."

Frank didn't answer for a moment, but Cassy didn't take her eyes off Jason when Frank finally did reply. "It doesn't escape my notice that those who needed your help were better off taking it than not."

Oscar chuckled, but it wasn't a menacing sound. "You're smart, I'll give you that, Frank. If we can help people, we aren't willing to let them suffer their own foolish pride. We'd very much like to hang out for a few days, get to know your people and the culture you've grown since the EMPs. Everyone has been different, so far. I guess the pre-EMP notion that we're all one culture was way off the mark. A useful fiction, I suppose. We are currently asking your permission to stay awhile, maybe a few days to a couple weeks. We'll work the fields with you, or whatever we need to do to pay our way while we're here. But I'd like to see for myself whether we can be friends."

Cassy found herself nodding without realizing it. Fear, she decided, but maybe her fears were well-founded. She fought to keep her voice even as she said, "I would not be so rude to the official representatives of another survivor community. Of course you can stay, so long as you earn your keep while you're here. I have only one... 'request,' as you say."

"And what's that?" Oscar asked.

"I ask that you be courteous guests and not hammer my people with questions or snoop around unescorted. If you're unfamiliar with our farming methods, you could accidentally fall into danger and we wouldn't want that." Nor did she want them mapping their booby traps on Clanholme's approaches. "If you, the representatives of the Empire, have any questions you need to ask, pose them to Frank or myself as the representatives of this community."

"Oh, of course, Miss Shores. We would not dream of being bad houseguests, so to speak. If I have any direct questions, we will be sure to ask you."

Yeah, right... but she didn't figure he'd turn down the chance to hear what her people thought while working with them, either. And she didn't miss his refusal to use the more traditionally polite "Mrs." form of address when "Miss," in a patriarchal culture, would imply she was vulnerable. Not to mention, their refusal to tell her what they would want in return for their "friendship" was alarming, to say the least.

She felt suddenly quite certain that she swam in a much bigger and deeper ocean, now, and these were circling sharks.

***

1230 HOURS - ZERO DAY +176

Jaz sat next to Choony with her tray—bright red plastic now instead of a wood trencher, since some of the scrounging parties had the super bright idea of taking stuff from fast food joints all over the place—and nudged Choony with her elbow. "We shoulda thought of these ourselves, you know."

Choony set his fork down on his own red tray. "I don't know. The wooden trenchers had a kind of charm to them, I think. They felt better. More real."

"Only because you hug trees and stuff. You can't honestly tell me you'd rather wash the wood ones than these plastic things when it's your turn for KP. Plus I hear they're going to be super useful for seed beds in the cold frames."

Choony smiled and tapped his finger on his tray, like he was testing it. Weirdo.

"Yes, I can see how they'd be useful for that," he said. "But we only have KP once a month, so it isn't that bad."

She shrugged. "So what do you make of the Empire people? They're always asking questions about everything we do. Whoever is working with them gets an earful, all questions and no conversation. Makes the job take forevvver." Jaz took a bite of bread and caught the unmistakable flavor of cattail pollen. It was light, but noticeable.

She'd gotten used to the pollen flavor and now sort of preferred it to the straight-flour bread. Plus grinding the flour was hard, and the pollen was ready-made. It cut the labor in half, so they ended up getting twice as much bread for the same effort. No more bread rationing...

"It can't be changed, though," Choony said. "They are here until they decide to leave or Cassy decides to risk war by kicking them out."

Jaz rolled her eyes. "Puh-lease. We're going to war in the spring anyway. Everybody knows that. They want access to the farming area, and we're in the way when they want to come get it."

Choony didn't reply, and they ate lunch in a comfortable silence. It was nice, spending time with Choony, because he didn't feel like he needed to talk constantly about himself, and she found herself okay with just being quiet and spending time with him.

Since the EMPs and the Clan, she hadn't really found herself attracted to the rough kind of guy anymore. Maybe the rough edges were a way to be sort of free in the old world, like you could do what you wanted around those guys without getting lectured, but these days? These days, those guys did a lot of dying. Couldn't fit in, couldn't go along to get along.

Choony once told her that when water was scarce, deep roots were needed to survive. They had been talking about how it wasn't so bad being in the Clan, even if most days were packed with chores from dawn to dusk just to survive. Jaz's old "type" didn't have any roots, much less deep ones.

But Choony totally wasn't like the thugs she'd known on the street. He had grown his deep roots days after getting here—it had taken her longer than it took him, really. And he was non-violent. In the old world she'd have thought him a coward, but she'd seen him run *toward* the enemy to grab a wounded Clanner. So he was one of the bravest of them all, really. Maybe that was what made her so interested.

Whatever the reason, she loved his company. She did catch him watching her when he thought she wasn't looking, like most guys did. But this was different. And he wasn't afraid of dying so he couldn't be afraid of her the way some dudes were. It wasn't cowardice. Respect, maybe? She could probably approach him if she wanted to, but she'd have to be serious. That was the problem; the whole "serious" part made her nervous as hell.

Soon enough, lunch was over and then it was time for her to do "farm stuff" while Choony cleaned up the horse stalls. He sure liked the animals, all of them, and they seemed to like him. She hoped she and Choony would both be to dinner at the same time tonight.

* * *

"...isn't like they're going anywhere," Frank said, and Cassy rubbed her temples in frustration, trying to concentrate on what he was saying. "We're going to have to fight them, and here we are giving their scouts all the intel they could want. Didn't even have to take the effort to actually spy, just changed their title to 'envoys' and we invite them in, instead of taking them to the Smoke Shack like the last two spies."

Michael said, "You know I agree with you, Frank, but can we stop them? If it's hopeless, then it's better to bend over for them than fight them, if they're just going to have their way with us anyway. It hurts less if you just relax."

Frank groaned. "God, Michael, must everything be a joke? Besides, that shit's not funny."

"No, it isn't. But if we pick fights we can't win, then we're *literally* going to get bent over and screwed."

Frank didn't reply, his lips pursed and eyebrows furrowed. Michael shrugged and turned to look at Cassy. She could only shrug.

Cassy said, "Listen, I'm going to make the decision I think gives us the best risk and reward ratio. I'm not playing the long odds with our lives as the stakes, got it? But if I think we have a chance to resist, or to negotiate an advantage, I'm damn well going to. If I think we can get them to just take a slice of our pie and leave us alone with the rest, we'll give up the slice before we lose half our people winning a war, much less risk losing everything. I—"

There was a loud knock at the door. Cassy frowned, irritated. "Come in, dammit."

The door opened and Joe Ellings stepped in, wiping his boots on the mat first. "Afternoon, y'all," he said as he closed the door behind him. "I was hoping to have a word with you, Cassy."

"Go ahead, Joe," Cassy said, reining in her irritability.

"I been thinking about this Empire problem we got coming. 'Member how them 'vaders used to fly around gassing everyone, dropping bombs and whatnot?" He stopped and cocked his head, waiting.

Oh, so it wasn't a rhetorical question. "Yes, Joe, I remember. I'm sure we're all glad their jets are gone, or things would have gone a lot differently this winter."

"Well that's right, of course. But what if all them airplanes ain't gone? And what if they could be ours, not theirs? You reckon that's something?"

Cassy had frozen, staring at Joe. What the hell was he talking about? "Well... yeah, Joe. Of course. But the jets are dead, just like most of the cars and everything else. Unless you know something I don't?" she asked quietly.

"Well now, picture it. What if we get all them 'vaders lined up out in the field like so much stalks of corn. What do you do with a field o' corn?"

"Cut it down," Frank said.

"But before you get to harvesting, ya gotta do something else first," Joe said, raising an eyebrow. "Ya gotta dust the bugs off of 'em. And I reckon to do that, you gotta have crop-dusters. Probably hundreds of them old crop-dusters lying around now."

"Aren't those planes dead?" Cassy asked.

"The spray systems and what not are probably dead, but a lot of 'em still got old mechanical flight systems. Especially if you can rustle up one of them old biplanes. And they don't run on that fancy gas jets use, no ma'am, they'll burn just about anything."

Frank nodded, smiling.

Joe continued, "Now follow me here, okay? I reckon out of all us White Stag people that done joined with y'all, at least fifteen of us knew about flying them things. I been dustin' since I was eight or nine, same with most of them others."

Cassy's jaw had dropped and now her eyes lit up. What. The. Hell. Why didn't *she* think of that? Of course not, she wasn't a farmer. "Holy hell, that's genius! Joe Ellings, I think I do love you," she shouted, grinning, and wrapped her arms around him.

Joe stood up, blushing, and looking not at all comfortable with the display of affection. "Just a regular old idea, Cassy. I'm just glad I could be useful."

"Oh, you brilliant, brilliant man! You know what you've done here, right? You just reshaped the whole damn situation!" Cassy grabbed him up in another bear hug. She glanced at Frank and Michael, and they were on their feet, mouths open and eyes aglow as well.

"You can't tell *anyone* about this, do you understand me, Joe Ellings? Especially not those Empire guys. Keep it to yourself!" When she let him go, he was grinning. The Clan would have an air force! They'd only get the drop one time, but damn if the Clan didn't have one hell of a brand new ace up their sleeve now.

* * *

Colonel Taggart ducked his head as he entered the big masonry-and-earth root cellar he was using as a temporary HQ. He'd banged his head a couple of times at first, and now ducking was a habit. "What do you have for me, Eagan?"

"Sir, I'm glad the runner I sent found you. We have traffic from your friend Dark Ryder."

Taggart frowned. He'd just had traffic a few days ago—the orders to abandon this area to the enemy, leaving nearly two million Americans enslaved. "Alright, get it decoded."

Taggart sat in his rescued swivel chair and leaned back, letting out a moan of appreciation to be off his feet for the first time in two days, it seemed. They'd been hungry for revenge after finding thirty thousand murdered slaves—murdered *Americans*—and went after the units that did it. Unfortunately, the invaders had a head start, and Taggart and his units kept missing them.

Everywhere they went, the civilians were gone and the whole place was on fire. That told him they were closing in. They must have been confident of outrunning him or they'd have left more fields of the dead. But then he found a warehouse with hundreds of bicycles among the dead computers and other items being shipped everywhere and anywhere from there. He put some of the new members of his units, the released slaves, on those bikes figuring they'd be hungry for revenge.

Well, they had been—they encircled a few enemy units and waited. When the units attacked their slaves, surprise surprise, the slaves attacked back, causing enough distraction for Taggart's men to close in. Then the battles became short and bloody. They'd repeated the process for the last two days, and Taggart had been kept busy keeping everything organized.

"Here we go, sir. They're from the *real* Dark Ryder this time. Shall I read them?"

Taggart, leaning back in the chair and rubbing his fatigued eyes vigorously, muttered that he should. Eagan cleared his throat, and Taggart heard the sound of his staff sergeant ruffling through the sheets one at a time.

"Interesting, sir. It's from the C-in-C again. I guess he figured we never left, but we knew he'd find out eventually. His new orders are to head to a small town called Lititz, or actually just south of it a bit. It says that there are small units coming through the region. Loyalists. I guess that means loyal to *him*. He wants us to go meet them, gather with them in central Pennsylvania east of Reading, and prepare for a major op in spring. His units will filter through for the next couple of months. We're to strengthen our control of the Lititz region for his loyalists and allies."

Eagan stopped abruptly and the room went silent. When Eagan didn't continue, Taggart looked up, saw his aide watching him, and said, "Yeah, I caught that too. Allies. Who the hell are the 'allies' of his loyalists? If they follow his orders, shouldn't they all be called loyalists, too?"

"Sir, maybe so, but the allies still have to be other Americans. I mean, Canada and Mexico didn't invade us or something. They got hit with EMPs, too."

"Affirmative," Taggart said with a sigh. "So some other region has gotten themselves organized somehow and is taking orders from General Houle—the only allies he'd take would be obedient ones. That's my take on it, anyway."

"You'll need to decide whether we migrate over there or stay here, sir. It's a tough choice—follow orders or do what's needed here despite orders."

"I know one thing, and that's that I am not trying to wander all over Pennsylvania with damn near a division of guerrillas, most of 'em not even military. Not when I'm actively engaged with the real enemy already. And I'm not eager to babysit Regular Army units and *their* guerrillas until the weather warms up. No way."

"I was hoping you'd say that. I'm looking forward to Operation Little Blue Engine Who Could." Eagan smirked and gazed innocently at the overhead.

Taggart snorted. "Ain't that a mouthful of stupid. I'm not saying that every time we talk about this. Operation Jesse James fits a lot better. Nice and historical, too. We know where their key railway stations are, where they keep their herds of horses and hide stockpiles of food or whatever they're moving on these railways. We're going to strike those and cripple the enemy's transport and logistics. Those same railways will let us strike hard and deep and quick."

"Keep them squealing from the feeling, sir?"

"Do you ever get tired of irritating me? Isn't it exhausting?"

"Yes sir, but totally worth the effort."

Taggart tried to suppress a grin, but failed. It was hard to yell at someone when grinning, so he gave up on the idea. "Fine, fine. Okay, new plan. We're going to send them a company—a platoon of troops with military experience and two platoons of the civvy fighters. Tomorrow they can leave to head toward this place... What was it called?"

"It's called Penryn. It's south of Lititz, sir."

"Okay, we'll send them to Penryn. They can handle babysitting the General's troops and guiding them up to northwest Pennsylvania. That's where a lot of the fighting is, according to the scuttlebutt I get from Dark Ryder, and it gets the General's people out of our damn way."

"Scuttlebutt is the Squids and Jarheads, sir. In the Army we just use real English and call them rumors."

Taggart clenched his jaw as he turned to write out the orders. "Find me that company and go be useful for once," he snapped, but Eagan still smirked as he saluted and left. Damn, that kid really was like a little brother. Only more irritating. But he trusted Eagan to pick the best people he could for the mission.

* * *

1330 HOURS - ZERO DAY +178

Cassy jumped a bit as her radio crackled and then Ethan's voice came through. "Cassy, be advised, Taj Mahal is reporting they encountered a squad of Army Regulars from out west. They say they're supposed to meet with our friend Taggart at Clanholme and will wait here until he arrives. The Indians have a guy escorting them to the copse of trees north of us. You know, where Choony hid out when Peter was here."

Cassy frowned. Army? There was still a U.S. Army? Ethan hadn't seemed surprised about this. Must be something he knew but hadn't seen a need to share. "Copy that. A platoon incoming. Get Michael and our Marines up and ready to go meet them in ten mikes."

Cassy hurried into her house and threw on clothes better suited to riding and—God forbid—fighting, along with her rifle and her 72-hour backpack, and headed to the stables. Her usual horse was already being saddled, and she made a note to thank Ethan later for thinking of that detail. Michael was the first there, but the other Marines he'd tagged were straggling in. They all wore civilian clothes, and she frowned. She should have thought of that. No need to advertise that the Clan had its own Marines who no longer operated within the traditional chain of command. She hadn't thought there *was* a chain of command anymore.

Ten Marines, with Michael and Cassy at the head, rode out toward the copse of trees. They spread out enough so that anyone firing on them could only take down one at a time. Michael set the pace, and it was quick but not so fast that the Army squad might feel like they were getting attacked out there in the middle of nowhere.

They'd been holed up in the Mountain this whole time, loaded with food and provisions and sitting out the apocalypse in comfort and safety. God only knew how insulated Houle's soldiers had been from the horrors of this new reality, out here in the world. She had low expectations for their attitudes and she worried about how they might behave. Trying to remember the attitudes and behaviors of people prior to the EMPs now kind of made her blood boil. It's a lot easier to be rude if you don't really believe the other person might simply bury a hatchet in your skull rather than try to deal with you…

As they approached the copse, Cassy saw ten "visitors," decked in their camouflage field uniforms—BDUs, Michael called them—loaded with packs and pouches. Their horses were tethered within the copse, and their saddlebags bulged. These guys were better off than ninety-nine percent of everyone out here, and probably didn't even appreciate their wealth. They were scattered a bit, in a defensive formation with rifles ready but not raised. That was a good sign. They looked as uncertain as she felt.

When they were some ten yards away, Michael reined in his horse and the others followed suit, then dismounted. Cassy climbed off her horse and walked toward the guy in front, but Michael walked faster. Well, if Michael felt it wise to reach them first, she'd play along. Keeping her safe was his job right now after all, and you never knew how it would go when you first met strangers.

Michael scanned the soldiers and diverted, ignoring the man in front whom Cassy would have talked to first. He went to a rather short woman in the main body and smiled. "Lieutenant, I assume this is your command? Welcome to

Clanholme. I've found it to be a good group of people. Loyalists should have no issues with these folks, in my experience."

Cassy eyed Michael, confused. Why had he separated himself from being introduced as a Clanner? Cassy noted that her own Marines were spreading out, probably unconsciously, almost mirroring the soldiers' positioning. She held her tongue, waiting to see what Michael had up his sleeve.

The woman removed her helmet, and Cassy saw that she had her brunette hair up in a tight, flat bun. Practical, with no pretense. That could be good or bad. "Lieutenant Mavis. Thank you for meeting with us. We were told we'd be greeted by the leader of this 'Clan.' Who might you be?"

Michael nodded. "I'm Captain Parker, under Major Taggart. He sent us out here to meet up with you. Pardon the civvy uniform, but seemed best to fit in and not stand out." He extended his hand toward Cassy, who nodded. "This is Clan leader Cassandra Shores. I asked her to come, since this is after all her territory that we're meeting in. I've found her a gracious host, but no-nonsense."

Cassy struggled not to lose her composure and kept her expression carefully neutral, but her mind was a jumble. Obviously, Michael was pretending to be one of Taggart's men, but why? It must have been a last-second decision on his part, or he would have warned her. Dammit, she'd almost given away the ruse, too! She watched Michael intently for cues as to what would come next.

The lieutenant's eyes roved over Michael for a moment. She was sizing him up in an instant, cold and calculating, and must have found him worthy or whatever. Then she looked over to Cassy and walked up to her. "Good afternoon, ma'am. I'm Lieutenant Mavis. It is a pleasure to make your acquaintance. America needs more patriots to step up and save what can be saved, like you have done. Your government thanks you."

Cassy grinned, but it was forced. "Good afternoon, Lieutenant. I didn't know you spoke for the government. The last I checked, we have none of the three legitimate branches of government, and even if there were, we have no president —no election, no Constitutional government. No such thing, at the moment."

Mavis frowned. "We're under Martial Law, ma'am. All Americans are duty-bound and obligated to obey the instructions of the legitimate Commander-in-Chief until the rebuild."

"Well, you're free to take that up in court, if you can find one that's legitimate. Since there's no Constitutional government, there's no new C-in-C. None legitimate, anyway. For now we're fine here without military rule, but thanks anyway for the dictatorship offer. It's good to know there's a U.S. Army still, though—when the government reforms, we'll need that to help restore order. *When* we have elections again, of course, we'll be thrilled to be part of a new America. I can't wait."

The lieutenant nodded once, curtly. "I see. Well, we're not here to subjugate survivors. Someday we'll enforce the law, even here, but for now we don't require submission to the lawful authority of the Commander-in-Chief in Colorado. We'd rather fight the real enemy, not misguided survivalists."

Cassy shrugged. "That's good, bearing in mind we're self-defending farmers, not pre-EMP skinhead survivalists. Required by Colorado or not, though, we're not really big on submission to unlawful authority. Misguided, maybe, but we'll wait for Constitutional government to return. In the meantime, we'll just be happy to still be alive when the Dying Time is over."

"Dying Time?" Mavis asked, a confused look on her face.

"Yeah. It's not over yet, as we keep seeing. It's a tragedy... All those poor *well-guided* people won't be around much longer. Or perhaps you aren't aware of the starvation, disease, and opportunistic violence out here in the real world —you've probably had it pretty cushy in Colorado, judging by your supplies and horses—but the rest of the country wasn't as lucky as you. So sorry, but I suspect that the other forty-nine states will pretty much think like we do about the whole military dictatorship idea. So what are you actually here for, if not to subjugate us?"

The lieutenant had stood still during Cassy's speech, eyes narrowed, but hadn't interrupted. Cassy figured she was cursing her for being a damned, dirty civilian, but that was just too damn bad.

Jaw clenched, Mavis replied, "Irrelevant. We have mission orders, which we'll adhere to, as much as I'd like to take my own initiative here. Colonel Taggart was supposed to meet us here."

"Yes, Lieutenant," Michael said, with a very slight emphasis on her rank so it sounded dismissive even to Cassy's civilian ears. Good, the snotty soldier deserved some lumps to her ego, as far as Cassy was concerned.

Michael continued, "Unfortunately, the realities of the conflict out here in the real world, beyond the bubble you're used to, don't always allow us to do as we wish. For example, you wouldn't much like the result if you took some impulsive hostile action against Mrs. Shores and her Clan—they've come through much tougher trials than a junior officer's pique. As for Colonel Taggart, op tempo and enemy action meant he was only able to exfiltrate one unit, under my command. Had a hell of a time getting here, too. However, I'm now familiar enough with the area to guide you where you need to go and to keep you out of trouble while you learn to fight and survive out here."

"Right. So, you'll guide us to him. I take that to mean he's not in this operational area as per his orders, so our going to him is now a problem. If I follow orders by meeting him where he is, I violate my orders to station in this region and establish operations for future ops against the enemy."

Michael nodded with a sympathetic shrug. "Sorry, Lieutenant. We have a fluid situation here, and adaptability is a necessity if you want to survive outside your nice warm barracks. We've been out here actually *fighting* for months and months."

"Yes, but Headquarters said—"

Michael interrupted, "Listen, it's the old thing about HQ never knowing what it takes to win in the field and never recognizing their own ignorance or respecting the operational knowledge of those on the lines who actually fight. Every war has that problem. But don't worry. It won't take long for you to adapt to the reality outside of Colorado Springs. Well, you'll either pick it up quickly or you'll die, but either way, this world—out here, the rest of the country—doesn't much care about your orders from Colorado, Lieutenant, nor what you or your HQ command wish the strategic situation might be as opposed to what it really is. However, I have some good news."

Cassy smiled as Michael dressed her down—chewed her out—in his not very subtle military style. She figured there was a lot more going on under the surface here that she couldn't see or understand, as a civilian, but even the part she could see made her pretty happy. She really didn't like this self-important lieutenant. Self-righteous little—

"So," Michael continued, interrupting Cassy's thoughts, "the new plan for you is either go home and get new orders, or adapt to the situation and maybe achieve the intent of those orders."

"And what is the intent of these orders, Captain Parker?" she said to Michael. It seemed a challenge but she looked a lot less self-assured now, and Cassy suppressed an urge to grin.

"From what the colonel has said—and he was a major when I left—the intent is to secure the main remaining food producing areas of Pennsylvania for use by the Army and some loyalist allies. I don't know who these 'allies' are, but that's what we were told. And I know where the food areas are, so you can still infiltrate and rally to work toward your mission objective of securing the food production areas and kicking out the invaders."

"The allies are loyalists, Captain, of a new republic building in Indiana and surrounding regions. They fall under the legitimate U.S. chain of command, having properly understood that Martial Law has made all able-bodied Americans de facto soldiers in this war under the authority of General Houle, the commander-in-chief of the United States. Your Clan here could learn something from these patriots. So where is it you *suggest* that we establish our theater of operations?"

Michael showed no expression of anger or irritation, only a bored indifference as far as Cassy could see. He replied, "Mrs. Shores has made a fairly compelling case about the status of America's continuity of government, all wishful thinking aside. Regardless, we're on the same side, or should be, and I follow Colonel Taggart's orders either way. The unfortunate facts are that the enemy has rendered much of this region barren with a brown haze they sprayed. Most of the land remains contaminated, even if the immediately lethal effects of the chemical have dissipated enough to allow travel."

The lieutenant frowned. "So you're saying the land around here is compromised?"

Michael nodded. "That's why the enemy has redeployed to the area of northwest Pennsylvania, which is part of what has caused problems for the colonel with trying to disengage. The OpFor scorched this AOI and then retrograded, basically. I'll be happy to show you a couple of points of interest that really make it clear the kind of devastation they wreaked in this area. Lancaster, Adamstown, some others."

The lieutenant nodded. "I see what you mean. That completely changes things. Operating without regular comms with HQ requires a certain tactical flexibility, I suppose. Yeah, I can see that. My men and I need to resupply from local resources and get at least a twenty-four-hour R-and-R before proceeding, since we find ourselves a bit adrift. Then one of your men can guide us toward the op area Colonel Taggart has identified."

Michael said, "Absolutely, Lieutenant. These people don't have much, but we'll find a way to compensate them somehow while we wait for additional units in our op area. Any idea how many units are transitioning through here and what the timetable is?"

Maven shrugged. "We're coming through in units ranging from squad to platoon. A new one every three days, until we get our battalion mustered in the new op area. I'll leave written instructions for units that follow. Now... Any chance there's an actual shower? We haven't had a shower in two weeks, and we're feeling the grunge."

Cassy smiled and stepped forward, trying to make her eyes light up too—pretending wasn't easy when she wanted to gouge the woman's eyes out. "Oh, yeah. You're in luck! We have wood-heated water and an outdoor shower. We'll bring you and your men through in twos, and return them to you with supplies. Whatever we can scrounge up, anyway. It'll drain us, but we'll make do."

Inwardly, Cassy seethed. Self-righteous, soft-skinned

pampered bitches, the lot of them. Well, they wouldn't be soft for long, not if they survived being outside their cushy Colorado mountain base.

- 20 -

1230 HOURS - ZERO DAY +179

OVER A LATE lunch, Cassy sat talking with the Council and eating constant stew as usual, with what was left of the fresh bread. Today, however, thanks to their new cold-frame grow beds, they had a fresh pile of micro-greens, even after the rest of the Clan had eaten. The baby spinach, succulent kale, and tender sprouts they now grew in the middle of winter were a very welcome addition to their usual tedious winter diet. They wouldn't have them daily, but every week or two they'd be able to harvest a new batch. Soon they'd start staggering grow-bed starts to different days and have fresh salad more often.

The fresh salad had put everyone in a festive mood. They usually ate the bare minimum their bodies required, being tired to their core of barley or oatmeal for breakfast and constant stew the rest of the time, but today it was amazing how appetites picked up when the kitchen simply added something new to the menu. Cassy would never have thought she'd crave a fresh green salad quite so much.

Standard manners went out the window with fresh greens on the table, and Cassy cheerfully asked between mouthfuls, "So, Ethan, what's the status out east?" Another bite of greens quickly followed.

Ethan stopped himself from chomping down on a forkful of salad and set the laden fork down with a look of utter longing. Cassy, enthusiastically chewing her own forkful of fresh greens, resisted the urge to smile.

"First item up is the troops from the Mountain. They're passing through regularly and will keep passing through. They're predicting an entire battalion will filter through here, a few at a time. Michael managed to get the first unit, breathing down our necks, to divert from here to northwest Pennsylvania. Let them be someone else's problem."

Michael added, "More will come, though. Ethan has a plan to deal with that."

Ethan cleared his throat, nodding. "Yes, we've got handwritten orders from this unit's C.O. to whoever follows, with directions to follow and rally around a town up that way. The idea is, they'll leave us alone for a while and go fight the enemy up where they're stronger anyway."

Cassy said, "Alright, so that's dealt with for the moment. What of the Empire's spies, I mean envoys?"

Frank raised his hand pleadingly while he finished chewing a mouthful of greens. Then he said, "Sorry about that. So, the envoys are still hanging out with our work crews, but from what I understand they're getting stonewalled. People talk about the weather, about the enemy, but never about the Confederation or our operations. Still, someone has likely slipped up here or there. We should *assume* the envoys know more than they let on."

Joe Ellings said into his salad, "Wish we could just take them out. They ain't gonna be missed, I reckon." He hated meetings, but attended the regular ones as the White Stag survivor's representative.

Michael said, "Maybe not, but they'd send more

eventually—and those ones would be on edge, looking for trouble. That makes it hard to be buddy-buddy with them, which is what we want to do, for as long as we can do it. Open and honest farmers, that's us. PsyOps do matter."

"So, we'll divert them as long as we can," Cassy said, "and in the meantime the Confederation grows stronger. We have to deal with the Empire and the Mountain, but we want to do it separately, not together. I figure we can delay things, but eventually we'll have to deal with both and doing it separately will help."

Ethan half-raised his hand, then looked embarrassed. Cassy grinned, but didn't say anything—this wasn't a classroom. He said, "One more thing. Taggart, who we've been in touch with for months, turns out to be waging a very successful guerrilla war in New Jersey, thinning General Ree's forces dramatically while we've been doing the same job here in southeast Pennsylvania. Almost like a new America."

Michael, sitting upright and even leaning forward to hear this military news update, commented, "That's good news for the future, but does it help us directly?"

"Well, for one thing, we have a strong trust relationship with Taggart. He has no use for the Mountain since they tried to rope him into an ambush by Ree's troops. I warned him and he turned it around on the North Koreans. I didn't think it meant much for us at the time or I would've told you all about it sooner. Turns out, he just got orders to join the Mountain's troops here and decided to keep fighting the 'vaders instead. He says he's responsible to engage the enemy for the American people, not to let some power-hungry desk jockey, hiding in a hole, send him back behind the lines. Taggart and I talk a lot now, back-channel. He's got a thousand trained troops with him and thousands more in militia units he formed. How's that for an ally?"

Ethan paused to chomp on another forkful of salad and added, "He's going to send a few troops this way in order to look cooperative. Not many, but they'll winter over with us if they can get away with it and establish direct comms between the Confederation and his own operations. We may be able to call upon him if we plan ahead and spot the critical moment. Every war has critical moments, when everything can turn on a dime. Think Gettysburg—we've all been on the tours, right? That battle decided the course of the last chapters of the Civil War. When it comes time for our own Gettysburg, we're going to want him and his troops on our side."

"War of Northern Aggressin', that's the real name," Joe Ellings corrected, smirking.

Cassy laughed. "The War Between the States isn't going to help us now, but I get what you're saying. Turning points matter, and we have a very good shot at being ready for it when one comes along, providing we work with this Army general and prepare as best we can."

"He's a colonel for now," Ethan said, "but he's been skyrocketing rank since all this began. Probably be a general before long, if he can keep Houle away."

Michael smiled at that and added, "With Adamstown burnt to the ground by the 'vaders when they ran, we're having a much easier time of things around Brickerville and Ephrata. The plague in Hershey ran its course mostly, but the survivors aren't so eager to tangle with Liz Town anymore. Less pressure on them, east and west."

"What of the north end?" Cassy asked and shoved another giant forkful of salad into her mouth.

Frank said, "Falconry is fine, too, and doing well as the region's neutral trading port. They've even had a few private caravans from the Empire, trading lots of manufactured goods for food and a couple gasifiers."

Cassy nodded. "Frank, see if we can't get them to trade those to us first. Our redneck engineer can build them now but lacks parts. He's better equipped to improve theirs than to make new ones. So, if Falconry is trading some, we can use them. Speaking of which, we need to set up a big depot of wood cut to size for those gasifier things."

"Sure, I'll ask them to trade with us first. And I'll see about Brickerville setting up that wood depot, being close to the forest and all. It'd strengthen our ties to give them a more solid economic base."

Cassy tapped her chin with her finger for a moment. "You know, we should send a consultant up there to help when they get started, and as many cloned fruit tree starts as we can spare from our fruit and nut trees. We can help them set up an agroforestry program—their own food forest—while they're clearing trees for the wood. Teach them how to cut their own clones once our donations grow a bit and get established."

Frank looked thoughtful. "I think I know just the person. You remember Dennis Blake? He was a supervisor under Peter when we were occupied by White Stag and Dennis was one Joe's people working to undermine Peter. He's been fascinated by your permaculture ways and spends most of his free time just... watching things. How they grow, where you planted what, and so on."

"You're right," Cassy said. "He's always asking me questions about why we do this one way, or do that another way. Perfect for this mission. Good call, Frank."

"That's why you keep my gimp ass around, right?" Frank asked, grinning. "I'll talk to him about it and get back to you."

"One more thing." She shifted her gaze to Ethan. "What have we heard from Lebanon?"

Frank interrupted and said, "I got that one. I've been the

one mostly 'diplomatting' with them. Since the plague, Hershey isn't putting as much pressure on them to the west. The Confederation has cleared up the area to their south, more or less, and they say the armed hordes of hungry people from Reading and so on aren't coming on as thick anymore. They think Reading must have gotten hit by the 'vaders or something, but we don't know for sure. Lebanon's northern borders are unchanged, but they expect more pressure from the 'vaders up there—it seems they've been acting more coordinated lately—yet with the pressure off them from other directions, Lebanon hasn't had much problem fighting off the 'vader border probes."

Cassy chuckled. "So, they're doing fine. Good! We should consider sending a scout east, though. Or maybe Ethan can ask his Army friend to have his people scout it on their way here." Ethan nodded. "Only one thing left, then—Choony, what's the status of our outreach program?"

Choony made a slight bow with his head—a mannerism he'd taken to lately—and replied, "Of the dozen or so other survivor groups who didn't make it to the Confederation meeting, Jaz and I have contacted six. Three of those are interested, and we're negotiating. We will have to visit them again a few times until we know which way they go with that. Two others were dead, one by plague some time ago, the second by cannibals more recently."

Michael added, "Ethan has sent out alerts about the new cannibals. Now that everyone is aware of them, they shouldn't last long."

Choony nodded, then continued, "And the last group declined, saying they hadn't made it this far needing some 'fancy-pants confederation.' Their words, not mine. I think if we hadn't just left right away they might have grown aggressive. I noted their location for Ethan to put on the map as an unfriendly red zone. Jaz had the impression that they were hiding something, and my gut says they're the cannibals."

Cassy listened patiently as Choony rattled off the details of his recent trips and frowned as he got to the last part. When he was done, she said, "Michael, send a pair of scouts to keep an eye on them for a few days. If they get the chance to safely scout their camp, do so, but otherwise stay undetected. We need to know. If they're cannibals, we'll have to deal with that."

Michael nodded, and Cassy wrapped up the meeting.

* * *

A couple hours later, as Cassy wrote in the Clan's ledger updating production and consumption figures—never her favorite task, but important—there was a knock at her door. "Come in," she called.

The door opened and Michael entered, smiling. When Nestor followed him inside, her jaw dropped. "You're alive! Where have you been?" she cried, bolting from her seat to rush over to him, where she shook Nestor's hand vigorously.

Nestor's face showed surprise, then a grin, and he shook hands enthusiastically. "I'm alive, yes. I got separated during the raid on the 'vader camps, but I gathered up quite a crew of Adamstown slaves. Rescued them, took a bunch of guns from the 'vaders and a big old supply wagon, and fled."

"Why didn't you come back sooner?" Cassy asked, still grinning. Her excitement at seeing a survivor they had thought lost was bubbling over, and infectious apparently because Nestor grinned back at her, a big sloppy grin.

Nestor took a step back, still smiling, and said, "We were having too much fun out there slaughtering 'vaders. You may have noticed they decided to take a vacation from invading our piece of Pennsylvania? That was after we took out probably a third of them. The way they were scattered made them easy targets for guerrilla raids, and Brickerville was striking out at them, too. The 'vaders thought we were vengeful ghosts, somebody told me."

The Night Ghosts they'd been hearing about lately, Cassy realized. How about that—those Adamstown survivors who had come storming into the quarry, inadvertently saving her life, had been Nestor's people.

"Nestor, I have to say you've helped more than you can possibly imagine," Cassy said, adoration in her gaze. "If it wasn't for you and your people, I'd probably be dead. Thank you."

Nestor nodded. "Don't mention it."

"So what are your plans now, friend?" Cassy asked. "You have a place here, though you know we can't take in Adamstown survivors, even though they burned away a lot of bad blood by coming to help at the quarry battle. But we've already set some Adamstown survivors up with a nice gig at Liz Town, where they get to earn their keep. Your Night Ghosts would be welcomed."

Nestor replied, "We heard about that. About half of those ones left and joined with us out there in the field. They didn't care for Liz Town, but I can't say I blame them. Those people are weird. So I doubt my people will want to go. And I can't just leave them out there—they look to me to lead them and to keep them fed on something other than people. It turns out they never did embrace that. Just did it out of necessity."

"So you're staying out there in the winter cold, doing... what, exactly?" Something struck Cassy as odd with that setup. Not her danger sense going off, exactly, but it didn't make her comfortable, either. Something just felt off plumb.

"Right now we're hunting some cannibals that have been raiding the few homesteads still out there. We're hot on their trail, too, and when we catch up, we'll put a stop to them.

Other than that, when the 'vaders send scout units around these parts we're usually the ones to find them. Then we chew them up and spit 'em out, take their gear and their supplies. Rinse and repeat. That loot is kind of why I'm here, actually."

"I imagine you have more gear than you can use and want to trade," Cassy said. "You do know that the Falconry have set themselves up as a trading hub, right?"

Nestor shrugged. "We go there when we have to, but I'd rather trade with you first and take what's left to Falconry. I owe you people my life."

Cassy nodded slowly, thinking. He'd never quite fit in at Clanholme. But he'd proven her wrong, and her earlier suspicions about how things went down during the Adamstown raid on the Clan a while back were therefore probably wrong. So he hadn't killed the Clanners after all.

"Sure, Nestor. I'll have Frank take a look at what you have to trade and see about setting you up with what you need. Although now I owe you my life as much as you owe me yours. Your support at the quarry battle was more timely than you know. You made a big difference out there, though I'm not sure you know how much of a difference. We may have caught up with all those retreating 'vaders and slaughtered them, but without you out there beforehand, killing them wholesale, they wouldn't have run and we couldn't have ended them quite so decisively. So now you're Nestor the Friendly Night Ghost, huh?" She grinned.

Nestor laughed. "I guess if the North Vietnamese could be afraid of a 'white feather' then these North Koreans can be afraid of a 'night ghost.' "

Cassy spent the next half hour chatting with Nestor over tea and a snack, then sent him on his way with Frank to take a look at his wares. The Clan could spare some wheat and barley to keep Nestor's band of guerrillas fed and in supply, and everyone benefitted from what he was doing. A pretty good bargain, all in all. And even if she didn't like to admit it, something about the guy, or something he'd said, still kind of made her uneasy, even if she was genuinely happy to see he had survived. She couldn't put her finger on the problem, though.

* * *

1045 HOURS - ZERO DAY +184

Taggart grinned as the recon-in-force came down the road toward his encampment. "Eagan, our boys and girls are back, it seems. They have a wagon with them that they didn't have when they left a couple weeks ago—I wonder what's in it. Don't just stand there, go welcome them back."

Eagan left in a hurry to meet the returning unit. Twelve had left, and twelve now returned. Whether or not they had succeeded in making contact with the Clan—and apparently Dark Ryder was one of them—Taggart could at least be grateful for that.

He watched as they came up the road toward him and then made his way down a slight embankment to meet them at the road. "Lieutenant! You've made it back. Congratulations. How was the mission?"

The young officer almost saluted, but remembered Taggart's field orders at the last moment. "Sir, thank you. We're glad to be back. We only spent a night and a day with those people, but it was educational."

Taggart turned to walk toward his HQ station, and the lieutenant followed while Eagan was focused on whatever was in the wagon. As they walked, he said, "Educational how?"

"Sir, these Clanners, as they call themselves, use a

unique method of farming. I wouldn't even call it organic, but more like... natural, maybe. They go out of their way to copy how things grow in nature. The list of benefits is a mile long. Harvesting is more labor than the normal way of farming, but everything else is mostly hands-off. Nature takes care of itself."

"I wonder if it would still be more labor-intensive now that there aren't any tractors," Taggart said. Something about what the lieutenant had said tickled at the back of his mind for a moment, and then it hit him suddenly. "Do they use fertilizer? Farms need fertilizer or the soil gets barren."

"I spent a lot of time with their manager, a man named Frank, asking questions. I don't know much about farming but this seemed like it might be vitally important somehow, so I even wrote it down. Frank said they don't need fertilizer. It's a long explanation, but the short version is that with the way they farm, it fertilizes itself. Everything kind of folds in with everything else. I'll write up everything I can about their ways in a separate report."

"Very well, Lieutenant. Well done. I suspect it's going to be more important than we know, come spring planting. Maybe we could get them to send us an advisor on their methods."

"Sir, that leads me to the next part of my report. You'll find this amusing, I think."

Reaching the HQ area—a pavilion tent set up beside several wooden picnic tables, where all the accessories to commanding a regiment were in use—Taggart sat on one bench and motioned the officer to sit with him. "Very well. Go ahead."

"They gave us a different HAM radio, something with more oomph and an antenna, which is part of what is on that wagon. The rest are supplies they gave us for the journey, more than we needed obviously. They also gave us one of those little netbook computers and a satellite uplink device. They only had a couple, but they wanted you to have one."

"And why is that?" Taggart asked, mind racing over the possibilities provided by a working computer. Logistics, spreadsheets, reports...

"They're calling your area New America. As opposed to some military operation out west, which they call the Mountain. The Clan doesn't trust those people. Believes they're working to reunite everything they can, both directly in the area from Colorado to Louisiana, and through a group they call the Empire, operating out of Fort Wayne, Indiana. The Empire actually had a couple envoys at the Clan's base while we were there, and we had to pretend to be residents. I didn't want to give away that you were in communication with the Clan."

A small alarm rang in Taggart's mind. If Dark Ryder was his usual contact, and if the 20s and Houle knew where the Clan was through this Empire, then could they already know that he and the Clan were in touch. He'd have to be very careful never to tip them off or suggest that it was more than a matter of simply receiving orders from the Mountain. "Of course, Lieutenant. Well done. But why would this Empire send envoys to the Clan? My understanding is that they're actually a small group in that region. Why would they not send envoys to the bigger groups?"

"It seems this Clan's leader has more influence in the area than their numbers would indicate. She's become the unofficial leader of the entire region. All the survivors there have their own enclaves, of course, but they are unifying into a confederation to fight off the Empire if needed and handle the various spats that happen between different survivor groups. Or enclaves, these days—I suppose it's not such a small world anymore."

"So they have a unified structure, they call us New

America, they sent us comms to coordinate with them, and only Reading, Allentown, and Easton are between us and them. That sum it up?"

"More or less, sir. One last thing—the computer they sent us is set up somehow to videoconference with them. Their computer whiz—Dark Ryder, who didn't reveal his real name for OpSec reasons, sir—is an elite hacker, and he set it up so that it would be almost impossible to find the connection, much less hack it, so long as we don't leave it open. They'd like us to be available every evening at nineteen-hundred hours to participate in the Clan's daily leadership meeting."

"Thank you, Lieutenant. And what of General Houle's units?"

"We got there after General Houle's first troops had passed through already. They were supposed to meet us there, but the Clan convinced them you were upstate dealing with another 'vader general. They'll keep sending Houle's troops that way for as long as they can."

Taggart nodded. "You're dismissed. Get some chow and clean up before you start on your reports. You can get those to me in the morning. Tell your troops you've got light duty for the next three days. You've all earned it."

That was all fascinating. With the computer they'd sent, they could coordinate in as close to real-time as was possible these days—daily, in fact—without the slow process of sending files embedded and back-channel as he and Dark Ryder had been doing. And they might as well have put a sign up saying they'd bow to his authority if he could get some sort of governance set up. They'd at least coordinate with him. And if they were going to have to deal with this Empire in the spring, which seemed likely, then just maybe the sudden appearance of a battalion of his civilian-soldiers could make a difference at some key point. Yes—they must have that at least partly in mind. He'd have to consider whether he really liked being at the focus of their play.

Eagan trudged up the embankment toward the HQ and grinned when he saw Taggart. "Well, sir, it seems you'll have a lot to think about," he said as he sat down.

"Indeed. I'm sure the returning troops told you about the laptop and the video conferencing this Clan wants to do. I want you to attend to those for me. I'm making you our envoy when I can't attend, which will probably be most of the time. Tell their leader—Cassandra?—that I'd like to make her the Secretary of Agriculture for our New America. We need her knowledge. I hadn't thought of it before, but she may be right. If the 20s and their overlord, Houle, are complicit in this whole end-of-the-world scenario, they can't be allowed to take over. Twenty years from now, I want a new America, not more of the worst of the old. The Clan's methods may well be the only way we can really grow enough food to save enough people to build a New America in twenty years and not be left with just a patchwork no-man's land for the next century."

Eagan, who had listened carefully to the monologue, nodded. "Yes, sir. I see what you mean. In the meantime, I'll increase our scouting runs into the region between us and this confederation. Eventually we'll have to deal with whatever's in between us if we're to link up to the Clan."

Taggart nodded, but then an idea struck him, and he grinned at Eagan. "You know, with rail transport, we can strike just about anywhere we want, quickly, and vanish just as fast. Get me a map of the railways, and put a priority on locating railway stations."

Eagan left to follow orders and Taggart followed his thoughts. Could he really rebuild the country, or maybe an improved facsimile of it? Maybe, with the right allies and a little luck, he could. He'd have to make all the preparations possible before winter ended, because springtime was going to be a critical window of opportunity. He just had a feeling much would be decided sooner rather than later. They had to get it right.

* * *

1300 HOURS - ZERO DAY +184

Down in the bunker, Ethan grinned, his face lit by his monitor. Cassy had taken the Empire's reps to see Adamstown yesterday, and they'd been shocked and horrified by the slaughter and dismayed at the destruction. The town was mostly a cinder, and the bodies had been too many to do anything with so they'd been left to rot where they lay, lined up along both sides of the highway. Cassy had told the reps that the 'vaders were still active and that their supply lines ran east and then north to Lewisburg. It was probably even true, though they had no real way of knowing what that region was like now. This morning, having learned probably everything they needed about the Clan, the Empire's envoys had traveled north to investigate. With any luck they'd die up there, the bastards.

Houle's soldiers kept filtering in and they, too, had been directed north to Lewisburg. "If you can cut their supplies there, they won't be able to keep hitting us here like they did Adamstown," Cassy had told them. Between that and the handwritten statement the first of Houle's soldiers had left, it was easy to divert them. For now, at least.

Only one last thing remained, and that was to convince the 20s of all that bogus intel. If the ruse held—and it might, since it was probably close to true—then it would divert much of the Empire's forces, Lewisburg being closer to Fort Wayne. Uncomfortably close, in fact—a straight shot along Interstate 80—and they'd have to divert forces to defend themselves. Every unit the Empire put up north was a unit the Clan wouldn't have to face when spring rolled around.

Best of all, if the Empire was General Houle's lapdog like Ethan suspected, then they'd confirm independently what Ethan was about to tell the 20s. Houle would get intel from his own troops, the 20s, and the Empire, all pointing toward imminent danger *north and far away* from the Confederation's territory. It'd still be a hard fight, if it came to that, but it would certainly help the Clan's odds of surviving a war intact and free. "Confusion to thine enemy," he murmured with a half-smile.

And then there was Taggart, who would finally be in contact with the Clan directly if he decided to lead the New America cause as he and Cassy hoped. Taggart was a wildcard, of course, but Ethan thought him to be a genuine patriot, and Taggart's response to Houle's manipulations supported his opinion. If the Clan could now maneuver his interests into line with their own, it opened up a world of new possibilities at the very least. A New America sounded just fine, after all—one based on people, not power; citizens, not money. He and Cassy had decided to call it New America partly to help get Taggart's cooperation. Ethan figured that Taggart couldn't be bought, based on how he was reacting to Houle's orders, and if the Founder's Principle he'd read about held true then it would be like a reset after the corruption and poison that had ultimately killed the old America.

Ethan put the finishing touches on his Dark Ryder reports for the 20s—many were falsified, with maps and scanned documents to add to their credibility—and then encrypted them for transmission.

He turned to Amber, who had made some time that afternoon to spend hanging out with him. "You want to do the honors? I'd love to have a woman hit 'send' on America's future."

Amber smacked his shoulder. "You're so melodramatic. We still have to survive springtime, and a lot could go wrong. But for the first time, I feel like we might have a future that's brighter than what we left behind." Her half-smile became a full smile.

"So you don't want to hit send on America's future?" Ethan said sadly.

"Shut up." She laughed, and reached over to press the Enter key. "I guess that makes me a Founding Father of New America."

"I guess it does," Ethan said, and grabbed her around the waist. Against her mock protests, he dragged her through the curtain and into the bedroom beyond.

* * *

Jaz bounced around on the wagon's wooden seat next to Choony, but for this trip they'd added a pillow someone had made for them, stuffed with the fluffy seed head fibers from cattails. They had a nice quilt stuffed with it, too, and it was amazingly warm. Who knew? She glanced behind them at Clanholme's food forest, shrinking slowly behind them.

"Choon Choon, do you think we'll be back before spring?" Jaz asked.

"I don't know. But we have plenty of supplies in our little covered wagon. It feels like we're in the Old West, heading toward the Oregon Trail. But for a while we'll still be in Confederation territory, as safe as it gets these days."

"Don't worry," Jaz replied, grinning. "I'll protect you if we come across any wannabe Red Locusts."

"Wow, Jaz, don't even joke about cannibals! The thought makes me shudder. And I don't *want* you to protect me. Violence against others harms you, too. You should know that by now."

Jaz pulled the quilt up over her shoulder and leaned her head against Choony's. "I know. But someone has to do it, or the evil in the world will take over."

For a while, they rode on in silence. She was content to just enjoy the closeness. And maybe she'd had enough time away from the trauma that had defined her life before and right after the EMPs. Time enough to heal a bit, grow stronger. When she thought back, the Jaz who had first met Cassy while hiding from looters right after the EMPs, *that* Jaz was like a stranger now.

The rolling of the wagon was kind of hypnotic, and she found her eyelids drooping. Sure, they would be away from home for a while as they made their way as far south as they were able, looking for other survivor groups, but Clanholme would be there when they got back. Clanholme was home. Her family lived there. Her real family.

She smiled a little as she sank deeper into sleep.

# # #

To be continued in
EMP Resurrection (Dark New World, Book 5)

About the authors:

JJ Holden lives in a small cabin in the middle of nowhere. He spends his days studying the past, enjoying the present, and pondering the future.

Henry Gene Foster resides far away from the general population, waiting for the day his prepper skills will prove invaluable. In the meantime, he focuses on helping others discover that history does indeed repeat itself and that it's never too soon to prepare for the worst.

For updates, new release notifications, and more, please visit:

www.jjholdenbooks.com

Printed in Great Britain
by Amazon